SUMMER DARKNESS, WINTER LIGHT

Sylvia
HALLIDAY

DIVERSIONBOOKS

Also by Sylvia Halliday

My Lady Gloriana
Gold as the Morning Sun
The Ring
Dreams So Fleeting

The French Maiden Series
Marielle
Lysette
Delphine

Diversion Books
A Division of Diversion Publishing Corp.
443 Park Avenue South, Suite 1008
New York, New York 10016
www.DiversionBooks.com

This is a work of fiction. Names, characters, places and incidents either are the product of the author's imagination or are used fictitiously. Any resemblance to actual persons, living or dead, events or locales is entirely coincidental.

For more information, email info@diversionbooks.com

First Diversion Books edition January 2015.
Print ISBN: 978-1-68230-216-3
eBook ISBN: 978-1-62681-542-1

Chapter One

The wrought-iron gate was newly painted. Allegra ran her fingers over the smooth curliques, followed the cool, sinuous curves to the oval medallion that held the Baniard coat of arms. The carved leopard still raised a broken front paw. But after more than eight years of fresh paint—glistening black layers piled one upon another—the jagged metal edges had become rounded, gentle.

"Curse them all," Allegra muttered. "Every foul Wickham who ever lived." She clenched her teeth against the familiar pain. If only sharp memories could be as softened and gentled as the old iron gate. She reached into the pocket of her wide seaman's breeches and pulled forth a worn, lace-edged square of linen, yellow with age and mottled with stains the color of old wine, the color of dead leaves. Papa's blood—staining the proud Baniard crest embroidered in the corner.

Wickham. Allegra's lip curled in silent rage and bitterness. If there was a God of vengeance, a just God, her prayers would be answered today. Her stomach twisted with the pangs of hunger, and her feet—in their broken shoes—ached from the long morning's climb through the Shropshire hills, but it would be worth it. She reached under her shabby coat and waistcoat and fingered the hilt of the dagger tucked into the waistband of her breeches. All her pain would vanish when she confronted John Wickham, Baron Ellsmere, false Lord of Baniard Hall. When she saw his look of surprise, then fear, then abject terror in the breathless, time-stopped seconds before she plunged her dagger into his black heart.

A sour-faced manservant came out of the lodge next to the high stone wall that enclosed Baniard Park. A thickly curled gray peruke covered his round head, and he wore a handsome livery of blue velvet trimmed with crimson—the Ellsmere colors, no doubt. He squinted up at the morning sun, peered through the bars of the gate and shook his fist at Allegra. "Get off with you, boy. You have no business here."

Allegra jammed her three-cornered hat more firmly over her forehead to shield her face from the gatekeeper's gaze. Her masculine guise had protected her clear across the ocean and through the English countryside all the way north from Plymouth. Still, to be discovered now, when vengeance lay so close at hand…

"I ain't doin' no harm, your worship," she mumbled, keeping her naturally husky voice pitched low, her accent common. "Just come up from Ludlow, I did. It were a long climb. And I'm fearful hungry. Thought I might beg a farthing or two of His Lordship."

"Pah!" said the gatekeeper with a sneer of contempt as he scanned her stained and ragged clothing. "Do you think milord can be bothered with the likes of you? A dirty-faced whelp?" He scowled at her dark eyes, her raven-black hair braided into a tousled queue, and her face still deeply tanned from the Carolina sun. "Leastwise not someone who looks like a black Welsh Gypsy," he added. "Be off, lest I give you a good rap on the ear."

Years of cruel servitude had taught Allegra how to feign humility, even while her heart seethed with rebellion. "Have a crumb o' pity, your worship," she whined. "I be but a poor orphan lad."

"Be off, I say." He pointed across the narrow, dusty road to a footpath that wound its way through a small grove of trees. "That way lies the village of Newton-in-the-Vale. There's a fine workhouse that will do well enough for you. A good day's work for a good day's bread, and none of your sloth and begging."

Allegra rubbed at her hands, feeling the hardness of the calluses on her palms and fingers. She wondered whether this self-satisfied, overfed man had ever known *real* work. Heigh-ho. There was no sense in quarreling with him. She shrugged and plodded across the road. The trees were thick in the coppice, crowded close together; their dark, summer-green leaves and shade soon hid her from the gatekeeper's view. She waited a few minutes, then stepped off the footpath and doubled back through the trees, treading softly so as not to alert the servant. Just within the shelter of the coppice, she found a spot that concealed her presence while commanding a clear view of the gate.

By King George upon his throne, if she had to wait all day for Wickham she would!

She heard the noise of a coach from somewhere beyond the gate—the rattle of harness, the squeaking of wheels—as it made its way down the long, tree-shaded drive that led from Baniard Hall. In another moment, the coach appeared in view and stopped at the gate;

the team of horses snorted and stamped, eager to proceed. At once, the gatekeeper hurried to take hold of the iron gate and swing it wide. Allegra heard the word "Milord" uttered in deference, noted the blue and crimson Ellsmere colors on the coachman's ample body. Wickham's very own coach. Without a doubt, the villain himself was within.

Allegra's heart began to pound in her breast, like the thud of distant thunder before a storm. After all this time...She started to rush forward, then checked herself. No. No! She mustn't let her impatience cloud her judgment; she must think clearly. The coach was moving quite slowly through the open gate. Out of the view of the gatekeeper and coachman, she might be able to hoist herself onto the empty footman's perch in the rear and cling to the coach until it stopped and her enemy alit. But that might not be until they reached a village and the coach was surrounded by crowds. And then the job would be impossible.

She remembered a crumbling section of the wall that surrounded the park, where the stones had loosened. Perhaps she could make her way onto the grounds from there, wait for Ellsmere to return. No. The wall might be repaired after all this time. And, besides, she couldn't wait another minute. She laughed softly, ruefully. She had endured the long, slow years, the years of nurturing her hatred in patient silence. And now, to her surprise, she found that the thought of a few hours' delay had become unbearable.

What to do? The frown faded from her brow as a sudden thought struck her. She would accost him now, present herself as a harmless lad, win his sympathy, worm her way into his favor. He wouldn't recognize her after all this time. And then, when his guard was down, her dagger could do its work.

"Milord!" she cried, and dashed in front of the carriage. The coachman shouted and tried to avoid her; she held her ground and leapt away only at the last second. It had been such a narrow escape that her shoulder burned from the friction of rubbing against a horse's flank, and a passing harness buckle had torn the sleeve of her coat.

She began at once to howl. "'Od's blood, but my arm be broken!"

She heard a string of foul curses from within the coach, then a deep voice boomed, "Stop!"

As the coach drew to a halt, Allegra clutched at her arm and bent over in seeming pain. Though she continued to wail, all her energies were concentrated on observing the man who sprang from the coach. She'd seen him once before—that long-ago, sweet summer at Baniard Hall. The summer she'd turned nine. The summer before the nightmare had begun. A man of stature, proud and haughty and cruel.

He was even taller than her misty memory of him, and the years had clearly treated him with kindness. His dark-brown hair was still untouched by gray. He wore it simply, unpowdered and tied back with a black silk ribbon. His pugnacious jaw had a bluish cast, as though he'd neglected to take a shave, and his dark and somewhat shaggy brows were drawn together in a scowl, shading pale-brown eyes. His well-cut coat and waistcoat of fine woolen cloth covered a solid, muscular torso, and his legs were strong and straight. The fact that he looked so young made her hate him all the more: Papa had aged a dozen years from the time of the trial to the day they had been herded aboard the convict ship.

"Damned fool," growled the man. He sounded more annoyed than angry, as though it was a bother merely to deal with the lower classes. "Why the devil did you run into my coach, boy? I should break your neck, match it to your arm." He stepped closer and thrust out his hand. "Show it here."

The simmering hatred became a red mist before Allegra's eyes: the red, bloody dream that had kept her going through all the hellish years, through the shame and the suffering and the loss of all she'd held dear. She felt strength coursing through her body—the strength of righteous anger that poor Mama had never been able to find.

Now! she thought. For her pledge to Mama. For all the lost Baniards! There would never be a better opportunity. The gatekeeper was busy with his gate and the coachman was too fat to scramble down from his perch in time to save his master.

Allegra snaked her hand inside her coat. A quick thrust with her dagger and then—in the chaos of the unexpected, the confusion of the servants—she'd make her escape into the woods. "Die like the dog you are," she choked, and drove the knife upward toward his breast with all her might. With all the fury in her pent-up heart.

"Christ's blood!" he swore. He wrenched his body to one side and just managed to dodge the murderous blade. At the same moment he caught Allegra's wrist in a punishing grip and twisted it until she was forced to drop the knife. His lip curled in disgust. "Good God. You're not a fool. You're a bloody lunatic! Do you fancy the gibbet, boy?"

She bared her teeth in a snarl. "It would be worth it, to see you dead."

He laughed, an unpleasant sound, lacking in humor or warmth. "What a tartar. How does a boy learn such passion at such a young age?" He drawled the words, as though strong emotions were scarcely worth his own effort.

"I learned from villains like you," she said. She eyed her dagger lying in the dusty road. If she could just reach it...

"Oh, no, boy. You'll not have a second chance." Reading her intentions, he quickly stooped and retrieved the knife.

"Curse you!" Allegra felt her stomach give a sickening lurch. She had failed them all. All the ghosts waiting to be avenged. How could she have been so hasty and careless? Would there ever be another chance to redeem herself? Another chance to do what she must, and then learn to live again? In her frustration, she raised her hands to spring at the man's throat; she grunted in surprise as she felt her arms caught and pinioned behind her back. She struggled in vain, then twisted around glare at the man who held her—a somber-looking young man who had stepped from the coach behind her. He was dressed in a plain dark suit, the garb of a steward or clerk.

"Hold your tongue, bratling," he said, "unless you mean to beg His Lordship's mercy."

"His Lordship can rot in hell, for aught I care!" She turned back and spat in the direction of the tall man. "In *hell*, Wickham! Do you hear?"

"Wickham?" The tall man laughed again and idly scraped Allegra's blade against the stubble on his chin. It made a metallic, rasping sound. "Wickham? Is that who you think I am?"

"You're the Lord of Baniard Hall, aren't you?" she challenged.

"That I am. But Wickham was ruined by debts nearly two years ago. The last I heard, he was in London."

"No!" She shook her head in disbelief, feeling her blood run cold. "Curse you, villain, you're lying to save your skin."

The steward gave a sharp jerk on her arms. "I told you to hold your tongue, boy," he growled in her ear. "This is Greyston Morgan, Viscount Ridley. Baron Ellsmere sold the Hall to His Lordship a year ago."

"I don't believe you." But of course there was no reason to doubt him. She examined the tall man more closely. What a fool she'd been, allowing her passion to blind her to reality. He didn't just appear younger; he *was* younger, and considerably so. Perhaps in his early thirties. Wickham would be almost as old as Papa would have been today, or at least nearing fifty. She'd forgotten that, still seeing the man through the eyes of her childhood.

All the fight drained out of her. She sagged in the steward's grip, filled with an aching disappointment. To have come so far, and then to find another obstacle in her path, another barrier before she could sleep in peace…She stared at the viscount, her dark eyes burning with frustration and resentment. He should have been Wickham. "I curse you as well, Ridley," she said bitterly. "A pox on you."

"Now, milord," said the coachman, climbing down from his box, "if this isn't a rascally lad who needs a few hours in the stocks to teach him manners! Shall we deliver him to the beadle in the village?" He looked for agreement toward the gatekeeper, who had finally joined them.

Ridley looked down at Allegra's petite frame and shook his head. "He's just a slip of a boy. The stocks would kill him. A mere ten minutes with a mob hurling garbage and filth…"

"But you can't let him go, milord. He tried to kill you!" said the gatekeeper.

Ridley smiled, a sardonic twist of his mouth. "So he did, Humphrey. And I note you took your time coming to my rescue." His icy glance swept his other servants as well. "The lot of you. Slow as treacle on a cold day. Very shortsighted. If you'd let him kill me, you'd have had to seek honest employment for a change." He shrugged, ignoring his servants' sullen frowns. "Well, the lad wasn't the first to wish me dead. However"—he slapped the broad width of Allegra's dagger against his open palm—"the boy does have an insolent tongue, and for that he should be made to pay." He nodded at his steward. "Loose him, Briggs. I'll deal with him myself."

"But…" Briggs hesitated. "Do you think you're fit, milord?"

A sharp laugh. "Sober, you mean?"

"I didn't mean that at all," said Briggs in an aggrieved tone.

Ridley's eyes were cold amber. "What a damned bloody liar you are, Briggs. Now, do you want to keep your position? You'll not find another master willing to pay so much for so little. Loose the boy, I said."

"As you wish, milord." There was pained resentment in the steward's voice, but he obeyed.

The moment her arms were freed, Allegra looked wildly about, seeking a path to safety. There was none. The three servants hemmed her in, and Lord Ridley stood before her, a cold smile of determination on his face. He slapped the flat of Allegra's knife more sharply against his hand. Again, and then once more—a decidedly menacing gesture, for all his smiling. "Damn me to hell, will you, boy? Spit on my boots, will you? Someone has neglected your education, it would seem. I intend to remedy that." He slipped the knife into his boot top and advanced on Allegra. His long arm shot out and wrapped around her waist. With the merest effort, he lifted her and tucked her under his arm, like a farmer carrying a squirming pig to market.

Allegra writhed in his strong grip. "Bloody villain. Spawn of hell! Put me down!"

"If I were you, boy, I'd hold my tongue," he said dryly. "I have all day to educate you, and every fresh insolence will only earn you another painful lesson." He turned toward the woodland path.

"Where are you going, milord?" asked the gatekeeper, Humphrey.

"To find a suitable 'schoolroom.' Don't follow me. Grant the lad privacy in his humiliation." Ridley laughed, a sharp, sardonic bark. "Besides, you shall hear his howls anon."

He carried Allegra into the grove of trees and stopped at last when he found a fallen log in a small clearing. He sat down and slung her across his knees with such force that her hat flew from her head and landed in a patch of bright green ferns.

Allegra grunted and wriggled in powerless rage, punching his legs, his thighs—anything within reach of her flailing fists. It was like beating back a tempest with a lady's fan. His strong arm held her firmly against his lap. She felt his other hand her rump, turning up the skirts of her coat; then his fingers we curled around the top of her breeches.

She struggled more violently to free herself. She didn't feel the thrashing—not even with the flat of her own knife, which the villain clearly intended. Punishment was nothing new to her. But if he saw the pale flesh of her backside, the womanly curves, he'd guess at once. And then what? What could she expect from this cold-hearted devil of a viscount? God save her, she hadn't guarded her virtue against the greatest adversities only to be raped by a man with nothing better to do on a July morning! With a superhuman effort, she wrenched herself from his lap and tumbled to the ground.

He reached down to pull her back. By chance, his hands closed over her breasts. "Christ's blood," he exclaimed, and dropped down beside her. "A *woman*, begad!" While she struggled in helpless frustration, he rolled her onto her back, straddled her and pinned her wrists over her head. With his free hand he explored her body, threw open her coat and tattered waistcoat and fondled her breasts through her full linen shirt. It was a leisurely, searching examination that clearly amused him. His mouth twisted in a smirk. "A very pleasing shape. May I assume your other parts are equally feminine? Or shall I find out for myself?"

She squirmed in disgust at his touch, her eyes flashing. "Let me up, you plaguey dog!"

He shook his head and laughed. "To think I very nearly beat you like a child. I should have realized...all that passion. Not childlike at all. But why waste your fire in anger? Why foul your lips with curses, when they could be put to better use?" He bent down, his face close to hers. His

11

breath smelled of liquor, sour and pungent.

"Cursed rogue," she muttered. "Drunken sot. I would rather the beating than the kiss."

"Perhaps I can oblige you with both," he said, and silenced her mouth with his.

His lips were hard and demanding, rapacious in their greed, the desire for self-gratification. And when she groaned and bucked beneath him, Ridley chuckled deep in his throat, as though her struggles only increased the enjoyment of his mastery over her. Without releasing either her lips or her hands, he shifted his body so his considerable weight pressed upon her breast and his free hand rested on the juncture between her legs.

Allegra had a sudden, terrifying memory of Mama, gasping in pain and grief as Squire Pringle violated her frail body. She could hear again the animal sounds she'd heard, night after night in the dark. Hear her mother's heartbroken sobs as the master, satisfied once more, slunk away to his own bed. *No!* It mustn't happen to her. She was stronger than Mama. Hadn't she survived until now?

Despite her rising panic, she forced herself to think clearly. If Ridley wasn't completely drunk, he'd certainly had a great deal to drink this morning. His senses would be dulled, his reflexes numbed by alcohol. Surely she could outwit him if she put her mind to it.

With a sigh, she relaxed under him in seeming surrender. She even managed a moan of pleasure when he began to stroke her inner thigh, his large hand hot through her breeches. He grunted his contentment, softened his kiss, eased his hard grip upon her wrists. How easily gulled men could be, she thought. And if he was anything like the lecherous pigs in Carolina, no doubt he enjoyed kissing in the French manner. She prayed it was so. She parted her lips beneath his, hoping he'd understand and respond to her invitation. To her satisfaction, he immediately opened his own mouth and thrust his tongue between her lips and teeth. She waited a second—fighting her disgust—them bit down with all her might.

He let out a bellow and flew off her as though he'd been shot sitting up to clutch at his bloody mouth. "Damned bitch!" he roared.

She gave him no chance to recover. She scrambled to her knees and drove her fist into his diaphragm with all her strength. He recoiled in agony and doubled over, gasping for breath. She was on her feet in a flash. She snatched up her three-cornered hat, pulled her knife from his boot top and turned toward the footpath. Her mouth was bitter with the taste of his blood; bitterer still with the knowledge that time was passing and she was no nearer her goal. Her stomach burned with hunger, and London and Wickham were long miles and days away. Somehow, that made her hate Ridley all the more. Ridley, with his careless, shallow lechery. What did he know of true suffering?

She retraced her steps to where he still sat, rocking in pain. "Filthy whoremonger," she said, and spat his own blood upon his bent head. When he looked up at her, she was pleased to see that the cold, indifferent eyes were—for the first time—dark with rage. "Laugh that away, Ridley," she said. "If you can." She turned on her heel and made for the safety of the trees…and the direction that would take her eventually to London and Wickham.

And bloody vengeance.

Sir Greyston Morgan, Lord Ridley, late of His Majesty's Guards and survivor of many an incursion against the Mogul Empire, gingerly rubbed the sore spot beneath his ribs and muttered a soft curse. He pulled out a handkerchief and wiped the spittle from his hair, grunting at the pain that small effort cost him. The absurdity of the whole episode served to temper his anger. "Ambushed, begad," he said, beginning to laugh in spite of his discomfort. He stuck out his tongue and dabbed at it, marveling at the amount of blood on the snowy linen. It was a wonder the virago hadn't bitten his tongue clean off!

"Are you hurt, milord?" Jonathan Briggs stood on the edge of the path, frowning in concern.

Grey struggled to his feet and glared at his steward. It was one thing to be outwitted by a wench. It was quite another matter to be caught at it by a servant. "Damn it, I thought I told you not to follow."

"We heard you cry out, milord." Briggs looked around the small clearing. "Where's the boy?"

Grey took a tentative step forward, relieved to discover that he could breathe almost normally again. "The 'boy,' Briggs, turned out to be a woman." His tongue was still bleeding; he stopped to spit a mouthful of blood against the base of a tree. "And a damned shifty bitch at that."

Briggs watched in dismay. "Was the wench responsible for his? I'll send Humphrey after her."

"No. Let her be. I'll wager she's halfway to London by now."

"What's to be done now, milord?"

Grey moved slowly to the steward and leaned his arm on the man's shoulder. "Help me back to the coach and open that bottle of gin."

Briggs shook his head in disapproval. "But, milord, do you think it wise, so early in the day?"

He swore softly. "You tell me what's worth staying sober for, Briggs, and I'll stay sober. Until then, you'll keep me supplied with all the drink I need. And no insolence. Is that understood?"

Briggs pressed his lips together and nodded.

By the time they'd reached the coach, Grey was feeling a good deal better. At least his tongue and his ribs were feeling better. He wasn't sure of anything else. There was something disturbing about the woman. Something about her eyes, so large and dark and filled with pain… "Damn it, Briggs," he growled, "where's that gin?" He snatched the small flask from the steward's hand and took a long, mind-numbing swallow. Why should he let the thought of a savage creature with a dirty face get under his hide?

"Do you still want to go down to Ludlow, milord?"

"Of course. The blacksmith promised to have that Toledo blade repaired by today."

"Are you sure you don't want someone to go after the woman?"

"I told you, no!"

"But she tried to kill you. What if she should return and try again?"

"She wants Ellsmere, not me." He smiled crookedly. "I pity him if the witch should find him." He took another swig of gin and shrugged. "Besides, if she should return to kill me, I'm no great loss."

"Nonsense, milord. You're a great man, admired and respected by your tenants and servants. Everyone in the parish honors Lord Ridley."

Grey threw back his head and laughed aloud. "Such kind flattery, Briggs. You do it well, as befits a man of honor. But how difficult it must be for you. To serve a man you don't even like. You're the second son of a knight, aren't you? You were predestined to inherit nothing from your father except his good wishes. Well, a house steward is a fine calling for a man with few prospects and a good education. And money speaks with a loud voice, as I've learned." He leaned back in his seat and tapped his long fingers against the bottle of gin. "How much am I paying you?"

"Forty pounds, milord," murmured Briggs. He watched in silence, his solemn eyes registering dismay, as Grey downed the last of the gin.

The liquor stung Grey's injured tongue, but he was beginning to feel better and better. He chuckled softly. "What a disappointment I must be to you, Briggs. I think your upbringing was better than mine, though I, too, was the second son of a title. I regret that I don't suit your ideas of proper nobility here in Shropshire. But if you can learn to hide that look of disgust on your face, I give you leave to take another thirty pounds per annum. If not"—he shrugged—"it's simple enough to buy loyalty elsewhere, if one has the money." He laughed at the sullen look Briggs shot at him. "God's truth, I think if my brother hadn't died and left me his fortune and title, you'd be pleased to knock me to my knees at this very moment. But you're too much a gentleman for that. Too respectful of a man's rank, even if he's undeserving. Eh, Briggs?" He laughed again as the steward reddened and turned away.

Grey closed his eyes. The rocking of the coach soothed him. And the gin had done its work. It was good to feel nothing but a comfortable hum in his brain. There was a surfeit of passion in the world, a stupid waste of emotion. He hated it. Hated caring, hated feeling. It was better to be numb than to suffer with rage and pain, one's soul exposed to the agony of the human condition. Raw flesh held to an open flame. Like that ragged, dark-eyed creature, who burned with an intensity he couldn't begin to understand. That he didn't *want* to understand.

"Briggs," he said suddenly. "Do you remember the red-haired serving wench at the King's Oak tavern in Newton? Find out if she's still as agreeable as before. If so, pay her double what you did last time. Then see that she's waiting in my bed tonight."

"Yes, milord." Briggs's voice was sharp with disapproval.

Grey opened his eyes and smiled cynically. "She's a shallow, greedy whore, Briggs. I know. But—like the gin—she gives me what I want. Forgetfulness."

And plague take all sad-eyed creatures who overflowed with more passion than their hearts could safely hold.

Chapter Two

The warm noon sun sparkled through the leafy trees, and the thicket hummed with insects. Allegra stopped to lift her cocked hat and mop her damp brow with her sleeve. Then she replaced the hat and peeled off her coat. She was beginning to feel lightheaded. She had begged a bowl of thin soup at a tavern near Ludlow last night, but it had scarcely filled the vast emptiness of her belly. And this morning she'd found no one with a scrap of charity, or even bread, for a ragged, filthy urchin who had spent the night in a ditch. She tossed her coat over one shoulder, casting her eyes to either side of the footpath as she resumed her walk. Surely this wasn't her lucky day. Not even a patch of berries to ease her hunger.

She sighed. She should have filched a copper or two from Ridley's pocket as he sat helpless and writhing on the ground. It was the least she was owed. The fat burghers in Charles Town had been willing to part with *silver* for a slobbering kiss and a sweaty hand to her breast. She sighed again. Heigh-ho. She'd have to make the best of it. Ridley's gatekeeper had spoken of a workhouse in Newton. If she couldn't beg a meal or a coin in the village, she'd spend a precious day and toil for her supper. It was one more delay, of course, but what could she do? She had to eat.

"Patience, Anne Allegra," her mother had admonished her, each time she had waited for Papa to return from London bearing gifts for his little princess. "The Baniards know how to bide their time."

Aye, Mama, she thought sadly. Eight long years of patience.

She emerged from the trees to a narrow road that bisected the path and curved away down a steep hill. The far side of the road was bordered by a dense hawthorn hedge that blocked the view beyond. A crumbling section of an old wall, gray-green with moss, stood beside the continuation of the footpath like a sleepy sentry. Over the top of the wall Allegra could see the whole valley laid out below her: lush green farmland, hedged-in pastures dotted with the white puffs of sheep, and—off in the distance—the small cluster of buildings that was Newton-in-the-Vale.

"Godamercy," she breathed, and leaned against the wall, trembling with feelings that had nothing to do with hunger. Curse her memories, that brought such pain. How often had she come here as a little girl, marching along the road or through the woods, her hand enclosed in the strong fingers of her big brother? "Lift me up, Charlie," she would say, standing on tiptoe to crane her neck over the wall that was always and forever too high. And Charlie would swing her up and seat her on the old stones, his arms wrapped protectively around her to keep her safe while she took in the view.

She inhaled a deep, steadying breath and closed her eyes. It was foolishness, to allow the past to crowd back and unnerve her. How was she to do what she must, if she allowed herself womanly weakness? She had no right even to think of herself and her pain—not while there was vengeance yet to be done. She opened her eyes with reluctance to the sweet, familiar vista and sighed. It was no use. Here—amid the hills she had called home, the green stretches and the scented thyme, the rolling crests of Wenlock Edge that rose to a vivid blue sky and the song of the summer larks—it was impossible to hold back the memories.

She saw Lucinda's face, beautiful at sixteen, her eyes shining with joy as Papa spoke of the marriage he intended to arrange for his elder daughter. He'd found a wonderful suitor: a handsome and important young duke, who didn't feel degraded to marry the daughter of a mere baronet. Not when the daughter was as exquisite as Lucinda. And Charlie had teased Lucinda when she blushed, rosy as the summer sun setting over the chimneys of Baniard Hall. And Papa had spoken briefly and indifferently of the political quarrels that raged in London between the Tories and the Whigs—so far from the serenity of their lives—and had called for supper to be served on the lawn under the ancient oak trees.

There had been enough of politics in the past, when the great civil wars had torn apart the countryside. Grandfather—like most of his Shropshire neighbors—had been a Royalist, supporting the king. The Wickhams, upstarts come down from Chester, had thrown in their lot with Cromwell. They had become fat and rich under the Protector, carving out a large estate in the next parish, acquiring titles and lands far beyond their expectations. The Ellsmere Barony for a family of mere clerks!

And when King Charles had been restored to the throne, the Wickhams had managed to survive—reduced to a small manor house, but still as proud and overbearing as they'd been in their prime. And Grandfather and the old Lord Ellsmere had kept the hatred and the animosity alive through the years, vying with each other at Court, quarreling each time they met at Shrewsbury or Ludlow.

Papa had been made of different stuff. He had avoided the bitter poison of politics, content to live in peace with his neighbors and whomever sat upon the throne. He had even invited John, the new Baron Ellsmere, to visit at the Hall. A generous gesture, though Wickham had been rude and surly all afternoon, Allegra remembered.

When the German George had been brought from Hanover to wear the English crown as George I, Papa hadn't cared. Not if it meant peace and stability for England. He had ignored the pleas of his old Tory friends to join the Stuart cause and fight for James in Scotland.

"A lost cause," he had said. "The Stuarts have had their day, and the world moves on. They can bring nothing but grief and dissension now to England." And surely the abortive uprising in the winter of 1715 had seemed to bear witness to Papa's wisdom. After James Stuart had been defeated and his partisans executed, peace had returned to the country.

And then...the arrest. The incriminating letters—that Papa swore were forged—tying him to the Jacobite cause. The trial and conviction. John Wickham's reward—Baniard Hall—for his loyalty to the new king. For his exposure of the wicked plot, his fortuitous "discovery" of the letters.

And the sentence against the whole Baniard family, traitors all, in the eyes of the court: transportation to America. For Papa, life slavery on the plantations. Seven years of bondage for Mama and Charlie. Even soft, gentle Lucinda hadn't been spared the sentence of bond servitude.

Allegra, a happy child soon to turn ten, had suddenly found herself drowning in bewilderment and terror, hearing snatches of conversation she didn't understand, watching Mama weep in despair, Charlie rage against the Wickhams, Papa mutter to himself, like a walking corpse. Everything had changed. Her sweet life had vanished. She had clung to her family—her rock and support—as the world had crumbled.

And even they had been taken from her.

She shook off her melancholy. It accomplished nothing to dwell on the past. The sooner John Wickham was dead and buried, the sooner she could lay the Baniard ghosts to rest. She turned her head away from the familiar old wall and regained the footpath.

After a few minutes, she came to a halt and held her breath, listening, her senses suddenly alert. A soft rustle was coming from a thicket at a small distance from the path. If English rabbits made the same noises as American creatures, she thought, that was surely her dinner, somewhere under the trees. She moved cautiously toward it, holding her coat outspread and at the ready. She stopped. In a moment, a small brown-and-gray rabbit appeared, scampering toward her, its large ears twitching. As it stopped to sniff the air, Allegra froze. Hunger made her senses sharp, honed the skills of survival she'd learned through the years. Gammer Pringle had always tempered her cruelty if there was a rabbit stew bubbling on her Carolina hearth.

The rabbit, satisfied of its safety, continued on its way. *Here*, thought Allegra grimly, scarcely daring to breathe. Come this way, you sweet, tender morsel.

The creature was not two feet from her when she pounced, falling to her knees and throwing her coat over the rabbit at the same time. It struggled in vain to free itself. Allegra pressed her hands against the squirming body, sought—through the folds of her coat—the vulnerable neck, and gave it a violent twist. The animal lay still. Cautiously, Allegra lifted her coat and held up the warm body by its ears.

"Now what am I to do?" she muttered. She had her knife to skin the little thing. But not a tinder box to make a fire. And she wasn't of a mind to eat the coney raw, no matter how empty her belly. Well, if she could practice Baniard patience for a little longer, she'd trade the rabbit in Newton for a good hot meal. Her mouth watered with the thought of it. She rose to her feet.

"Now here be a thieving, poaching cove, Lord love me."

Allegra's head snapped up in surprise at the soft voice behind her.

"Turn slow-like, my gallows-bird," continued the voice. "I have a pistol what is aimed at you."

Allegra turned. The soft-voiced man was tall and sinewy, with a coarse face at odds with the gentleness of his voice. He was dressed in the homespun of a simple farmer—dull, earth-toned linen; the felt hat on his head was shapeless, and the pistol in his fist looked like a relic of a past war.

Allegra scowled at him from under her cocked hat. If he was a footpad, he could be dangerous. "What do you want o' me, mate? A poor lad that never done you harm?"

"Why, as to that, you be poaching in these woods, be you not? That be against the law."

At least he wasn't a robber. Only a simple man with a conscience. Allegra contrived to look woebegone. "Where's the harm, mate? One little rabbit? And I be fearful hungry."

The farmer smiled. "Never a better reason to poach, my lad."

"Then you'll let me go?"

"Not I, Lord love you."

Allegra held out the rabbit. "Look. It be a fat one. Enough for two. Will you share, mate?"

The man shook his head with reluctance. "No, more's the pity. And I can't let you go. Sir Henry will be wanting to meet you."

"Sir Henry? Who's that?"

"A stranger here, are you? Well, lad, Sir Henry Crompton be the man what owns this very wood."

That took Allegra by surprise. These woods had been part of the Baniard lands. "This…Sir Henry is the lord of these woods?"

The man nodded. "Aye. Leastwise, this side of the road. And the justice of the peace in the parish, besides."

This time, Allegra's woe was genuine. "Justice of the peace? Godamercy. You wouldn't see me clapped in irons, would you?"

"Why, as to that, lad, I mean you no harm. Nonesoever. I have a boy at home what's near as big as you. But Sir Henry gives a shilling for every poacher brought in. And my Betty is off to church with her young man on Saturday next. A shilling will buy a nice bride's cake, don't you see?"

"I beg you, let me go." Desperation made Allegra's voice catch in her throat.

"I can't, lad. It be my bounden duty, as one of Sir Henry's cottagers, to keep his law. Now, if you'll hand over that coney and trot afore me…" He gestured toward the footpath with his pistol.

Reluctantly Allegra complied, wondering if she could break away and outrun him. But his strides were long and he'd surely overtake her almost at once. Besides, she wasn't sure whether Sir Henry's reward wasn't payable for a dead—as well as a live—poacher. And the pistol, though old, was primed. Sick at heart, she stumbled along the path. She made one more attempt to win the farmer's sympathy. She glanced back at him, her mouth twisted in an unhappy pout. "I be just a poor, hungry orphan, mate. A stranger to these parts, and at your mercy. Will Sir Henry take pity on an orphan, do you suppose?"

"Lord love you, no," said the farmer cheerfully. "Sir Henry be a fair tiger when it comes to poachers. He eats 'em up. Swallows 'em whole for breakfast, he does. But don't you fret, lad. I'll speak for you with Sir Henry. You mind your manners, and make a leg to him, and I'll speak for you."

Heartened by the man's words, Allegra allowed him to march her down the path until they reached the valley and the road that led to Newton.

Just outside the village was a snug inn that squatted by the side of the road like a plump, contented magpie, its black timbers and white plaster bright against dark-green trees. In the yard was a table, before which sat a very fat, very red-faced gentleman wearing an exuberant periwig of foaming curls and ringlets. The table was set with an elaborate meal, which the man ate with such gusto that his powdered curls brushed across the food each time he bent forward to sample another morsel. He stopped only long enough to signal his hovering servants to refill his tankard with wine, then he resumed his guzzling. The innkeeper stood nearby, beaming his approval, his sharp eye on the sack of coins next to the gentleman's plate.

The farmer pushed Allegra forward. "Be not afeared, lad," he whispered. "Make your bow to Sir Henry."

Allegra watched Sir Henry stuff a chunk of roast beef into his mouth. The juices ran down his chin and stained the white napkin at his neck. She swallowed hard, twisting her coat in her fists to keep from snatching at the plates of food. She took a hesitant step and bent her leg in a bow. "Your worship," she said.

Cheeks bulging, Sir Henry looked up and frowned, clearly vexed to be disturbed at his table. He chewed hard and swallowed, then took a large gulp of wine from his tankard. "Well, Jenkins, what is it?" he growled to the farmer.

"I found this lad in your woods, sir. With this." Jenkins held up the rabbit.

Sir Henry's red face turned a deeper shade. "Poaching, you mean to tell me? Upon my honor, I'll not have it!" He fixed his eyes on Allegra. They were small and dark and greedy. "What do you mean, you young rapscallion, poaching in my woods? Don't you know that's a serious offense?"

Allegra hesitated, then shook her head. "No, your worship." Maybe she could talk her way out of this. "I be new to these parts. In Carolina, the woods belong to everyone. And the rabbits. I hunted free all the time."

Sir Henry bit down on a meat pie. The steam wafted a spicy, tantalizing aroma to Allegra's nostrils. "Ignorance of the law is no excuse," he muttered.

"If you please, Sir Henry," said Jenkins, touching his hat politely, "this be a good lad. And his catch be yours now." He held out the rabbit toward one of Sir Henry's servants. "So what's the harm? No need to bring the law into it."

"Hmph! He should be made to pay. When winter comes and there's not enough food on my table because of poachers like him, what am I to do?"

"I could give his breeches a good dusting, don't you see, Sir Henry? Would that serve?"

"Well, he's only a boy…I don't wish to see a boy in irons."

Having narrowly escaped one thrashing this morning, Allegra didn't fancy the prospect of another. Besides, Sir Henry was beginning to look bored with the whole matter, and eager to resume his feed. Perhaps a bold attack…She jutted her chin in defiance. "I didn't harm you nowise, your worship. The rabbit didn't come from your land. I took it from Lord Ridley's wood."

Sir Henry glared at Jenkins. "Is that so?"

Jenkins kicked at a clod of dirt in the yard. "Well, I didn't rightly see him *kill* it, sir. But the coney were still warm…"

"Ridley," said Sir Henry with a sneer. "Why the devil should I care about his property? That cowardly knave doesn't have the stomach to prosecute on his own behalf. It's a wonder the whole parish doesn't make off with all he owns. It was different when old Ellsmere was alive."

"What?" Allegra gasped and fell back a step. "What did you say?" Her brain whirled with confusion; surely her lack of food was beginning to affect her hearing. "Ellsmere not alive? John Wickham…not *alive?*"

Sir Henry shrugged. "He's been in his grave for nigh on to two years now."

Allegra clenched her fists till the knuckles gleamed white. "You lie, rogue. Wickham lives!"

Sir Henry rose to his feet, his face darkening to crimson. "You dare to show me a temper, sirrah, when I've just spared you a prison sentence? I tell you the man died peacefully in his bed."

I'll go mad! thought Allegra. His words were knives, tearing at her heart, slicing it to little pieces. "He can't be dead!" she cried. "The black-hearted devil can't be dead! He sold Baniard Hall only last year."

"That was his son, Thomas. The new Baron Ellsmere."

She refused to believe it. After all this time, the years of waiting, it couldn't be so. It couldn't! Sir Henry was lying only to torment her. "Liar!" she shrieked. "Knave. Villain!" In a frenzy of rage and torment, she turned to the table, picked up a platter of roasted pigeons and hurled them in Sir Henry's face.

He sputtered in fury, wiping the grease from his cheeks. His eyes were bright, like dark, hard coals glittering in the fleshiness of his face. "Now, boy, you'll learn what it means to insult me! Jenkins can't swear that the rabbit was mine, and I've no mind to prosecute for Ridley. You're safe from prison, at least. But, upon my honor, you'll pay for your insolence before I release you!" He snapped his fingers at his two manservants and pointed to an iron ring set into the side of the inn. "Tie the wretch there, and bring me a whip!"

"No!" Allegra reached for her knife as Sir Henry's servants charged toward her. She tried to slash one of them across the forearm, but the other gave her a slap to the side of the head that knocked off her hat and sent her sprawling to the ground. Still dazed from the force of the blow, she felt herself hauled to her feet and dragged to the side of the inn. Rough hands pushed her face against the wall, stretched her arms above her head, bound her to the iron ring with a rope that cut into her wrists. She heard the tearing of her shirt and waistcoat and felt the sudden warmth of the sun on her bare back. She grunted and struggled against the cords that held her fast.

One of the servants snickered. "He has the skin of a girl. All pale and soft where the sun didn't get it."

"But he's just a little thing," said Jenkins in his soft voice. "Be merciful, Sir Henry."

Sir Henry was beginning to puff with the mere effort of walking across the yard. "Merciful? For the insult to my person, to the memory of my good friend, John Wickham?"

Wickham. At the sound of the hated name, Allegra felt her rage ebbing, to be replaced by a cold numbness. John Wickham was dead. She cursed herself. Her failure. She should have come home sooner. She should have returned to England as soon as she'd buried Mama. Even if it had meant whoring to earn her passage.

She ceased her useless struggles. It no longer mattered, what happened to her. John Wickham was dead, but—God forgive her—not by a Baniard hand, as she had pledged to Mama.

Well, she would begin again, with fresh resolve. Thomas Wickham had done his evil part, hadn't he? Though still a youth, he had spoken at Papa's trial. Added the final, damning testimony that had sealed the case against her beloved parents. She would endure Sir Henry's beating. When it was over, she would go to London and seek out Thomas Wickham for her revenge. If not the father, then the son. She would... *"Godamercy!"* she cried, as the whip tore into the flesh of her back. She clenched her teeth, fought to ignore the searing pain.

"Spare the boy, sir," said Jenkins, clearly suffering along with her.

"Not yet," panted Sir Henry.

The whip fell again. Allegra cried aloud, a deep groan torn unwillingly from her throat. Her back burned like fire, but she could hear Sir Henry's labored breathing behind her. She prayed the punishment would be brief, that Sir Henry wouldn't have the strength or the wind for more than a few savage cut with his whip. She held her breath, awaiting the next blow.

"What the devil are you doing, Crompton?" The voice was deep and faintly slurred. And familiar. Allegra stiffened, straining her head to see the speaker over her shoulder. Ridley! Behind him, she could just glimpse his carriage stopped on the road, his frowning young steward hurrying forward to join his master.

"Stay out of this, Ridley," growled Sir Henry. "The boy's a poacher of rabbits, and a damned insolent whelp besides."

Viscount Ridley stepped closer to Allegra. His mouth was twisted in an arrogant smirk and he appeared to be even more intoxicated than he had been this morning. "I myself can attest to the creature's insolence and savagery," he drawled. "But, for the rest, you are in error." His hand shot out, a knife flashed, and Allegra found herself freed of her bonds. None too gently, Ridley spun her around to face Sir Henry. "This is no boy, Crompton." He reached for Allegra's already torn shirt and waistcoat and stripped them down to her waist, exposing her full breasts. Ridley smiled in pleasure, his eyes focused on Allegra's womanly curves.

She gasped and wrapped her arms around her nakedness, trying in vain to shield her body. Sir Henry gaped in amazement, his slack jaw hanging open, while his servants laughed and poked each other in the ribs. Jenkins looked disconcerted and Ridley's steward turned red.

Ridley himself seemed to find it all a capital joke. "Poaching rabbits? You're full of the devil, aren't you, girl? Well, I'll save you, if I can."

"A pox on you," she muttered. She wasn't sure whether she wasn't safer with Sir Henry Crompton and his whip than she'd be in the care of Lord Ridley, with his cruel mouth and his lustful eyes.

Sir Henry was beginning to recover from his surprise. "Maid or knave, she took a rabbit from the woods," he began.

"Is that so, girl?" asked Ridley. He swayed unsteadily from side to side.

"I was hungry!" Allegra burst out. She had begun to shake. She didn't know if it was from rage or hunger or the shame of being exposed in this fashion with no one to care. "And I've learned to fend for myself. Surely *you've* discovered that by now, milord," she added with a touch of malice.

Ridley laughed and rubbed his mouth with the back of his hand. "To my sorrow," he said. "I fear I'll not eat a solid mouthful for days. But if you were hungry, girl, it seems to me you could have found other ways to earn a crust of bread. I myself would be willing to offer…" He smiled suggestively and reached out a languid hand; one long finger stroked

Allegra's bare shoulder, followed the line of her collarbone to touch the soft hollow at the base of her neck.

She cringed away, feeling trapped. "Curse you. Curse all of you!" she cried defiantly. She was feeling too miserable and discouraged to remember her humble station.

"Here, miss." Ridley's steward stepped forward and pulled off his coat, frowning as he helped her into it and she winced in pain. He seemed embarrassed by the whole ugly scene. By his master's careless drunkenness and lechery.

Ridley turned to Sir Henry. "You've had your sport, Crompton," he said. "Give the wench over to me now."

Sir Henry thrust out his fleshy lower lip. "Have you forgotten the Black Act, Ridley? The girl had a knife. She was dressed as a boy. And she admitted openly to me that she took the rabbit. I'm the justice of the peace in this parish. Not you. And I say that the damned thief should be bound over to the assizes."

"Don't be hasty, Crompton. Perhaps I can—"

"You can leave me in peace," Allegra interrupted. The thought of a villain like Ridley negotiating on her behalf made her stomach turn. God knows what he might expect in return! And she didn't need him to speak for her. Sir Henry had already said he didn't intend to send her to prison. It was only his dislike of the viscount that was persuading him to change his mind. She glared at Ridley. "Go away. I don't need your help!"

He swore softly, took her by the arm and gave it a savage shake. "Little fool," he muttered under his breath. "Are you so careless of your life? I'll try to save you, if I can. But only if you control your saucy tongue!" He turned toward Sir Henry and managed a bored smile. "Now, what will it take for you to change your mind?"

Crompton smiled in his turn, suddenly aware of his unexpected power over the situation. "Why should I change my mind?"

"Because the wench interests me."

Crompton's smile deepened and he put his hand on his sword hilt. "Would you be willing to fight for her?" His voice was as silky as a snake writhing through the grass. "I see you're not armed, milord. But I can send one of my servants to fetch a weapon."

There was a stillness about Ridley that was frightening. "No," he said softly. Allegra suddenly wondered if he was as drunk as he appeared.

Crompton chuckled, an ugly sound that came from deep in his throat. "As white-livered as they say? If I call you craven, leave my glove in your face, will you fight me?"

Ridley forced a laugh. "No."

Crompton slapped his thigh in delight. "By my troth, it's true! The coward of Baniard Hall." He grinned at his servants, savoring his triumph.

Ridley's steward growled and leaped forward, his hands curled into fists. "Milord, will you not answer the insult?" he cried.

Ridley sauntered to the table and picked up Sir Henry's tankard of wine. He took a deep draught, rubbed his hand across his lips and shrugged. "Why should I? All I want is the girl. She's not worth a fight." He made a face at the tankard and motioned to the innkeeper. "Bring me some gin. Not this watered slop." He looked at his steward, ignoring the expression of dismay on the man's face. "Briggs, take the girl back to the Hall. I'm sure Sir Henry and I can settle this business like gentlemen."

"No." Crompton shook his head. Ridley's lack of shame at his own cowardice had clearly taken the edge off Sir Henry's victory. "There's the matter of a poached rabbit. The law says…"

Ridley silenced him with an impatient wave of his hand. "There's no cause for an arrest. The rabbit was mine. From my woods. The girl had my leave to take it. I'll swear to that in court, if I must. Do you understand?"

Crompton wasn't about to give up so easily. "You can't prove it," he said. He pouted like a spoiled child. "And the insult to my person, my pride…"

Ridley's mouth twisted in a sardonic smile. "Think of how your pride will be salved when you go to London and tell them that Viscount Ridley wouldn't fight you."

"Well…" Crompton hesitated. "There's some satisfaction in that, I suppose, but…" He frowned in thought and scratched at his fat chins.

Ridley strode toward Allegra and his servant. "Quick now, Briggs, while he's wavering," he said in a low voice. "Into the carriage with you. Take the girl back to the Hall. See she's fed and dressed in proper woman's fashion."

"But how will you get back, milord?"

"Send a groom with a horse for me. In the meantime," he grinned goatishly as a pink-cheeked serving girl came out of the inn bearing a flask of gin, "I'll find my own amusements."

"There's no need for you to trouble yourself, milord," said Allegra. She hoped she sounded deferential enough. Defiance had earned her nothing. But perhaps the man could be persuaded to be reasonable. "Just let me go and I'll be on my way. Neither you nor Sir Henry will ever see me again."

Ridley shook his head. "Not just yet. You intrigue me. What's your name?"

"Allegra…" she hesitated. She'd be safer if no one knew she was a Baniard. "Mackworth," she finished. That had been Great-grandmama's name.

He smiled, his eyes narrowing. "Well, Allegra Mackworth, go back to the Hall with Briggs and wait for me. I'm not done with you yet."

He was not about to be reasonable. Allegra glared at him. She hated his smirking face, the pale, cold amber of his gin-glazed eyes, the cruel sensuality of his mouth. And her back had begun to throb and she was faint with hunger and John Wickham was dead. She groaned. "Godamercy, what do you want of me?" she said wearily.

His lecherous glance flickered over the exposed skin of her neck and throat and came to rest on her mouth. "I can think of any number of things," he said. His voice was thick with drink and lust.

"Curse your soul!" she cried, and raised her hand to strike the ugly smile from his face. But her strength gave way; her arm dropped to her side. She blinked in desperation, fighting the waves of dizziness and nausea that threatened to overcome her.

"Here you are, miss. Lean on me." Briggs put his strong arm around her waist, supporting her when she would have fallen.

Ridley laughed. "Always the gentleman, aren't you, Briggs? *You* would have taken Crompton's challenge, I have no doubt." He laughed again as Briggs clenched his jaw and said nothing. "Ah, well. Let me see if I can persuade Crompton to my views. Take the creature home." He sniffed in distaste. "And, for God's sake, see that she has a bath!"

Chapter Three

Allegra dropped onto the seat of Ridley's carriage and closed her eyes. She felt wretched, her strong spirit beginning to fail her. She was near to swooning from hunger, and her limbs shook uncontrollably. Her back still stung from Crompton's lash and she ached with weariness. Worst of all, her mind was beginning to wander, playing tricks with her reason. Godamercy, now she even fancied that she could smell food!

"Here, Miss Allegra."

She opened her eyes as the carriage started off. Ridley's steward, Briggs, sat opposite her, smiling. In his hand he held a meat pie, wrapped in a snowy napkin. "I didn't think Sir Henry would miss it from his table," he said.

She was too overwhelmed with hunger to do more than nod her thanks. She snatched the pie from him and devoured it in a few frenzied seconds, scarcely stopping to chew—or even to breathe—in her haste to fill her empty belly. She was breathless by the time she had swallowed the last crusty bite and sucked the gravy from her fingers. She drew in a gasping breath and leaned back in contentment, smiling her gratitude at Briggs. "Thank you, sir."

"There will be more food for you at the Hall, of course," he said. "But I thought that a little prologue would not be amiss."

For the first time, she examined him with care. A very agreeable-looking young man, with soft gray eyes and a serious, thoughtful mien. Like his master, he wore his own hair—dark blond—tied neatly behind, but his clothing was of plainer stuff, as somber and restrained as his expression. Except that he lacked a white collar, he looked like a country parson. "You're the kindliest man I've met since I came to England, Mr. Briggs," she said.

He seemed pleased at that, but without conceit. "I thank you for the compliment, miss. You've come from the tropics, I should guess. Your dark complexion…" He paused delicately. Englishwomen guarded their fair skins from the sun.

"I've come from the Colonies, yes," she replied. That was enough for him and his master to know for now. She stirred in discomfort and felt a trickle down her back. "I fear I may have bloodied your coat," she said.

His jaw tightened. "Sir Henry is a savage."

She laughed dryly. "Sir Henry is a proud man, and I had just tossed half his dinner in his face. I scarce know if his anger was for the loss of his pride, or the loss of his meat. Don't grudge the man his full measure of wrath." She laughed again—a deep, throaty chuckle. "Besides, he gave My Lord Ridley the opportunity to play the part of a knight-errant."

Briggs frowned. "Play? His Lordship saved your life."

"Nonsense," she said, and accompanied the word with a snort. "Sir Henry eats too much for his own good. He could scarcely move. I warrant the man was like to have died of apoplexy ere he could deliver the next stroke. Let alone kill me with blows."

Briggs shook his head. "Don't you know of the Black Act? Well," he went on as she looked perplexed, "I suppose not, if you've been in America. It was passed last year. To stem the tide of poachers in the land. Under the Black Act, poaching is against the common good, and a hanging offense now."

She stared in astonishment. "But there have always been poachers! No less than highwaymen and thieves. And a fair sight less threatening to the common good."

"But of late there have been whole gangs of men abroad," Briggs elaborated. "They break into enclosed parks and invade private forests to spirit off deer and game. They even took to wearing disguises, blacking their faces, so as not to be recognized. That didn't sit well with our esteemed minister, Walpole, and his friends. It was decided that poaching should become a capital offense, at least when committed by armed felons in disguise."

Allegra nodded in understanding, aware at last of the danger she'd been in. "Felons in disguise, you say. And that would include women dressed as…?"

"Young lads," he finished. "Aye. Even though the purpose of your disguise, I should guess, was to ensure your safety. You see my point. But for Lord Ridley's intervention with Sir Henry you had more to lose than merely the skin off your back."

From one dilemma to another. Her mouth twisted in a bitter smile. "And now Lord Ridley expects me to pay for my life with my virtue?"

SYLVIA HALLIDAY

Briggs cleared his throat and stared down at the buckles on his shoes. "I'm sure His Lordship has no such thought," he said, reddening.

"He must expect *something* in return. To let Sir Henry shame him like that. The 'coward of Baniard Hall.'" Allegra frowned. The juxtaposition of the two words—coward and Baniard—seemed an affront to her family's proud name. "Is he?" she demanded of Briggs. "A coward?"

His cheeks were now a bright red. "Lord Ridley is a man of many fine qualities," he said.

"But is he a 'white-livered' coward, as Sir Henry said? Is he truly afraid to duel?"

"His Lordship...disdains to accept any challenges," he said stiffly.

"You're a very loyal man, Mr. Briggs, as well as a kindly one. I wonder you lower yourself to work for such an unworthy master."

"There is much in His Lordship that is admirable. And a man has a duty to himself—once he has been employed—to render service to the best of his ability."

"Are the rest of the servants at Baniard Hall so loyal?"

He scowled. "'Tis not in their natures, alas. They serve because they are well paid, and leave when they weary of...life at the Hall. But I was born a gentleman."

"And will remain so, I think. No matter your straitened circumstances."

He searched her face, his expression shrewd and filled with understanding. "As you were born...*what*, Miss Allegra? Surely not of common stock, for all your rags."

She sighed. "I was born to suffer, Mr. Briggs."

"At least until Baron Ellsmere is dead?"

She compressed her lips. "Pardon me, but that is none of your affair," she said softly.

He ducked his head, acknowledging her gentle rebuke. "And your name, Mackworth?" he said at last.

She shrugged. "Not my own, of course. I took it from a gravestone in a churchyard. It has a nice sound to it."

They rode in silence after that, climbing slowly to the long Shropshire ridge known as Wenlock Edge. Briggs watched Allegra all the while, as the carriage rocked and creaked its way through the hills. But it was a look of such benign good will—without a hint of disapproval or lechery—that Allegra soon relaxed and gave herself up to her musings. She wondered if the Hall had changed, if there were any servants left who had served the Baniards. She hoped not. It would only make matters more difficult for her, to be recognized. And eight long years, after all.

30

Surely Wickham would have replaced every servant loyal to the Baniards. As for Ridley's people, she had the impression from Briggs that they stayed for only a short time.

At last they reached the crest of the Edge and the gates of Baniard Hall. Humphrey, the gatekeeper, opened for them, then gaped in astonishment to see Allegra within the carriage. She ignored him, leaning forward to peer out the window as the carriage swept up the long, gently curving drive. They emerged from the trees, and Allegra held her breath for a moment, filled with cold dread and heart-stopping anticipation.

Baniard Hall. The place of her birth, her happy childhood. It sat in the middle of its park, commanding a view of the hills; for all the splendor of its setting, it was a modest old manor house of soft, honey-colored limestone and gray granite columns and pediments. The tall windows glinted like golden coins in the afternoon sun, and a thin wisp of smoke curled from the kitchen chimney. The lawn was a smooth green carpet, and the gardens stretched into the distance, their beds bright with summer flowers.

Allegra bit her lip as the carriage crunched over the gravel of the drive and swung around to the back of the Hall. No matter how hard she stared, her eyes absorbing every detail, it was just a manor house—beautiful, old, serene. Familiar, yet strangely distant with time. It stirred no painful memories. Moved nothing within her heart and soul. It was all she could do to remind herself that she'd lived here once.

She didn't know whether she was glad or sad. The memories had kept her hatred alive for all those years; now she felt oddly bereft. But perhaps the still-fresh recollections of her misery in Carolina would serve as well to strengthen her resolve against Wickham. She mustn't forget her duty to the ghosts.

There were clacking geese in the enclosed yard near the kitchen entrance, and several tethered mastiffs began to bark as the carriage came to a stop. A groom opened the door and grinned when Allegra stepped out. "Here's a draggle-tailed package, or I'm hanged." He raised a questioning eyebrow as Briggs followed. "And His Lordship?" he asked.

"Take a horse and fetch him at the Thistle and Rose."

The groom snorted. "Is he still able to sit a horse?"

Briggs scowled and his voice dropped to an angry growl. "Do you have the courage to suggest the contrary to his face? If not, do as you're told, and hold your tongue." Ignoring the groom's mumbled apology, he took Allegra by the elbow and led her into the house.

An elderly woman in a starched cap bustled toward them, her mouth set in a hard line. "Mr. Briggs, you really must try and speak to His

Lordship. Margery has been in tears for half the day, and threatening to quit, because of something Lord Ridley said to her this morning."

Briggs sighed. "Then let her go. We'll find another."

"But she's the third laundry maid in a month!"

Briggs puffed in exasperation. "Mrs. Rutledge, you're in charge of the house servants. Surely you can find a laundress who doesn't take offense at the thoughtless ravings of a man who…" He stopped, seeming to remember his position. "His Lordship isn't always himself," he went on more calmly. "The servants should be made to understand that. 'Tis their place to respect the master, not to nurse their grievances. In the meantime, promise Margery half a guinea as a sop to her pride. And begin to train another girl in case she leaves anyway. Now…" He gestured toward Allegra. "His Lordship wishes this girl to be properly tended. See that she's fed and bathed. And find clothes for her."

"A girl?" The housekeeper smiled, a malicious smirk. Her glance took in the shirt-sleeved Briggs and Allegra—in her tattered masculine clothing—still wrapped in the steward's coat. "It *has* been an interesting day for His Lordship, I take it, Mr. Briggs," she purred.

"See to your duties, Mrs. Rutledge," he said stiffly, and hurried away.

The housekeeper scanned Allegra from the top of her head to the dusty toes of her shoes. "You're a pretty one, I'll say that for you. Despite your browned skin and dirty face. You'll clean up right well. His Lordship has a good eye, whatever else one can say of him." She motioned toward an inner staircase. "Well, come along, girl."

The implied meaning in the woman's words touched the very core of Allegra's fear. "I'm not here to be His Lordship's whore," she said defiantly.

The housekeeper shrugged her indifference. "You could do worse. His Lordship, at least, is generous with his money."

But not nearly generous enough to buy his servants' loyalty, thought Allegra, hearing the sharp contempt in the housekeeper's voice.

Mrs. Rutledge led Allegra down a flight of stairs, past the kitchens and the large servants' hall, and settled her into a small, simple parlor. She summoned two young housemaids and gave orders in a crisp fashion. In a few minutes, Allegra was seated at a table in the parlor, enjoying her first full meal since she'd left the Carolinas. While she ate, the maids brought in a tub filled with lavender-scented water, lit a small fire in the grate, and fetched a simple blue gown, a petticoat, shift, and stays. They helped her to undress, clucking in dismay at the sight of her back, the two long whip strokes that made an ugly cross.

"'Swounds!" said one of the maids. "I knew His Lordship weren't the kind of johnny you'd take to church of a Sunday, but I didn't think he would do this. Not even him!"

"It wasn't Ridley," said Allegra. "It was Sir Henry Crompton."

"Oh, that one," said the other maid. She giggled wickedly. "Beg your pardon, miss, but you must have been trying to steal his food. That's the only reason *he'd* be in a temper."

The first maid laughed even louder. "My cousin Mary is in service to him. They all whisper in the servants' hall that when Sir Henry dies, they'll bank his coffin with cabbages instead of roses, and string garlands of sausages in the church!" She explored Allegra's back with soft fingers. "Well, it looks fair to heal soon enough, miss. And we've all had our share of beatings. Into the tub with you, now. There's only a few places where the skin is broke, so it won't sting but for a minute."

Allegra was grateful for their gentleness and thoroughness, for the comfort of surrendering to someone else's care. And though they exclaimed at the odd contrast of her pale body with the deeply tanned skin of her face and forearms, they had the kindness to leave her to her thoughts, working mostly in a companionable silence that soothed and lulled her.

By the time she was bathed and dressed—her stays laced loosely so as not to press against her sore back—she was beginning to nod, lost in a drowsy haze. She sat on a stool before the fire, her eyes closed, while the maids dried and combed her freshly washed hair, which fell in dark, abundant curls almost to her waist. She drifted on a warm tide of ease and contentment. It was an unfamiliar luxury. Tomorrow she would think of Wickham and her duty. Tomorrow she would resume her journey. But today…She yawned and sighed, her head dropping forward on her breast. Today…

She was aware suddenly that the combing had ceased—and more than a few minutes ago. That the room was very quiet. Her eyes flew open and she jerked upright. Ridley leaned against the mantel, watching her through half-closed eyes. The servants were gone. The door was closed.

Ridley shook his head and smiled lazily. "Burn me, but you're a fine-looking wench."

She jumped to her feet and glared at him, her body tense with the wariness of a cornered animal. She wished that the maids had given her a handkerchief to wrap around her neck and shield her bosom. She was painfully aware that her full breasts—lifted and cradled by her stays—

swelled enticingly above the frilled edge of her shift, the low-cut bodice of her gown.

Ridley was equally aware. His glance lingered on her bosom for a long, slow minute while his sensual mouth curved in a smile of pleasure. Then he ran his eyes over her body, from top to bottom, and back again—a frank and open appraisal.

Allegra shivered. It reminded her of the auction block at Charles Town. She remembered how Ridley had stared when he'd stripped her in front of Crompton. "Vile man," she muttered. "Plague take you and your wicked eyes."

He grinned. "Nothing, I see, will daunt that passionate spirit. Barbara...the little maidservant who tended you," he explained, "tells me Crompton's whip didn't do too much harm. Show me. Loosen your shift and turn around."

"I will not!" She clenched her teeth in defiance.

The smile faded from his face. "I'm not in the habit of being disobeyed. Turn around, I say."

Allegra swallowed hard. At this moment, she couldn't imagine why they called him coward. Not when his very aspect was intimidating—the cold amber eyes, the set of his jaw. The sense that he was capable of sudden violence. Ah, well. If she had to fight him, it was sensible to choose her battles with care. And this wasn't the time. She sighed in resignation, fumbled with the strings of her shift and presented her back to him.

He lifted her heavy curls from her shoulders, running his fingers sensuously through their length before tucking them to one side. He pulled down her gown and shift in back, the better to assess the damage from Sir Henry's whip, and gently stroke the bruised flesh. His hand was warm and soft on her skin—more a caress than an examination.

Allegra found herself trembling, caught off guard by the strange feelings he stirred within her. It had been such a long time since she'd known a tender touch, a kindly hand.

His voice was soft behind her, as warm and unsettling as his touch. "It will heal without scarring, I hope. It would be a pity to mar such beauty. Scented velvet." He bent and pressed his lips against her neck.

Allegra shivered at the feel of his burning mouth, then stiffened in sudden alarm. Godamercy, she must be mad! To allow herself even a moment's weakness? Was she such a fool to forget what the rogue wanted from her? And to let him accomplish his lechery through a tender seduction! Sweet heaven. Where was her Baniard pride?

She pulled away, hastily refastening her shift, and darted around the table. It was scarcely a safe barrier, but at least it would keep him at a distance while she marshaled her scattered wits. Her eyes cast wildly about the room as she searched for an escape, weapons, *something*. "Devil take you," she said. "I'm not a meek she-goat, to go to slaughter without a battle!"

Ridley began to laugh. "So I've discovered." He stuck out his tongue and scraped it with his thumbnail, grunting in discomfort. "Still…" he continued, "you're a challenge, Allegra Mackworth." He edged around the table toward her, his eyes gleaming with hungry desire. "And worth the battle."

She circled in her turn, backing away to keep the table between them. They watched each other warily, adversaries at a deadly tournament. Allegra was filled with dread. He could rush her, leap across the table, overpower her in an instant. And then what? A moment's careless triumph for him, soon forgotten. For her, shame and humiliation. As it had been for Mama. Her shoulders sagged in resignation and weariness. She couldn't endure any more today. "You monster," she whispered.

If she didn't already know that he was a callous and self-interested devil, she might have thought she had touched his conscience. He shrugged, smiled nonchalantly and backed away from her. Then he rubbed his hand across his face, and she saw that his eyes were bright and glassy. It wasn't conscience that had stopped him; it was the effect of too much gin. "Another day, perhaps," he muttered. "We both bear too many scars from this day's battles." He pulled out a chair, sat down, and slapped a piece of paper onto the table. "To business, then. One hundred pounds."

"What?" She stared, shaken by his abrupt shift of mood.

"It cost me a hundred pounds to buy your life and freedom from Crompton." He smiled pleasantly. "I expect to be reimbursed, of course."

A hundred pounds! She sank into a chair opposite him. "But I don't…I can't…" she stammered, almost too stunned to speak.

"No, of course not. I didn't think so. Which is why I had Briggs prepare this paper."

"What is it?" Her voice was a croak of dismay.

"An indenture contract. For a year. It will scarcely repay my hundred pounds, you understand. But it will serve."

"No!" she shrieked. She leapt to her feet, shaking her head in a frenzy of helpless rage and disbelief. "No, no, *no!*"

He seemed unmoved by—or indifferent to—her passion. "I should have thought that you were no stranger to work." He shrugged. "And it's only a year, after all…"

"Work?" She spat the word. "Curse you, villain, I can tell you about work. Look!" She thrust out her hands, palms up, before his face. "Three years. Three years of indenture, to earn my passage to England! *Three years* of field work and shame and degradation!"

"Sweet Jesu," he swore softly. He reached out and stroked the calluses on her hands, and when he looked up at her his eyes were filled with unexpected pity. "Then we shall have to find softer work for you here," he murmured. "Can you read?"

"Yes," she answered sullenly.

"Good. I'm sure Mrs. Rutledge can find something useful for you to do." He frowned with a sudden thought. "You're not a runaway, are you?"

"No. I served my time to the last bitter day."

"We'll try to make your stay here more pleasant."

She glared at him. She'd never hated anyone more in her life, except Wickham. Ridley was stealing a whole year from her. A whole year! And he sat chatting as though they were negotiating a lease on a piece of property. "What if I should refuse to sign?" she challenged.

"Then I should be forced to take you back to Crompton, with his whip and his thirst for justice and his assizes. And perhaps more. He has other appetites besides his love of the trencher, so I've heard." He paused to let his meaning sink in. "But if you sign you'll be under my protection. And safe from his predations."

She groaned in anguish. Did he leave her any choice? "Why are you doing this? You don't need the money. Your servants talk of your generosity."

His mouth twisted in a sardonic smile. "'Tis the only kind thing they *do* say about me."

"Then why? What can it matter to you...a hundred pounds?"

He chuckled. "I must have Scottish ancestors. All that thrift. Besides, I thought I might buy Wickham one more year of life."

She gasped. *"Wickham?"* It was all coming clear. "You torment me and make me your unwilling servant to save a friend. Is that it?"

He shook his head. "I scarce know the man. I met him but once. But I thought to give you time to reconsider your folly."

"Reconsider? Never!"

"Well, then, time to let your passions cool a bit. If you try to kill Wickham in as rash a manner as you came at *me* this morning, you'll be caught, tried, and hanged. And there's an end to it."

"Why should I care, so long as Wickham is dead first? And why should you care what happens to me?"

"No man's life is worth destroying your own," he said with a careless shrug.

"Is that why you refuse to duel?"

He stiffened at her words, and Allegra was dimly aware that she'd somehow cracked his mask of indifference, if only for a moment. He rose from his chair and went to stand at the mantel, his head bent toward the fire, so that she couldn't see his eyes. "You'll find it's hard to sleep at night, with blood on your hands," he muttered. "A moment of madness…and you're damned for all eternity."

She heard the pain in his voice and felt an unexpected rush of sympathy. "Milord…" she began.

He seemed to recover himself. He turned and grinned; it was an ugly, artificial smile that reminded Allegra she didn't like him. So why should she care what lay behind the mask?

"I'll enjoy killing Wickham," she said, her words a cold challenge to Ridley's interference in her life.

The grin deepened. "But 'twould be a pity to see you hanged for murder. To extinguish that passion and fire. At least not until I've warmed myself at your hearth." The grin had become a satyr's leer.

She gasped in dismay. The rogue didn't deserve her sympathy. Not when he could negotiate so cruelly for her virtue. "Curse your eyes and liver," she said bitterly. "Is that what you expect, with your evil contract? Well, you may have bought my time. But never my body or my soul."

He ran his hand back and forth across the mantelpiece as though he were caressing a lover. The erotic movements of his long, sensuous fingers were spellbinding. Allegra could almost feel them on her flesh—stroking, soothing, stirring her senses with unknown joys. She felt an odd jolt, a quivering in the pit of her stomach. Ridley's voice dropped to a seductive growl. "Not even if I showed my gratitude by shortening the term of your bondage? I might be persuaded, you know."

His words brought her to her senses. Was there ever a man more heartless than this devil? Giving her a choice that was no choice at all. "Must I be an unwilling whore to earn a reprieve?"

"No. I should want you compliant, or not at all."

"Then it will be not at all," she said firmly. "Unless you have a mind to rape me," she added, her eyes opening wide with the sudden, dreadful thought.

He smirked, a wicked smile. "What an unkind notion. You cut me to the quick. But 'tis not in my nature to take a woman against her will."

"And this morning, in the woods?" She could scarcely conceal her contempt.

He threw up his hands in a playful gesture of innocence. "I merely wanted a kiss or two. And you repaid me most cruelly."

She rubbed her fingers across her eyes and sighed in resignation. "You may be enjoying this game, but not I. Can we not return to the business at hand?"

"Of course." He took an inkstand from the mantel and set it on the table. "Are we agreed to the terms?"

"A year of my life for a hundred pounds?" Her voice cracked as she thought of the postponement of her hopes and dreams. "A whole year?"

"I feel sure your hatred of Wickham will burn like a beacon through the long year." He lifted her chin with his fingers and stared into her dark eyes. "Indeed, there's no danger of that passion burning out." His mocking tone vanished. His expression was suddenly solemn and filled with bewilderment. "My God," he muttered, "where does it come from— all that intensity? And what did Wickham do to earn such hatred?"

She moved away from his hand, his probing eyes, and reached for the quill pen. "A year," she said crisply, evading his questions. "And I need fear no sudden ambush in the night?"

He shook his head and laughed, the rakehell once again. "Not from me. Though my offer stands. You give me a willing woman—and I consider amending the contract. I might even buy you a silken gown or two. Something low cut, to display that fine bosom."

"Though I'm sorely tempted," she said with sarcasm, "I shall remain steadfast for the full year."

He smiled lazily, reached out and wrapped one of her dark curls around his finger. "I warn you, I shall try to woo you into my bed. You're a devilish tempting morsel."

She shook her head free. "I'll resist you at every turn."

He grinned. "Then it will be a year of sweet battles. That thought alone excites me." He laughed at the look of disgust on her face. "I trust you won't be foolish enough to run away. 'Tis a capital offense here in England. For bond servants to flee their masters."

"Until Wickham is dead, I'll guard my own life. I have no wish to hang as a runaway." She dipped the pen in the ink, bent over the table and signed the accursed contract. Ridley had her trapped, and they both knew it. She sighed. Heigh-ho! She'd waited this long to avenge the family. She could practice Baniard patience for one more year. That is, if she didn't end up killing this devil Ridley before the time was out!

He folded the contract and slipped it into the breast of his coat. "One more thing," he said. "A trifling matter, you understand. But since the rest of the servants at the Hall are hired, only you and I and Briggs need know of this agreement. He will arrange a small salary for you. To prevent gossip."

He seemed a bit too offhand. Allegra wondered if he felt a twinge of conscience, after all. "Are you ashamed of this arrangement?" she asked softly. "Or concerned for *my* shame?"

He laughed, a hard, mocking sound. "God's truth, not at all. But I still hope to persuade you into my bed before the year is out. I feel sure you'll want to…" he laughed again, "…'negotiate' for an early release long before next summer comes to these hills. And I shouldn't want the other servants to think you were coerced by the terms of a foolish contract. Far better that they should think you found me irresistible."

Allegra snorted in disgust at his smug arrogance, but said nothing.

He raised a sharp eyebrow. "You disagree? Very well, then. I give you leave, whenever you wish, to tell them that I bought you, hoping to make you my whore."

She flinched at the naked cruelty of his words. She was beginning to understand why everyone at Baniard Hall seemed to hate the master. Well, she thought, steeling herself to ignore his venom, the villain wouldn't reduce *her* to tears! Not like poor Margery. "It will remain our secret," she said. She bobbed a stiff curtsy. "May I go and find Mrs. Rutledge now, milord? I'll need a bed, if I must stay a year."

"Tell her to inform me where she intends to put you. There might come a time when…" He leered wickedly.

Curse him. She'd be revenged for his cruel words, whatever it cost her. She gave him a cold stare. "I scarce believe that will happen, milord. On my oath, but with your fondness for the bottle I wonder you can find your *own* bed by the time night falls. Let alone another's." She curtsied again and was pleased to see his arrogant smile turn to a frown as she fled the parlor.

Allegra grunted and sat up in bed, blinking against the night-black room. She grimaced and flexed her shoulders. Perhaps it was her sore back that had awakened her. For surely when Mrs. Rutledge had led her to this little room under the eaves, and she'd stretched out across the soft bed as twilight darkened the dormer window, she had thought she'd sleep for days. At least until morning, when she would be assigned her chores.

She frowned, peering into the gloom. No, it wasn't her back that had disturbed her rest. There were sounds, voices, coming from somewhere beyond her door. For just a moment's panic, she wondered if Ridley had changed his mind about attacking her in her bed. Then she shook her head and laughed softly. Ridley wouldn't be shouting like that if he intended to creep into her room!

She stood up and made her way to the door. Her room was at the head of a small staircase that led down to a wide passageway on the floor below. She opened the door and padded down the stairs on bare feet, her shift billowing softly around her legs. Ridley's voice was louder now—unintelligible but blended with other masculine cries and shouts.

The passageway was a scene of chaos. There were chairs overturned, mirrors smashed. Candles blazed from one end to the other; even as Allegra watched, another footman rushed in, bearing more lights. A side door opened and Briggs hurried forward, carrying several lengths of rope. Other servants cried out, and ran helplessly back and forth like skittish horses in a thunderstorm. One candlestick had been knocked to the floor, igniting the edge of a carpet; a footman beat frantically at the flames.

And in the middle of all this tumult was Ridley. His coat and boots were off, and his shirt hung loose from his breeches. His hair ribbon was gone; his long brown locks drooped about his face, damp with sweat. Even as Allegra watched, trembling in terror, he let out a roar, picked up a chair and crashed it against a large painting. Then he turned and lurched in her direction.

"Godamercy," whispered Allegra, and pressed herself against the wall.

Ridley stopped in front of her and stared. His eyes were bloodshot, and he reeked of liquor. His mouth hung slack, oozing with spittle, and his expression was so frightening that Allegra threw her arms in front of her body to ward off the expected attack.

Then his expression changed, and a slow, sad smile spread across his face. "My Lady of the Sorrows," he said hoarsely, gazing into Allegra's eyes with a look of such pain that it nearly broke her heart. "Have you come to weep with me?"

"M-milord..." she said with a stammer, confused and bewildered.

"Sir Greyston." A small, dark-skinned man had stepped forward and put his hand on Ridley's arm. "Come to bed now. The moon is being full on the Ganges." His voice was a soothing singsong, sweet and faintly foreign. "Come, Sir Greyston. To bed. And I shall light the incense and fill your dreams with the sweetness of the lotus blossom."

Ridley nodded and turned, his steps shaky. Then, in a frightening transformation, he suddenly shook off the other man's hand, raised his fists in the air and began to bellow, his face contorted in fury.

"Now!" cried Briggs, motioning to the servants. "Take him now!"

Several footmen rushed Ridley, clutching at his arms, his twisting body, his legs. He kicked and bucked, cursing them all the while. After a few moments of fierce struggle, he was pinned to the floor, his arms and feet bound with Briggs's rope. Writhing in fury and still shouting curses at his captors, he was carried down the passageway and into his rooms.

Allegra sagged against a table, her body shaking uncontrollably. She heard a soft laugh and looked up. The two maids who had served her were coming down the stairs.

"I remember the first time *I* saw that," said the one called Barbara, with an air of superiority.

"Dear heaven," said Allegra, wrapping her arms around herself to still her trembling. "How often does it happen?"

Barbara shrugged. "Once a month or so." She turned to her companion. "Isn't it so, Verity?"

Verity giggled. "Once a month…like the full moon on the Ganges."

Allegra was horrified at their lack of concern, their want of compassion. "But that's dreadful!"

Barbara tossed her head. "He'll remember nothing of it in the morning. He'll be as cruel as ever, finding fault with the housemaids and insulting the grooms."

Allegra was still thinking of the frightful scene she'd witnessed. "But why does it happen?"

"Even *he* can drink too much, once in a while. And then he needs that ugly little valet of his to put him to bed."

"He's from India, isn't he?" Allegra remembered once seeing a sailor from Calcutta in the harbor of Charles Town.

"Aye. His name is Jagat Ram. Strange, dirty little man. I don't like him. But he's the only one Lord Ridley wants with him, when he's like that."

"Why does he drink so?" asked Allegra. She remembered the scene with Sir Henry. "Does he run from his own cowardice?"

"No. 'Tis his dead wife," said Barbara. "At least *I* think so. Don't you, Verity?"

Allegra felt a twinge of pity. Even Ridley didn't deserve such torment. "Does he mourn his wife so deeply, that he must rage like that?"

"*Mourn* her? It isn't grief that moves him. 'Tis guilt!"

"But why?"

Verity shuddered and turned to go back up the stairs. "I don't like this place. Good wages or no, if I can get another position, I will. Come, Barbara. To bed."

"Wait." Allegra put her hand on the girl's arm. The long passageway still seemed to echo with Ridley's agonized shouts. "Why should he feel guilt over his wife?"

Verity's eyes opened wide in superstitious horror, and she glanced nervously about. "Fortune preserve you and me," she whispered. "They say he killed her."

Chapter Four

"To begin, you will sup at the lowest table in the servants' hall, with the dairy maid and the scullions. So long as you are under my dominion, you will *earn* the right to improve your station, and not a moment before." Mrs. Rutledge's voice was cold and pinched. What little civility she had shown the previous day had vanished before Allegra's new and servile position in the Hall.

Allegra gave an uneasy curtsy. "Yes, ma'am." What had she done to earn the woman's obvious disapproval? She guessed it must be because Ridley himself had brought her into the household without consulting his housekeeper. A slap at the woman's haughty authority in the Hall. Surreptitiously she scanned Mrs. Rutledge's room, centrally located on the lower ground floor next to Mr. Briggs's office. However much the housekeeper might hold her employer in contempt, it was clear that she had profited mightily from her service here. The room was lavishly furnished; a snug alcove separated a velvet-curtained bed, polished tables, and comfortable chairs from a solid and workaday desk, covered with ledgers and schedules and the various accouterments that attended the running of a large household. Even there, however, nothing had been spared: the inkstand was of silver, not brass, and the armchair upon which the housekeeper sat was upholstered in a handsome crimson mohair.

Mrs. Rutledge opened a little enameled box on the desk and popped a sucket into her mouth. "Have you served in a great house before?"

"No, ma'am, but I'm not a stranger to work."

"So His Lordship has indicated. And yet I have been instructed that you are not to be given any excessively heavy work." She searched Allegra's face as though she were seeking clues to the mystery. "You're not sickly, are you?" she asked with suspicion.

"I'm as fit as any servant here." It was difficult to keep the edge out of her voice. The last thing she wanted was favors from Ridley. "I can work as hard as the next girl."

A slow, crafty smile spread across the housekeeper's face. "But for a great deal less. Three pounds. An insulting pittance, I should say. I wonder why you accepted it. Or why His Lordship didn't offer more." She waited expectantly, her eyes bright with curiosity, for Allegra's response.

Wait in vain, thought Allegra. I'll tell you nothing.

After a long moment of silence, Mrs. Rutledge shrugged. "Well, who knows what goes on in that man's head?" she said, her lip curling. She took another sweetmeat. "As to your duties, you will work as a housemaid, unless you prove yourself apt for more taxing responsibilities. Follow Verity's lead. She's an industrious girl, and a good example." Mrs. Rutledge's lips puckered in sudden displeasure. For a moment, Allegra wondered if the sucket was made of lemon peel. "Mr. Briggs tells me you can read and write," the older woman went on sourly. "I trust that will not prompt you to give yourself airs above your station. Or lord it over the other girls. I can make your life very unpleasant here, if I choose." She twirled an imperious finger in the air. "Now, turn. Let me look at you."

"Yes, ma'am." Allegra swallowed her resentment. It would be foolish to make an enemy of the woman. She turned slowly, allowing the housekeeper to assess her costume. Before they'd gone down to a hearty breakfast in the servants' hall this morning, Barbara had given her several additional pieces of clothing—a neckerchief that modestly covered her breasts and tucked into her stays, a small white linen cap to perch on her pinned-up black hair, and a crisp apron. Though she was dressed in the usual habit of a housemaid, it was far grander than anything she'd ever worn in Carolina. Gammer Pringle had been as stingy with clothing as she'd been with food. Or kindness.

Mrs. Rutledge frowned. "The sun has scorched you to a parchment. You're scarcely fit to look upon." She nodded her head for emphasis. "Well, a few good scrubs with fuller's earth and sand should take off that color and make you as white as a summer lily."

Allegra frowned in her turn. She was here to be a servant, not a pale-faced flower. Godamercy! She had a sudden, dread thought. "Is it His Lordship's wish?" she asked with some heat. "Does he still hope I'll play the lisping, mincing trollop for him?"

The housekeeper's cold eyes narrowed. "You will not speak to me in that way again, miss! His Lordship likes pretty wenches around him. What he does with them is entirely his affair. 'Tis not my place to question. Nor yours, the good Lord knows! But I do not intend to bear the brunt of his sharp tongue if you are not fit to be seen! You will scrub your face twice a day, without fail. Or I shall have the cook and her helpers do it for you. Do you understand?"

Allegra bowed her head in defeat. "Yes, ma'am," she murmured.

Her tone seemed to placate the other woman. "If you mind your manners," she said more kindly, "you will find life pleasant enough at the Hall. At least below stairs." She hesitated, toying with her quill pen. "His Lordship…I mean to say…that is, Mr. Briggs tells me you were present last night." She lifted her chin and stared directly into Allegra's eyes. "You saw?"

Allegra nodded, the color rising to her cheeks at the memory of Ridley's dreadful humiliation.

"His Lordship is given to…occasional outbursts of that sort. You will have to learn to accept it. And hold your tongue outside of the Hall." The housekeeper's voice deepened with scorn. "Whatever one may think of such behavior, His Lordship's shame is ours while we serve him. I will not have it noised around the parish, to add to all the other things they say about him."

Allegra nodded again, but kept silent. Mrs. Rutledge was certainly not the one to ask about Ridley's reputation as a coward, no matter how curious she was. Barbara and Verity seemed more likely to share the local gossip with her. "Where shall I begin this morning, ma'am?" she asked.

"Have someone direct you to His Lordship's apartment. He was particularly fitful last night. There is much work to be done. You will find the other girls already there." The housekeeper dismissed her with a wave of the hand.

There was no need for Allegra to ask directions. Ridley's rooms had been Papa's apartment. She climbed the main staircase to the ground floor, went along a wide passageway past open salons and drawing rooms, and mounted the back stairs to Ridley's rooms on the floor above. It gave her an odd sensation, to pass through the house this way. She tried to picture herself as a young child—skipping in these passageways, sneaking down to the kitchen for a treat from the kindly cook, trailing worshipfully behind her grown-up brother and sister. But her memories were too dim, washed away by the horrors that had followed.

Moreover, everything within Baniard Hall was changed. The paneling was new, the wall-papers freshly hung, the furnishings far more showy than Mama's elegant taste would have approved. Here and there, in passing, she thought she recognized a piece of furniture—a table, a carved chair—but she couldn't be sure. And the paintings on the walls were, for the most part, unfamiliar to her. She sighed, feeling an odd sense of guilt. Of unworthiness. Why did *she* have to be the only survivor? Mama wouldn't have felt so remote from her own house. Nor Lucinda, or Charlie.

A half dozen footmen were busy in the passageway in front of Ridley's apartment when she reached it. They bustled about like bees in a hive, sweeping up the debris from the night before, removing the charred carpet, replacing broken chairs and mirrors. A workman with a bucket of plaster and tools was attempting to restore a chipped piece of molding around a doorframe, and a fresh-faced young boy scrubbed diligently at a stain on the painted wainscoting.

Allegra skirted a smashed marble bust that lay in front of Ridley's door and stepped over the threshold into his private drawing room. The havoc here matched that of the passageway. Overturned furniture, broken porcelain, candles and candlesticks scattered to every corner. There were three maids in the room, hard at work; the only one Allegra recognized—Barbara—was on her knees near the door. She held a small knife, which she was using to scrape at hardened candle-drippings on the polished floor. She looked up as Allegra entered and scowled. "Do you always dawdle?" she asked petulantly.

"Mrs. Rutledge kept me. I'm sorry." Allegra glanced around the room and clicked her tongue. "Godamercy, what a mess."

Barbara snorted and jerked her chin in the direction of an inner door. "The bedchamber is worse still. He wanted a doxy last night, but changed his mind when he saw her. He drove her away in tears, then began to pour bottles of claret all over the place. One for his gullet, one for the room. Lord knows how long it went on. The boys carried out a tub piled with empty bottles this morning. The bed is stained beyond belief—linens, hangings, everything. Even the draperies at the windows!"

Allegra shook her head in amazement. "How can a man spend good money to furnish his house and then befoul it? Drunk *or* sober."

"They're not *his* furnishings. He never bothered to change a thing when he bought the Hall, Mrs. Rutledge says. What's here belonged to the last lord of the manor. Baron Ellsmere."

"I've…heard of him," said Allegra. "Wickham was the family name, wasn't it? Or so they say." She tried to sound offhand. It was best she learn to hear and say the hated names without flinching. She was suddenly curious about the current parish gossip. "Did the Ellsmeres always own the Hall?" she asked.

"No. The Baniards were before them. A long time ago. That's where the Hall gets its name. They're all dead now. And good riddance. Traitors to the Crown, they say. I never knew a one of the rascals, myself. Though there be a man or two in Newton, and a few of the older cottagers, who still speak kindly of the family." She frowned and scratched at the stubborn wax on the floor, then threw down her knife and rose to her feet. "This will never serve. Perhaps a firkin of green soap and a good scouring with a brush…" She made for the door, pointing toward the bedchamber as she went. "Verity is inside with Margery. Go and help them."

The one called Margery—the laundry maid—was bending over a large, canopied bed and complaining as Allegra opened the door. "Oh, Verity," she said in a soft whine, "I'll never get this damask clean! What am I to do?" She stripped the stained coverlet from the bed, then began to pull off the sheets.

Verity was perched on a tall ladder that leaned against the bedframe; she unhooked a length of pale-gold silk from the tester and sighed. "'Odds fish, Margery. Don't start in to wailing again. Mrs. Rutledge don't expect miracles. If it comes clean, so be it. If not, maybe Mr. Briggs can talk His Lordship into buying new goods."

"But you don't understand!" Margery's lower lip had begun to quiver. "He took me to task only yesterday. Called me a stupid, clumsy girl who couldn't keep his linens clean. And after I'd dipped them in blueing three times and all, and scrubbed my fingers raw…" She fluttered helplessly with her hands, gesturing toward the piles of gold damask on the floor; the delicate silk was mottled with dark-red stains. "Now, what am I to do about all of *this?*"

"Don't you fret, Margery." Verity turned, saw Allegra and nodded. "See? Here's another pair of hands for us. This is Allegra, the new girl."

Allegra smiled a greeting. "If you wish, I'll fold the draperies as you take them down," she said, to be helpful. At Verity's nod, she set to work, folding the heavy lengths as the other two women stripped the bed and the windows.

"They were talking about you at breakfast," said Margery at last. "And that cruel Sir Henry."

"Wicked man," muttered Verity. "With wicked hands. I met him in Ludlow on market day last month. He tried to…" She shuddered.

"I can't believe Lord Ridley came to your rescue, like a champion of old," said Margery, shaking her head. "Not a man who speaks such hurtful words as that one does."

Verity snorted. "Champion? Farmer Jenkins told Humphrey that His Lordship wouldn't take Sir Henry's challenge. Not even fat Sir Henry, that a lad of ten could fight! His Lordship could drub him with one hand, if he had a mind to it. 'Champion,' indeed."

"'Tis true, then?" asked Allegra in dismay. "He'll never accept a challenge?"

"I don't know why," said Verity. "But they say when he ventures to London everyone makes sport of him. There's never a man who fails to throw his glove at Lord Ridley's feet. Just to see him turn tail and run. Why, I remember once, in Newton…"

"Enough!" said Allegra. "We'll never finish if we chatter." She didn't know why she should suddenly feel so vexed about Ridley. Why should it matter to her if he chose to act the coward? To drink his life away. Because he was favored by fortune and handsome and rich? Because it seemed such a waste?

She worked in angry silence, folding and stacking, until the room had been completely stripped of its fabric and Verity had descended from her ladder. The maid bent and lifted an armful of drapery. "Margery and I will take these to the wet laundry and start in on the scrubbing. There's fresh linens for the bed. There—in the corner. After that's done, you can come and help us. Come, Margery."

Margery picked up the remaining fabric, but Verity's words seemed to have reminded her of the hopeless chore that lay ahead. Her mouth collapsed into an unhappy pout. "I'll never get them clean. What shall I tell him, when he complains?"

Useless man, thought Allegra, still feeling anger at Ridley. To dissipate all his advantages, when others had so little…"Tell him to do his own washing!" she snapped in a loud voice.

Verity gasped and pointed to a small door in the corner of the room. "Shh! He'll hear you," she whispered.

Allegra stared in surprise. "He's in there?"

"'Tis his private closet. There's a little bed there…" Verity moved toward the drawing room door. "Finish this chamber. Then come to the laundry."

"And don't disturb the master," breathed Margery, her eyes wide with fear.

"Wait a moment, Verity," said Allegra. She was bursting to ask. And didn't the girl seem to know all the gossip? "Who is the 'Lady of the Sorrows'?" It had haunted her dreams—his heartbreaking words, the look in his eyes when he'd called her by that name last night.

Verity shrugged. "I don't know. I never heard of her. Come, Margery." They left Allegra to her work and her troubled thoughts.

It took no time for her to make up the bed, to smooth the sheets and fluff the pillows. She was used to far harder work. She glanced at the door to Ridley's closet, hesitated, then shook her head. She really should go down to the wet laundry. Still…just one peep. What harm?

The sweet, musky scent of incense wafted to her nostrils as she opened the door cautiously. "Godamercy," she whispered, staring in surprise and wonder. This room surely was Ridley's doing, not Wickham's. The man who had furnished the rest of Baniard Hall in such a commonplace manner would never have chosen *this* style!

The room she had entered was as strange and exotic as anything she had ever seen. The morning light filtered through delicately carved sandalwood shutters at the windows, and the floor was covered with a thick, luxurious carpet in a multihued design of intertwining leaves and flowers unfamiliar to Allegra. The single large armchair, which sat near a window, seemed more like a collection of silk-covered pillows attached to a wooden frame than any chair an English gentleman would choose. And the unusual yet harmonious colors of the individual pillows—saffron and sharp yellow and the bright scarlet of a tropical bird—seemed to speak of distant lands and mysterious climes.

There were several round tables inlaid with mother-of-pearl, three or four straight-backed chairs of carved and pierced teak with silk-cushioned seats, and a parade of ivory Indian elephants marching across the mantel. The various candelabra and vases and incense bowls that decorated the room were of exotic shapes—shiny brass etched with fanciful designs.

Strangest of all was the display on the wall above the hearth: a mounted collection of swords and knives, their hilts studded with precious stones, their polished blades chased and embossed with all the skill of the swordsmith's art.

Allegra bit her lip in dismay at the imposing array of weapons—forceful, challenging, bellicose. What was in the man's heart, she thought, that he should torment himself with such a reminder of his own cowardice?

Viscount Ridley lay uncovered on a small, upholstered couch to one side of the room, breathing gently. With his pallid face and white shirt, he looked strangely vulnerable against the vivid, patterned silk. He lay on his back, his eyes closed, his limbs relaxed in the softness of sleep. There was no sign of the ropes that had bound him the night before; perhaps his valet had removed them once he'd fallen asleep.

Allegra crept near the bed and studied him with curiosity. His wide brow was as smooth and free from care as a child's, and his long, dark eyelashes curled against his cheeks like delicate, fringed feathers. He was in need of a shave, though it detracted not one whit from his superb good looks. The bluish line of his stubble curved down in graceful scallops from his ears to his chin, and circled his mouth in a symmetrical oval that was extraordinarily pleasing to the eye; it made Allegra want to trace the pattern with her fingertip. His mouth—the cruel mouth that could curl with scorn, or utter harsh insults, or take hers with rapacious abandon—was now so sweet and tempting in its repose that Allegra had to fight the mad desire to bend and kiss it. Had there ever been a time, she wondered, when the man's nature had been as young and innocent and good as now his face was in sleep?

I should have liked to know you then, Greyston Ridley, she thought with a pang of yearning. To call him sweet friend, and joke and laugh, and flirt a little. And perhaps to exchange tender kisses with that mouth. They might even have been neighbors, had her life been different.

What nonsense! She smiled ruefully at her own foolish fancies. One would think she had never seen a man before, to indulge herself with such daydreams! Their worlds were as different as day and night, and she was a goose for allowing his handsome face to set her heart to pounding.

Still…She sighed for what might have been, and could never be, and then—feeling more than a little wicked—continued her shameless examination. His ruffled shirtfront was torn, and gaped open almost to the waist; Allegra's eyes followed the path from his chin, with its slight indentation, down the sinews of his neck to the patch of dark-brown curls on his chest, and on to the sleek ridge of muscle below that rose and fell with his soft breathing. The sight of his strong torso only increased the thumping in her breast; she dared not cast her eyes beyond the waistband of his breeches.

She gasped in sudden shock as she felt a band of steel clamp around her wrist. Her glance flew back to Ridley's face. Though he still lay in the same position, he was now awake and alert; he had wrapped his strong fingers around her wrist and was pulling her toward him.

Time seemed to stop. Allegra caught her breath, enchanted by what she saw. His eyes were like golden honey, liquid amber that warmed and bathed her with a tender light. His mouth hinted at a smile, and his full, soft lips invited intimacies of which she could scarcely dream. She trembled in every nerve of her body.

Then—it was an almost imperceptible shading, like the wisp of a cloudlet across the sun—everything changed. The amber crystallized. Those melting eyes were now the eyes of a tiger ready to pounce; they belonged in this exotic room. The soft curve of his mouth, which had stirred her but a minute before, now became a wolfish smirk. His eyes boldly dropped to her bosom, then returned to her face. He ran his tongue across his lips in a gesture that was hungry, sensual, mocking.

Allegra was suddenly aware of the heat of his burning hand on her wrist. She felt a prickly sensation on the back of her neck that was fear and a strange longing all at once. "Please, milord, let me go," she murmured.

He chuckled softly. "The fair Allegra." His voice was a whispered, seductive croak. "I knew that you would come to me sooner or later. But I scarce expected that you were as eager as this."

He couldn't possibly believe that she had come to offer herself! She was too dismayed to do more than stammer. "But, milord...I did not... it isn't so..."

He grinned. "Has the heat of your passion tied your tongue?"

"You misunderstand, milord," she said, more anxious than ever to make him see that she hadn't come to submit to his desires. Nor ever would, God save her! "I...only came into your closet because I wondered if I could be of service."

The grin deepened into a leer. "Yes. My point precisely. There is but one worthy service a beautiful woman can render to a man. And here you are."

She cursed her own stupidity, her unwise choice of words. Her cheeks burned with embarrassment. "I told you, milord, I'll not be—"

"My whore? Yes, I remember. But perhaps I want you to be my *lover*." He purred the word, his eyes scanning her face. "There is a world of difference, you know. Begad, 'twould be very agreeable to wake in the morning with you beside me in a bed, warm and contented after a night of passion. To hear that deep, musical voice of yours as I struggled up from a dream."

She hated him for his despicable attempts at seduction. For tender words that only a fool would trust. Why was he any different from the indolent, lecherous landholders she had seen in the Colonies? From Squire Pringle, who had been content to use her mother as though she were no more than a device for his pleasure? Ridley was probably a good deal worse than any of them—with his gin and his claret and his carnal self-indulgence. "I think it more likely you would struggle up from a drunken stupor than a dream, milord!" she said sharply.

His hand tightened on her wrist with such savagery that she flinched in pain. His eyes flashed in warning. "I expect more civility from you, now that you belong to me," he growled. "My property for a year, lest you forget. I have the right to lay hands on you as I wish, to ensure your obedience. Do I make myself clear?"

She felt a thrill of terror. The brute was physically powerful and dangerous. Capable of beating her, or…who knew what? They were quite alone, with no one to restrain him. And, God help her, *had* he killed his wife, as the rumors said? She tried to keep the fear from her voice. "Will you show yourself to be no better than Sir Henry?" she asked, hoping the memory of Crompton's cruelty would shame him.

The man was incapable of shame, that was apparent. He shrugged in indifference. "You're scarcely worth the effort it would require. Or the ruin of a good riding whip. However, I could order Mrs. Rutledge to punish you for your saucy tongue. She's an unpleasant woman, with a sharp temper besides. And a hunger for gold that would do King Midas proud. I'm sure, for a crown or two, she would do whatever I asked. Hot pepper on that tongue of yours, perhaps. Or a sound thrashing, so you couldn't sit for a few days." His mouth twisted in a sardonic smile and he stared at her, seeming to gauge her reaction to his threats.

No, by heaven, she thought. If he was waiting for her to cringe or beg for mercy, it would be a cold day in hell before she would show fear! Not to this devil! She kept her expression bland.

He began to laugh. "Egad! Not a flutter. Fearless, aren't you? Perhaps we shall have to resort to boiling oil, or some such." He laughed again. "On the other hand, I might spare you—for a forfeit. Give me a kiss."

She drew in a shocked breath. "Beg your pardon, milord, but I will not."

He grunted in annoyance and gave a sharp twist to her arm. She cried out. She found herself forced to bend low, her face just above his, merely to keep him from snapping her bones like kindling. "I shall not let you go," he said coldly, "until I get my kiss."

It was madness to fight him. Clearly he had no scruples about breaking her arm. Ah, well. What did it matter? A moment of unpleasantness, and then she could escape him. She sighed and planted her mouth on his.

She was totally unprepared for the sweet gentleness of his mouth. It moved softly under hers, as though he were seeking the precise angle at which their lips would be perfectly joined—one rounded swell pressed against the other as though they had been formed for just this divine union. She felt his other hand at the nape of her neck—stroking, caressing, his long fingers cool on her bare flesh as he held her head to his. If he meant to prevent her from raising her head, it was a wasted gesture. Nothing would have persuaded her to end the kiss. Heaven help her, if he wished to keep her lips on his until the end of time she would be willing! She had never thought a man's kiss could stir her so.

She felt abandoned when he suddenly jerked his head away from hers, pushed her upright and released her wrist. It was so brusque and surprising that she nearly toppled backward. But surely he had felt something of what had moved her. The thrill of surprise and discovery that left her still quivering. "Milord..." she whispered.

He groaned and rubbed his hand across his eyes. "Go away," he said tiredly. "I'm finished with you. My head hurts."

"You will be needing your breakfast, Sir Greyston." Ridley's valet, Jagat Ram, stood in the doorway. His voice was gentle, and his liquid, deep-set eyes were warm with concern. He bore a tray that held a cup and saucer, a chocolate pot, a plate of buttered sweet cakes, and a small flask. Behind him stood Briggs, with a sheaf of papers.

Grey shifted his body on the couch and groaned again. "Help me to sit up, Ram. And put away that bloody tray. I've not felt so vile in a long time. My head, my guts...Not even the thought of that gin holds any appeal." He glanced at Allegra. His lip curled in supreme boredom. "Are you still here, girl?" he drawled.

She glared at him, wondering if he could see the hurt, the anger, on her face. It had been deliberate—his cruelty. He wasn't a fool, after all. He had to know what he'd done. The seductive words, the sweet kiss, and then—when she was trembling, humbled, almost willing to abandon herself to him—the blunt, brutal dismissal. She scowled at him in pure hatred. It would be worth even a beating to speak her mind.

"If you must get drunk, milord," she said, "you had best stay with gin. Too much claret is poison for your head and guts. It dries out your brain and corrupts your liver. Any half-wit in an alehouse knows that!"

Briggs looked alarmed at her insolence to the master, but Grey only laughed. "Are you a storehouse of rustic lore as well as a saucy wench?" he asked.

"I only know common sense. Have your stillroom maid mix you up something for a good vomit. Then you'll be restored. To your usual disposition, milord," she added sarcastically. She gave a halfhearted curtsy. "I'm needed in the laundry," she said, and swept out the door into Ridley's bedchamber.

"Allegra!" Briggs came hurrying after her.

She stopped, and bobbed politely. He, at least, deserved a respectful greeting. "Mr. Briggs."

"You spoke of the stillroom. Are you yourself trained in the arts of distilling and perfumery and cures?"

She nodded. "At my previous employ, I was expected to know all the skills of a goodwife. And there was a library of old herbals, as well as secret family recipes, that I was permitted to use."

"And do you remember them?"

"A great many. God has blessed me with a clear memory."

He smiled in pleasure. "Good! Mrs. Rutledge will be relieved. The last stillroom maid left a week ago, and we have despaired of finding another. Come with me. You'll concoct Lord Ridley's cure, and then we shall speak to Mrs. Rutledge about your new duties."

The stillroom to which Briggs led her—an airy little space off to itself on the lower ground floor—was in a state of disarray. A jumble of porcelain bowls, glass beakers, and mixing spoons was spread across the shelves that lined the room. Some of the vials and bottles that held curative powders and other ingredients were lying open, their contents scattered. Although many of the containers were identified by crude, scribbled labels affixed to them with paste or tied on with string, more than a few bottles were unmarked. Bunches of dried herbs hung from the ceiling beams, but they were so old and faded that Allegra supposed most of them were useless by now. The large work table in the center of the room held several alembics, the cone-topped tin vessels used for distilling; they seemed serviceable, but sorely in need of polishing. And the equipment for making complicated confections—molds for jellies, cutters for marzipan, flat pans for candying nuts and fruits—was stacked in a chaotic pile. There was a small, open charcoal stove, placed under the latticed window so that the dangerous fumes given off by the coals as they burned would be dispelled; no one, it seemed, had bothered to rake out the old cinders or sweep away the ashes.

"A fine enough stillroom," said Allegra. "Though it wants a bit of orderliness," she added with a smile that held a gentle reproach.

Briggs looked embarrassed, his cheeks turning red. "Yes...well, there have been a number of girls...and the last one left in rather a haste."

Allegra snorted. "His Lordship's exceeding charm, no doubt?"

The blush deepened. "His Lordship's example, I fear. The creature had a fondness for the cordials she distilled."

Allegra reached up to one of the shelves and took down several small bottles, which she unstoppered. "I hope she has left me with some kind of ardent spirits, at the very least." She took a deep sniff from each bottle, then nodded in satisfaction. "Yes. Good. This one is a strong aqua vitae, I think." She poured a little of the liquor into a clean glass, then rummaged among the shelves for the rest of her ingredients, murmuring their names aloud to herself as she searched and sniffed. Now and again she dabbed her finger into a powder or liquid to place it on her tongue and taste. "A spoonful of stonecrop. Alum. Is there mustard here? Yes. Here it is. A drop of verjuice. Let me see…what else? We shall make His Lordship well in no time, Mr. Briggs."

He smiled uneasily as she mixed and stirred, adding strange ingredients of various hues. "So long as you don't kill him with the remedy!"

Allegra laughed. "For a few moments, God knows, he'll wish he *were* dead. But perhaps 'twill lead him to more wisdom the next time he is tempted by a bottle of claret or sack."

By the time they returned to Ridley's closet, he was up and sitting in a chair. He had a cloth tucked around his neck, and his valet was just finishing his shave. It was the first time Allegra had seen him with smooth cheeks; he was even more handsome than before. "I've brought your cure, milord," she said, holding out the glass.

Briggs cleared his throat and waved the papers that he still held. "Shall I return for your decision on this when you're feeling better, milord?"

"No. Stay." Ridley pulled off his neck cloth and reached for the glass. "This won't take long, will it, girl?"

"No. But I should have a basin nearby, if I were you."

He smiled in mockery and nodded toward a small open door. "I shall retire to the privacy of my dressing room when the moment arrives. You shall not be privy to my discomfort, however much it might please you."

"I take no joy from others' distress," she said tartly. "I had thought to go to the kitchen, to have them prepare a water-gruel and some broth for you." She scowled at the flask of gin from Jagat Ram's tray, placed close to Ridley's elbow. Was the man ready to begin drinking again, as soon as he was cured? "A sensible diet, for one day at the very least, wouldn't be amiss," she scolded. She swallowed her anger at his stupid self-destruction, curtsied and turned to go.

His voice, cold and dark with malevolence, stopped her. "Did I give you leave to depart, girl? You will stay, damn it, until you are dismissed!"

Allegra turned, her heart contracting in sudden fear.

He had risen from his chair, and now towered over her. "Did you think to get off scot-free?" he asked. His eyes bored into hers, filled with menace and danger. "You will stay. If your cure works, I shall forgive your presumptuous manners. After that you may go to the kitchen and arrange my diet for the rest of the day. If it doesn't work…what had we decided? A good thrashing? Boiling in oil?"

Despite his intimidating height and the satanic gleam in his eye, she was beginning to wonder if his bark was worse than his bite. He was free with his threats, that was sure. But Squire Pringle would have long since blackened her eye for speaking out of turn as she had.

She stared defiantly at Ridley, her chin set, and willed her body to still its frightened trembling. He glared back at her; she surrendered before his superior power and dropped her glance. "I trust you will be cured in no time, milord," she murmured.

He laughed, an unexpected response. "What a contradiction. Brazen one moment, and servile the next. What do you *really* think of me, I wonder?"

She smiled blandly. She would reveal nothing that this devil could use against her. "The sooner you take your potion, milord, the sooner you will be restored."

"Indeed." He took a tentative sip of the liquid, made a face and closed his eyes. He inhaled a deep breath, as though he were working up the courage, then downed the contents of the glass in one long gulp. He shuddered, grunted, opened his eyes and curled his lip in disgust. "Could you not have contrived to make it taste better?"

The cool smile remained on her face. "Yes," she said softly. She ignored Briggs, whose eyes seemed to beg her to remember her place.

Ridley's hands knotted into fists, and his dark, shaggy brows came together in a fearful scowl. "Now, by God," he thundered, pacing the floor from one side of the small room to the other, "you will stay until this is done, and then we shall deal with your insolence! I'll not tolerate the brass of an impudent little baggage who hasn't the sense or wit to be grateful that I've saved her life! Crompton would have skinned you alive, whilst I am expected to endure insults—not the least to my stomach and palate! Well, by heaven, I…Christ's blood!" He gasped and gulped and clutched at his belly, then dashed for his dressing-room door, Ram following close behind. The sounds of violent retching came from the little room.

Briggs glared at Allegra. "Are you quite mad?" he said in a low voice.

She sighed. What was it about Ridley that kept her from guarding her tongue? Always before, she'd had the sense to know when to be humble, when to defer to the master. She sighed again. "No doubt I am, Mr. Briggs."

"Well, I think he can be soothed. I've seldom seen him strike a servant, for all his bluster. And never a female." He smiled ruefully. "Of course, there is always a first time. And you seem to have touched a rare anger in him. You would be wise to keep a distance between you whenever you can, and mind your manners when he is near. Don't speak unless you are spoken to. Wait for permission to leave his presence. And, for the Lord's sake, hold your saucy tongue!"

The unhappy sounds from the dressing room had stilled. After a few minutes, Ridley came staggering back to the closet and sank into a chair. His face had gone white, but his eyes seemed brighter and more alert. He looked past Allegra as though she were invisible and smiled wanly at Briggs. "The chit at least has healing skills to match her impudence. Give her a shilling for her trouble. Now, what were those papers?"

Allegra waited while Briggs explained the correspondence, which seemed to have come from Ridley's secretary in London. It was clear that she was expected to stay until Ridley chose to speak to her or let her go. Perhaps the humiliation of being ignored, of being treated like a piece of furniture in the room, was to be her punishment. Or perhaps he had something worse in mind. She bit her lip in consternation. Baniard patience or no, she would almost have preferred a quick cuff on the ear and an immediate dismissal to this waiting and wondering. And dreading.

"If you will but read through these letters, milord," said Briggs, ending his report by proffering the papers he held, "you will see that the sale of that piece of land in Windsor will earn you a nice profit."

Ridley dismissed the papers with a bored wave of his hand. "I take your word on it. Gifford agrees on the wisdom of selling now?"

"Yes. The price won't go any higher, he says. And the land itself isn't prime."

"Then sell. Have Gifford send me the papers to sign." He laughed——a soft, mocking sound—and shrugged his indifference. "How much richer shall I be, Briggs?"

"You should see a profit of two thousand pounds, I should imagine. Nothing of which to be ashamed." Briggs's soft gray eyes were dark with reproach.

"Ah, well. 'Tis only money." Ridley looked at his steward's expression and laughed again. "Shall I forever be a disappointment to you, Briggs? Because wealth matters so little to me, while you—gentle-born though you are—have nothing?"

Allegra could hear the crunch of Briggs's jaw as he ground his teeth together. "I am content, milord," he said at last, in a strangled voice.

"You're a poor liar, Briggs. Content to serve *me?* When you might have a home, and a wife and family—if you could afford it?"

"I shall take whatever God gives me in this life, milord." Briggs looked as though he were in physical pain. It was all Allegra could do to keep from rushing to his defense in the face of Ridley's cruel and unwarranted attack.

Ridley's mouth twisted in mockery. "A noble answer from a noble man. But you would do better if your brother were to graciously die and leave you his title and his fortune. As mine did, for me. At the least, you should marry an heiress, as I did. Then you will go through life without a care. Without a care," he repeated bitterly, as though he were saying the words for himself alone. He scowled, reached for the bottle of gin, and drank deeply of its contents.

Briggs gave a curt bow. His soft young face was a mask of controlled anger and despair. "By your leave, milord. I shall write at once to Gifford." He bowed again and hurried from the room.

Allegra stood like a stone, seething with suppressed outrage. To shame Briggs that way…

Ridley continued to ignore her. He stood up and stretched, a long, lazy, indolent gesture. He unbuttoned his ruffled shirt cuffs then, and pulled off the garment. His arms, beneath a menacing thatch of dark-brown hairs, rippled with bulging muscles as he moved, and his back and shoulders were sleek and powerful-looking. "Lay out my clothes, Ram," he said to his waiting valet. "I feel fit as a fiddle." He turned suddenly and caught Allegra with his piercing glance. "Well?" he demanded.

She gulped in uneasy fear. Did he want her to leave? To stay and endure a beating at his hands? To beg his pardon or—God save her—be forced to watch him as he stripped naked and dressed afresh? "Well, what, milord?" she ventured.

"What are you thinking at this moment? I should like to hear."

She looked away. "Nothing, milord."

"Damn it, don't insult me further by lying," he growled. "Your eyes are guarded, but they speak volumes. I would know your thoughts. You can speak freely. I give you leave."

She hesitated, then faced him boldly. "Well, then. Mr. Briggs is a good man."

"That he is."

"You are the master. You can do and say what you wish."

He shrugged, his eyes heavy-lidded with boredom. "Indeed, I can. The privilege of rank."

She didn't know whether she was angry at his callous indifference or still suffering for Briggs's humiliation and pain. Her eyes filled with hot tears. She pointed to the array of knives and swords upon the wall. "You scarce need those weapons," she said, her voice catching. "For you have learned to wound in a more terrible and cruel way. With your words. Such words as break the heart of every person who comes within your sway. And for that, I despise you." She brushed angrily at her eyes. "*That* is what I'm thinking at this moment, milord."

His face turned a bright scarlet and he took a step toward her. For one terrible moment she feared he would strike her. Then he whirled away and slammed his fist on a small, carved table. It collapsed into splinters. "Get out, girl," he said in a choked voice, then turned to his valet. "I shall go to Ludlow, today, Ram. Do you understand?"

Ram nodded. It seemed to Allegra as though a secret message had passed between them. "Of course, Sir Greyston," he said. "I shall be having your horse saddled at once. But what of your meeting with the rector in Newton?"

"Not today." Ridley shook his head, then suddenly groaned and buried his face in his hands. When he spoke, his voice was muffled and filled with deep grief. "God preserve me, I *must* go to Ludlow today. Or go mad."

Chapter Five

Grey Ridley stumbled along the night-dark passageway in his stocking feet, holding his candlestick aloft with an unsteady hand. He stubbed his toe against the unseen edge of a table and muttered a curse under his breath. This was madness, and he knew it—at least in the part of his brain that hadn't been numbed by an excess of drink.

He was sorry now that he had started in on the gin. His visit to Ludlow yesterday had been good for his soul. It had brought him peace, at least for a little while. He had come back late to Baniard Hall, eaten his supper with more appetite than he'd had in a long time, and then gone to bed and slept like a baby. The sleep of the innocent, sweet and untroubled by dreams.

It was a nightingale that had wakened him. Some time after four, he guessed, when the moon had set. The bird and its song had started him to thinking, there in the dark quiet of his bedchamber. It was rare to hear nightingales at the beginning of July. Their spring songs were done; their mating completed. The young were already hatched, and the family settled in its nest. The parents. The offspring. Together, as Nature intended.

And that thought, of course, had reminded him of Ruth. And of the gray and lifeless baby he had held in his hands while the bitter tears flowed. A boy. A son. A child who might have been toddling by now, instead of lying beside its mother in a moldering grave.

And suddenly the gin had seemed the warmest comfort in his cold and empty world.

But then, after a while, he had thought of the girl. A strange, intense creature. She burned with the flame of life, sending out sparks of warmth. They touched him, ignited him—even when he didn't want to be touched. He hadn't thought he was capable of any feelings anymore. God knows he didn't *want* feelings. He'd spent too long numbing his heart with gin and indifference and ready women. Constructing a safe, thick wall of dispassion that brought him a certain release. Now, because of the girl, he had felt rage more than once in the past few days. Rage, hot and fierce—the deep, frightening, and unfamiliar sensation of human emotion. He didn't like it at all.

But the girl was all emotion, pure and instinctive, without regard to reason. She had wept, for the love of God, merely because he'd spoken to Briggs with sarcasm! What was Briggs to her, that she should care? For that matter, what was he himself to her? He had given her no cause to love him, with his indenture contract that thwarted her plans of revenge. And yet he had seen concern in her eyes when she had ministered to him. A rare warmth and compassion that flowed from her, whether he deserved it or not.

Even the intensity of her hatred for Wickham was extraordinary, no matter what the man had done. He guessed, of course, that Tom Wickham had ruined her. That was the usual story. In the Colonies, probably, where the girl came from; he'd heard that Wickham had spent some time in America or the West Indies. But it must have been years ago, since the girl had clearly forgotten what the man looked like, and had mistaken *him* for Wickham the day she'd attacked him. Years ago— and still her hatred burned brightly. It bewildered him, but fascinated him as well. All that passion and fire. A glowing rocket of incandescence. How could she live with it, without being consumed?

The window at the end of the passageway showed a sky already beginning to turn gray. It would soon be dawn, and the Hall would stir to life. Madness, indeed, to be found this way.

But…what the devil. He had come this far. And he wanted to see her. He felt drawn to her like a moth to a flame. What did he see in her? His destruction? Or his salvation? He couldn't begin to tell; he only knew she had haunted him from the first moment he had gazed into those dark, sad eyes.

He climbed the back staircase to the servants' quarters in the attic story. Her room was here, just at the head of the stairs. He chuckled softly. Rutledge must have guessed what was in his thoughts when she'd conveniently put the girl into a room by herself. Not that it took much guesswork: his interest in beautiful women was common enough knowledge in the servants' hall. And Allegra had an exotic beauty that was heart-stopping, a lush body that would take any man's breath away.

He wanted her, that was for certain. But—unlike the parade of whores and agreeable serving girls who had warmed his bed since Ruth had died—he wanted more than just a night's casual amusement. As absurd as it was, it seemed suddenly important that this one should bring all her fire and all her passion to their encounter. And for that he was willing to wait—to entice her, torment and tease her, beguile her, until she was madly eager to yield all to him. Until she could admit what he was sure he had already seen in her—a weakness for his touch, for his kiss. However much she tried to deny it, even to herself.

She was lying curled on her side when he crept into her room and set down his candle. The night had been warm; she had pushed off her sheet as she slept and now lay uncovered, her legs tucked up, her head resting on one hand. She reminded him of a kitten, small and soft and adorable. He felt his body growing tense with desire, just looking at her.

Her raven hair was braided into a single plait down her back, and it lay like a dark bridge between the bronzed skin of her face and neck and the paler flesh below. Her shift was tousled and draped loosely around her, exposing her soft shoulders and tantalizing him with a glimpse of one full breast. He rubbed his hand across his mouth like a thirsty man and lowered himself carefully to the edge of the bed. The movement disturbed her without waking her. She sighed and turned onto her face, uncurling her legs and stretching like a contented cat before settling back into sleep. The edge of her shift just covered her firm, rounded bottom; her legs were bare and spread invitingly. A small pulse throbbed softly in the hollow at the back of one knee.

Grey caught his breath, the blood pounding in his temples. She was as provocative and alluring as any woman he had ever seen. Sweet and ripe and fragrant, like a summer fruit waiting to be tasted. He burned with the desire to crush her in his arms, to explore every inch of that body with fervent hands. To force her to yield. To…

He shook his head. No! Surely he'd had too much to drink. To take her against her will? Was he a complete idiot? He hadn't sunk that low yet. He had enough on his conscience without attempting to rape the girl. There wasn't sufficient gin in this world to drown that additional sin, if he was fool enough to commit it. He reminded himself that he had come only for a kiss or two. Because the memory of her tender mouth still lingered on his lips.

Carefully he placed his hands alongside hers on the bed, ready to pounce the moment she awakened. He smiled in satisfaction, bent down, and planted his eager lips on the line of feathery wisps at the nape of her neck.

Someone was kissing her. Her neck and shoulders, the corner of her cheek, a sensitive spot beneath her earlobe. Delicate kisses that made her quiver with delight. It was the sweetest dream she had ever had, strange and new and thrilling. So unlike the cold meanness of her life that she prayed never to waken. She moaned, a soft, throaty murmur, and wriggled under the gentle assault. She felt a warm hand at the back of her thighs, sensuously stroking the bare flesh. It moved upward and fondled her buttocks through her shift, probing intimately and insistently where the soft mounds came together. She shivered. Oh, heavenly dream! The hand moved on and caressed her back. Even with the protection of her shift, she could still feel the soreness from Crompton's whip.

Crompton's whip? Godamercy, this was no dream! She blinked open her eyes to the dawn. Fighting her sleepy confusion, she tried to roll over and sit up. Instead, she found her wrists suddenly pinned to the bed, her movements restricted by the force of the hands that held her down.

She heard a soft laugh above her. "I wondered how long it would take you to become aware," said a mocking voice. "Not that it hasn't been pleasant for me…"

"Ridley!" she cried, frightened and surprised in equal measure. She grunted and struggled desperately against his pinioning hands. The growing awareness of her peril only added to her frenzy. She tossed her head from side to side in frustration; it was useless. She couldn't even turn enough to see his face. He would be smirking, no doubt, the lecherous devil! "Curse you, villain," she said, and pounded her feet in impotent fury against the bed.

"Be still," he said. "I have the advantage, and you know it."

By the faint slur in his voice, she could tell that he had been drinking. She wriggled again. "Cowardly rogue. Let me go!"

He laughed. "I'm content to let you struggle until you are quite spent. But I should warn you that each time you twist, it raises your shift a trifle higher. A futile effort for you, but a feast for my eyes. I think the most seductive part of a woman's body is at the end of her spine. A place of soft hills and dales. Very captivating."

Allegra gulped, remembering the sensual feel of his hand on her buttocks. She cursed the weakness of her body that had enjoyed such an immodest caress. She felt her face flame red and tried to hide her head against her pillow.

"Your blush is charming," he said with a chuckle, "but I only meant that I like it if a woman has dimples there. Do *you* have dimples there?"

"Do you hope to find out this morning?" she asked bitterly, feeling as helpless as Mama must have felt with Squire Pringle. "Was your drunken promise worthless? Did you come to rape me, after all?"

"Not at all. I wanted you willing, and I still do. But you crept into my room to look at *me* as I slept. Yesterday morning. I thought to return the favor. And then I couldn't forbear the desire to do more than merely look. 'Tis a pleasant way to waken, is it not? With the softness of kisses?" He brushed his lips against her bare shoulder.

She tried to shake him off. "A pox on you, you plaguey dog." It was madness to speak so boldly to him, but her anger was driving out her fear, her common sense.

"Why do you resist me? Is it that you fear to succumb to my charms?" His voice was filled with mocking humor.

"'Od's blood, no! Never in all this world," she added scornfully.

"Then grant me my few kisses, without so much stir. And then I'll go on my way."

She was beginning to realize that he enjoyed tantalizing her as much as anything else. It was chancy to trust him, she supposed. But her instincts told her that she was probably safe from rape, as he had sworn she would be. At least if she didn't fight him or anger him. And what did it signify, a few kisses? The sooner he was satisfied, the sooner he would leave her in peace. She sighed tiredly and relaxed against the bed. "Take your pleasure, milord. I cannot prevent you."

Allegra waited for the touch of his lips on her flesh. Instead—and without releasing her wrists—he curled his fingers around her hands until they reached the tender vulnerability of her palms. He scratched gently, a delicate, tickling sensation that sent unexpected thrills racing through her body. God save her. How could she be so weak, so susceptible? She closed her eyes and turned her head away from him, lest he see how easily she could be beguiled. And when he bent again to stroke her neck and back and shoulders with warm, velvety lips, she prayed he wouldn't know that she had begun to tremble inside. "Have you done yet, milord?" she said, forcing her voice to sound hard and indifferent. She bit her lip in helplessness and buried her face in the pillow.

He laughed, clearly aware of her weakness. "The fair Allegra. Your ears are charming. Did you know that? Golden shells, like ripened apricots from the sun. And behind your ears, where the sun never touched you… pale crescent moons, cool and inviting…"

She suppressed a gasp of pleasure when she felt his lips on her ear, the tantalizing current of his breath as he blew softly across the whorls and passages until they tingled, alive with feeling. Aroused by his skillful seduction, it was impossible for her not to luxuriate in this sweet torment. To give in to the gentleness of his mouth. She had known only the lecherous mouths of the men of Charles Town—hungry, greedy, selfish. They had wanted a passing kiss, no more, for the payment of a few coins. But Ridley wanted her surrender. And he seemed willing to pay in time and patience until she crumbled.

His voice at her ear was as seductive as his lips. "You enjoy this, do you not?" he whispered. "Does it make your body feel warm? Are your breasts swelling against the bed in hungry desire? Your breasts are very beautiful. I picture myself touching them, kissing them…Can you imagine it now? The feel of my lips upon your breast?"

She could imagine it…and more. She had never been more aware of her body than at this moment, even as he reminded her of it. She was vividly alive to every sensation—the tense fullness of her bosom pressing against the mattress, the pounding of her heart, the strange and wonderful fluttering deep within her vitals. She groaned in frustration. She couldn't endure any more of this torment. She was only human. "For the love of God…stop!" she cried.

He gave a bored, drunken laugh and released her wrists. "I think you will be remarkably easy to seduce."

He was enjoying her suffering, the villain! She couldn't prevent the tears from filling her eyes. "You devil," she said, choking back a sob. She struggled to turn and sit up. Dear heaven! She looked down at herself in horror. Would her humiliation never end this morning? Her shift had slipped off one shoulder, exposing her breast. She wanted to die.

Before she could adjust it, Ridley—a lazy smile on his face—reached out and pulled up the garment so it covered her modestly. Then he stood and bowed, the mocking, florid gesture of a cavalier. "I bid you good morrow," he said, and left her alone.

She was shaking so hard that her bedstead creaked. He had said that he planned to seduce her into his bed. He had promised he wouldn't rape her. But where was the need for rape? He clearly had realized—from that first trembling moment when he'd examined her back in the kitchen parlor—that she was vulnerable to his kisses and caresses. She was filled with self-disgust. She rubbed an angry hand across her tear-stained face. Little fool! Where was the need to take her by force, when she would be undone by her own weakness?

She was suddenly grateful that all the Baniards were gone. It was too shameful to think how far she'd strayed from her purpose. To let a drunken lecher make her forget that this was a year simply to bide her time with Baniard patience, just as she had done in her dreadful years with Gammer Pringle. To bide her time until she could fulfill her purpose and justify her existence. It was the only reason that God had left her alive out of all the family. To destroy the Wickhams.

Anything else—happiness, peace, the enjoyment of that devil Ridley's kisses—was no more than wicked self-gratification.

Allegra raised herself on tiptoe and stretched her arms to the topmost shelf. Even with a high stool to elevate her, she could just reach to the back corner of the plank. She swept off the thick dust with a little straw brush, placed it on the shelf below and then wiped the spot again with the damp rag she held in her other hand.

What foulness, she thought with a click of her tongue. From the yellowing labels on the bottles, she guessed that the stillroom hadn't had a competent maid since Wickham had sold Baniard Hall to Lord Ridley a year ago. And the dirt and filth only confirmed her belief. She had spent the whole morning cleaning and scrubbing. She had managed to lay out the various powders and liquid ingredients in some sort of rough order on the work table; she hoped to sort and label them afresh before nightfall.

It felt good to be busy again. The sea voyage from Charles Town had taken forever, with nothing to do but dwell on the painful past and nurse her grievances against Wickham. But there was a rhythm about working that had always pleased her, however hard her tasks; while performing her chores, she could clear her mind of whatever thoughts weighed heavily. She sighed, turned her rag to the clean side, and wiped the shelf once more. But this time the blessed forgetfulness of work eluded her. She could scrub furiously until midnight, and still her brain would teem with the memory of Ridley's invasion of her room this morning. God help her, did he plan to do it every day until she succumbed to him?

"Godamercy!" she cried, and dropped her rag in surprise. Strong arms had wrapped about her hips like a vise. She found herself lowered to the floor, turned around and captured within the solid embrace of Grey Ridley. "Let me go," she said, and wriggled against his arms.

He smiled down at her. His golden eyes were sly, catlike…and faintly unfocused. Allegra wondered how much more he'd had to drink since their dawn encounter. "The fair Allegra," he drawled. He held her squirming body more closely to his breast. "'Tis a stillroom. Can you not contrive to keep still?"

She was determined that this time he wouldn't have his way so easily. It was one thing to be caught unawares from a deep sleep. But now she had her wits about her. If she made it clear to him, by word and deed, that she didn't intend to be seduced, perhaps he would find someone else to torment, and leave her alone. She forced her body to go rigid, and kept her expression as cold and stiff as she could make it. "Did you wish something from the stillroom, milord?" she asked.

His mouth twitched. "Wish something? Of course. I came to refresh your memory of something that I have not forgot. Something that I should like to repeat. A sweet kiss, given in my closet."

"I have no remembrance of it, milord," she said in a frosty tone. "I can only recall a very unpleasant kiss in the woods, the other day. Would you care to repeat *that*? Or will you let me go?"

He laughed aloud. "A hit, or I'm damned! That brazen answer has earned you your freedom." He released her and fished in the pocket of his waistcoat. "In point of fact, I came to give you something." He pulled out a gold coin and held it out to her. "No doubt you will refuse it, and say that I'm trying to bribe you. To ease my conscience after this morning," he added sarcastically.

"Not at all, milord," she said, taking the coin from his hand and putting it into her pocket. "I'm not too proud to take it." Though her voice was even and calm, she found herself quivering with anger. He insulted people shamelessly, and then threw them a sop, as if gold could salve hurt pride. Reckless of her safety, she lashed out with the only weapon she had—her words. "Besides, how can it be a bribe? I consider that I earned it by enduring your presence in my chamber this morning." Instinctively she ducked her head, half expecting a blow to her ear.

Instead, he smiled and moved closer to her on unsteady legs. "Then your pleasure in it was a bounty, was it not?" he murmured. "And you *did* take pleasure, by my troth." His voice was low and seductive, mocking her with the memory of her own weakness. She would have turned away in anger, but he stopped her with a hand on her arm. "I brought you another gift. Here." He pressed a key into her palm. "For your chamber. So that you need not fear unwelcome visitors."

It seemed too simple—that he would concern himself with her welfare. Not *this* drunken scoundrel! "And do you have its mate in your pocket?" she said with a snort.

"No. What need I for another key? I know that, sooner or later, you will open for me. *In every way*." He laughed wickedly when she blushed at the pointed crudeness of his words.

She was suddenly filled with a deep heaviness, a despair that clutched at her heart. He would never leave her in peace. He would persist in his unwanted attentions, and torment her with his cruel words, until she had learned to hate him as much as everyone else did at the Hall. Or until she learned to hate herself because she couldn't resist his seductive entreaties. She remembered Mama and Squire Pringle. At least Mama had been forced to submit, to play the whore against her will and strength. But how would she justify it to herself if she surrendered to Ridley? She sighed heavily, feeling defeated. "By your leave, milord, let me be. I have my stillroom duties waiting."

The arrogant smirk faded from his face. "Why do you have such pain in your eyes?" he asked, scowling. "We only jest, you and I. There's nothing deeper in our discourse. Not for me. Don't you know life is to be laughed at?"

She blinked against the unexpected rush of tears. "Life has taught me other lessons."

For the first time, his eyes focused clearly on her face, as though the solemnity of her pain had sobered him. He reached out and brushed a crystal droplet from her cheek. The touch of his finger held the tenderness of a loving parent. "Tell me, fair Allegra," he murmured, "why are your dark eyes so sad?"

She stared at him in confusion. Who was this man? So mocking and cruel, so shallow and dissolute? Scarcely worthy of anything save her hatred. And yet, in her short stay at the Hall, she had caught a few glimmers of another man. The man who now smiled so gently at her, and touched her cheek. A man as different from the profligate Ridley as the Angel Gabriel was from Lucifer. A man whose merciless tiger eyes could turn suddenly soft with concern, dark with shared pain. Those eyes seemed now to reach into her very soul, to invite her confidences.

She was torn with the mad desire to throw herself into his arms and pour out her sad story, to weep the ocean of tears she had suppressed for so long. She had lived with her heart in isolation, alone and friendless, since Mama's death. Perhaps—because of that—she was even more vulnerable to Ridley's brief flashes of humanity than to his caresses. Or perhaps, out of her own need, she only imagined that spark of warmth in him. "Milord…" she said, trembling.

"Lord Ridley. Your pardon." Briggs stood in the doorway of the stillroom, an uncertain smile on his face. "I have no wish to intrude, milord. But Colonel Lane has come up from Diddlebury with that pair of horses you wished to buy. Will you look at them again before I count out the guineas?"

Ridley twitched with annoyance at the interruption, then shrugged. "Do you fear he will cheat me, Briggs?"

"'Tis common knowledge in the parish that he has been known to substitute an inferior animal."

"Is there an honest man in this whole world? Or a good one?" He gave a sharp laugh and a bow in his steward's direction. "Besides you, of course, Mr. Briggs. Ah, well. You were born a gentleman. Perchance, in your commendable upbringing, you learned to judge horseflesh. I leave the final decision to you." He started to dismiss Briggs with an impatient wave of his hand, then checked himself and frowned at the expression on the man's face. "Is there more?"

To Allegra's surprise, the normally composed Briggs seemed somewhat agitated. "It can wait, milord…A letter…" he stammered.

Ridley raised a mocking eyebrow. "A *letter?* This sounds fateful. From whom?"

Two small spots of color appeared on the steward's cheeks. "The Most Honorable Lord Richard Halford, Marquis, writing on his own behalf and that of his sister. Lady Dorothy Mortimer."

Was Allegra mistaken, or had the tone of Briggs's voice subtly changed when he uttered the lady's name?

"Christ's blood," growled Ridley. "Meddling fools. What do they want now?"

"They wish to visit. In little more than a fortnight, according to Lord Halford."

Ridley slammed his hand against the edge of the work table. "Again, damn it? What is it…three months, four, since last they were here? Why the devil must they plague me again?" He ran his hand through his hair in exasperation. "God save me from old friends!"

"Lord Halford writes that they have been in London. Renewing old acquaintances that had faltered while they were in India. And Lady Dorothy, I understand, has opened up her late husband's townhouse. But they wish to leave London and seek the comfort of their country estate. To escape the heat of the city."

Ridley snorted in derision. "A poor excuse to come interfering in my affairs. London in July and August is a damn sight cooler than Calcutta. Do they think I've forgotten that? Well, tell them not to come. I don't want them."

The flush had reached the roots of Briggs's hair. "But, milord," he said in a pained tone, "how can I tell an amiable gentlewoman such as Lady Dorothy that she is unwelcome? That is…Lord Halford, I mean… he considers himself your friend!"

"Sometimes, Briggs, your sense of honor makes me want to choke. Tell them I've grown another leg and have taken to hopping about like a bloody toad. Tell them *anything*, for God's sake. But I do not want them at Baniard Hall again! Lie to them, if you must. If you can prevent them from coming, there will be fifty guineas for you, in gratitude. Now, get out. And see if you can manage my affairs without disturbing me when I have other business on my mind."

Briggs's frown was matched only by Allegra's as the steward bowed stiffly and left the stillroom. "Do you take pleasure in that, milord?" she muttered.

Eyes glowing, Ridley reached out and gave a savage tweak to her ear, wringing a grunt of pain from her lips. "I did not give you leave to tell me your opinion today," he said coldly. "How I deal with Briggs is my affair. Remember that. In the meantime…" Though he still held fast to her ear, he relaxed into a careless smile. "I was only sharp with him because I wished to be alone with you." He softened his cruel hold and caressed the delicate skin of her ear. "Charming. Not only will I consider shortening your indenture, but I'll buy you pretty eardrops if you agree to…" He allowed his hungry, lecherous expression to finish the thought.

She pulled away in dismay. Had she been foolish enough to imagine—if only for a brief moment—that there was a human being hiding beneath the surface of this monster? "You must have better things to do than to torment me constantly, milord."

He grinned. "*Is* it torment? Then succumb to it."

It was exhausting just to keep him at bay. "Why me?" she asked with a weary sigh.

He shook his head, the cynical smile vanishing, to be replaced by bewilderment. "God knows. You're a strange creature. Sometimes I think that we have met before. What is it I see in you that so bewitches me?"

"The same thing you see in all women, I warrant," she said bitterly. "Find another who is more willing, and leave me in peace." She glared at him, defying him with her glance.

For a moment, she feared that he would explode into a rage. Then he laughed and shrugged. "I can wait for your surrender. I sought you out for another reason. Are you skilled at distilling cordials?"

"Yes, of course, milord. I told that to Mr. Briggs."

"What can you concoct for me, then? I should like something interesting for tonight. To aid in my digestion and help me sleep."

She eyed him doubtfully. Despite his drinking habits, he seemed as sound as a bull. More likely, he enjoyed the strong spirits for entirely different reasons. "It will take at least two days, milord, before I can produce anything. I haven't yet examined the alembics, to be sure that they are still sound. However, if you must drink…" She tried to hide her disgust as she pointed toward the work table. "I found several cordial waters that your last maid must have distilled. A fine aqua mirabilis. There, in that crock. 'Tis a trifle heavy with the taste of cloves, but quite pleasant for all of that. What I concoct for you will depend on what herbs I find in the cook's garden. At least until I can grow my own. I know the plants from the New World. I beg your indulgence until I learn what I can use here."

He nodded in satisfaction. "Good. Each evening after supper you will attend me in my drawing room, bearing whatever you have distilled that day."

"Will I be expected to stay until you have quite drained the beaker?" she asked, reluctant to be a party to his drunkenness night after night.

He clearly chose to interpret her question differently. His mouth curved in the familiar lustful smirk. "Only if you wish it. Do you?" He laughed at her silence. "An eloquent answer."

She pretended not to hear. It seemed the safest course. She turned to her work table and poured a bit of water from a pitcher into a small basin. She retrieved her cleaning rag and rinsed it out. "Is there anything further, milord, before I return to my work?"

"Yes. You have fine healing skills—to those I can surely attest. You cured me of too much claret, God knows," he said fervently. "But now I'm wracked with pain. 'Tis a very delicate part of me—I hesitate to speak of it. But it brings me suffering that will not cease. I know that you are the only one who can cure me."

She understood enough of nature to know that a man's body could physically suffer if his carnal hungers were not satisfied. Clearly, the sly rogue meant to take another tack on the way to his vile seduction. Would he be crude enough to uncover himself next? "I fear I cannot help you, milord," she said firmly.

"But surely…" he began. He ambled over to the work table beside her and perched on the edge of it so that his eyes were level with hers. Golden, liquid eyes, filled with wicked laughter and desire. "'Tis my *tongue*," he said softly. "It still hurts from the other day. Look. When I move it like this." He stuck out his tongue and ran it across his lower lip. It was a gesture that was so bold and deliberately seductive that Allegra fought to contain the sudden thrill that tugged at her vitals, a longing that took her breath away.

Longing was followed by anger. How dare he? "I am not a surgeon, milord," she said through clenched teeth.

"But you are so skillful. And, since you were the cause of my distress, I thought you might be the cure. Surely there are many healing potions here." His tongue, as he slid it across his lips and thrust it suggestively toward Allegra, was pink and moist and sensuous. His eyes smoldered with passion.

Allegra gulped and shivered in spite of herself. He seemed to know just how to tantalize her. Curse the man and his teasing ways! Well, she *would* be revenged. She moved closer to him and forced a smile of concern. "Perhaps there is some cure after all, milord." She ran her finger along the top of his tongue. He shuddered in pleasure and closed his eyes. "Poor tongue," she murmured. "This will help you to forget your pain." She reached for the bitterest salts she could find on the work table and dumped a generous handful into his unsuspecting mouth.

He choked and gasped and jumped to his feet, his eyes springing open in fury. He snatched up the water pitcher and poured half its contents into his mouth, frantically swirled the liquid around, then spat the residue to the floor. He turned on Allegra, his eyes burning with a frightening intensity that made her quake in terror. "Damn you!" he roared, and struck her savagely across the side of her face.

She staggered backward from the force of the blow. Only the work table kept her from falling to the floor.

In a moment—and to Allegra's astonishment—the rage in his face had crumbled into remorse. He turned away, shoulders sagging, and groaned. "My God, what is happening to me?" He took a deep, steadying breath, then turned back to face her. The unexpected smile on his face was brash, arrogant, and artificial. He shook his head. "Egad! You're like a contagious malady! A disease of wild passion that seems to have infected me, willy-nilly. 'Tis a danger to succumb to it. I shall have to be more careful." He reached for the crock of aqua mirabilis, took a deep swallow of the liquor, and swaggered to the door. He wobbled slightly, seeming more drunken than he had been just a moment before. He turned and grinned again, but Allegra thought she could read apprehension in his eyes.

"'Tis a wonder you didn't try to poison Wickham rather than stab him," he drawled. He strutted from the room, all male pride, leaving

Allegra to rub the side of her face and wince in pain.

"I curse you with every breath, Ridley," she whispered. She wondered if she would have any hatred left for Wickham by the time this ghastly year was done.

Chapter Six

Chapter Six

Allegra finished setting the last of her seedlings, tamped the soil around the tender shoots, then rose to her feet and brushed the rich, damp earth from her hands. It was late in the season to start herbs, but a few weeks of good growth before autumn would give her enough—between the distillations she could make from the first few plants and the drying of the remainder—to supply her stillroom through the winter.

She squinted up at the early-morning sun. It shone bright and clear, promising a hot August day. If her garden continued to be blessed with the same happy combination of sun and rain that it had received for the past four weeks, there would be mature plants in no time. Heaven knew she could use the ingredients; the kitchen garden was as sparse and carelessly tended as much else at Baniard Hall seemed to be. Nothing was done with any pride in the work: only those rooms that were likely to catch Lord Ridley's eye were properly cleaned, and the cook made do with the same tiresome cuts of meat and limited herbs night after night. The kitchen chimney smoked, and the footmen fell asleep at their posts. But why should anyone care, when the master went around with a bottle of gin in his hand and cruel insults on his lips? Mrs. Rutledge was content to sit in her office and indulge her taste for sweetmeats; the rest of the servants followed her lead in sloth and indifference.

Only Jonathan Briggs seemed to perform his duties with any sense of obligation. But since he kept all the accounts and oversaw the entire estate outside of the house servants—the tenant farms, the vast park and gardens, the stables with their dozens of horses and carriages—he was sorely pressed to ensure that Mrs. Rutledge ran the Hall with any degree of efficiency. Moreover, to add to his burdens, Ridley expected him to fill the position of personal secretary as well.

Allegra shook her head, thinking of Grey Ridley. She didn't envy Briggs. In the month or so since she had arrived at the Hall, she had begun to wonder if there wasn't a kind of war going on between the two men. At least on Ridley's part. The kinder and more considerate became Briggs's behavior toward his master, the more he was rewarded with cruel and mocking words. They were usually followed by a purse of gold, which probably was—for a man of Briggs's honor—more insulting than the words themselves. Allegra sighed. Welladay, there was nothing she could do about it, however much it pained her to see a decent man affronted.

She was grateful, at least, that Ridley's romantic overtures toward her had ceased after that day in the stillroom, though she still took pains to lock her room every night. With nothing but her instincts to guide her, she felt in some odd way that Ridley had come to fear her—or at least to fear giving in to his strong emotions, as he had that day. She had begun to suspect that his shallow, careless demeanor was a pose. Or perhaps a shield. Sometimes it made her curious to find the true man behind that pose.

Every night, at his bidding, she attended him in his rooms, offering the day's distillation—one night a spicy cinnamon water, the next a mint-and-wormwood cordial or a beaker of Barbados water, rich with orange and lemon peel. He drank them in silence, ignoring her until he was ready to wave her away with a bored flick of his hand. If he liked the cordial she had prepared, he would send a penny to her the following day; if not, a farthing. She would copy the favored recipes into a little book and retire the others.

Most of Ridley's days were spent wandering around the Hall in a haze of gin, or riding in the park if he wasn't too unsteady to sit a horse. There had been no repetition of the wild, drunken scene that had so frightened Allegra on her first night at the Hall; for that, she was grateful. There had been no more visits from the local whores, either, which caused much comment in the servants' hall.

During the past month, Ridley had made two more of his mysterious trips to Ludlow. Mysterious because he always returned sober, which elicited even more comment. No one, not even Verity or Barbara with their noses for gossip, seemed to know precisely where he went on those trips. Not to his usual haunts, it was agreed—the taverns, the brothels, the swordsmith, for the repair of one of his ornate blades or knives. But Ludlow was a large town, the largest in Shropshire, outside of Shrewsbury. It would be simple enough for a man to get lost there, if he chose.

"Allegra!"

At the sound of her name, uttered in a biting tone, Allegra turned. Mrs. Rutledge stood frowning at the edge of the garden, arms across her chest. Allegra curtsied uneasily. "Ma'am?"

"Do you think, because you have insinuated yourself into His Lordship's favor and wheedled Mr. Briggs into giving you the stillroom, that you can do as you wish, Miss Malapert? Do you fancy yourself behind *my* desk one of these days?"

"Have I done something wrong, ma'am?" asked Allegra, bewildered by the woman's unprovoked attack. She certainly had no wish to become housekeeper here. "Has His Lordship complained about the cordial waters?"

"Why should he?" was the sneering reply. "You tarry in his rooms every night; we have all marked it. I have no doubt you give him a little 'sweetening' along with his drink."

"That's not so!" Allegra bit back sharper words. With Ridley's reputation, who would believe her denials?

"Spare me your protests. Your traffic with His Lordship matters not to me. You're not the first petticoat to turn his head, nor scarcely the last, I warrant. My quarrel is with you, miss."

"Have I been remiss in my duties, ma'am?" Surely the woman couldn't complain of her complexion; she had scrubbed it diligently for weeks. And though by nature she would never be pale, the deep rosiness of her skin—absent its dark tan—was now softly feminine. "How have I displeased you, ma'am?" she asked.

"You went to the apothecary and the lace seller in Newton on Friday last. Did you not?"

Allegra nodded, mystified. She had made several trips to Newton, seeking supplies for her stillroom; it seemed only decent to offer to run Mrs. Rutledge's errand this last time. The bills would have arrived from the tradesmen by now. But she had scarcely been extravagant in her purchases, buying only those rare and exotic ingredients that she couldn't produce herself. "I thought you were pleased with the lace I bought for His Lordship's shirts. Was it the wrong kind?"

"I most emphatically directed you to Mr. Buel's shop, in the High Street."

"But…if you examine the bill, ma'am, you will see that Mrs. Simpson gave me a better price. And the quality of her lace was much finer."

The housekeeper's eyes glowed with anger. "You were to go to Mr. Buel!"

Why was the woman making such a fuss? "To spend His Lordship's money foolishly?" she asked with indignation. "I'm sure that wouldn't please Mr. Briggs, who is the soul of prudence."

The expression on Mrs. Rutledge's face changed, the scowl giving way to a sly smile that reminded Allegra of a cat who had just crept out of a birdcage, licking its whiskers. She patted Allegra on the hand. "Come, come, girl. You're not a fool. No need to go to Mr. Briggs. He will pay whatever the bill says. He has no wish to quarrel over pennies or disturb the master with unnecessary details. And the right tradespeople can be quite grateful for His Lordship's custom. Merely because Mr. Briggs is too proud to 'shoe the mule' from time to time, it doesn't mean that we must do without a little extra, and to spare. Do you understand what I'm saying?"

Allegra felt like an innocent, blindly ignoring what any idiot would have understood. Since mules were not regularly shod, a charge for "mule shoes" was likely to be false. No doubt there was a great deal of "shoeing the mule" that went on at Baniard Hall, from Mrs. Rutledge to the cook and down to the lowliest servant sent on a purchase. But of course it was far easier to cheat in a large household than in a small one. It would have been impossible in Charles Town, even if it had occurred to Mama. Squire Pringle had doled out every shilling as though the coins were stuck to his fat fingers.

Mrs. Rutledge smiled, one conspirator to another. "Next time, see that you shop where I send you, and you'll find a copper or two under your pillow at the end of the week." Verity had told Allegra that the housekeeper was the first servant Ridley had hired after he had bought the Hall a year ago; Mr. Briggs had taken his position some months later. Allegra had often wondered what kept the woman servile in the face of Ridley's insults. Willing to keep her post no matter what she endured. She certainly wasn't cut from the same noble cloth as Mr. Briggs. Now it was coming clear: Mrs. Rutledge intended to depart the Hall a rich woman, and not a moment before.

Well, why should she care? Allegra thought. It was Ridley's problem, if he chose to concern himself with it. Not likely, of course. Didn't he himself already use his money in a vile way—to buy loyalty? If he lost more through the sharp practices of his scheming servants, what was it to her? She nodded to Mrs. Rutledge. "Certainly, ma'am. As you wish."

Mrs. Rutledge preened as she led the way back to the kitchen entrance. "With my training, I think you will serve very well. If you don't try to rise above your station," she added. There was a sharp edge of jealousy in her voice. "Now," she went on more kindly, "His Lordship's guests have been at pains to inform me of their pleasure at your skills. Lady Dorothy swears she has never tasted finer marzipan, and Lord Halford is convinced that the imperial water you gave him on Friday after his ride in the rain prevented the ague."

"I'm pleased to serve them," Allegra murmured. *Someone* had to make them feel welcome. In the two weeks since Richard Halford and his sister had been at the Hall, Lord Ridley's behavior had become more loathsome than ever. He tormented Briggs with cruel words, and castigated the man for being unable to prevent the visit. He ignored his guests, leaving them to amuse themselves, and spent his days in his rooms, drinking and breaking into bawdy song whenever Lady Dorothy ventured past his door. He played unwilling host to his friends only at the evening meal, then invited them into his drawing room or closet for cards and insults.

Allegra felt her face growing warm with shame. It didn't seem right that she should be a party to it—forced to be a witness to the humiliation of Ridley's guests. But each night, after she had presented him with his cordial, she had been obliged to stand in attendance during the whole long evening. To listen in pained silence while Ridley mocked his friends, and watch him drink until he could scarcely utter a clear word.

And when they played cards, he defeated them without mercy, then jeered at them for their clumsy play. It bewildered her that they should even desire to befriend such a monster. "Lord Halford and his sister are charming people," she said with some heat. "Why shouldn't we treat them with honor?"

"Why not, indeed?" purred Mrs. Rutledge. "If you continue to please them as you have, the gratuities they bestow at their leaving will be the larger. For all of us." She seemed almost to be licking her chops in anticipation of the windfall, then she sniffed in disgust. "There are precious few vails for people in service when the master is too indisposed to invite guests to call." She waved Allegra toward the stillroom. "Well, go on with your duties. It will be warm today. I trust the cordial you plan to bring His Lordship tonight will serve to refresh him, and keep his mood civil."

The day proved to be sweltering, the air close and humid. All afternoon the clouds had rumbled and darkened, promising a storm. By the time Allegra knocked softly at the door of Ridley's closet that evening, she was drained and exhausted from the heat.

It seemed to have affected the guests as well. Lady Dorothy Mortimer, a pretty, willowy creature with soft brown hair and blue eyes, wandered aimlessly about the small room as though she were a helpless animal in a cage. Several times she frowned at Lord Ridley, seeming about to speak, then turned and resumed her pacing.

Her brother, Lord Richard Halford, sat across from Ridley at a small card table set in the center of the room. With each play, he slapped the cards to the table and muttered darkly. "Damme, if I have any luck tonight," he said at last.

Ridley grinned—a sardonic smile—and helped himself to the gin at his elbow. "Richard, you could hang a dozen hare's feet on your waistcoat and still play a vile game of all-fours." He looked up and acknowledged Allegra with a careless nod. "But here is our fair stillroom maid with her nightly elixir. Perhaps she can improve your luck. With a smile if not with her brew. Come, fair Allegra. Smile for our guest."

Halford fiddled with the stack of coins before him and cleared his throat. "For God's sake, Grey, don't behave like a drunken ass," he muttered.

Grey roared with laughter. "Have I struck a nerve? Girl, I order you to stand very close to me tonight, so that Richard may watch you as we play. You'll either bring him luck, or distract him to such a degree that I'll drub him even worse than usual."

Allegra clenched her teeth to keep from speaking out of turn. Whether or not Lord Halford had taken notice of her was no cause for Ridley to bait him. "Shall I pour the cordials all around, milord?" she asked tightly.

She served the drinks at his bidding, then stood beside him as he directed. Halford scowled and shuffled the cards furiously, taking care to avoid looking at Allegra. The game resumed; Lady Dorothy continued her pacing, stopping occasionally to pick up a carved statue of an elephant or a tiger and turn it idly in her fingers. Allegra swayed on her feet, feeling suffocated by the heat and the heavy scent of incense that lingered in the room and clung to the silken hangings. Would this dreadful evening never end?

"God's teeth, Dolly," growled her brother, "stop pacing. Join us for a hand."

Lady Dorothy shook her head. "No. Forgive me, Dick. I'm too restless tonight." Her voice was sweet and soft. She reached above the mantel and took down a knife from Ridley's collection. It was a finely carved blade, its hilt studded with jewels. "I remember when you came by this one in Calcutta, Grey. A gift from the Nawab of Behar, wasn't it? But I didn't know you had taken a fancy to collecting knives." She indicated the wall with a graceful sweep of pale white fingers.

He stared at her, one eyebrow arching sharply into the smoothness of his broad forehead. "'Tis a new amusement of mine. In the event I should want to use one of them on myself someday."

Brother and sister exchanged worried glances. Halford threw down his cards. "Enough of this pretense! For God's sake, Grey, how much longer are we to act as though nothing is different? Come back to London, I pray you. Open Morgan House again. I still remember the happy times we had there. Before you and Ruth…" He stopped abruptly when his sister put a silencing finger to her lips.

Ridley reached for his glass of gin and drained it at a gulp. When he spoke at last, his voice was filled with dark pain. "That was a long time ago. In another life." He forced a laugh and shrugged. "Besides, I like Baniard Hall. The solitude. 'Tis why I bought it."

"Is it solitude you seek? Or escape?"

Lady Dorothy clasped her hands in supplication. "Tell us what happened, Grey. It *can't* be true, what they're saying in London."

Grey's eyes were half closed in seeming boredom. "Why not?" He shook his head. "Poor Dolly. You always try to see the best in everyone. I remember that Peter used to tease his soft-hearted wife. And I would defend you. But he was right, I think."

Lady Dorothy buried her face in her hands. "Far better that he died of the fever last year. It would break his heart to see you today."

Grey sighed in disgust. "Christ's blood. Don't weep for me, Dolly. You're not a fifteen-year-old anymore, smitten with a brash soldier of twenty-three."

She looked up, her face streaming with tears. "I thought of you as my dear, brave brother."

"Then you were a fool," he sneered.

Dolly paled at his cruel words. She gulped, brushed at her tears and took a steadying breath. "I'm very tired. If you will excuse me. Grey… Dick…" She turned and fled the room.

Halford jumped to his feet, smashed his glass to the floor and glared at Ridley. "Damn it, what the devil happened to you, Grey? Your drinking, your insults…Don't you know this is killing Dolly?"

Grey stretched and eased himself lazily from his chair. He ambled to the window, opened the sandalwood shutter, and stared out at the dark night. Thunder rumbled in the distance. "Are you unhappy here, Dick? Then go. Take Dolly and go. You aren't here at *my* bidding, God knows. I could understand it, when you came in March. You were on your way home from India. It was only civil of you to stop on your way."

"*Civil?*" Halford's voice was heavy with reproach. "We came to offer our sympathy. Because of Ruth."

"And now? Is there more to add?" Ridley drawled. Even with his back to them, Allegra could imagine the cold gleam of his amber eyes.

Halford moved toward Grey and put his hand on his friend's shoulder. "The stories we heard in London, Grey…"

Ridley shook off his hand and turned, snarling. "They are none of your affair! Go home to Coventry and enjoy your country house. And leave me in peace!"

Halford's face twisted in despair. "Grey, I beg you. Speak to me. We were friends for years. You and I and Peter Mortimer. How can you cast aside those years?"

Allegra struggled to draw a breath, her head spinning. She was beginning to feel faint. She didn't know whether it was from the oppressive heat, or from standing motionless for so long, or from the anguish of being privy to a discourse she had no right to hear. "Please, milord," she whispered, "may I go?" She took a step toward the door, faltered, and would have fallen. But Halford reached her and supported her within the circle of his arms.

"Thank you, milord," she said, struggling to regain her balance. She stared into his face. His eyes were as blue as his sister's, and soft with concern. He seemed unwilling to release her.

Behind them, Grey laughed. "So that's how it is? I warn you, Richard. If you want her, you had best take care. The wench is a tartar."

At the mocking words, Halford stepped back from Allegra and drew himself up, all aristocratic pride. "Go to your room, girl," he said gently. "'Tis late. You must be tired. As for you, Grey…" he bowed stiffly in Ridley's direction, "I leave you to your gin, since you've become so fond of it. I shall seek my own bed, and pray not to dream of a past that is dead."

Chapter Seven

"May I come in?"

The soft voice interrupted Allegra at her work. She put down her beaker and turned, smiling. "Lady Dorothy. You are always welcome," she said with a curtsy.

The young woman took a turn about the stillroom, her wandering glance taking in every detail. The morning sun streamed through the open casement and sparkled off shining copper pans. "What a cheery place!" she exclaimed. Her voice was filled with an admiration that seemed excessive for such a humble chamber.

"Aye, my lady. I like it."

"And what a pleasant breeze! I was so very grateful for the rain last night. It took away the dreadful heat."

Allegra eyed the woman with curiosity. She flitted around the room like a butterfly afraid to light. Clearly, Lady Dorothy hadn't come to discourse on the room *or* the weather. "Is there something you wish, my lady?"

Lady Dorothy hesitated, then turned and faced Allegra squarely. Her eyes were puffy and swollen, with deep lavender circles beneath. "'Tis… 'tis only my eyes," she said with a bright smile of apology. "I need a cure from you. I fear it must be the weather."

Allegra wondered if the poor thing had sat up all night weeping, after that terrible scene in Lord Ridley's closet. But it wasn't her place to intrude. "Yes, of course. The weather," she agreed.

The brave smile faded. Lady Dorothy sank onto a stool and covered her eyes with her hand. "Or a surfeit of grief," she said, choking on the words.

Allegra stared at the unhappy woman. There must be more to Grey Ridley than there appeared, she thought, to cause a sweet creature like this to weep for him. The tears of a friend, not a lover. She was sure of that, after seeing them together last night. "'Tis just His Lordship's way, my lady. You mustn't cry."

"But it *isn't* his way! Or it wasn't. Now…I don't know."

"Perhaps—forgive my boldness, my lady—His Lordship changed when his wife died. Was he fond of her?"

"He adored her. We never met her, but all his letters to us in India were filled with praise for Ruth. Peter…that is, Lord Mortimer, my late husband, used to say he reckoned that Grey and Ruth were almost as happy as we were."

"How did Lady Ridley die?" She had no right to ask the question, but Lady Dorothy seemed eager to confide in someone.

"She lost his son in a stillbirth, then died of a childbed fever herself. Or so we were told."

"Some of the servants whisper that…that he killed her."

Lady Dorothy looked shocked. "Merciful heaven! How could anyone think…*Grey?* I've known him most of my life. It simply isn't in his nature." Her face fell. "But the stories they told in London weren't like him, either." She began to tremble.

"Here, my lady." Allegra poured a bit of soothing rosemary water into a glass and urged the young woman to drink.

Lady Dorothy's blue eyes were warm with gratitude. "You are very kind, Allegra. That is your name, is it not? Well, Allegra, if you should ever wish to go for a lady's maid, you may seek me out in London. Bloomsbury Square. Near King Street."

"Thank you, my lady." She hesitated. It was none of her concern, but she wanted to know. It suddenly seemed vital to know. "Lord Ridley… the stories in London…?"

"This is only between us, you understand. But…they said he was challenged to a duel. He had killed a man in a previous duel, and the man's friends demanded satisfaction."

"Was it in his nature to quarrel often? To duel?"

"Not at all. After his years in the Army, Grey always said that he preferred peace. But…" Lady Dorothy turned anguished eyes to Allegra, "he was never a *coward!* Nor yet a drunkard. But they say he came to the field of honor so intoxicated he could scarcely stand. And when the signal was given, he…he dropped his sword and ran away."

Allegra bit her lip in dismay. She didn't want to hear this. She realized with a start that she had hoped it wasn't true. Hoped that they were mistaken, the people who had called him the coward of Baniard Hall. It was mad and foolish of her, but she was desperate to defend him. "A temporary lapse," she insisted. "Surely the gin must have clouded his judgment."

Lady Dorothy shook her head, her face a study in misery. "It happened again and again, they say. Until he became the laughingstock of London. Young bucks vied with one another to challenge him. To call him craven and strike him in the face. To visit upon him every indignity. He allowed it all. Their mockery, their insults. He could only slink away to the sound of their taunts." She sighed, fighting against fresh tears. "They called themselves the three Princes of Camelot—my Peter, and Richard and Grey. But we all knew that Grey was the natural heir to Arthur's throne, a king among men. And now, to see him so low…" Her voice caught on a sob.

Allegra felt helpless, aching for the woman's pain, suffering even more for Lord Ridley's humiliation, though she couldn't understand why. She put her hand on Lady Dorothy's shoulder and managed a gentle smile. "Please, my lady. Don't begin to weep again. I can distill a soothing water to take away the redness from your eyes. But it will be useless if you continue to cry."

"Lady Dorothy! Has something distressed you?" Jonathan Briggs hurried into the stillroom and glared at Allegra. "Have you allowed your saucy tongue to get the better of you again, girl?"

Allegra stared in surprise. Mr. Briggs had never spoken so harshly to her before. And for so little cause.

Lady Dorothy composed her face, rose from her stool and smoothed her brocaded skirts. "You are mistaken, Briggs," she said. "I am in no distress. 'Tis merely an inflammation around my eyes that Allegra has vowed she can cure."

Briggs clapped his hands together in annoyance. "Then do it at once, girl! Don't keep Her Ladyship waiting!"

"I shall need time to prepare…" began Allegra.

He refused to let her finish. "Then bestir yourself!" he said, pacing the floor impatiently. "Why do you dawdle all day long? When our guest has need of your services."

"Please, Briggs," said Lady Dorothy in her sweet voice. "For my sake, don't scold the girl. I'm sure she will send the balm to me as soon as it is prepared." She turned and made for the door.

Briggs stopped pacing and bowed deeply. "Of course, my lady." He bowed again, cleared his throat and bowed a third time. "I will see to it personally, my lady."

Lady Dorothy suppressed a smile. "Do so," she said. "But spare me further bobbing up and down, or I shall soon grow quite giddy." When

Briggs blushed at her words, her gentle smile broke through—a teasing sparkle of blue eyes and white teeth. She nodded at Allegra and left the room.

In the silent minutes that followed her departure, Allegra crumbled a handful of herbs and dried blossoms into a stoneware crock and poured in a few drops of sweet oil. She took a small pestle and began to grind the ingredients into a paste.

Mr. Briggs sighed and gazed up at the beamed ceiling. "I behaved like a damned idiot," he muttered at last.

Allegra had to agree. It was scarcely like him, to rail like a fishwife and bow and scrape in a flurry of servility. Not calm, reasonable Jonathan Briggs! Unless…Allegra stared, her jaw dropping open. "Mr. Briggs, can it be that you have lost your heart to Lady Dorothy?"

"Don't be absurd," he growled. "'Tis entirely unsuitable. The woman is a lady in her own right, and the widow of a marquis besides. I'm the second son of an improvident knight, who wasted half of his inheritance long before my brother and I were born. I have neither the title nor the riches to approach a woman of Lady Dorothy's rank."

"I didn't ask what was suitable," she said softly. "I asked if you had a fondness for her." His embarrassed silence told her all. She laughed in tender understanding. "I wonder if you truly tried to urge them not to come."

"I serve my master first, whatever my own desires," he said indignantly, as though he couldn't imagine any other way to behave. He sighed. "But, yes. I was glad I could not dissuade them from coming." His soft gray eyes were filled with longing. "She has only been at the Hall twice. Yet I feel as though I have known her forever. A lovely creature who makes the humblest rooms glow with her charm."

"Does she return your sentiments?"

"I know not."

"Then why not show her your heart?"

He frowned and waved his hand as though he were brushing away a foolish thought. "'Tis not to be. We'll speak no more of it."

"But, Mr. Briggs…" It didn't seem fair that such a kindly man should suffer the pain of hopeless young love.

He drew himself up. "No. You forget yourself, girl. I have my honor. And my duties. As you have yours. Now—Mrs. Rutledge tells me you wish to go to Ludlow tomorrow."

He was right. It was none of her concern. "Yes," she answered. "I need to go there. The apothecary in Newton has too limited a trade to properly supply my stillroom. I need ambergris and Florentine iris, as well as other substances."

"Ludlow is not Newton. A person—were she so minded—could vanish there. I trust you will not forget the contract you signed with His Lordship."

"Mr. Briggs," she said sharply, "I was raised with as much honor as you were. I will 'vanish' when Lord Ridley releases me from my contract, and not before! Do you think I'm like the other servants here, a flock of do-naughts, loiterers, and scoundrels?" She felt her anger growing. She pounded her herbs as though she meant to murder them. "Have you no care? They steal from His Lordship and you don't even see it!"

Briggs scowled. "I see it," he said bitterly. "But when I try to tell Lord Ridley, he laughs and makes a jest of it. If I persist, he tells me to leave the servants to the care of Mrs. Rutledge. I think he knows very well what goes on at the Hall—sober or not. I suspect it amuses him. Sometimes I even think he encourages the dishonesty. He sends a footman to buy a handkerchief, bearing a sack of coins fat enough to purchase a whole suit of clothes. And never asks for any return. I know he's not blind to the cheating and thievery." The scowl deepened. "So *I* must pretend to be, to satisfy him."

Allegra felt a pang of remorse. Mr. Briggs had scarcely deserved her condemnation. After all, the master of the estate, not the steward, set his seal on the character of the household. And if Ridley courted financial ruin, what was Briggs to do? "Forgive my outburst, Mr. Briggs," she said.

He tried to look stern, but his gentle voice put the lie to his expression. "You must learn to guard your tongue. If not, it will bring you grief. His Lordship is a man of strong passions, for all his seeming indifference. There is anger sleeping within him, I think. And you have roused it more than once. I fear you could goad him into a thrashing one day." He searched her face, then shook his head. "You have no fear of that, have you? I see it in your eyes."

Her mouth twisted in a wry smile. "Shall I tell you about grief, Mr. Briggs?" she asked.

He laughed softly. "Am I to learn of the mysterious Allegra Mackworth at last?"

She looked toward the open door through which Lady Dorothy had passed. "'Tis a day for hearts to be opened, perhaps."

He looked disconcerted. "I'll guard your secrets, if you will mine."

"Fair enough. Well, then…When I was a child, I lived with my mother in the Colonies. She was an indentured servant. Housekeeper to a rich squire who had bought her contract for seven years. And every night, until she died, the fat pig would come to our room and rape her. Afterward, she would creep to me in my little trundle bed and hold me. And weep until she had no tears left."

Briggs's gray eyes were soft with sympathy. "Allegra…"

She gulped, surprised at the depth of her pain, even now after all these years. "'Tis still so real. So fresh. I think it will haunt me forever. She was such a frail creature. I did her work—as much as I could—to spare her. I thought, in my child's way, that Squire Pringle would see how hard we worked for him and leave her alone at last." She laughed bitterly. "A child's dream."

"You had a good heart, even as a child, I think."

Allegra shrugged. "Good hearts are for fools. *She* had a good heart. But not the strength to save herself. She died, quite worn out, with two years yet to serve of her contract. The debt had become mine, the squire said. What could I do? I signed his accursed paper. And another as well, in which he agreed to pay my passage to England in exchange for a year's labor."

"Three years?"

She nodded. "Three years. But it wasn't long before he began to notice that I was no longer a child. I swore he wouldn't ill-use me as he had my mother. I swore I would kill him or myself first."

"And did you sway him with your determination?"

She shook her head. "God's faith, no. He was an evil man. Quite heartless. But a cowardly bully as well. He tried to take me, but I fought him off. He saw that I would never break, as had my mother. He had taken pleasure in making her weep, a hundred times a day, with his cruelties. But I would not."

"And still will not," he said in wonder. "Your eyes are dry even now."

"I weep for others, Mr. Briggs. I have no tears for myself." She sighed. "But he longed to crush my spirit. And so he gave me out in rent to his spinster aunt who had a farm just outside of the town."

"A simple old woman? To break your spirit?"

"That 'simple old woman' was the devil incarnate. Gammer Pringle was born with a twisted foot and an abiding hatred of the world and all in it. She had a large farm and a miserly nature. She could not see why two servants should not be enough."

"For both house and farm?" he asked, incredulous.

"Indeed. My partner in misery was an old Negro. A slave. We worked from sun rising to sunset, bending over the fields to plant and hoe and weed. And when we could do no more for weariness, she expected the old man to tend the livestock and see to the repairs, while I was cook and scullion and housekeeper. And lady's maid to her vanity. And once a month, when she came from church inspired by the sermon to root out evil and sin, she would lay us across a bench and whip us with a switch until the blood ran down our legs."

Briggs cursed softly. "But there are laws against such oppression and hard usage!"

"For bond servants, but not for slaves. I protested only once. She beat the old Negro twice as savagely, and swore he'd bear my punishment henceforth, if I refused to submit." Allegra's memories were suddenly sharp talons, clawing at her heart. She pounded the herbs with her pestle—again and again in a fierce rhythm—and squeezed her eyes shut to close out her pain. She felt a soft hand on her wrist, stilling her frenzied movements.

"God give you peace," murmured Briggs.

The moment of weakness had passed. She opened her eyes and made a feeble attempt at a smile. "Don't pity me, Mr. Briggs. Pity that poor old man instead. I knew there would be an end to my torment. Only death will release *him*."

"Have you ever known happiness?" His voice was deep with concern.

She turned and stared out the casement window toward the gardens of Baniard Hall. They thronged with ghosts. "Once, a very long time ago," she whispered.

No! She mustn't falter! She shook off the past. She had meant just to tell him a part of her story, not to give in to the frailty of her sex. Memories served only if they fueled her righteous anger, not if they made her weak. Her mouth twisted in a self-mocking smile. "'Twas not all misery, Mr. Briggs. Once a fortnight we would go to market in town. I soon discovered that the good burghers would pay me well for a kiss, or an arm around my waist. And every coin I put in my pocket brought me closer to England. And so I saved and endured. And so I dreamed of Wickham and the day when…"

"My God," he breathed.

She laughed softly. "Hatred, you see, is better than despair. 'Tis how we survive in this world." She heard a throaty chuckle from the doorway and turned, surprised.

Ridley lounged against the doorframe, shaking his head in disbelief. In his hand was a bottle of spirits. He hadn't even bothered to put on waistcoat and coat this morning. An added insult for his guests, no doubt. "Such a surfeit of passion in you, girl," he said. "I shall never fathom it. All that hatred." He lifted the bottle and took a deep swallow of its contents.

"'Tis my strength, that hatred," she said tightly. She prayed Ridley hadn't overheard her tale to Briggs. It was an advantage she didn't want to give him.

"And Wickham? Was he one of your good burghers in the market? Did he take more than a kiss, and pay less?"

Her heart sank. He had heard at least a part of her confession. Well, she wasn't about to tell him anything further. She was already regretting her frankness with Mr. Briggs. "Wickham is my affair, milord," she said with finality.

"You must have been quite young when you met him," he persisted.

She had only a misty recollection of Wickham's face. But she could still see clearly the smile of welcome on Papa's dear face as he greeted the new Baron Ellsmere on the steps of Baniard Hall. *To put aside the animosity of our fathers,* he had said. *And learn to live in harmony.* "Aye," she muttered. "I was quite young."

"And you hate him still."

"I hate him always and forever."

Ridley laughed aloud. "Is this not a paradox, Mr. Briggs? Here is a creature who tends her garden with loving hands, who ministers to our disorders here at the Hall. A creature who suffered cruel punishment to spare an old man. And yet—were I to give her one of my blades and put Baron Ellsmere in her path…" He laughed again. "I suspect she would rip him from his throat to his navel without a moment's hesitation. Do you think it not ironic that she knows the healing arts, yet holds life so cheaply?"

Briggs scowled at the bottle in his master's hand. "If I may say so, milord, I think that you…"

"That I've had too much to drink? God's blood, not yet! But 'tis early in the day. And I need my wits about me. I've come to try and seduce this charming young thing." He put down his bottle and moved toward Allegra. "I'll not need your good offices this morning, Mr. Briggs. In a word, go away."

Briggs bowed with stiff dignity. "As you wish, milord." He allowed himself a brief, uneasy glance toward Allegra before he left the room.

"And now, my sweet…" Ridley reached out a languid hand and stroked Allegra's bare arm.

She pulled away, frowning. Was it to begin all over again? She felt angry and reckless. He might be afraid to duel with blades, but he enjoyed attacking with words, seeking the constant advantage, the weakness that would allow a fatal blow. Well, she would match him thrust for thrust, and devil take the consequences! "I prefer my seducers sober," she snapped.

He laughed, undaunted. "I'm as sober as I want to be. As I *need* to be," he added with a lecherous smirk. "You'll not find me lacking to satisfy you, when you finally surrender."

She snorted. "And what do you buy with your bottle?"

"Joy and good spirits." His mocking smile belied his words.

"And *peace?*" She could tell by the startled flicker in his eyes that she had hit home. Perhaps now he would go away.

Instead, he turned her words against her. "Peace?" he repeated with a sneer. "What do *you* know of peace? You, with your burning eyes. My hundred pounds have bought Wickham a year of life. No more. Will you be at peace with your conscience when he's dead? You would find more peace here. In my bed."

She flinched and turned away. He would win every pass. She was no match for a tormenting rapier wit that had vanquished every soul in Baniard Hall. But perhaps if she continued with her work and moved around the room, she might succeed in keeping him physically at a distance, at least. She pulled down a small jug of white wine, poured a goodly quantity of it into a shallow earthenware bowl and scraped her crushed herbs into the liquid. "I should have guessed that my story wouldn't move you," she said in disgust. "Is gin your armor against sentiment as well?"

"You mean the tale of your lustful squire? I didn't hear it all. Only that he wanted you, and you refused, and were forced to pay for it. Very touching. But what has that to do with me? He hoped to force you into his bed, willy-nilly. I wish merely to persuade you." He scratched his earlobe and grinned. "I had thought to be successful by now. More than a month. But perhaps my lack of persistence…"

"For which kindness I am humbly grateful, milord." There was nothing humble in her angry tone.

He scanned her lazily. "I didn't spare you to be kind," he drawled. "In point of fact, I had lost interest. And then I saw the way Richard looked at you. It reminded me of your charms. And that you might be worth the effort after all."

She bit her lip in dismay at his deliberate insult, then silently cursed herself. She was a fool. Didn't she *want* his indifference? And hadn't she endured the sharpness of his tongue often enough to ignore it by now? Why did she allow him the power to hurt her? She threw him a glance of outrage and cast his venom back at him. "Can it be you are human enough to feel *jealousy*, milord? Does the green viper gnaw at your cold heart? I think you fear I'll succumb to Lord Halford while refusing you still!" She waited, anticipating his sarcastic retort.

Instead, his face turned red and his hands curled into fists. "Now, upon my faith!" he cried. "Insolent chit, you are too forward to be endured!" He glared at her, then turned away, seeming to contain his fury only with the greatest effort of will. He growled deep in his throat, like a wounded animal—a long, drawn-out sound that was half rage and half anguish. After a few moments, his heaving shoulders stilled, and the bright flush of color faded from his skin. When he turned back to Allegra at last, the mocking smile had returned to his face, a transformation that left her astonished. "No, girl," he said. "You'll not goad me into anger this time. Not this time."

If she had doubted her instincts before, she was sure of them now. He *was* afraid of her. In some strange way, there was something in her that managed to reach him, to open doors that he wanted to keep tightly closed. The door to rage. And now—clearly—the door to jealousy. And desire? Could that be why he had stopped pursuing her these past weeks?

She eyed him warily. This was a frightening man; she baited him at her own peril. Best to keep silent and hope he would leave. She turned back to her work table and tried not to make her silence a challenge as she resumed her task.

She stirred her concoction, then put it aside to prepare her still. She removed the cone-shaped lid of the alembic; the bottom, a shallow pan, she filled with several inches of sand. She set her mixing bowl upon the sand and replaced the tin lid. Dipping a linen cloth into a paste of flour and water, she wrapped it tightly around the joining of the two parts as a seal. Finally, she placed the alembic over the burning charcoal stove, and put a beaker under the spout that came from the cone top to catch the distillation as it formed.

She was aware, all the while, that Ridley watched her. His face was dark with hidden thoughts, a brooding intensity that made her uneasy. What was it about him that *always* made her uneasy? Whenever she was in a room with him, she was conscious of his eyes on her. She found herself moving differently, behaving strangely, saying things that she shouldn't. Perhaps it was those eyes of his—tawny golden and beautiful—that unnerved her and gave her a thrill of fear. Dear heaven, she thought, feeling as though she were ready to jump out of her skin, would he never say anything? Or leave? She turned away to keep from being burned by those eyes.

"Take off your cap," he said. She jumped in alarm. His voice was so close behind her that she fancied she could feel his breath on the nape of her neck.

"Milord?" Heart pounding, she turned. His face was inches from hers, his eyes crystal amber, glowing with a strange light.

"Take off your cap," he repeated. "And let down your hair. I want you to wear it loose henceforth."

She didn't know what to make of this sudden odd request. Nervously, she touched her pinned-up hair and the trailing lappets of her linen cap. "But, milord, everyone else…Mrs. Rutledge…" she stammered.

A small muscle twitched along the side of his jaw. "I don't want you in a cap."

"Milord, how can I work…?"

"Damn it, *I don't want you in a cap!*" he cried, and snatched the offending garment from her head. He plunged his fingers into her hair in a frenzy of searching and pulling. While she cried out in terror and tried to back away, he tore the combs from her head, then tangled his hands in the heavy, cascading curls. He held her tightly, his hands at her temples, and tilted back her head to meet his penetrating gaze. She trembled at the look on his face, at the whirlwind of passion that had suddenly been unleashed. His eyes were clear and alert, but she wondered how much gin he had drunk this morning. If he was more intoxicated than he seemed, there would be no escaping him this time. Not if he chose to take what he wanted. The drink, and the madness that had come over him would vanquish her.

He searched her face. "Who are you? Why do I think I know you?" he said wildly.

She felt helpless, her head imprisoned by his savage grasp. "I'm only your humble servant, milord." Her voice quaked. "Please let me go."

He shook his head and groaned. "God's blood, you'll drive me mad. You haunt me day and night. I see you in my sleep, like a dark-eyed wraith. I hear your voice in my dreams. As rich and beautiful as a sobbing harp. I ache for you and wake to pain." His face twisted in anguish. "You've bewitched my soul. I can no longer look at another woman. I need you alone." He groaned again. "Will you never give in? Release me from this torture?"

His distress touched a chord of sympathy within her. She was torn with the mad desire to surrender and erase the misery from his face. Then she remembered Mama and Squire Pringle. "Must I lose my honor to quiet your dreams?" she asked bitterly.

He stared at her—the tormented look of a drowning man. "Close your eyes," he said. "They tear out my heart with their pain."

She was trembling so violently she could scarcely stand. His mouth hovered above hers, soft and inviting. "Milord..."

"For God's sake, Allegra, close your eyes," he whispered.

She sighed and did as he asked. At once, she felt his mouth on hers, soft and sweet. He moved gently, brushing against her lips with his own—a tender caress of warm flesh that sent shivers racing up her spine. She moaned and sagged against him. In response, he slid his hands down her arms to circle her waist and support her quivering body.

His mouth released hers to trail feathery kisses across her cheeks, the tip of her nose, her closed eyes. He moved to her chin and throat, planting kisses in the soft hollows of her neck. He buried his face in the linen neckerchief that covered her bosom; even through the fabric she could feel the heat of his breath.

He lifted his head from her bosom. One hand left her waist, parted her neckerchief, slid beneath her shift to cradle her breast and stroke it with teasing, sensual fingers. She felt as though she were falling, down and down. Lost in the exquisite thrill that followed every kiss and caress. And when he tugged at her shift and gown to release her breasts from their confinement and closed his hungry lips around one straining nipple, she gasped in helpless pleasure. In another moment, she knew, they would be on the floor—she, beneath him with her skirts up, begging him to take her. And she didn't care. She didn't care! There had been too much misery in her life. She deserved whatever joy she could find.

"Grey, you Judas!"

Allegra gasped at the harsh voice, her eyes flying open. Instinctively, she pulled away from Ridley and frantically attempted to cover her shameful nakedness, tugging at her tousled clothing and hair with shaking hands.

Lord Richard Halford stood in the doorway, glaring fiercely at the man he had called his friend. "You Judas," he said again, his mouth curling in bitterness. "Was this what you wanted me to see, when you invited me to the stillroom?"

Ridley frowned and ran his hand through his hair. "Richard, you were only meant..."

Halford laughed sharply. "Don't trouble to explain. If the wench finds you more enticing than me, 'tis *her* loss. But you might have told me direct, instead of playing out this disgusting scene. I shall order my coach at once. Dolly and I will leave you to your solitude, and whatever hell you've built for yourself. You've chosen to destroy our friendship. I'll not see Dolly hurt further. Let it be ended." He bowed, his face like stone, turned on his heel and stalked away.

Allegra stared at Grey Ridley, the horrible realization dawning on her. To kiss her like that, to make her think he cared…It had all been pretense, a cynical, vicious game he'd devised to drive away his friends. He hadn't wanted his visitors in the first place. How simple it had been for him—to play upon Lord Halford's interest in her, to use her as nothing more than an instrument for his own purposes.

She clenched her fists to her sides to still the shaking of her hands. She felt dirty, used, naked. As humiliated as if he had raped her. She saw his ashen face through a haze of tears.

"You monster." She choked on the word.

He reached out to hold her. "Allegra…"

"No!" she shrieked, and struck him across the face as hard as she could. The sharp crack of flesh against flesh brought her to her senses. Was she mad? This was the master, and the owner of her bond for a year. No matter what he had done, she could go to prison for lifting her hand against him. She shrank back, fearing the violence of his retaliation.

He advanced on her, but his golden eyes were soft, not filled with anger. What did she see in their topaz depths? Gratitude? Remorse? He reached for the offending hand that had struck him, turned it over and planted a tender kiss on her palm.

"It was all a mistake," he whispered. He smiled gently—a sweet, painful smile—turned and hurried from the stillroom.

Trembling in confusion and grief, she sank to the floor.

"And Venice turpentine, I think. The coachman is complaining of stones." Allegra nodded her satisfaction as the apothecary wrapped her purchases and tucked them into the basket she had set on the counter of his shop.

The man smiled and rubbed his hands together. He had the sly face of a ferret beneath his ill-fitting periwig. "Thank you for your trade, miss. 'Tis always a pleasure to serve someone from Baniard Hall. Mrs. Rutledge is well?"

Mrs. Rutledge had insisted that Allegra patronize this apothecary shop in Ludlow, and no other. She smiled wryly. "Mrs. Rutledge is well. And prospering," she added. She tied her broad-brimmed straw hat over her linen cap and hooked the basket on her arm. She glanced out of the open door of the shop to the sunny street. It would be a long walk in this heat.

"Pardon me, miss," said the apothecary, "but I see that you hesitate. Do you return to Baniard Hall on foot?"

She shrugged. "'Tis the way I came."

"But on such a hot day." The man's smile was becoming an oily smirk. "Allow me, then, to be of some service to you, miss." He came around from behind his counter and took Allegra's arm.

She felt the first stirring of alarm. Would he demand a kiss—or worse—for whatever was this "service?"

He guided her to the door and pointed toward a small wagon with a single mule that waited just down the lane. Beside the wagon stood an old, bearded man, bent with age. "Yonder is Old Bibby," said the apothecary. "He runs my errands and delivers goods for some of the shopkeepers. I know he goes to Wenlock Edge today. It would please me to prevail upon him to let you ride along."

He still held fast to her arm. She pulled away and eyed him with suspicion. "And what will it cost me?"

"My dear child," he said, "I only wish to be your friend. You are new to Lord Ridley's employ, I think you said. I trust that there will be many, *many* ingredients you need to furnish the stillroom to your satisfaction. And that when you do, you will remember your friend."

Allegra could almost have laughed her relief. His interest in her was financial, not carnal. "I thank you for your kindness," she said. "I shall indeed remember you, sir." And shop elsewhere, she thought grimly. Still, it would be pleasant to ride today. "Will Old Bibby object, do you suppose?"

"Not at all. But I must warn you that he is very old, and very slow. And he likes to stop now and again on his rounds. To lift a pint with a friend. You'll not return to Baniard Hall much sooner than if you walked, but at least you'll be spared that long climb."

Old Bibby proved to be a cheery companion. Allegra was grateful for his simple goodwill. Her solitary walk down from the Hall in the morning had given her nothing but time to relive the horrors of the day before: Ridley's kiss and that dreadful scene with Lord Halford, the chaos of their guests' hasty departure, the shouting and the running about. And—most heartrending for her to see—the desolation on the face of Jonathan Briggs as he watched Lady Dorothy depart.

Allegra had pinned up her black hair again, and gone about her work as though nothing had happened, but she felt the pain of Ridley's betrayal like a knife to her soul. When she had brought him his cordial last night, he had glanced in silence at her hair and cap, then waved her from his rooms. There had been half a dozen empty gin bottles outside his door this morning.

"Well, now," said Old Bibby as he came out of a draper's shop with a large bolt of cloth and tossed it into the back of his wagon. "That be the last of my stops but one. And then us be out of Ludlow. The Edge for me, and Baniard Hall for ye." He scrambled aboard, spry for his age, and picked up the reins.

She glanced at him out of the corner of her eye as they made their way up Broad Street. "Did you…did you know the Baniard family that lived there?"

"Only met His Lordship but once. A fine man, he seemed. I were to deliver a chair that come from London. A gift for his little daughter. All carved, it were, wi' a letter wrote into the design. 'Anne,' it stood for. So they said, me not bein' able to read and all. Anne Baniard. That were the little girl's name."

She gulped. Anne Allegra Baniard. She had almost forgotten the sound of her own name. But the chair…"I don't remember a chair like that," she said without thinking. Then quickly added, "That is, I've never seen one in the Hall."

He shook his grizzled head. "Upon my honor, I give it him. But 'twere the day afore they drug him off to prison. Likely there weren't no time to give it to little Anne. Poor thing. They be dead now, all of 'em. So said Lord Ellsmere, when he kept the Hall."

Allegra bowed her head, overcome with memories of the child she had been. Her chair must be long gone by now, tossed into a fireplace to warm the toes of that villainous Wickham, no doubt.

"Here, now, ye be flaggin', miss," said Bibby. "'Tis the heat." He wagged his finger at her like a gently scolding grandfather. "Heed Old Bibby, now." He pointed to the Church of St. Lawrence, its square tower rising high above the surrounding shops and buildings. "Yonder be the church. And the almshouse. There be a fine garden out back. Shady and cool. Sit ye there, whilst I deliver this parcel. Then, if it be all the same wi' ye, I'll just pop 'round to the Feathers on Corve Street for a dram of ale wi' me old friend Joshua. And then, faster than ye can wink, us be on our way to the Edge."

The gardens behind the almshouse were dappled with the shade of old, sprawling trees. Gravel walks surrounded neatly tended flower beds, and clipped yews formed a wall of serene isolation. The silence was broken only by the trill of a summer lark and the hum of bees among the roses. Allegra was content just to sit and drink in the sweetness of the day.

"God be with you, Daughter."

She looked up. A clergyman stood before her, an angelic smile on his face. He wore a long cassock with white bands at the neck, and a lightly powdered wig on his head. Allegra rose to her feet and curtsied. "Good afternoon, Reverend."

"Can I be of service, Daughter?"

"No, sir. I came only to enjoy the peace of your lovely garden for a little while."

"A worthy aim. I myself have been known to slip away for a few moments of quiet contemplation, when the burdens of the almshouse weigh too heavily." He sighed. "There are so many who need us. The old and the sick, the poor, the needy. Ah, well. We do what we can. And if we bring them closer to God, we are doubly blessed."

Allegra scanned the long, low stucco building with its black timbering stark against the whitewash. The walls were bowed with age. "'Tis very old, your almshouse."

"Hosier's Almshouse, they call it. Some three hundred years ago, there was a good man of that name, a rich cloth merchant who wished to pave his path to heaven. We bless him every day."

She laughed gently, noting the timeworn state of the old building. "And pray for a new angel of mercy as well?"

"Angels come in many guises, Daughter," he said softly. "Lest you doubt, we have one among us today. In the trappings of a mere mortal. He comes when he can, and does the work of ten. There is no task too menial or lowly for him. No work too difficult. He offers to do it all, with a generosity that inspires the rest of us to toil the harder. He nurses the sick. He cheers them when they feel pain and cleans them when they foul themselves." The rector spread his arms and indicated the flower beds before them. "This garden is his. When he first came to us, it had almost gone to seed. And now, you see what he has wrought."

"But who is he?"

The rector shrugged. "A man of no importance, I should guess. Merely a man. But God makes no distinctions. A learned man, to be sure. Sometimes, late at night, before he leaves, I will find him beside the bed of a dying creature, reading the Scripture aloud for comfort."

Allegra shook her head. It still surprised her, that there could be goodness in the world. "I should like to see this saint."

The rector led her to a side door that opened onto a large dormitory room. It stretched the length of the building beneath ancient roof beams; a door at the far end led to a small chapel. The room was crowded with cots on which lay the poor unfortunates who had found refuge within these walls. There were some who slept, and some who babbled aimlessly, and some who wept or cried aloud. The blended sounds made a low hum in the room—a soft, collective moan of pain.

Near the door to the chapel, a man was kneeling on the floor, a bucket of water at his elbow. He was dressed in old, tattered clothes, and his hair hung loose and unbound, in the manner of a country plowman. He scrubbed the old planks vigorously with a stiff brush, his head bent in concentration, his dark hair obscuring his face.

Just then, an old woman in the bed near him cried out and tried to sit up. Immediately, he rose to his feet and hurried to her side, soothing her and gently stroking her white hair until she calmed and lay back again on her pillow.

Allegra gasped and shrank into the shadow of the doorway. She shook her head in disbelief. It couldn't be! She must be losing her reason. "He shows such mercy and serves without complaint?" she whispered to the rector.

The clergyman smiled. "I told you he was our angel. There is no shame or pride in our Mr. Morgan. God has blessed us by sending him."

Mr. Morgan, the reverend had called him. Her eyes had not deceived her. It was he.

Sir Greyston Morgan, Viscount Ridley. Monster of Baniard Hall.

Chapter Eight

"I wish I could persuade you to come to Ludlow today, Mr. Briggs." Allegra clambered into the small cart, sat down and smiled at Jonathan Briggs beside her.

He sighed and clicked his tongue at the horse. It tossed its mane in impatience, then started down the long drive of Baniard Hall at a lively pace. Briggs sighed again. "'Tis merely market day."

"Merely market day? 'Tis Bartholomew-tide! And every soul who hasn't gone to London for the great fair will be in Ludlow!" Allegra grinned, surprised at her own rising excitement. She hadn't thought she could feel such joy. Not ever again. Surely it must be the relative ease of her days at the Hall—after the misery of the Carolinas—that had so heartened her, helped her to look for the sweetness in life again.

Or perhaps it was the memory of Grey Ridley, bent with concern over an old, sick woman. It had been nearly a fortnight since that afternoon at Hosier's Almshouse, and still the scene warmed her thoughts. She smiled to herself. What a soft fool she was becoming! He had scarcely ceased to be the monster of Baniard Hall. The man who seemed to enjoy tormenting everyone. Why should one chance glimpse change her opinion of him?

Still…to know that he had a spark of goodness within him, a secret life of charity, had pleased her beyond measure. Beyond all reason. She had slipped out of the almshouse without his seeing her that afternoon, then had taken a rose from "Mr. Morgan's" garden. A fragile blossom gently nurtured by his own hands. She had kept it in her room, marveling at its fragrance, until it faded.

Its presence had made it easier for her to endure Ridley's sullen silences and sharp words, the memory of her humiliation before Lord Halford. She found herself remembering, with a thrill, the searing fire of Grey Ridley's kisses, and forgetting that he had used her to drive away his friends. Stroking the velvety rose across her lips, she had half persuaded herself that Ridley's passion and his burning, needful kisses had been genuine, at least.

And then…did she only imagine it? Had he become kinder, these past few days? Less disposed to scold and criticize? He had been quiet and withdrawn since his friends had gone. Scarcely a serenity, but at least there was peace in the Hall. Moreover, he seemed more temperate lately in his need for intoxicating spirits. She could never forgive him for using her as a dupe, she told herself. But perhaps the knowledge of his secret goodness would help her to view him with more tolerance.

The cart passed through the iron gates of the Hall and made its way along the narrow road that followed the crest of Wenlock Edge. Allegra adjusted the ribbon of her wide straw hat and took in her surroundings with satisfaction. It would be hot later, but now the sweet morning spread its glories before her.

Scented fruit was ripe on trees and bushes; apples and plums and blackberries blended their aromas with the gentle breeze. The rich hues of purple thistle and red, ripe sumac twinkled like jewels amid the dark-green foliage of late summer, joined by the second bloom of spring blossoms—bright yellow dandelions, poppies, and fragrant honeysuckle. The hay had already been harvested, and the empty fields that dotted the hillsides were a pale, shimmering gold, like a child's freshly washed hair spread out in the sun. With a trilling, whirring sound, startled flocks of hedge-sparrows fluttered up to the tops of the bushes as they passed. Allegra smiled at a farmer leading his milk cows to an emerald patch of grass.

"Such a lovely morning. Why won't you change your mind, Mr. Briggs? Come to Ludlow Market after you've seen to His Lordship's business. It will be as jolly as any fair ever was."

Briggs snorted. "Pickpockets. Thieves. Wild seekers after pleasure. And highwaymen waiting on the London road to waylay the revelers as they leave town. That's your jolly fair."

Allegra laughed gently. "Are you Job's comforter, that you can see naught but gloom and misfortune in a fair?" She looked sideways at his sweet young face, twisted in misery. She felt helpless before his distress— distress that had deepened at an alarming rate since Lady Dorothy's departure. "In the name of mercy," she said at last, "*write* to her. Or else forget her."

He turned and stared at her with pain-filled eyes. "Forget her? Have you lost your wits?"

"But if you refuse to speak openly to her, what choice have you? Better to forget her. Find the daughter of a prosperous squire, with a good marriage portion."

"Don't be absurd." He cleared his throat and stared up at the limpid blue sky. His soft gray eyes were unnaturally bright.

Allegra sighed. It was useless to urge him to swallow his pride and pay court to Lady Dorothy. His sense of honor was as great as his prospects of fortune were small. "Why did you choose to work for His Lordship?" she said. "If I may be so bold as to ask."

He gave her a fleeting smile. "You have never quite known your place, girl. But, as to His Lordship…he pays me handsomely."

"Have you no ambition in this life beyond that of steward?"

"I had hoped once to study for the law. But my father gambled away my inheritance—such as it was—long before he died."

"And your brother, the knight? Can't he help you?"

Briggs shrugged. "He himself struggles along as best he may. Our father was very democratic in his profligacy. He managed to impoverish both our legacies."

"And so you stay with Lord Ridley."

"He's quite generous. Lavish, even, with his gold. Perhaps if I save enough, I might yet take up the law someday."

That seemed so mercenary, coming from a man like Briggs. "And so you endure his insults and stay at the Hall for money alone?" she said sharply.

He drew himself up, clearly offended by her question. "I told you long ago, I think, that His Lordship has many fine qualities. I should not serve him else!"

Perhaps it was the look in his eyes that put the thought into her brain. "By all the saints," she said, shaking her head in sudden comprehension. "You *know* where he goes in Ludlow. Don't you?"

His face turned red. "'Tis not for me to say," he muttered.

She smiled at his loyalty. "Of course. But I, too, think there is much to admire in His Lordship. Not that I would venture to guess where he goes. 'Twould be presumptuous of me." It seemed prudent to say no more.

"Indeed?" He searched her face, clearly trying to guess how much she knew. They stared at each other in silence for a long time, as the cart rocked gently down the hill under the morning sun. At last Briggs nodded, as though he had decided something in his mind. "We will speak no more of it. 'Tis His Lordship's secret. But—under the circumstances—it might please you to know that Lord Ridley gives vast amounts of money to the churches and hospitals and workhouses in the county. All anonymous, you understand. I must carry out his wishes with discretion. But I thought you might like to know."

"I'll honor your confidence with my silence," she said. She found herself suddenly grinning. What nonsense! As though Ridley's generosity should matter a tinker's curse to her! But the grin held all the way down the hillside and up to the town wall of Ludlow. It seemed that nothing could spoil her well-being on such a fine day, or cast a shadow on the foolish joy that crowded into every corner of her heart.

Except, perhaps, the memory of a grief-filled cry.

"Mr. Briggs," she said, as she climbed down from the cart, "do you know aught of the Lady of the Sorrows?"

He frowned in thought. "Not a whisper. Who is she?"

Allegra sighed and turned toward the Corve Gate. "Another of His Lordship's secrets, I suppose." She waved a farewell to Briggs and passed through the gate, making her way down Corve Street and turning west at the Beastmarket onto the High Street. The decaying towers of Ludlow Castle rose in the distance, dominating the town and countryside as they had since the time of the Norman conquest. The Council of the Marches had ruled all of Wales from those towers. But with the centralizing of the government in London under William and Mary, the castle—though still the property of the Prince of Wales—had fallen into disuse and ruin, plundered by looters for decades.

Allegra had been awed by it as a child, but now its crumbling stones and roofless battlements saddened her. Had not the Baniards once stood as tall and as proud as those soaring walls? And now were as dead and lost to time as the glories of that castle?

She sighed again and shook off her dark thoughts. She wouldn't let her rage toward the Wickhams spoil her lovely day. Mrs. Rutledge didn't expect her back until suppertime, and Lord Ridley had gone out riding early and would scarcely need his stillroom maid until his evening's cordial. Allegra had only to make her few purchases at the apothecary, and then she'd be free for the rest of the day.

She stopped at the Beastmarket for a few minutes to admire the livestock: squawking ducks and turkeys, milk cows and oxen, a pair of tired-looking draft horses. A pig woman with a dirty face, her animals tethered to the ground beside her, clutched at every well-dressed person who passed and begged their worships only to imagine a fine roasted pig at Christmastide.

Within a small, fenced-in ring, a magnificent bull paced back and forth, angrily snorting and pawing the ground. Just outside the fencing stood a man with a stout staff in his hand; the staff was attached to a short length of chain that ended in an iron ring looped through the snout of a large, brown bear. Each time the maddened bull lunged toward the bear, only to be stopped by the palings, the man tugged on the chain.

In obedient response, the bear rose to its hind legs and roared ferociously, scratching at the fence with its sharp-clawed paws, which only enraged the bull further. Spectators crowded around, enjoying the torment of both bull and bear; they applauded and occasionally tossed a coin to the man. Allegra turned away. This cruel sport was not to her liking.

Near the edge of the Beastmarket, two bewigged and powdered jack-a-dandies—swords protruding from their velvet coats to show their aristocratic standing—were haggling over the price of a chestnut mare. One of them turned and gave Allegra a salacious smile as she passed. "Ecod!" he exclaimed. "But here's a fine wench!" He reached out to slip his arm around her waist, but she ducked away.

"Not for you, sir," she said, giving him an insolent curtsy. "I can do better."

He muttered an oath and advanced toward her. Before she could evade him again, he had clamped his hand around her wrist. "By my faith, here's a doxy who deserves a lesson in civility."

Allegra struggled to release his savage grip. The High Street was bustling enough for her to lose herself in the crowd. But not if she couldn't break away from this perfumed lecher. She was considering taking a bite out of his hand when his companion clapped him on the shoulder.

"Let the wench go, Billy boy. There will be petticoats aplenty as the day wears on. And more agreeable ones than this. But if your cousin Crompton sees this most excellent mare before you can buy it, you'll regret it for the next six months."

The first man grumbled and glared at Allegra, then reluctantly let her go. "Now, wench," he said, "you may tell your fellow whores that Sir William Batterbee of London was merciful to you."

"Oh, Sir William, you have my undying gratitude," she said with a smirk. She gave him another mocking curtsy and skipped away into the throng. She wasn't about to wait around to meet Sir Henry Crompton again. Certainly not after insulting his cousin!

Farther along the street, near the old High Cross, amusements of all descriptions were in progress, and the air rang with music and laughter and the shouts of the crowd. Men bedecked in ribbon streamers and bells were doing a lively morris dance to the tunes of a piper, while children gathered around a puppet show and squealed at the antics of the little figures. Before a closed stall advertising a waxworks, a thin and ragged little boy beat a drum and pointed to a wax model of a buxom woman beside him. Showcloths, hung above a hastily erected platform, announced the offerings for the day's theatrical performances.

Near the town fountain, a bagpiper played a skirling tune for his dancing monkey. The tiny creature, clad in a red cape and a miniature sword, pranced about on his hind paws, doffing his feather-trimmed hat to every passerby. Allegra laughed in delight at his antics. In the shadow of the High Cross, an angry farmer was quarreling with a mountebank who had cheated him in a game of dice, and the bailiffs were dragging off a costumed actor for an unpaid bill.

Allegra lingered for a few minutes, scanning the showcloths and wondering if she should spend a few pence on a theatrical performance later in the day. It would be crude, no doubt. And a waste of money. But she was feeling so strangely contented that she was tempted to indulge herself. Then she shook her head. It was too frivolous. She'd be better off spending her coins on useful goods, or even something special to eat.

She moved toward the covered stalls that lined this part of the High Street on either side and extended as far as the entrance gate to Ludlow Castle. She wandered up and down the long rows of shops and stalls, admiring gloves and mirrors and trinkets laid out for sale, stopping to sniff a basket of ripe pears and to chat with a seller of curds and whey. When she grew thirsty, she avoided the ale stalls, whose tented interiors were already beginning to fill with boisterous patrons; she chose instead a mug of good local cider, sold by an old man with a wooden cask on his back.

That whetted her appetite for more indulgence. She was about to purchase a crisp and sweet Shropshire cake, pricked and marked off in its familiar diamond pattern, when two gawky farmboys caught her eye.

Giggling like schoolgirls, they knelt before a mangy dog. A stray, from the look of it. While it whimpered and squirmed, one of the boys pressed it to the ground and held it fast; at once, the other boy produced a string of fireworks. Before Allegra realized what they were doing, they had broken off a few crackers from the string, tied them to the tail of the unfortunate dog, and lit them with a piece of smoldering hemp.

"You rascals!" Allegra cried. She lunged for the dog as the boys raced off down the High Street. She managed to pull the burning squibs from the animal's tail and stamp on them, but not before the first cracker had gone off with a loud pop and a bright flash of flame. The dog gave a yelp of terror.

"Oh, you poor thing." Allegra scooped the animal into her arms and held it close, feeling the trembling of its thin body. She glared in the direction in which the boys had vanished. She could hear the intermittent snap of fireworks all the way to the end of the High Street. She hoped that someone would stop the little monsters and give them a good rap on the ear!

"Godamercy!" A high-pitched scream filled the air, drowning out every other market noise. It sounded like the voice of a tormented soul who was being torn asunder. Allegra dropped the dog and began to run in the direction of the Beastmarket, whence had come the scream. She shuddered as the cry was repeated again and again. She elbowed her way through the milling crowd and stared in horror.

If there was a God of retribution, he had surely taken his revenge. One of the dog-tormenting farmboys lay on the ground, beneath the paws of the great brown bear. His face and chest were slashed and bloody; one side of his lip was torn and hanging slack. Each time he tried to wriggle out from under the bear, the savage creature would roar and swipe at him with a razor-sharp claw, bringing forth another cry of agony.

Only one link of the chain still remained attached to the ring in the bear's nose; from the handful of spent fireworks that lay nearby, Allegra could imagine what had happened. The sparks and the sharp noise had clearly enraged the bear, who had snapped his chain and turned on his tormentor.

The bear's owner stood above him, clutching his broken stick and chain. He shouted curses at the animal, and beat him with the stick. It was a futile effort. The bear merely shook him off and returned his attention to his prey. He bent his massive head and began to gnaw on the boy's shoulder.

The boy screamed piteously. "Oh, masters! Help me! Have mercy. Oh, sweet Jesus!"

In response to the boy's plea, there was the stir and rumble of horrified conversation among the onlookers, and a chorus of sympathetic groans. Several merchants turned about and tried to urge their neighbors to action. But nobody moved to help.

"For the love of God, someone fetch a net or some ropes!" Grey Ridley's angry voice rose above the crowd. He pushed his way through the cringing spectators, threw down his cocked hat, and strode to the bear and his trainer. Snatching the staff from the man's hand, he put it around the bear's neck and tugged on it with all his strength.

With a ferocious growl, the bear rose to its full height, nearly lifting Ridley off the ground. He wrestled valiantly with the beast, trying to keep behind the animal and evade those sharp teeth, the vicious buffets of the paws that swung at the stout staff and his vulnerable arms.

Allegra held her breath. At times it seemed like such an uneven contest that Ridley would surely fail. But still he clung tenaciously to the creature, the muscles in his neck bulging with the strain of his superhuman effort.

At last—and to Allegra's relief—men came running with ropes and a large net. In a few minutes, the bear was subdued and contained. Gasping to catch his breath, Ridley shook off the thanks of the crowd and urged them to see to the boy, who was now moaning in an extremity of pain. He retrieved his hat and limped away, still breathing hard from his struggles.

Allegra followed him down the High Street. She was sure he hadn't seen her in the throng, but she wanted him to know how much she had admired his bravery. How moved she had been by his nobility and strength of purpose. She hurried up beside him, then hesitated. She felt timid and awkward at the last moment. "Milord..." she began, tugging at the cuff of his coat.

He stopped and looked at her. He seemed almost sober, which heartened her. "What? Is it the fair Allegra?" he said in a teasing voice. "And frowning on such a fine day?"

"I...I saw what happened. You might have been killed."

"Would you miss me? More to the point, would you miss my kisses?" His sensuous mouth twisted in a mocking, lecherous smile.

"Milord...I..." She bit her lip in dismay. She had wanted to be kind, and he was turning her solicitude into a cruel joke. She curtsied, meaning to leave him. "By your leave, milord. Find another to torment."

He stopped her with a gentle hand on her sleeve. His eyes were unexpectedly warm, searching her face as though he hoped to read her heart. "No. Don't go. I should thank you for your concern, not vex you." He sighed. "Upon my oath, I think that if I were to die tomorrow, you would be the only soul who would come and put flowers on my grave." His hand slipped from her sleeve to caress the bare flesh of her forearm, then to take her fingers in his.

She trembled and looked away from his glowing-amber gaze, dropping her eyes to the hand that rested on hers. She gasped aloud. "By all the saints, you're hurt, milord!" Blood was seeping from beneath the ruffled cuff of his shirt.

He pulled his hand away and hid it behind his back, like a little boy embarrassed to be caught fighting. "'Tis of no consequence."

She scowled and snatched at his other arm. "And this one, as well! How can you be so foolish? Come and let me tend you."

"I haven't heard such a stern voice since my last nursemaid," he said with a slow smile that lit up his face. "Will you scold me if I refuse?"

"As your servant, I haven't the right, milord," she said with dignity.

He chuckled. "But, as my saucy stillroom maid, who never flinches from insolence…" He laughed again, a lovely sound, friendly and enveloping.

She melted and returned his laughter with a smile. He was sober, praise be to God, the day was beautiful, and he had done a good and brave deed. "As your stillroom maid, who must devise cures if the infection sets in," she corrected him, "I give myself leave to insist. Come and let me tend your wounds."

"Fair enough." He nodded and allowed her to lead him to the High Cross, which was now almost deserted, the crowd having rushed to see the drama at the Beastmarket. While Ridley took off his coat and seated himself on the steps, Allegra moved to the fountain opposite.

She removed the large linen square that modestly covered her bosom and tore it in half, tucking one piece into her pocket and moistening the other in the crystal waters of the fountain. "Now," she said, as she returned to the Cross, "let me see the damage."

She sat on the step above him and placed his arms on her lap. His shirtsleeves were rent with several long gashes, as though someone had taken a knife to them, and their snowy whiteness was stained with drops of blood. Gently she unbuttoned his ruffled cuffs and tucked them back to his elbows. She was relieved to see that the scratches from the bear's claws, though numerous, were not very deep. She sponged away the blood with her wet cloth, working as carefully as though she herself felt the sting of each cut. "I'll bind them to keep them clean," she said, "and mix up a healing salve when I return to the Hall."

She finished her task, then examined his arms once more to be sure that she had found every scratch. His right forearm bore a deep scar that ran from elbow to wrist—a thick ridge upon which the dark, curly hairs no longer grew. It looked as though it had been a cruel and painful wound. "Where did you get this?" she asked in sympathy.

He shrugged. "Fighting against the Old Pretender in Scotland."

"You were a soldier?" Lady Dorothy had told her so, but somehow she had never connected Ridley to the reality of an actual battle.

"Does that surprise you?"

Everything about him surprised and bewildered her, she realized with a start. But how could she begin to ask him about the contradictions she saw in him? She busied herself with her work, at a loss to think of what more to say. She tore the rest of her neckerchief into strips and wrapped them around his forearms, pulled down his sleeves and carefully refastened them. For the first time since she had begun her work, she allowed herself to look him full in the face.

He was watching her with an intensity that made her shiver. Head down, eyes glowing beneath his dark, shaggy brows. She was suddenly aware that her bodice—stripped of its covering handkerchief—exposed far more of her swelling breasts than she would have wished. Had he been staring at her all this time? She blushed furiously.

Godamercy, she thought a moment later. She was behaving like a goose today. In another minute, he might think that she actually gave a fig whether or not he looked at her! He was already beginning to smirk. Best for her to say something—anything!—before he turned her blush to his advantage. She cleared her throat and willed her foolish cheeks to cool.

"That was very courageous of you, milord," she said. "To wrestle with such a savage animal." It seemed sensible to turn the focus back to him. A little genuine praise to soften his sharp wit. She had no wish to be humiliated for her weakness. "I'm sure that everyone at the Hall will be pleased to learn of your bravery."

If she was hoping for a simple acknowledgment of her words, she was disappointed. The smirk deepened, the devil peeped out from his golden eyes. "What? Compliments for a monster?"

"No…milord, I…" she stammered.

"Don't deny it. You have called me monster. And upon more than one occasion. I *do* remember what happens, even when I'm drunk." He chuckled, a surprisingly unpleasant sound from deep in his throat. "And now you praise the monster? What do you hope to gain? A month from your bond contract? Two, perhaps? For such a piddling compliment?"

She felt helpless and defeated once more. "By your leave, milord," she said with a sigh, "I have purchases at the apothecary." She started to rise, but he clasped her hands and pulled her down beside him.

"No. Wait. Stay with me for a little." He scanned her face with eyes grown suddenly serious, then looked away. "God help me," he muttered, "sometimes I don't know why I say the things I do. Stay, I beg you."

How could she refuse when she heard the pain in his voice, felt the warmth of his hands, the throbbing of his fingers in hers? "As you wish, milord."

"No. Not milord. Call me Grey. Just once. Let me hear you say my name. As though we were equals, friends. Lovers."

"Oh, I cannot, milord," she said, startled by such an intimate request.

"Please. Grey. 'Tis not so difficult." He leaned toward her; she could feel the silken caress of his breath on her cheek.

She was blushing again, frightened and stirred by his sudden and unexpected tenderness. "Grey," she whispered at last.

He smiled into her eyes. A smile of warmth and gratitude. And something else? She dared not guess at what she saw in those liquid depths.

Gently he pushed back her straw hat and smoothed a stray curl at her temple. "Do you know how beautiful you are?" he said. "There is healing in your face as well as your hands. It soothes my soul just to look upon you. Your nightly visits to my rooms—I wonder if it's the cordial or that lovely face I so anticipate. Do you know how much I watch you while I'm enjoying your concoctions?"

Her face was now on fire. She had known he watched her, of course. But she had always thought that the intensity of his gaze held nothing more than lust. She was moved and touched that he would admit to something deeper in his need of her. She remembered his kindness in the almshouse, his secret charities, and her eyes filled with tears of frustration at his willful self-destruction.

"Why must you drink so, milord?" she burst out. "You're a good man, I think. 'Tis only the drink that makes you cruel. If you would put aside your gin, I would stand before you all day, still as a statue, to bring you peace." Helpless to stop them, she felt the burning tears fall from her eyes.

He stared at her, awestruck. "*Tears? For me?*" He brushed her cheek with the pad of his thumb and rubbed the moisture between his fingers, as though he were a miser who doubted the worth of his gold. He shook his head in amazement. "There's an ancient Irish tale about a maiden who wept on the eyes of a blind man and restored his sight. Are *your* tears magical? Will they restore me? Will they be my salvation?"

Her voice shook with grief and pity. "If it would ease your pain, milord, I would weep an ocean of tears."

"Oh, God," he said with a groan, casting his eyes to the cross above him. "Is there hope for me yet, do you think?"

"Oh, milord. Don't give yourself to despair. Take my tears to heal your soul." She ached with the desire to hold him in her arms and comfort him against the unknown sorrows he bore.

He lifted her hand to his lips and pressed a burning kiss into her palm. "Sweet, generous Allegra. I have my horse. Come with me. Weep your tears against my breast. If God forgives me, you may yet be my cure."

She pulled her hands from his and stood up, blotting at the tears on her face. She felt the first stirrings of unease. "Come with you?"

He stretched out his arms to her. "Come with me. Lie with me. We'll find a meadow of sweet clover on the Edge. Come."

She frowned and backed away from him down the steps. He was clever and he wanted her. Was this just another of his attempts at seduction—to play the tormented soul and win her sympathy? His pain had truly seemed genuine. But what did she know of the ways of clever rakes? Of men who would try anything to satisfy their hungers?

She hesitated, torn by the longing to give in, to taste again his sweet, hot kisses. She yearned to believe the words he spoke—to think that she, above all women, could restore his wounded heart. But perhaps she was only a fool and a dupe.

She gasped in sudden shock. She felt a strong hand grab her around the waist, and another snake over her shoulder to plunge into the bodice of her gown and clutch at her breast. As Ridley jumped to his feet in alarm, Allegra was pulled against a hard, masculine body. She breathed the sickly scent of heavy perfume, and heard a rasping voice behind her ear.

"Now, you insolent chit," said the voice, "I intend to take my pleasure of you."

Chapter Nine

Allegra recognized the voice of Sir William Batterbee, the jack-a-dandy from the Beastmarket. The ruttish pig! She tugged at his hand, striving in vain to pull it from her bodice.

Grey Ridley bounded down the steps, his eyes as cold and hard as stone. "If you value your life, you will release my servant at once, sir," he said through clenched teeth. He stood tall and threatening, a match for any man.

With a languid movement, as though it signified little to him, Batterbee removed his hand from Allegra's breast. But his voice, when he spoke, was filled with false bravado; he was clearly intimidated by Ridley's tone and bearing. "And who might you be, sir?" he drawled.

"The man who will batter you to a pulp if you don't remove your other hand from the girl's person. *Forthwith*."

Batterbee laughed nervously, relinquished his hold on Allegra, and gave Ridley an apologetic little bow. "A jest, you understand, sir. I meant merely to frighten the girl. She was insolent to me."

Ridley curled his lip in disdain. "Insolent? My servants are never insolent. I have no doubt you provoked her. Give her a guinea for her pains."

Batterbee's jaw dropped. "By God, sir, I will not."

"By God, sirrah, you will!" Ridley strode forward and clutched at Batterbee's lace cravat with his two fists, lifting the man bodily off the ground. Batterbee squeaked in alarm. "You mangy cur," growled Ridley. "I'll not have my servants pawed by the likes of you."

"'Odds fish, Billy boy. Will you get yourself into mischief the minute we turn our backs?"

Allegra whirled to see Batterbee's companion, hands on hips, grinning at his friend's predicament. Sir Henry Crompton, his large bulk swathed in velvet, came puffing up beside him. He mopped his red face with a lace handkerchief and scowled. "Ridley? Begad, is that you? What the devil are you doing to my cousin Batterbee?"

"Teaching him manners." With reluctance, Ridley lowered the other man to the ground. "But, since he's your cousin, I give him over to your care and instruction."

Safely on terra firma, Batterbee found his courage again. "Who do you think you are, to insult the person of Sir William Batterbee of London?"

Ridley gave him a mocking bow, making obsequious circles in the air with his hand as he bent low. "Greyston, sixth Viscount Ridley. Of Calcutta, London, and Shropshire. Your servant, sir."

Batterbee sputtered in outrage. "'Tis no wonder your servants have learned to be insolent, sir!" He took an angry step toward Ridley.

Crompton put a hand on his cousin's arm. "Come, come, Billy. This is my neighbor. We must live in peace, side by side, long after you've returned to London." He held out his arms to the three men—an expansive gesture. "Gentlemen. Can we not find a tavern and share a good claret together? A joint of mutton?"

Ridley shook his head. "Not until we've concluded our business. There's the matter of a guinea, which your cousin owes to my maidservant here."

For the first time, Crompton peered closely at Allegra. "Damme, but I know that wench." He smiled a hungry smile, his small, dark eyes appraising her thoroughly; then he smacked his lips. "She's a damn sight better looking today than when first we met. You must keep her content, Ridley." He turned to his friends and grinned. "He paid me for the jade. A hundred pounds."

Allegra cringed at his words. He made her sound like a whore.

Ridley was clearly aware of her distress. He turned to her and gave her a crisp nod. Master to servant. "I dismiss you, girl. See that you stop at the apothecary on the way back to the Hall. I'll need that salve." He turned to the other men. "A most excellent stillroom maid, Sir Henry. I thank you for the opportunity to bring her into my service."

Batterbee snickered. "But…a hundred quid! What else does she do, to give you your money's worth, Lord Ridley?"

"Now, God damn you, you mongrel!" Ridley leapt for Sir William and drove his fist into the man's face. Batterbee went down with a grunt of pain, blood oozing from his mouth. "Get up," growled Ridley. "You deserve at least another."

Batterbee licked at his lip and struggled to his feet, vainly holding his arms before his face to shield it from another blow.

"Your sword, Billy boy!" shouted his friend, as Ridley struck again, sending Batterbee staggering backward. "Use your sword!"

Batterbee shook off his daze, fumbled with his sword, and drew it from its scabbard. He pointed it unsteadily toward Ridley. "I challenge you, sir."

Ridley stepped away from him and spread his hands—a gesture of cool indifference. "I am unarmed, sir."

"Arm yourself, then."

Ridley shrugged. "I choose not to."

"Do you refuse my challenge?"

"Not at all." Ridley pointed toward Ludlow Castle. "There's an open field just beyond the porter's lodge. Quarterstaffs. It would please me to crack your pate."

Suddenly, Crompton stepped forward, his eyes glittering like hard coals. "No. Swords."

Grey Ridley laughed. A harsh, strange sound, it seemed to Allegra. "I prefer quarterstaffs," he said. "Though I don't mind rapping Sir William's empty head, that coat of his is too fine to cut with a blade. Good tailors are harder to come by than lousy noblemen."

"By God," said Batterbee, beginning to sheathe his sword, "it matters not to me what we use. Just so I teach this braggart a lesson!"

Crompton's smile had become a sly smirk. "No, Billy. Swords. This is Lord Ridley of *Baniard Hall*. You will recall I told you of him?"

"Ecod!" Batterbee slapped his thigh in pleasure. "This is the man? Then swords it is. Give him your blade, Cousin."

Crompton drew his sword and held it out, hilt first. Ridley flinched, took several shaky steps backward, and wiped his hand across his mouth as though he were desperately in need of a drink. Allegra stared in horror. What was happening to the man?

He glanced briefly at her, then looked away, the color rising to his cheeks. "I shall not fight you, sir," he said. "'Tis scarcely worth my effort." Allegra heard the tremor in his voice, and wondered if the three men could hear it as well.

Batterbee's friend began to laugh. "Is this nothing but a toupet man?" he taunted. "A mincing coward who is less than a man?" He pointed down the street. "Yonder is a monkey with a sword, Billy boy. *He* would make a more worthy foe than this lily-livered craven."

Crompton poked the hilt of the sword at Ridley's lax fingers. "Take it."

Ridley pulled his hand away; he was beginning to tremble slightly. "I shall not."

Batterbee's friend reached out and slipped his arm around Allegra's waist. "A kiss from the wench as the prize."

Allegra broke away from him and turned to Ridley. He mustn't be forced to fight on her behalf. Not when he was so clearly unwilling. And afraid? She was reluctant to accept the word, but surely that was fear on his face. She searched her brain to rescue him from this dilemma.

"You needn't duel on my account, Lord Ridley," she said, the words tumbling out of her in an anxious rush. "I'm to blame. Wholly to blame. I did insult Sir William." She curtsied to Batterbee. "For which I humbly beg your pardon, sir. There's no need to trouble my master further. Put up your sword."

He sneered. "Shall I have you on your knees next, begging for your master's life?"

She glanced again at Ridley. That *was* fear in his eyes. An unreasoning terror that had reduced him to helplessness. "If I must," she whispered.

"Enough," said Ridley. His voice was low, his face a mask of tired resignation. "Give me the blade, damn you." He took the sword and held it firmly for a moment in a white-knuckled fist, his jaw clenched in determination.

Then he groaned, lowered the blade and began to shake—a violent quivering and trembling that buffeted him from head to toe. He had become as pale as a ghost. The corner of one eye twitched and beads of sweat appeared on his broad forehead. He was now shaking so violently that the sword point tapped against the ground in a sickening rhythm. His chest heaved as though he were having difficulty breathing, and soft, agonized grunts came from his throat.

Allegra gasped and covered her mouth with her hands. The transformation was so complete and appalling that she wanted to die. This was far more dreadful and bone-chilling than anything Lady Dorothy had told her of his behavior. It shamed her to watch him. Shamed her even more to guess that her own presence must be adding to his humiliation.

The more he crumbled before their eyes, the more his tormentors taunted him; the air was poisoned with their laughter and their insults. Allegra couldn't bear another moment. She pushed aside Crompton and Batterbee, snatched the sword from Ridley's hand, and threw it to the ground. She glared at the men and indicated Ridley's bloody sleeves. "Can't you see that His Lordship has been hurt?" She put her arm around Ridley's waist. "Come away, milord. Let me tend your wounds."

He stared down at her. His eyes were blank and lost, like a man who had suffered a mortal blow and still couldn't believe it.

"Please, Your Lordship. Grey. Come away."

He clung to her. She could feel the helpless quivering of his limbs. "Gin," he said hoarsely.

She guided him to an old, out-of-the-way tavern, suffering—as though the pain were hers—the taunts and laughter that followed them down the High Street until they turned a corner.

Ridley seemed incapable of conducting his own affairs; Allegra hesitated, then fished in his waistcoat pocket and pulled out several gold coins. "Here," she said to the tavernkeeper. "A private room. And a dram of gin to start. And send a boy to the High Cross to fetch His Lordship's coat and hat."

The private room in the rear of the tavern was small and cheerless. Grey Ridley staggered to the single decrepit armchair, threw himself down, and glared at Allegra. "Go away."

She gambled that he was too devastated to care that she was merely his bondservant, who owed him perfect obedience. She shook her head. "No. I shall stay."

"Then stay and be damned," he said, and closed his eyes. He was still pale and shaking when the landlord shuffled into the room a few moments later, bearing his coat and hat and a flask of gin. He opened his eyes and curled his lip in disgust. "Did you have to send to London to get it, fool? If you expect to be paid, you will fetch me another flask of gin at once. In *timely* fashion, you understand. I'll not pay for a sluggard. Now, get out."

He lifted the flask with a trembling hand and poured the gin down his throat. Allegra watched the bob of his Adam's apple as the liquid sought its terminus. He scarcely seemed to stop for breath. But when he lowered the flask at last, the color had returned to his face. He paused for a moment, then returned the bottle to his lips. He drank steadily and silently, by the time the landlord returned, bearing the second flask of gin, Ridley had drained the first.

About to start on the second bottle, he looked at Allegra and frowned. "Why do you stare at me in that fashion?"

"Please, milord," she whispered. "Don't drink so much."

He gave a sneering laugh. "Such a humble plea. Landlord, in honor of this sad-eyed creature, bring me six more bottles of gin."

She sighed, feeling helpless. There must be something she could say that would ease his pain, turn him from his self-destructive course. "If I may be permitted, milord," she began in a faltering voice. "I have never seen such bravery as yours. The boy would have died else. No one would have saved him from the bear. But you…you risked injury… ignored the danger…"

"Injury?" He laughed and held up his bandaged arms. "I've had worse scratches from a whore. And enjoyed it almost as much. Do *you* scratch a man when he's swiving you?"

She lowered her eyes, shocked by his crudeness. He was determined to be cruel. Best for her to hold her tongue.

He finished the second bottle of gin, watching her uneasily all the while, as though he expected—or dreaded—that she would speak. "Come here," he growled at last, and pointed to a spot on the floor in front of his chair. When she obeyed, standing before him with downcast eyes, he stuck out his chin as though he were challenging her. "Do you think I give a damn what they think of me?" he demanded.

"No, of course not, milord." But of course he did. She sought desperately to give him back his pride. "They were as lowbred and coarse as the lowest rogues in the land. What should their opinions matter to a man like you?"

"And *your* opinion?" He searched her face, his amber eyes glowing with intensity. He seemed almost to be holding his breath, waiting on her answer.

She had a sudden wild thought. Would he have felt so humiliated if she hadn't been there to see it? God forgive her, but perhaps he would have refused the sword except for her presence. Surely he had only accepted the challenge because she was there. Yet why should he care what she thought of him? She was only a lowly servant. But, clearly, he did.

She felt a pang of guilt; if it was her fault, how could she lessen his shame? And then she remembered "Mr. Morgan" at the almshouse. She would praise him, confess that she knew of his secret life of benevolence, his noble deeds. Far more the mark of a truly brave man than a momentary weakness in the marketplace. "You're a good man, milord," she began. "Whatever your…difficulties in the face of a challenge…"

His mouth curved in a bitter smile. "My dishonor, you mean. My cowardice."

"No!"

He shrugged. "Call it what you will. I can live with it."

"If you can live with it, why do you need the gin?"

"What would you have me do? Cut off my offending right arm?"

"No." She sighed heavily. "Only learn to accept whatever is past."

A cynical laugh. "As you have, with the flame of hatred burning in your heart?"

She gulped back the tears. What could she say? He twisted every bit of comfort she tried to give him.

He laughed again and picked up a bottle. "This is where my succor lies."

"Please don't," she murmured.

He rose to his feet and towered over her, staring down at the rounded swell of her bosom. He raised a mocking eyebrow. "If you can give me something better to do for the next quarter of an hour or so, I'll not touch another drop."

She backed away. This was not where she had wanted to lead his thoughts. If she could get him to his horse, send him back to the sanctuary of Baniard Hall and the care of Jagat Ram, she might keep him from further harm. And herself, as well, God knows.

She turned and picked up his coat. "Come, milord," she said briskly. "Come home. You'll have a fine supper, and I'll bring you your cordial. I have a new concoction I think you'll enjoy. And, if it will comfort you…" She smiled shyly, hoping she could remind him of the tender moments they had shared. "I remember what you said at the High Cross. If it will comfort you, I'll stay in your rooms for hours and let you look at me."

He sneered. "I must have been mad when I said that. The only way you could comfort me is if I found you in my bed naked and willing."

She stared at him in hurt and dismay. "But…you said…my face…"

"You're merely another petticoat," he drawled. "If I could have your body willing, you could come to my bed wearing a mask." He laughed bitterly. "At least, in *some* ways, I can still prove that I'm a man. You see?"

His hand shot out and clamped around her wrist; with a cruel wrench, he pressed her palm against the hard fullness of his groin. "You see?" he said again. "Am I a man?"

"For the love of God!" she cried, cringing at the savage intimacy he had forced upon her. "Let me go."

His eyes glowed with pain and rage. "*Am I a man?*" he repeated.

She twisted her hand from his grasp. "You're a monster!" she cried, and burst into tears. "And not deserving of a minute's pity!" She threw his coat to the floor and rushed from the room. From the tavern. From the town.

From the grief that tore at her heart.

• • •

"You silly creature! Just because I saved your tail, will you follow me all the way up to Wenlock Edge?" Allegra sat down on a patch of grass beside the dusty road and held out her arms to the thin dog. She had paid no notice to the animal on her hasty flight from Ludlow. She had been filled with too much misery for anything but the thought of escaping Ridley.

But the dog had remembered her. And followed, wagging its tail in happy loyalty. Now, it barked softly and burrowed in her arms, tucking its head against her neck.

Its fur was as warm as her flesh, reminding her that she had kept her large hat hanging by its ribbon down her back since Ridley had pushed it from her head. She should have been wearing it all this time. The climb in the sun had been too hot for her to go uncovered. Perhaps that was why her head was beginning to throb.

She got to her feet and looked around. She must be near Culmington by now. She seemed to remember from her childhood that there had been a brook, running through the village and into the woods. A cool drink would revive her spirits. At least if she could stop thinking about Grey Ridley.

The woods were cool and refreshing when she turned off the road. There was even a footpath; others, no doubt, had been drawn to the stream on hot August days like this. With the dog scampering at her heels, she came to a small, open meadow, bright with flowers and sweet, scented grasses. It reminded her that she had forgotten her visit to the apothecary in her haste to leave Ludlow.

"Well, dog," she said to the animal, with a laugh, "my mother taught me to be practical as well as patient." And surely there were enough plants and flowers in the meadow to stock a dozen apothecary shops.

She pulled off her hat and looped the ribbon over her wrist, making her way through the tall grasses to poke and search and discover the treasures that lay all around her. Yellow-flowered gentian, for ills of the stomach, eyebright and maidenhair fern, fragrant thyme, shepherd's purse for the flux. She filled her hat with flowers and stems and leaves, grasses and berries. She brushed away the humming bees from a patch of clover and smiled in satisfaction. Even the unhappiest of days could yield its small rewards. If Lord Ridley's scratches festered, she would need a poultice. And the clover was her chief ingredient. She plucked handfuls of the scented blossoms and added them to her store.

By the time she reached the edge of the meadow and heard the gurgle of the stream beyond, she was feeling a good deal better. She would think no more of what had happened. There was no way that she could help Ridley, so why should she suffer on his account? She had her own life. She had her own griefs. She would forget the despair she had read in his eyes, the softness of his lips, the warmth of his hands.

She knelt and drank from the stream, then followed it deeper into the woods. It widened suddenly into a little pool, shaded by a large ash tree and glinting with sparkles where the sun broke through the leaves and touched the placid surface of the water.

It looked cool and inviting. Allegra hesitated, then put aside her hat, and pulled off her clothing—gown, petticoat, stays, and shift. The summer breeze was gentle on her naked body, sweet after the heat of the day.

The dog watched her, its head cocked to one side, as though it thought her mad. And when she put a tentative foot into the water and gasped at its icy coldness, she was tempted to agree with the animal.

Still, it seemed foolish to lose her nerve now, when she had gone to the bother of disrobing. She screwed up her courage, took a deep breath and plunged into the pool. By all the saints, she *was* mad. She splashed wildly about to warm her blood and accustom her heated flesh to the frigid water. It was refreshing, but she didn't intend to linger for any length of time.

The pool was not very deep—reaching only to her breasts— which was just as well; she wasn't a good swimmer. Gammer Pringle had discouraged her from swimming in the farm pond even on hot days, fearing she might someday leap into the harbor of Charles Town and escape.

The dog stood on the bank and barked at her. She laughed and threw handfuls of water at it, which sent it scurrying behind the large tree. In a moment it emerged, returned to the bank and began again to bark. Again she splashed, again it retreated only to return, barking furiously. It was an amusing game, one that seemed to delight the dog as much as Allegra. She hadn't played like this since she was a child. That thought sobered her for a moment, and she shivered—as much from her painful memories as from the cold water. The dog stood watching her, barking to remind her of their game. She shook off her dark mood and splashed the animal with water once more. It vanished.

She waited. She could hear the rustle of branches in the thicket beyond the tree. "Well, dog," she called, "have you tired of our frolic?"

"I could hear his barking all the way from the road. My horse frightened him away."

Allegra gasped in surprise and ducked in the water up to her shoulders. Grey Ridley, astride his horse, moved to the edge of the pool and looked down at her, a sly smile on his face. His clothing was in disarray, and his eyes were unnaturally bright, like glittering chips of amber.

"How many bottles of gin have you drunk since I left?" asked Allegra in disgust. Oddly, she felt more anger than fear.

He looked pleased with himself. "Not nearly enough."

She tried to shield her nakedness from his gaze, but it seemed a pointless effort. The water was far too clear to afford her much modesty. Besides, he had seen her breasts before. What did she care? She stood straight and tall and proud, defying him. "Go home to the Hall while you can still sit your horse, milord," she said sharply.

He laughed and dismounted, his movements unsteady and graceless. His riding whip hung from his wrist; he raised it to smack the horse on its flank. "Let him go home alone. Together, you and I will walk back to the Hall." He leered. "*Later.*"

She gritted her teeth. Why did drink always bring out his lechery? "I'm no more willing to be your whore today than I was yesterday. Or will be tomorrow."

He shrugged. "Then I see no point in inconveniencing myself." He turned and tied his horse to the tree, then ambled to the bank and sat down at the edge of the pool. He slapped idly at the water with his whip, watching Allegra with eyes that told her nothing. Was she in danger? Or was this just one more of his teasing games? Like the morning when he had come to her room.

She waited, refusing to break the silence. It felt like a battle of wills, as though the first one to yield, to speak, would somehow be the loser. Even moving about in the water seemed an admission of weakness. But surely he would tire of the game and leave. In his present condition, he would soon crave his tipple back at Baniard Hall. She could be patient.

The gentle, rhythmic splash of the whip was the only sound in the shady stillness. Grey Ridley smiled like a mocking devil, clearly enjoying the state of affairs. Curse him! she thought. She fought the sudden wild urge to reach out and pull him into the icy pool. *That* would sober him right quickly, the wicked rogue! But it would also put him into the water beside her naked body—a proximity that could lead to unwelcome consequences. No. She would wait for him to leave.

She began to shiver with the cold, and still he would not move or speak. This was madness. Her foolish pride. She glared at him. "The water is very cold," she said with reluctance.

He grinned in triumph. She had surrendered first. "And?"

"I wish to come out. Please go away."

"No."

She sighed. He was determined to stay. To look at her nakedness, to disconcert her as much as he could. Ah, well, what did it signify? Was it better to risk her health than her dignity? As though there was a loss of dignity in dealing with a man like Ridley! She moved to the far edge of the pool and stepped up onto the bank, her chin held high and proud. She would dress as though he were not even there. As though his presence meant no more to her than the dragonflies that hovered above the surface of the water. She picked her way across a pebble-filled clearing to reach her clothes.

Considering his state of intoxication he was surprisingly agile. He jumped to his feet and barred her way.

The villain! By heaven, she would serve him the most vile-tasting cordial tonight! "'Tis cold, and I am very wet, milord," she said, fighting to contain her anger.

Nothing seemed to daunt him. "So you are." His eyes ranged her body, a searching appraisal that made her feel as though he could see clear through to her bones. She shivered with the cold…and the look in his tawny eyes. "Very wet, and very beautiful," he went on. "I had not guessed that you were so lovely." His voice was a sudden rasp of passion. "I want to see all of you."

She eyed him warily as he began to circle her. If she made a move toward her clothing, he might be tempted to stop her. And if once he put his hands on her body…who knew what would happen? She stood still and allowed him his examination.

He laughed softly behind her. "Yes. You do. Have dimples, as I surmised. Captivating. Just here."

She gasped as she felt the touch of his whip on the small of her back, a gentle stroking that felt like the flutter of a bird's wing on her naked flesh. She whirled in alarm and anger, glaring at him with an outrage that came as much from an awareness of her own weakness as from his taking advantage of that weakness. "If you try to rape me," she cried, "I swear I'll make you pay!" She cast her glance wildly about. There was not even a large enough rock or branch to strike him down.

His eyes widened in surprise. "Rape? I told you, long ago, that was not my way. But you want your freedom, no doubt. And I'm still willing to negotiate. And to see you like this…so beautiful…" He ran his tongue across his lips. "You have the advantage at the moment. I think I'd grant you anything in exchange."

"Only let me return to the Hall in peace," she said with a sigh. She was exhausted. There had been more than enough drama today. She had seen him at his best, and at his very worst. She couldn't play out another scene.

He ignored her words. He touched the tip of his whip to the outside of her ankle, and ran it slowly up her calf to her knee. He stilled his movements for a moment watching her intently, then stroked her thigh and her rounded hip. "A charming limb," he murmured.

She trembled, wondering why her flesh was so weak, so soft and vulnerable to his caresses. Even his voice seduced her, deep-pitched and rich, throbbing with desire.

"Would it be so difficult for you to surrender?" He returned the whip to her foot. But this time he sought the inside of her ankle. She held her breath as he moved the whip upward. Surely he wouldn't be so bold...he couldn't!

"Oh, Lord," she breathed, and shuddered in terrified, wonderful expectation.

Slowly he moved the whip to the juncture between her legs, stroking, gliding, rubbing against the delicate, sensitive flesh. Again and again, each stroke more insistent, more impatient, more tantalizing than the last.

She trembled in an agony of joy, her body on fire with strange and thrilling and frightening sensations.

He watched her through half-closed eyes. And still his whip did its work, rousing her to the verge of madness; she could no longer think clearly. "Would it be so difficult?" he repeated in a whisper. "Your body is willing, is it not? 'Tis only your pride that rebels. Is it that you fear to surrender to a coward?"

She felt herself crumbling in a helpless confusion of longing and fear. He was drunken and cruel, and this was not the way it was supposed to be. She moaned softly. Dear God, if he was sober, tender, kind, she would fall into his arms in a moment. But when he could only behave like this...

With a despairing cry, she pushed the whip away and covered herself, one hand flying across her breasts, the other protecting her loins against further assaults. "Do you want me to *hate* you?" she choked.

He stepped back at the harsh word, his eyes wide and bewildered.

She stared at him in sudden knowledge, filled with the most extraordinary notion. Perhaps it was his stillness. Perhaps it was the odd, haunted light in his eyes. And perhaps it was that intuition that had been in her from the very beginning, that had seen something more in him than the angry, cruel face he presented to the world.

"Yes," she said in wonderment. "Yes, you do! You've *always* wanted my hatred. You've courted it from the first. Was that what you saw in me? Was that why you bought me? You were jealous of Wickham! Did you hope that some portion of the hatred I feel for him could be yours?"

"What nonsense is this?" he muttered.

"You treated me in a vile manner. You used me to drive away your friends. You torment me like this, play your games of seduction, shame me with my weakness. Not because you want me. But because you want me to hate you."

He glared at her. "Hold your tongue, girl."

She shook her head. Her growing awareness gave her the strength to defy him. Why hadn't she seen it before? Why hadn't she realized? "My God, it isn't only me. You court all the world's hatred. Every servant, every tradesman, every friend. Your sharp words, your insults, your careless cruelties. All with the same end. To make them hate you. You waste your money like a fool, you let Mrs. Rutledge and all the others cheat you. And you know they do. And you welcome it—their scorn and their laughter, behind your back."

His eyes were beginning to glow with a dangerous light. "Be still, I say. I shall not tolerate such treason. Such wild ravings! Why should I care if I'm despised? I live my life. If they hate me, if *you* hate me, it matters not a whit to me!"

"Are you blind as well as cruel? Or do you drink to hide the truth from yourself?" She was starting to weep, though she couldn't begin to understand why. "And poor, honorable Mr. Briggs. You reserve a special hell for him. And reward all his goodness with venom. Is his hatred the most precious of all to you? Does he remind you of what you could have been? And are not?"

"By God, I've heard enough!" he roared. "You will be silent!"

She was fearless. The angrier he became, the more she guessed that she had touched on the truth. A truth, perhaps, that he himself hadn't faced. She remembered his dreadful humiliation in the market, his cringing cowardice. She remembered, as well, "Mr. Morgan," who abased himself to work as a menial. The poor tormented man. How filled with self-loathing he must be.

She sniffled, fighting to stem the bitter tears. "You take all that hatred, I think, and lay it against your soul. For a healing poultice. Does it help to draw out the pain, the one hatred you cannot live with? The festering sore?"

"What do you mean?" he growled.

"The hatred of the one person who despises you the most," she said, brushing at her tears, which now flowed unchecked.

His lip curled. "You?"

"No. Yourself."

He flinched as though she had plunged a knife into his heart. Then his expression hardened and he raised his whip. "Now, by God," he said, "I'll give you cause to hate me, girl."

Despite his savage words, there was desperation in his eyes. She spread her arms to receive the blow, open and willing. "Strike me, if you must. If you wish. If it will ease your suffering. But I'll not hate you, Grey Ridley."

The tears had turned to sobs. She knew now why she wept. "I shall pity you, Grey. And weep for your tortured heart. But I'll not hate you. If hatred is your absolution, you must find it elsewhere."

The whip wavered, dropped from his hand. "Damn you," he said in a strangled voice. Haggard, reeling, he staggered to his horse, mounted and vanished into the woods.

She covered her eyes with her hands and shook with wrenching sobs. How could she hate him, when she saw his pain and ached to comfort him? How could she hate him, when his torment broke her heart and she was powerless to help? How could she hate him, when she…

No. *No!* She shook her head. He had no right to draw her into his life, to trouble her heart, to tear her apart with longings. Until the Wickhams were dead, every last one of them, she had no life of her own. She had no right to it. She had sworn an oath.

Weeping, she gathered her clothes to her bosom. If only she could run, hide, escape.

She saw his face, his haunted eyes. She felt again the press of his burning lips on hers. "Leave me alone, Grey," she whispered. "In the name of mercy, leave me alone."

Chapter Ten

"About time you got here, girl." Humphrey, the gatekeeper, scratched his ear under his wig and scowled at Allegra.

She glanced up at the rising moon, a pale, silvery disk against the still-light sky. "I'm sorry," she said. Where had the time gone? She had wandered through the woods, and sat and wept and thought about Grey Ridley.

Humphrey grunted. "Sorry? Hmph! And all the while a body's waiting to lock the gate and be done for the night."

Allegra knew from Barbara's gossip that Humphrey abandoned his lodge almost every night to meet a farmgirl—one of the cottagers' daughters. She shook her head in disgust. Another servant who took as much as he could from Lord Ridley, and gave back as little. "She'll wait, Humphrey. Even for you."

"Don't get saucy with me," he growled, "or I'll tell Rutledge. She's fairly itching to take you to task."

"Fortune preserve me, what have I done now?"

"You're far too thick with the master, to her way of thinking. And I'm not the only one is wanting to finish his chores. Andrew fed the dogs long since. He's only waiting on you before he gives 'em the run of the park."

"His Lordship came home, I take it."

"Hours ago. And drunk as David's sow. With his sleeves all bloody, and swearing like a sailor. There's been the devil to pay all evening. And Mr. Briggs!" Humphrey rolled his eyes. "He's sent Verity down here every quarter of an hour to find out if you come back yet. He and His Lordship seemed to think you run off."

She sighed. "Perhaps I wish I had."

He shrugged. "'Tis all one to me." He beckoned impatiently to Allegra. "Come inside." When she complied, he leaned against the large gates, closed them behind Allegra, and threw the heavy iron bolt. He nodded to her, disappeared into the lodge, emerging a minute later on the side that faced the road, his cocked hat atop his peruke. He locked the outside lodge door, pocketed the key, and ambled down the road toward Diddlebury, whistling as he went.

Mrs. Rutledge nearly pounced on Allegra as she came in at the kitchen entrance. "Where have you been, girl?"

Allegra held out her hat filled with flowers and herbs. "Gathering plants for the stillroom."

"You've missed supper. Mr. Briggs told Cook to put aside something for you. *I* wouldn't have. You've given yourself far too many airs in this household—you and your high-flying ways." She sniffed her disdain. "Well, go along with you."

Allegra sighed. "I'm not hungry." She had supped on a few berries in the woods, but the long, torturous day had robbed her of her appetite. "I'll just go and fetch His Lordship's cordial. He'll be wanting it soon."

Mrs. Rutledge smiled, her eyes crinkling. She reminded Allegra of a cat about to pounce. "His Lordship doesn't want to see you tonight. He was quite specific about that. He wished to be informed when you came in, but he didn't want to see you. 'Keep that wench out of my sight,' he said. His very words. 'Out of my sight.'" The sly smile deepened. "Have you fallen out of his favor at last?"

She was tired. She had had enough grief without having to deal with this jealous old dragon. "I've told you before, I don't want your position, Mrs. Rutledge."

The older woman's face twisted into a sullen pout. "He might give it you, willy-nilly. The way he looks at you. Men are always fools for a pretty face—even when they're sober. And *that* one…" she tossed her head in the direction of Ridley's rooms, "he hasn't been sober in ages."

Allegra chewed at her lip. Between his shameful display of cowardice in Ludlow and that dreadful scene at the pool, Grey Ridley must be in a low state by now. "Is he drinking heavily tonight?"

"Like a condemned prisoner on his last day. His arms are all scratched up, as well. Barbara saw them when she brought his supper." Mrs. Rutledge snorted. "No doubt he had a tussle with some doxy in a tavern."

Allegra felt a rush of anger at the woman's disdain for her master. The housekeeper was growing very rich at Ridley's expense; the least she owed him was respect! "Mrs. Rutledge," she snapped, "he saved a boy's life today in Ludlow! At great risk to himself. You might tell that to the others when you're all sniggering behind his back." She turned on her heel and stomped toward the stillroom. "His Lordship will need a salve for those scratches."

She worked quietly in the stillroom for hours, glad to be alone. She chopped a quantity of herbs and leaves, using the freshest of those she had gathered in the afternoon, then mixed them with a pinch of saffron and chopped suet and put them to the boil. When it was done, she took the mixture—it had turned a lovely golden color—and strained it through a fine linen cloth, then set it to cool. While she waited, she busied herself with the rest of her day's pickings. She hung some of the herbs and flowers from the beams to dry, and distilled the rest into infusions that she could use at another time.

When her amber liquid was cool enough, she added yellow wax, a bit of Venice turpentine and olive oil, and beat the mixture with a whisk until it had become a smooth, creamy salve, which she scented with oil of roses.

No matter how hard she worked, however, she couldn't still her troubled thoughts. *He didn't want to see her.* Surely the words she had spoken had cut him to the soul. Sharp words and accusations she had no right to utter. He was the master, she the servant. But he was also a man who could bleed, and she had attacked him when he was most vulnerable. She cursed her intemperate tongue, wishing she could take back all the things she had said.

She packed the salve into a small, covered crock and climbed the stairs to Ridley's rooms. She would knock on his door and ask Jagat Ram to take the salve. She found herself hoping—wildly, foolishly—that Grey would receive it as a peace offering and ask to see her tonight.

The minute she stepped into the passageway leading to Ridley's apartment, she knew that something was dreadfully wrong. There were more footmen about than there ought to be at this time of night, standing silently and shuffling their feet—small gestures of helplessness and unease. And Mrs. Rutledge stood at the door to Ridley's drawing room, her ear pressed to the paneling.

Filled with dread, Allegra hurried to her. "Godamercy, what is it?"

The housekeeper sneered. "I knew he would drink too much tonight. He's having one of his fits. Listen."

She didn't need to put her head to the door. Ridley's agonized shouts and cries drifted out to the corridor. The sounds wrenched at her soul, and she moaned in sympathy. It was no surprise, of course. Not tonight. Not after today. But her heart ached for him. "The poor devil," she whispered, putting her hand on the doorknob. "Perhaps I can be of help."

"No!" Mrs. Rutledge's eyes flashed. "Do you hope to insinuate yourself once more into his good graces? I told you, he doesn't want to see you!" She peered intently at Allegra, her expression filled with sudden suspicion. "Did *you* have aught to do with this, miss?"

Allegra blushed, the hot flush of guilt. "I...I don't know," she stammered.

Just then, the door burst open and Jonathan Briggs rushed out, nearly colliding with the two women. "Good!" he cried, grabbing Allegra by the wrist. "You're just the one we need. Perhaps you can recommend a soothing water for Lord Ridley."

She thought quickly. "I'll do what I can, Mr. Briggs. But I should like to see His Lordship first. To judge his state. A soothing water is useless if he'll not drink it. Perhaps a narcotic plaster, bound around his temples to ease him into sleep, would be better."

Briggs nodded and indicated Ridley's drawing room. "I leave him to you and Jagat Ram."

"Let me help, as well, Mr. Briggs," simpered Mrs. Rutledge.

"It isn't necessary. See that the rest of the servants go about their business. 'Tis late. Let them seek their beds. I have work of my own." He returned the housekeeper's sour frown. "Lord Ridley scarcely needs idle observers to his distress! See to your duties, woman, and leave the man in peace. I'll do the same."

"But..."

Allegra closed the door on their dispute and crossed Ridley's drawing room to his bedchamber, cringing as his shouts grew louder and more desperate.

She was met at the open door by Jagat Ram. A fleeting smile crossed his face. "You will help, yes? I am not being able to calm him tonight." He stepped aside and motioned her into Ridley's bedchamber. She was almost suffocated by the musky, heavy scent of incense that assailed her nostrils.

Grey Ridley lay on his bed, thrashing wildly. His wrists and ankles were bound with rope, and he roared in frustration and strained at his bonds. "Damn! Bloody hell! For God's sake, let me free!" His words were slurred and indistinct. He twisted and grimaced, wrenching his body with such force that he would have tumbled over the edge of the bed to the floor but for Jagat Ram.

His valet leapt to his side and restrained him. "Please, Sir Greyston," he said in his singsong voice, "you must sleep. The Nawab of Behar is wishing to take you hunting for tigers in the morning."

Ridley stared at him, absorbing his words. A look of peace and serenity slowly spread over his face. He seemed for a moment to be far away, in a different time and a better place. A gentle smile hovered around his mouth.

Then, unexpectedly, his face crumpled into an expression of deep grief. His body began to shake with uncontrollable weeping. Great heaving sobs burst from his chest. "Why did she die?" he cried. "Why did she die? Give me my sword, and let me use it on myself." He laughed bitterly through his tears. "But I'm the coward of Baniard Hall. Don't you know that?" He curled himself into a ball of pain and began to moan, a haunted sound that seemed to come from the depths of a dark tomb.

Allegra touched his shoulder. "Milord…" she whispered, fighting back her tears.

As though someone had turned a key, closed a door, he sat up suddenly and glared at her. His eyes were filled with rage. She jumped back in alarm. "Will you mock me?" he shouted. "Will you scorn me? The girl said…" He shook his bound fists in her direction. "Damn you, damn you! *Damn you!*"

Jagat Ram sighed. "You see? He will not be quieting. Is there some medicine? Some cure?"

She shook her head. She alone knew the torments Grey had suffered today that had pushed him to the edge. Her grief and guilt and pity sat like a sharp thorn in her breast, a pain that would not cease. "No," she said, "there's no medicine. The only physic he needs is a human touch."

Despite Ram's warnings, she climbed onto the bed and pulled Ridley's body into her arms. He struggled fiercely, grinding his teeth in fury and bellowing curses at her. For a frightening moment, she thought he would break free and harm her, bound as he was. Then the anger gave way to sadness and he leaned his head against her breast. Fresh tears welled in his eyes and poured down his face.

"Hush, Grey," she murmured, rocking him back and forth in her arms. She could feel the trembling of his strong body. "Hush, my dear. Hush. Hush."

He looked at her, his golden eyes unfocused and filled with bewilderment. "Ruth?" he said—an agonized croak of pain. "Ruth? Forgive me, Ruth. Kiss me. Forgive me."

She hesitated for only a second, then put her lips on his. She kissed him as a mother would. Sweetly, tenderly. His lips, his cheeks, the graceful cleft in his chin. She closed his eyes with gentle fingers and kissed his lids, tasting the bitterness of his tears.

His trembling ceased, but still she rocked him, whispering his name and kissing him over and over again. At last she knew he slept. She laid his head on the pillow and looked at Jagat Ram. "Untie him, Ram," she begged. It seemed so degrading for a proud man to be bound.

Ram nodded and produced a strange, exotic knife from a hidden pocket in the skirts of his coat. The handle of the blade was shaped like a snake. Crossing to the bed, Ram slashed Grey's ropes and removed them. Allegra flinched to see the raw lines on Grey's wrists where the cords had rubbed. He had stripped the bandages off his arms, and the deep marks from the bear's claws were red and ugly. His violent struggles had started some of the scratches to bleeding again. His clean shirt was spotted with fresh blood.

It was too much for Allegra to bear. So much pain. Her own tears flowed. "I brought a salve," she said to Jagat Ram, her voice quivering. She pointed to where she had set her crock.

"I shall see that Sir Greyston uses it in the morning."

She rose from the bed and looked down at Ridley. She was reluctant to leave him. "Will he waken? Will you want a soothing cordial water for him?"

"No. He will sleep until morning."

"And forget all that happened tonight?"

His mouth curved in a knowing smile. "'Tis what he *says*. But perhaps 'tis only what he *wishes*."

She twisted her fingers together, feeling helpless. "If you should need me…"

"You can do no more. I am watching at his bedside all night. Come." He indicated the small door in the bedchamber that led to Ridley's closet. "We will go this way, through Sir Greyston's closet and dressing room. It is being more private. The maidservants can be unkind with their questions and gossip."

There was a candle still burning in Ridley's private closet. It lit up the array of knives and swords on the wall, glinting off burnished gold and glittering steel. After being a witness to that dreadful scene with Batterbee in Ludlow today, Allegra suddenly saw Ridley's collection in a new and awful way. The coward of Baniard Hall, who trembled at the touch of a blade handle, yet forced himself to dwell each day surrounded by the symbols of his weakness. It was more than just a cruel reminder. It was a punishment, like a flagellant doing penance at some ancient

Church rite, tormenting himself without cease. "Oh, alas!" she sobbed, covering her eyes with her hands.

Jagat Ram touched her arm. "I am thinking that you have a good heart. May Allah protect you."

"Oh, Ram," she said, lifting her streaming eyes to his. "Tell me about him."

"'Tis not my place to tell. Nor yours to hear."

"I know."

His liquid brown eyes searched her face. "But you have brought a rare light to his eyes. And you would not harm him with your knowledge, I am thinking, as some of the others might."

She gulped. "I wish to God there was strong enough medicine in my stillroom to cure his affliction."

"'Twas not always thus," he began slowly. "If the young Sir Greyston had a flaw, it came from his very perfections. He was a man who was favored by chance in every way. A man who succeeded in all he set out to do, with an ease that other mortals might envy. If he had weaknesses," he shrugged, "and I suppose he did—a little too much pride, a little arrogance, a certain lack of sympathy for others' imperfections—they came, I am thinking, from his ignorance of the pain and troubles of the world." Ram smiled in understanding.

"He led a charmed life. His natural skills and talents opened doors. Good fortune took care of the rest. He had friends at Court, the admiration of his fellows, the respect of all who met him. He was, you understand, simply Greyston Morgan, Esquire, a second son, with few prospects for wealth. His father had left him only a modest legacy. But he so distinguished himself in the fighting in Scotland that the king conferred upon him a knighthood, the Order of the Bath, as well as a large financial reward. With his usual faith in his good luck, Sir Greyston gave the money to his broker to invest, resigned from the Guards, sold his commission, and came to Calcutta as an officer in the East India Company. He was, of course, successful. Both in his business affairs and in the fighting that sometimes became necessary when rebellions arose."

"And there he employed you as his servant?"

Jagat Ram drew himself up, dark eyes glittering in the light of the candle. Despite his humble station, he clearly had pride to rival his master's. "I am not employed. I am a prince in my own country," he said softly. "Sir Greyston saved my life. I owe him a debt. I swore to serve him until that debt was repaid."

Allegra stared in astonishment. "But, such a sacrifice..."

"He gave me my life. I made a vow to Allah."

"How fortunate he is to have you, Ram." She was grateful that Ridley wasn't alone in his wretchedness. "Did he grow wealthy because of his work in India?" she continued at last.

Jagat Ram laughed. "No. It was the kiss of fate, as usual. Sir Greyston had meant to stay on in India for some time, making a modest livelihood. My country pleased him."

"He was happy there?" She didn't need an answer. The exotic room in which they stood was answer enough. "He finds his serenity here, doesn't he? In this room. And in the incense, and the reminders of the past you give him."

"Yes. Often." Ram sighed. "Or as often as he can find serenity."

"Then why did he leave?"

"His brother, the viscount, died, leaving him a title, a large fortune, and Morgan House. We came back to England. Sir Greyston felt that a viscount should not be dabbling in chancy ventures. He instructed his broker to sell his stock. This was in the summer of seventeen-twenty." Ram stopped and searched her face. "Ah, I see by your expression that you are not knowing of what I speak. The South Sea Bubble."

She shook her head, still mystified. "I was in the Colonies in seventeen-twenty."

"It was a great investment scheme that ended in ruin for many people. A scandal. Time has proved that there was chicanery in the highest levels of government. But when Sir Greyston innocently sold his holdings, the stock was paying a thousand pounds for every hundred invested. Scarcely a month later, the bubble burst. But Sir Greyston found himself with wealth far beyond his wildest imaginings. A fortune such as a man could not amass in half a dozen lifetimes."

"It sounds like a tale to dazzle children, with miraculous happenings and good fairies. Was he pleased?"

Ram's face darkened. "I think he was frightened, for the first time in his life. It had been too much. Too sudden. His brother's title and estate, and then this. There was an outbreak of plague in London that year. And the South Sea traders were denounced in the press and from the pulpit. Moral decay, they said. The evils of greed. Sir Greyston, I am thinking, had already suffered at the death of his brother, though he bore no blame for it. And now he felt unworthy of his windfall. He would say to me sometimes, 'Ram, the gods will punish me for my good fortune someday. You mark my words.'"

"But he had no part in any of it!" she cried. "Why should he feel guilt?" It seemed so tragically unnecessary.

"Why should any of us feel guilt when we are blameless? But we do. I shall stay here until I repay his gift of my life. Have you no whisper of guilt in your heart?"

She turned away and stared into the shadows of the room. All unknowing, he had touched her own raw wound. A part of her had always felt that she had no right to be alive. Not when all the other Baniards were dead.

There was a long silence. "But you will be wanting to hear the rest of His Lordship's story," said Ram at last. "Yes?"

She turned back to him. Forced herself to suppress her own pain. "Yes."

"We were in London. He had opened Morgan House. Enlarged it, refurnished it. He entertained in a most gracious way. Great personages were coming to call, writers and painters. Even Sir Robert Walpole, the prime minister. His old friends, Lord Richard Halford and Lord and Lady Mortimer, came from India for a brief visit. It was a pleasure to serve him at that time. He had begun to reconcile himself to his good fortune, and Morgan House was filled with laughter and gaiety. And then he met Mistress Pickering."

"Ruth?"

He nodded. "A lady of quality. She had come up from Kent with her family. In search of a husband, I am thinking."

"Was she..." Allegra hesitated. Why did the question catch in her throat? "Was she beautiful?"

"She was a goddess. Fragile, quiet, serene. She had a beauty that turned men's heads, and a sweet child's voice. She never raised it in anger. She smiled often. She hung on Sir Greyston's every word, her eyes shining in perfect devotion. He was captivated. He married her within the month."

"Did he love her?" she whispered.

"More than any man ever loved a woman, he often said."

Why did she resent a dead woman? "They must have been gloriously happy together. She sounds as perfect as he."

"Yes, perhaps."

She frowned at the odd shift in his tone. "Did *you* like her?"

His face was a mask. "It was not my place to judge her. She was my master's wife, and he was devoted to her."

"But surely you have an opinion..."

"When I return to my country, and choose a wife, I shall not want to be hearing that I have made a mistake. He loved her. That was enough. And when she began to grow large with his child, he would almost weep for joy at sight of her."

Allegra tried to picture a time when Grey was happy. He smiled so seldom now. But when he did—his golden eyes luminous and sparkling—it warmed her heart. "And then she lost his child," she said sadly. "Lady Dorothy told me."

"Not then. There was an older gentleman. A friend of Lady Ridley's, from her district, who came to visit. He and Sir Greyston quarreled over some trifle. Sharp words passed between them. A glove was thrown, and arrangements were made for a duel of satisfaction. Lady Ridley begged Sir Greyston to forsake the challenge. She wept and clung to him. The man had been her childhood friend. He was like an uncle to her. She feared to see him harmed."

"And His Lordship persisted in the duel, despite her pleas?"

"Sir Greyston is a proud man, and the gentleman had insulted him grievously. Moreover, he was, in those days, passionate as well as proud, and headstrong sometimes to the point of folly." Ram studied Allegra, a wise, knowing look in his eyes. "There is about you, miss, something of what *he* was, scarcely two years ago. I do not think he meant to kill the gentleman in the duel, but..." he gave a shrug of wry acceptance, "these things happen. The will of Allah."

"And Lady Ridley?"

"She took to her bed, refusing to see Sir Greyston. Within the week, she had lost the child."

"Merciful heaven." Allegra bowed her head.

"Her illness grew, and fevers wracked her frail body. Her shrieks of pain rang through the rooms of Morgan House."

"Oh, alas! How he must have suffered to hear them."

"Night after night he sat by her bed, nursing her, begging her to live. But when she did not scream, she cursed him. That gentle child's voice was filled with hatred. She cried out that he had killed her. That your God would never forgive him for what he had done." Ram shuddered, clearly remembering the horror of those days. "It was a mercy, the day she finally died. And when he came back from the church after he had buried her, he took his sword and snapped it over his knee."

"Do you..." she brushed at her tears, "do you really think he killed her?"

"There was talk of it. The suddenness of her affliction, her own dying accusations. And there are certain poisons…"

"Oh, no!" she cried. "He couldn't have."

"I do not judge. I merely tell you of the rumors at the time. He began to drink heavily then."

"And the second duel? Where he ran away? Lady Dorothy told me," she explained.

"A month later. A Pickering cousin, who had helped to spread the rumors of murder. Sir Greyston…" a flush of embarrassment darkened Jagat Ram's swarthy complexion. "Sir Greyston found himself…unwilling to fight the man. I will say no more, out of loyalty to Sir Greyston."

"He trembled and paled and dropped the sword, didn't he? And seemed to be stricken with the ague." She nodded at the look of surprise on Ram's face. "I saw it today, in Ludlow. That pig, Crompton, and his vile friends…"

"Ah," said Ram softly, looking toward Ridley's bedchamber, "I am understanding now. It has not happened for a long time. He has contrived to avoid such a scene."

"Oh, Ram, it was frightening to see!"

"It is frightening to Sir Greyston, as well. He knows not what takes hold of him. He is a man possessed by a demon in those moments, struggling against something in his nature that is beyond his power. He does not like to speak of it. His dread of a challenge. His helplessness. But sometimes, when the gin has loosened his tongue, he tells me that it is just as he foretold. 'Tis his God's punishment upon him."

"Can't he conquer it?"

Ram sighed. "He tried. In London, at first. He would provoke a challenge, hoping to overcome his weakness, his…cowardice, once and for all. But it grew worse. And that was when we came here."

"Where he seeks a false manhood in gin, and every woman he can seduce into his bed," she said bitterly.

"I am not being free to tell you," he said, his voice gently chiding, "but there are other ways in which Sir Greyston hopes to reclaim his pride."

She pretended not to understand. She wouldn't betray Mr. Briggs's confidence. Nor her own knowledge of the almshouse. "Is there nothing you can do to help him?" she said. "You say you owe him a life. But how can you save a man who is bent on his own destruction?"

"He has touched your heart."

"Of course not," she answered quickly. Her words sounded forced and strained. "Why should I care? His life is his own. I'm but a servant.

I have my own…his troubles are not…" She stopped, gulped back the tears, and closed her eyes for a moment. "Yes," she whispered at last, "he has touched my heart."

"And you have helped him."

She stared in surprise. "I?"

"Since you have come to Baniard Hall, he is smiling sometimes. He is drinking less. Your innocent cordials have kept him from the gin on many a night. And he speaks of you often. And in some detail."

"Wh-what do you mean?" she stammered.

He smiled. It was as sly an expression as she had ever seen on his open face. "You have a…birthmark, I believe."

Allegra gasped, her face coloring, and put a hand to her breast. It was just a tiny mark. What sort of man would notice?

Ram's smile deepened. "He finds it charming. And your eyes, and your hair. And the shape of your fingers. There is a scar on your right thumb, is there not? He hesitated to ask about it."

Her face was now on fire. She blushed to think that Grey had examined her with such care. "A burn from a skillet…Why should he…?"

"Who knows? We are strange creatures, all of us. I had despaired of him restoring himself. Putting his mourning aside and embracing life again. But now I am thinking that the kindness of one woman may yet be his salvation." He picked up the candle and gestured toward the door that led to Ridley's dressing room. "But it grows late. Come."

"One more question," she begged. "The Lady of the Sorrows. Who is she? He called me that once," she added, in response to Ram's questioning look.

He frowned. "How very odd."

"How so?"

"'Tis a painting of a woman. Sir Greyston found it when first we came to Baniard Hall. In the box room in the attic story. Among many others. He took a fancy to her portrait. There was tragedy in her face. And so he called her his Lady of the Sorrows. 'Ram,' he would say, '*there* is a creature who has known true suffering.' In the early days here at the Hall, he would sit and contemplate her for hours, drinking and gazing on the face of this long-dead woman. I think she brought him solace. Perhaps the sadness in her eyes helped him to forget his own wretchedness."

"Did she look like his wife?"

"No. Not a bit."

"Like me?"

He motioned to the door of the dressing room, holding his candle high. "Judge for yourself." He led her through the door and pointed to a painting on the dressing-room wall. She had never been in this room before; she examined the painting with care.

It was the picture of a young woman. In the time of the Tudors, Allegra guessed. She stood formally in her rich garments—a little woman, regal, proud, and distant—one jeweled hand resting on her bosom, the other holding a letter. Her oval face was pale and ghostly with powder, almost white, in the fashion of the time. Her hair was equally pale, a halo of tight blond curls. Her features were regular, neither plain nor beautiful. But her face—indeed, the entire portrait—was dominated by her large, dark eyes. They were soft as they stared out from the canvas, and filled with an inexpressible grief. For a fanciful moment, Allegra wondered if it had been the contents of the letter that had broken the woman's heart. Written across one corner of the painting were the words: "Ye Ladye Hilda Banyard."

Allegra suppressed a cry as she read the name. A Baniard! She remembered this painting now. It had hung in the great parlor. She could see no resemblance to herself in the picture. But surely that was Mama's mouth and chin, the tilt of Lucinda's head. Perhaps it was that family resemblance that Grey Ridley had seen in her own face, that night of his drunken raving.

Her eyes darted to Ram's face. Had he seen the resemblance as well? She couldn't allow it. For her own safety, for the success of her plan against Wickham, she mustn't be found out. She gave a scornful laugh. "Why should he have called me his Lady of the Sorrows? There's not one jot of resemblance."

"Of course not. She is pale, while you are dark." Ram shrugged. "But if Sir Greyston was in his cups when he said it...An honest mistake."

She eyed him with suspicion. She wondered if he had guessed the truth. Well, she thought, it was of no consequence. Jagat Ram was far too discreet to unmask her, no matter what he might suspect.

She went through the far door of the dressing room to the passage beyond, climbed the stairs to her room, and fell wearily into bed. It was hours before she slept. And when she did, she dreamed of Grey Ridley weeping over a coffin that held a woman who looked very like the Lady Hilda Banyard.

Chapter Eleven

The full moon was bright and dazzling. It transformed the road into a long, silvery thread that wound its way among the trees, and illuminated the length and breadth of the sky above the crest of Wenlock Edge. The moon was so near, the rolling hills so lofty, that Grey felt as though he were riding on the edge of the world. Surely he had but to stretch forth his hand to touch that shining globe. This was a place of enchantment. Even the darkness of the trees sparkled with fireflies, like diamonds against black velvet.

He slowed his horse and breathed deeply of the soft night air. He was glad now that he'd bought Baniard Hall. The serenity, the isolation of these hills, touched his spirit and warmed his heart. Lately he had even found himself noticing the sounds of birds in the trees, feeling the living caress of summer on his lifeless flesh.

He pulled out a ribbon from his pocket and tied back his hair, then took his cocked hat from its loop on his saddle and placed it firmly on his head. The hour was late, and most of the Hall would be abed by now. But he liked to avoid questioning eyes when he returned from the almshouse in Ludlow. Liked to look like Lord Ridley, not Mr. Morgan. He wrapped his well-cut cloak more closely around his shabby clothes to conceal them. His shirt was becoming quite ragged and threadbare. Impossible to work in. Perhaps he'd ask Ram to get him another from a secondhand shop.

He yawned and shook his head to clear it of its sleepy cobwebs. A few more minutes, and he would be home. The thought of his bed was a comfort.

It had been a difficult day. That poor old woman had died this morning, and he had been helpless to hold back the inevitable, to keep the spark of life from fading in her eyes. He had thrown himself into his work after that—scrubbing, climbing the roof to replace some thatch, hauling the dead stump of a tree from the garden. Good, honest labor. But it had failed to quiet his sense of impotence at the grandam's death. There had been no satisfaction in any of it.

"There was a time, Grey Ridley," he said bitterly, "when you could measure yourself by a battle well fought."

And now? He had crept like a thief into Ludlow this morning, dreading to find anyone who had been at the High Cross yesterday. Who had seen…He groaned aloud. He never should have taken Batterbee's challenge. He never should have allowed Crompton to force the sword on him. Hadn't he learned by now how futile it was?

But Batterbee had insulted her. Put his filthy hands on her sweet flesh. What could he do, when she looked at him that way? The last thing he had wanted to see was disgust, disappointment, horror in her dark eyes. He was a man. How could he not defend her, and still keep his honor?

He sighed and stirred in the saddle. His body ached. He should have stayed in Ludlow and found a tavern wench. He needed a woman tonight, to fill the vast caverns of dissatisfaction in his soul. But perhaps he had avoided a tavern because he knew that gin was no salvation for him tonight, either.

He didn't want *any* woman. He wanted *her.* He needed her. That face, those eyes. That graceful body. She had taken his breath away at the pond, standing tall and proud as a queen, clad only in the majesty of her naked perfection. He had yearned to pull the combs from her hair, to run his fingers through those thick curls. To lay her down on the grass and stretch out her hair like a dark halo around her head. To kiss that ruby mouth, that radiant face. He frowned. That face…It always reminded him of something he couldn't quite remember, something beyond memory. Perhaps he had dreamed her long ago. In a misty daydream.

The frown deepened into an angry scowl. But there was nothing misty about his memory of her insolent tongue! It was as real and as fresh as the water in that pond. Drunk or not, he had heard every saucy word. He wondered now why he'd tolerated such impertinence. And not only insolent. It was *absurd*, the things she'd said. That he courted her hatred? How vain and presumptuous of the chit, to think that she was the center of his world! What did he give a damn about her hatred—or anyone else's, for that matter? And as for welcoming it, as some sort of punishment…the girl was mad!

He closed his tired eyes for a moment, allowing his sudden, unexpected anger to cool. Perhaps her sharp words had only been meant as a kind of revenge. To repay his ill usage of her. She'd been deeply mortified and hurt, that day in the stillroom, when Dick had come upon them kissing. Grey sighed. He regretted that unfortunate scene. He'd wanted to drive his friends away, true enough. It was too painful, to see them and remember what he had once been. But he'd meant only for Dick to find him in the stillroom with Allegra, to think that he visited her every day. An intimate rendezvous.

And then he had seen her, the passion of her hatred for Wickham burning in her eyes like a vital flame. It had fired his own blood, reminded him of a time when he had felt life as passionately. And suddenly he had wanted to possess her, to warm his cold heart at that flame. He had forgotten everything but his desperate hunger.

He hadn't meant for Dick to see what he had seen. He hadn't meant to shame her. He had wanted to beg her forgiveness, but he'd never seemed to find the right moment. Or perhaps his pride had prevented it.

But she had forgiven him. He was sure of it. That sweet, generous creature. He had read forgiveness in her eyes yesterday, in Ludlow. And last night...

He had only a vague memory of last night. He'd always tried to forget those nights when he couldn't seem to control the demon in him. When the rage and the grief and the frustration—yes, and the gin—had overwhelmed him. But he remembered last night. Remembered tender kisses, a warm embrace, words that soothed him as much as the unguent she had brought for his scratches.

He smiled at the memory and rummaged in the pocket of his coat, pulling forth a small, carved object. It was a foolish thing, a child's toy, really, sold for pennies in the poorest quarter of Ludlow. A wooden flower, crudely fashioned and painted in bright colors. Each of the half dozen petals was attached with a strip of leather, like a tiny hinge. And when he folded them back, one by one, the painted face of a cherub was revealed, just in the center of the blossom. He laughed softly. He didn't know why he'd bought it. Why it had caught his eye. Absurd little thing. But perhaps he'd give it to Allegra.

He reined in his horse with a sudden jerk that made the animal snort in alarm. *A child's toy?* What the devil was happening to him? He'd bought a bloody toy for an impertinent servant? A bond servant, no less! She'd surely bewitched him, casting spells as magical as this dark night. With her eyes and her musical voice and her cordials.

God help him, he hadn't had a moment's peace since the day she'd come to the Hall. She had stirred up long-forgotten emotions, feelings he thought he'd buried with Ruth. Anger, jealousy. Assaulting him. Knocking at the closed gates of his heart. He had tried to ignore her, he had stopped pursuing her. And still he had seen her face before him, wherever he turned. And still the gnawing emotions had crept back. Longing. Desire.

And so much more. Pain. Oh, yes, pain, though he'd tried to push it away. He'd wept this morning at the old woman's death. A stranger, scarcely known to him. Yet he had stood in his garden, among his roses, and wept like a child.

He sighed heavily. He wanted peace again. He wanted the numbing indifference that had made his days bearable, swallowed up the empty nights. But now, thanks to the girl, work no longer comforted him. Gin had ceased to protect him against his turbulent emotions. Perhaps he was healing at last. Perhaps those feelings were like the irritating itch that comes with a wound on the mend. A vexatious reminder that he was alive after all.

He looked at the toy in his hand for a moment, then hurled the damned thing into the trees. He gave a cynical laugh. Or perhaps the sorceress was merely driving him mad!

Humphrey was waiting as he rode up to the gates. "Milord," he grumbled, touching his fingers to his hat. "'Tis very late. Mr. Briggs was concerned."

He was still feeling an edge of anger because of the girl. "Don't I pay you enough, Humphrey?" he said with a sneer. "God knows you have little enough to do. No doubt you'll make up for the hours of sleep you've lost tonight by drowsing all morning." He waved an imperious hand, ignoring Humphrey's black scowl. "Open the gate, damn it."

He started up the long, curving drive. It was darker here, hidden from the moon by the overarching trees. He slowed his horse to a gentle pace. He still saw Humphrey's face, twisted with resentment. What was it the girl had said—that he courted hatred? Ridiculous! Yet why had he spoken so sharply to Humphrey? After all, the man deserved a decent night's rest like any other creature. He frowned. It was a galling thought—that the girl might have spoken truth—and one he didn't want to entertain.

He looked up at Baniard Hall as he emerged from the trees. Most of the windows were dark; nearly all the lights came from the wing that held his apartment. There were a few lamps burning in the kitchens, and Briggs seemed to be working late, as usual.

And someone was moving around in the attic story. He could see the flickering light of a candle as it bobbed about, disappearing for a moment and then twinkling once more near the window. Strange. That wasn't one of the servant's rooms. That was where the box room was. He was almost sure of it. Who the devil could it be, at this late hour?

Perhaps, before he retired to his rooms, he'd go quietly up to the attic by a back staircase. If it was someone out for no good, he meant to surprise the wretch. His servants stole enough from him by cunning means. He didn't intend to tolerate an outright thief in his house!

He nodded at the groom who came for his horse, dismounted and strode to the steps of the Hall. The groundkeeper Andrew was waiting, holding his three watchdogs tightly leashed until the master should go in. Much to Grey's own surprise, he wished his servant a pleasant good night.

Allegra tiptoed softly into the box room, raising her candle aloft. This was folly. She should be in her bed by now, instead of prowling the ghost-ridden rooms of Baniard Hall. But there was no rest for her tonight. Not yet.

As she had gone about her work all day in the stillroom, her brain had teemed with the sad details of Ram's narrative. She had found herself grieving for Grey Ridley, brushing away tears of pity that sprang to her eyes each time she thought of his torment.

But by evening, she had become obsessed with something else: the Lady of the Sorrows, and Ram's story of its discovery. Among the paintings in the box room, he had said. She'd always assumed that Wickham had sold or destroyed most of the Baniard treasures when he'd redecorated the Hall. The thought that they might still be here had chafed her for hours, until she knew she couldn't sleep unless she satisfied her curiosity.

There was little danger of her being found in this place. Most of the servants were already asleep, except for those few who waited on Lord Ridley's return. He had gone to Ludlow at dawn this morning, Ram said. She was pleased at the news. She prayed that he would find solace in the almshouse, forget his humiliations with Batterbee, his dreadful drunken fit last night. He was particularly late this evening, she noted, which boded well for his serenity tonight.

She had another reason for being glad about his absence all day. The Hall had buzzed with malicious gossip since breakfast. Curse Humphrey and his tale-bearing paramour! He had sat over his breakfast ale and crowed his delight as he recounted the story of Ridley's craven behavior in Ludlow.

"The milk-livered coward," he had sneered. "I'll never lift my hat to him again."

Andrew had smugly announced that His Lordship had gone off early today; he himself had seen him creeping out of the Hall with his cloak wrapped about him. "No doubt to get himself primed to the muzzle with gin," he'd added with a snicker.

And Margery, the whining little laundry maid, had found the courage to giggle and swear she'd make a mouth to the cowardly rogue the next time he criticized her.

Allegra had scolded them all for their cruelty and mockery, wanting nothing so much as to box a few ears. How could they talk so? To find sport in the miseries of that poor man!

She sighed in unhappy recollection and moved into the large box room. It was less dusty up here than she would have supposed, after all these years. But perhaps Mrs. Rutledge dispatched a maid to this room from time to time for fear Lord Ridley, having once discovered the place, would return again.

The room was a jumble. Stacks of paintings leaned against the walls, furniture was piled helter-skelter, rolled-up carpets and little tables filled every spare corner. A fat upholstered settee squatted in the center of the room, partially covered with a linen cloth; it crowded up against a large japanned sideboard. A footstool, embroidered with prancing dogs, sat on a high-backed chair of faded red damask.

She moved about the crowded room—touching, searching, remembering. That had been Papa's chair. Mama's scrutoire, where she sat and wrote her letters. Allegra even remembered when Lucinda had embroidered the dogs, beaming in satisfaction at her first grown-up needlework.

She set down her candle on a folded gaming table and looked through the paintings, smiling as she came across old favorites. There was Grandfather, young and handsome in his starched lace collar and plumes, holding the sword King Charles had given him after the battle of Edgehill. There was the picture of Valiant, Papa's favorite horse, that had hung in the dining parlor. There was a long-forgotten Baniard cousin.

They were all familiar, yet all so impersonal. Like old, dear friends, separated by time and distance, that one remembered with fondness. Unexpectedly come upon—only to discover that one no longer cared.

She bowed her head, overwhelmed by an empty sadness. It was too long ago. That family, that little girl, Anne Allegra, no longer existed. The memories were as faded as the upholstery on Papa's chair. Only her hatred of Wickham was sharp and fresh. And the sight of Mama's drawn face in that last year in Carolina before she died. Allegra sighed, turned toward the door and reached for her candle.

The little chair rested against the wall, just to one side of the door. It was half the size of an adult's chair, a tiny thing, clearly meant for a child. The seat was upholstered in gold damask, and the back and arms and graceful legs were fashioned of dark polished oak. There were shells carved into the arms and the turn of the legs. In the fiddle-shaped back was the largest shell of all—a fluid scallop, surrounded by spiral waves and bearing in its center an elaborately carved letter. The letter A.

Allegra cried out, her hand flying to her mouth. Her little chair! Just as Old Bibby had described it. The chair that Papa had meant as a gift for her. The chair she had never seen, that had been delivered the day before Papa's arrest.

She felt a quivering jolt in the pit of her stomach, a flutter on her shoulder as though someone had touched her. "Papa?" she whispered, half expecting a reply. She shuddered and stared about the room in growing panic, feeling as though the walls were narrowing, the furniture about to smother her. The shadowed corners were suddenly alive. Papa, Mama, Lucinda, Charlie.

Oh, God! She heard their voices, heavy with sorrow, calling her name. *Anne Allegra! Annie! Anne!* They beckoned to her from the dimness, their ghostly forms swirling around her so she cowered in fear. The very whisper of breath from their mouths, their ancient, faded scents—caught in the folds of draperies and cushions, in carvings and paintings—filled her nostrils with the musty sweetness of the grave. She saw their eyes, burning with accusation. You still live, and have done nothing? they murmured. Remember us. *Remember us!*

She began to tremble in an excess of horror. All the long-dead memories, all the pain that she had denied, came crowding in with the specters of her family. She was in a world beyond tears. She sucked in great gasping mouthfuls of fetid air, her eyes wide and staring in terror; she wrapped her arms around her shaking body to protect herself from their onslaught. And still they crowded close, closer, beseeching her with their cries, their open arms.

She heard sounds coming from her own throat; they scarcely seemed human. A wailing, moaning cry that burst from her with every breath she took. "Oh! Oh! Oh!"

"My God, girl, have you seen a ghost?" Grey Ridley loomed in the doorway, frowning. He threw off his hat and strode into the room. He took her roughly by the shoulders. "What is it?" he demanded.

She shook her head. She couldn't speak. She couldn't stop her trembling. She couldn't drive away the ghosts. She continued to moan in helpless pain, her body shaking convulsively.

He muttered a curse and pulled her into his arms, pressing her against his breast. She felt his hands on her back—stroking, comforting. "Don't be frightened," he said. "There's nothing to fear." He held her more tightly as she continued to tremble. "Come now, what did you see? A harmless mouse? A shadow that frightened you? Was it a bad dream?"

He was solid and real. She clung to him in desperation, her fists clutching the front of his coat, her face buried in his chest, and willed the ghosts to leave her in peace. After a little while, her racing heart slowed, her quivering body quieted, soothed by his strong embrace.

A bad dream? God knows that was the truth. She nodded. "Yes," she managed to croak. "A bad dream."

He laughed gently. "'Tis a forbidding room even by daylight. You should never come here at night."

She lifted her head from his breast and looked at him. He was frowning in tender concern. But in another moment he might begin to wonder why she was here. And she hadn't regained her wits enough to invent a plausible lie. She stirred in his arms. "I've quite recovered, milord," she whispered. "Don't trouble yourself with me any further. I'll just go on to my room."

"Nonsense. You can scarcely stand alone yet. You're shaking like an aspen leaf. Come and sit down." Still holding her close, he led her to the settee.

She sat reluctantly, but made a feeble attempt to move away from him. "Truly, milord...I..."

He pulled her tightly against him once more. "I will not have disobedience. I *order* you to stay just so, in my arms, until you cease your trembling." Though the words were scolding, the voice that uttered them was warm and benevolent. "That's better," he said, as she relaxed into his embrace.

Surrendering, she nestled in his arms. He was a comfort against the fading specters—his words, his voice, his very corporeal presence. What harm to allow herself this ease? A few minutes, no more, and then she would find an excuse to leave. His hands were on her back and the nape of her neck, caressing her in a soothing rhythm. How sweet and pleasant. She had not thought she could ever feel so protected again.

His gentle hand moved around from her neck to stroke the side of her face; he cradled her jaw for a moment, then lifted her chin. He gazed into her eyes, his thumb making soft circles on her cheek. He ran his finger down the bridge of her nose and across her trembling lips, as though his fingertips meant to record her face. He traced the arch of her brows, ruffled the feathery fringes of her eyelashes. His delicate touch enchanted her, lulled her into a sweet, safe realm.

"So somber. So tragic," he murmured. "That lovely mouth." He sighed heavily. She could feel the rise and fall of his chest against her bosom. "The fair Allegra. What must I do to make you smile?"

She gulped, hot tears springing to her eyes. "I've almost forgotten how."

He sighed again. "Why are we slaves to our own demons?"

She felt his pain as sharply as her own. "'Tis very lonely, this life."

"It doesn't have to be. Not all the time. Even a hermit needs the sound of a human voice, now and again. The warmth of another hand." His eyes focused on her mouth. "And a sad-eyed woman needs to be kissed," he whispered. "If she will allow," he added, a flicker of doubt crossing his face.

She closed her eyes. He had always wanted her. She had seen his desire as a need—for whatever reason—to possess her and soothe his soul. But now she knew that her need was as strong as his. That her longing to be cherished again had become an open sore, a wound to her heart that would only be healed by a human bond. She opened her eyes and smiled at him. Tentative, and a little frightened. "Yes," she said softly. "She will allow. Grey."

He returned her smile. "How sweet to hear you speak my name." He put his lips on hers. It was a gentle kiss at first, the soft, soothing, comforting kiss of a dear comrade. But as she returned it, her eager mouth thrusting to meet his, his gentle kiss became a delirium of passion. He groaned with desire. His lips were suddenly hard, firm, demanding. Inhaling her own lips as though he were a desperate man satisfying a great hunger. Roughly, he pressed his finger against her chin, forcing her lips to part, and filled her mouth with his searching tongue.

She gasped in helpless pleasure and wrapped her arms around his neck. Every sensual movement of his tongue—a frenzied pulsing in and out—sent spasms of delight racing through her body. She moaned softly, lost in the wonders of his burning kiss.

Panting, he lifted his head from hers at last. "Oh, God. How delicious you are. Your mouth is honey. Nectar of the gods." He pulled the linen square from her neck, bent his head and kissed the swelling roundness of her breasts. His mouth was a searing flame on her skin and she trembled anew, her head thrown back in an agony of sensual pleasure.

She felt his hand on her knee, tugging at her skirts until his fingers touched naked flesh. He stroked her quivering thighs, fondling the firm young limbs while she writhed in exquisite joy. It was an intimate caress, new and wonderful and heart-stopping. Then his impatient hand clutched at her furry softness and she cried aloud. His fingers were hard, more demanding, more aggressive than his mouth had been; they rubbed against her delicate cleft, kneading and touching her in ways that set her body on fire. Her loins contracted in hot, eager spasms against his hand, and she gasped when he responded by thrusting his finger deep within her.

She tangled her hand in the hair at his nape and pulled his head up to hers, seeking fresh kisses. She was lost in a haze of ecstasy. She wanted nothing more than to return to him some measure of the joy he was bringing to her. She kissed him with all the passion in her, then pushed her tongue against his mouth, begging entry.

Instead, he released her body and her lips and stood up. "You sorceress," he said, his voice rasping with passion. "You tantalizing witch. Do you think I'll let you tease me with your kisses? When I've waited so long?" He fumbled at the ties of his cloak with shaking hands, and muttered a curse when the strings knotted.

Allegra lay back on the settee, waiting, watching him, trembling with longing. The light of the single candle was behind him; it cast his looming shadow across her where she lay. She shivered, feeling a moment's uneasiness and fear. He was so impatient. So hungry. And when he swore loudly, ripped the cloak from his shoulders and threw it to the floor, she shivered again. So impatient and hungry. And so filled with lust. Just like Squire Pringle?

She felt the excitement fading from her body. She turned her head aside as he knelt to kiss her again. By chance her eye fell on her little chair near the door. Dear heaven, how could she do this? Had she forgotten so soon? Don't die, Mama, she had pleaded. My life is yours until all the Baniards are avenged. I shall not rest. I shall not seek happiness for myself until all the Wickhams are dead. I swear it to you, Mama, she had wept.

Oh, God, what was she doing here except forgetting that vow, betraying the ghosts, shaming herself for a moment's pleasure? Of a sudden, she felt cold and drained. "No, Grey," she murmured, shaking her head. "No, I cannot…"

He chuckled and leaned closer, cupping his hand on her breast and squeezing gently. "You vixen. Are you determined to torment me?"

"No!" she said more firmly, and put her hands against his chest. "I shall not!" She struggled to sit up.

He grabbed her by the shoulders and pressed her back against the settee. "What new game is this?" he growled. "Must I woo you again with kisses?" He bent to take her mouth.

"*No!*" she cried, and pushed against him with all her might, hands and feet in concert to defend herself.

He teetered for a moment, thrown off balance, and then toppled backward. He fell hard, striking the back of his head against a sharp corner of the sideboard and going down with a groan. He lay curled on the floor, rocking in pain, his hands clamped tightly against his skull.

"Godamercy," breathed Allegra, dropping to the floor beside him. What had she done? "Are you much hurt, milord?"

He lifted his hands from his head and held them out to her. They shone darkly wet in the candlelight, stained with his blood. He glared up at her from beneath his brows, his eyes dark with fury. "You haven't addled my brains, or killed me, if that's what was in your mind. But, I swear by the Almighty, you've damn well come close to earning yourself a thrashing." He grumbled a curse and bent in distress, returning his hands to his head.

"I'll get help," she whispered. "Don't try to stand." She raced for the staircase and flew down the stairs, passing a startled footman on her way to Ridley's rooms. She tapped impatiently at his door and clutched at Jagat Ram's sleeve when the valet opened for her. Words tumbled out of her in a rush of panic and dismay. "His Lordship. The box room. He's been hurt. Bring lights."

Ram nodded and motioned to the footman, giving firm orders in his low voice. In a few minutes, the passage was alive with servants. Allegra hung back as they fetched candles and trooped up the stairs. She could hear the clump of their feet on the attic floor above. She breathed a sigh of relief when at last she heard Grey Ridley's voice from the staircase; it was filled with anger, but strong and vigorous.

"Damn it, Ram," he barked, "I don't need to be carried! Put me on my feet and fetch someone to take a stitch in my skull!"

Allegra waited only until she saw Grey, his head wrapped in a bloody cloth, come limping along the passageway, supported by Ram and one of the footmen. Then she fled. It was enough to know that he wasn't seriously hurt. Beyond that, she couldn't think clearly. She only knew that she had to get away. It wasn't a question of her freedom, though surely she could go to prison for harming her master. It wasn't even the threat of a beating. She could endure it, if *he* weren't there to see her shame.

She simply knew that she had to leave. Run, flee—as far away from Baniard Hall as she could get. She dashed down the stairs and into the dark night. For the first time, she blessed Humphrey and his dalliances. The gate would be unattended.

The moon was bright. Fearing to be seen from the Hall, Allegra avoided the gravel paths and the road. Instead, she raced through the vast park, dashing from shadow to shadow beneath the large and spreading trees, like a farmboy crossing a stream from stone to stone.

She reckoned she was halfway to the gate and the walls of Baniard Hall when she heard the dogs. Their frantic barking echoed through the still night, growing closer and louder. "Oh, sweet heaven," she whispered. They couldn't be coming after her! She increased her pace, hitching up her skirts to speed her progress. And still they came closer. She could hear them snarling now. The sound froze the marrow in her bones.

She reached an open clearing. The pounding of her feet on the greensward was echoed by the thud of her racing heart. Sweet God, if only she could reach the gate in time! She cast a wild glance over her shoulder. It was too late. She saw the dogs hurtling toward her, their massive bodies emphasized by the moonlight. The brightness glinted off their bared teeth.

Allegra shivered in terror. They would rip her limbs to shreds. There was no doubt of that. What to do? What to do? Desperately she scanned the nearby trees, looking for one that might afford her shelter, with a low enough handhold to climb it.

She whispered a prayer of thanks to Charlie when she saw the ancient oak. Old and sprawling and half dead. But Charlie had loved to climb it, and had convinced Papa to let it stand. Allegra leapt for the lowest branch, hauled herself up and scrambled into the leafy depths of the tree. She clung to the trunk, gasping for air and trembling in every fiber of her being. She had never been so frightened in all her life.

The dogs were now at the base of the tree, circling and baying up at her. They growled and barked and snarled, they took little running jumps against the tree trunk, they leapt high in the air in their futile attempts to reach Allegra. She clung more firmly to her branch, praying the animals would tire of their sport and leave her alone.

She heard Andrew's voice, calling to the dogs, and then she saw the flicker of lanterns through the trees. Her heart sank. There would be trouble now. How stupid of her to flee. What had she been thinking of? And where was her common sense in the attic, to allow Ridley such liberties with her body in the first place?

Andrew emerged into the clearing, followed by three footmen bearing lanterns. One of them carried a musket. Andrew whistled to his dogs, hooked their leashes onto their collars, and patted them until they quieted. Then he borrowed a lantern and held it high, peering up into the tree. "Who be there?" he called.

Her voice was still unsteady from her fright. "'Tis only me, Andrew. Allegra Mackworth."

"Get you down."

She clambered down from the tree and stood before him, taking care to put herself beyond the reach of the mastiffs. She giggled nervously. "I never would have gone out into the night, had I known the dogs were so savage." She hoped she sounded innocent and girlish enough.

His face twisted in a grimace of suspicion. "Where you been, girl? No one be allowed in this park afore dawn. Not when my beauties be out."

"I...I didn't know. The moon was so pretty, and I..."

"Mr. Briggs will have to learn of this."

She thought quickly, her sense of self-preservation reasserting itself. She was in enough difficulty with Lord Ridley now, without him learning that she had tried to run away. "Oh, please, Andrew," she begged. "Must you tell Mr. Briggs? If you come to the stillroom tomorrow, I can give you a tasty cordial that I made for His Lordship. Red mint and honey. It will warm the cockles of your heart. And take away that dyspepsia."

He hesitated, then shook his head. "I can't do it. It be against Mr. Briggs's orders. You find 'em in the park? he says. You bring 'em to me." He jerked his head in the direction of the footmen, who stood at a distance, wary of the dogs. "Besides, they saw you. One of 'em would tell Mr. Briggs, if I didn't."

She sighed and allowed herself to be marched back to Baniard Hall.

To her surprise, she was met at the door by Mr. Briggs himself. His normally pleasant face was set in a scowl, and his gray eyes were as cold as steel. He listened carefully to Andrew's story, his expression growing colder and harder. Then he beckoned to Allegra. "Come with me."

Filled with foreboding, she scanned his implacable face. "Where are we going?"

"Silence!" he ordered. "You will do as you're told."

God save her, he could be as imperious as the master, when he wanted to be! While she quivered in dread, fearing the worst, he led her up the back stairs. She breathed a sigh of relief when they stopped at her room and she saw that no one was there. She had half expected to find Mrs. Rutledge, on Ridley's orders, with a rod in her hand.

Briggs removed the key from her door and motioned her inside. She did as she was bidden; then, emboldened by her reprieve, if only for a little while, she turned and held out a supplicating hand. "Please, Mr. Briggs. Have a crumb of pity. Speak to me."

There was no warmth in his normally kind face. He was the steward of Baniard Hall, and no familiarity or friendship with her was about to sway him from his honorable duty. "I intend to lock you in this room until morning. And then we will get to the bottom of this. His Lordship was in no condition to speak of it tonight. And I was reluctant to question him. But I mark that Lord Ridley was found, sorely wounded, in the box room tonight. Found at your direction, Ram tells me. There was a woman's neckerchief beside him." He glanced briefly at her exposed breasts. "I note you are missing yours. And, perhaps most damning of all, you were attempting to run away, I think. Doubly damning, in view of your situation. A legally contracted bond servant with no rights of your own. I hesitate to accuse you of harming His Lordship, but the evidence would point to that conclusion. I'll say no more. You have betrayed His Lordship's trust. And mine."

She bit her lip, dismayed anew at what had happened because of her. "Wait. Please. Lord Ridley…is he…that is, his head…is it a grievous wound?"

"Mrs. Rutledge doesn't think so. A deal of blood, of course. 'Tis only natural, in that sort of injury. But she's putting in a few stitches, and thinks His Lordship will be fine in a day or two."

"Thank you," she said, sinking into her chair. Relief washed over her like a comforting tide. Thanks be to God he wasn't badly hurt. She bent her head and wept into her hands.

She went to bed exhausted, thinking she would sink into black oblivion until morning. But when she slept, she dreamed of Grey's kisses.

Chapter Twelve

"I want you to know that Margery is quite vexed with you this morning!" Barbara flounced into Allegra's room, carrying a tray with a cup of milk and a slab of bread. She set it down on Allegra's chair and smiled condescendingly.

Allegra fastened her apron over her skirt and sighed. "What have I done to Margery?"

"Your neckerchief." Barbara glanced at the white linen square folded across Allegra's bosom. "I see you have another. It's just as well. Margery says she can scrub until her hands are raw, but she'll never get the other one free of His Lordship's blood. They had to use it to wrap his head." Her smile deepened into a knowing smirk.

Allegra sighed again. The breakfast gossips had clearly been busy. "Tell Margery I'll wash it myself."

"It was strange that Lord Ridley was in the box room at that hour. And then to suffer such a wound...If he has told Mr. Briggs what happened, we'll never know. Mr. Briggs is as shut-up as an oyster."

She was grateful for Briggs's discretion. "So he is."

"Well? What happened?" Barbara leaned forward, eyes shining with expectation.

"If Mr. Briggs says nothing, I suppose we'll never know."

"Oh, come now! Do you take us all for fools? What were you and His Lordship *doing* in the box room?" The insinuation was sly and ugly.

She frowned at the girl. "Playing cribbage."

"Don't be high-and-mighty with me!" snapped Barbara. "You're the one has something to fear. Mrs. Rutledge has been at Mr. Briggs all morning, begging him to get Lord Ridley's permission to give you the thrashing you deserve. And Verity said..."

She pressed her hands together to still their sudden trembling. "I really don't care what Verity said."

Barbara shrugged. "Please yourself. I'll leave your door unlocked. You are to present yourself at His Lordship's chambers when you finish your breakfast. By the back entrance, Mrs. Rutledge said. You're not fit to show your face at the front door." She tossed her head at Allegra and swept from the room.

Impatient to be done with the whole business, Allegra left her breakfast untouched and went down the stairs to Ridley's rooms. The few servants she passed on her way stared at her and elbowed one another in the ribs. She felt like a condemned prisoner going to the gallows. Whatever His Lordship had—or hadn't—told about last night, all of Baniard Hall clearly assumed she was guilty. She gulped and tried to still her racing heart. God only knew what awaited her in Ridley's rooms!

She tapped on the door of the dressing room and was admitted after a moment by Mrs. Rutledge. The woman's tight mouth curled in a smile of victory. "I knew you would stumble at last. Not even a pretty face can make up for a vicious disposition. I'm only surprised that it took His Lordship this long to discover it." She motioned toward the door of Ridley's closet. "Come this way."

Viscount Ridley sat at an inlaid table in his closet, busily signing papers. As he finished each one, he would reach up and hand it to a waiting Briggs, and then bend again to his writing. He wore no bandage wrapped around his head, but Allegra could see the pale gleam of a small plaster on his skull, and a portion of his unbound hair seemed to have been cut away around the spot. He wore a brocaded morning gown over his shirt and breeches, and his feet were encased in velvet slippers. Jagat Ram stood near the door to Ridley's bedchamber, holding a tray that bore the remains of his master's breakfast.

Allegra was painfully aware that not a one of the three men had bothered to look at her as she came in behind Mrs. Rutledge. She had no friends in this room today.

The housekeeper hurried across the carpet to stand before Ridley and shake her head. "Oh, Your Lordship," she simpered, "you mustn't tax your brain so soon after your injury. I'm sure 'tis harmful." She clucked her tongue like a doting nursemaid. "How can I heal you, if you *will* be wicked and refuse to stay in your bed?"

He looked up at her and smiled. "You're such a good nurse that I think I shall heal in remarkable time, despite my folly." He turned to Briggs. "Have we shown our gratitude yet to Mrs. Rutledge?"

"I shall see to it this morning, milord."

Mrs. Rutledge rubbed her palms together, her eyes shining with greed. "It isn't necessary, Your Lordship. 'Twas my honor to serve you in your hour of need."

"Yes, I quite understand," he said dryly, handing the last of his papers to Briggs. "Now, I want to speak to this chit alone. You will leave me. All of you." For the first time, he turned and looked Allegra full in the face. His cold eyes held a challenge. "Ram, leave the gin." He smiled cruelly when Allegra frowned in dismay at his request.

"Yes, Sir Greyston." Jagat Ram put the large flask at Ridley's elbow, then left the room, followed by Mr. Briggs and Mrs. Rutledge. At the last moment, the housekeeper turned and gave Allegra a smug, triumphant smile.

Allegra stared down at her shoes, afraid to look at Ridley. She knew that she was quivering inside; she wondered if he was aware of it as well. But whether her trembling came from fear, or the memory of his burning mouth, his arousing hands, she couldn't tell. Her mind was awhirl with conflicting emotions.

His silence only added to her distress. She knew he was watching her; she could almost feel the coldness of his glance on her flesh. Perhaps she should blurt out an apology. Surely he must know that—whatever else had happened in the box room—she hadn't meant to cause him physical harm. She was about to risk speaking up, when his harsh voice cut into her thoughts.

"Come and stand in front of me. With your head up, if you please. I want to see your eyes."

She nodded and moved toward him, lifting her eyes to his face with some reluctance. Though he was seated, and the table was between them, she felt the frightening thrill of his virile, overbearing presence. There was violence locked within him, and she feared it.

He poured himself a glass of gin and raised it to her in salute. "To your health."

She felt a pang of disappointment. Would he debase himself with drink today merely to be revenged on her for last night? The tears sprang to her eyes. "To *your* health, milord," she whispered.

He bared his teeth in an ugly grimace. "I did not give you leave to speak." He stared at her for a moment, then downed the gin in one gulp. "They say eyes are the mirror of the soul. But yours tell me lies. Last night...No matter." He shrugged and poured himself another glass of gin. "You should account yourself fortunate that I chose to be merciful this time. I could have had you hanged for a runaway. All I need do is produce your bond papers, and the law would allow me to do anything I wished to you. Do you understand?"

She lowered her head briefly in acknowledgment of his words. She and Mama had had many grief-filled years to learn and understand the power of a bond servant's owner.

He laughed sharply. "Not that I wasn't tempted by Mrs. Rutledge's entreaties this morning. That charming woman begged to take a switch to you. I don't believe in drawing blood with a switch. But a good thick strap…" He paused to see the effect of his words. "Still fearless, I see."

She held her chin high. He would never know how much she feared him. At least she still had her pride.

"Let us speak now of your transgressions, so you know precisely how things stand with you in this household. This is between you and me. I choose to say nothing—not even to Briggs." His voice was cold and unemotional. It chilled her more than if he had been in a rage.

"To begin," he said, "your presence in the box room makes me suspect that you're a bloody thief."

Allegra started to cry out a denial, but he held up a silencing hand. "I cannot prove it," he went on. "I'll have the box room locked, in any event. But you've earned my distrust on that score alone. And then, of course, there was your attempt to escape. There can be no doubt about *that*. I've already instructed Briggs that there will be no more unescorted trips for you to Ludlow, or anywhere else. And kindly do not frown at me," he growled, as she drew her brows together in consternation. "You're lucky I don't get Andrew to make a leash for you, as he does for his watchdogs. I could call you my very own bitch," he added with a sneer.

She chewed on her lip in dismay. He had always had the power to hurt her with his sharp words, but today was different. There was coldness in his eyes. There was something that went beyond his sarcasm and his often cruel teasing, and his drunken hostility. Today there was outright hatred in his eyes. She wanted to die.

"If you attempt to escape again," he continued, "you will be punished. No. Let me amend that. After last night…" he touched the back of his head and winced, "I have a personal score to settle with you. Two, for that matter. I'm minded that you've managed to deceive me twice now. Gulled me into believing your sincerity. Or have you forgotten the first day we met? I haven't. The urchin who sighed so sweetly at my kiss, and then tried to amputate my tongue. If you try to escape again, this is how it will be. I myself will send for a strap, lift your petticoats, and blister your backsides. A stinging burn for a few hours might encourage you to regret your behavior."

Allegra gasped at his words and fell back a step. The blood drained from her face at the thought of being humiliated by Ridley, chastised by his very own hand.

"Ah," he said in satisfaction, "*that* frightens you. Good. Let that fear temper your perverse ways. You will continue to bring me my cordial each night. But you will not speak to me, nor linger. I shall have Barbara come and wait on me for the rest of the evening. You might take lessons in civility from her. An agreeable girl, don't you think?"

She nodded in misery. It was as though he were saying everything he could to hurt her. She wanted to cry out. To remind him of the dear words he had uttered last night, his tender kisses, his gentleness. Had he forgotten all of it? Had the accident of a blow to the head turned all that sweetness into the venomous hatred he now offered her?

He poured himself another drink, downed it and poured another. The silence was suddenly charged, different, ominous. "We turn now to the matter of last night," he said at last. His voice was deep, and tightly controlled. "I seem to have been your dupe for some time. You're either very skillful, or I'm more of a fool than I thought. Perhaps the gin has begun to corrupt my judgment. But I was mad enough to trust the look in your eyes, to think you returned my passion. 'Tis quite clear to me now that you were only intent on buying your freedom. From the very first. You simply chose to play the reluctant lover, to wait for the advantageous moment. To appeal to my sensibilities, my weakness for you, if you will, in order to negotiate the most favorable terms."

He *couldn't* believe that! It had been the furthest thought from her mind. Dear God, let him read the truth in her eyes. She shook her head vigorously.

His mouth curved in a twist of contempt. "Do you try to deny it now because you fear I'll rescind the conditions? And you'll have no chance to earn your freedom?"

"No," she whispered.

His amber eyes glowed. "I told you to keep still." He took another swallow of the gin and turned away, staring at the knives mounted on his wall. "But we were speaking of last night. I would have torn up your contract this morning. Did you know that? You had so bewitched me— with your lying eyes and your trembling lips—that I would have granted you anything." He sighed and swung around to face her again.

For the first time, Allegra was aware of how haggard he looked. His eyes were haunted and filled with despair. He reminded her of Papa on the convict ship. A proud man in whom all hope had died.

"Then you changed your mind," he said. His voice rasped with bitterness and pain. "Was it too distasteful, at the last, to submit to a coward? Even for your freedom? To give yourself to a craven fool? Did your flesh crawl at the thought of making love with…" he clenched his teeth and pounded his fist softly on the table before him, "with the man who disgraced himself before you in Ludlow?"

"No!" she burst out, her heart aching. "You cannot believe that! It had naught to do with *you*. I was not refusing you, I was only…"

He slapped his palm on the table to silence her. "Hold your tongue," he roared, "or I'll send for that strap upon the instant!"

She bowed her head. It was all clear now. His hatred, his coldness this morning. She had turned him aside last night. And in his tormented world of shame and humiliation, he had seen her rejection as an indictment: he was not manly enough to please her.

He emptied the bottle of gin and swore softly. "Will there ever be enough drink in this world?" he muttered. "Ah, well. To business." The cold, cynical voice had returned. He had closed the door on his pain. "Strange as it may seem, I still find you desirable. I wish to satisfy my lust. You wish to have your liberty. Very well. But, henceforth, if you choose to barter for your freedom, *you* will come to *me*. I will expect to be pleasured as though you were a Shoreditch whore. There will be no more soft wooing from me. You may boast, in years to come, that you bought your freedom with your body. But not that you made a fool of me to do so! Do you understand?" He leaned back in his chair and glowered at her. "I give you leave to speak now."

She was desperate to give him comfort. "I never meant to hurt you, milord," she whispered. "My refusal last night…" She brushed at the tears that had begun to fall. "It had nothing to do with you. I had no right…I could not…" Oh, God, how could she make him understand?

He curled his lip in disgust. "Spare me your tears. They're as dishonest as the softness I read in your eyes."

It was useless. She bobbed a curtsy. "By your leave, milord," she murmured, and stumbled from the room.

She climbed the stairs to her room, threw herself onto her bed and wept until she was spent. Her family, Grey. They were snatching at her from all sides, tearing her apart. Rending her into little pieces. Her heart, her duty, her obligations. Her desires. She wondered if this is how it would have felt—all this wrenching pain—if the dogs had reached her last night.

A year. It was too long to wait. A year of seeing him, watching him, aching to be his comfort. A year of sweet distractions, of tangling her life with his, while the memory of her family faded and her vow became a broken promise. She had already spent too much time at Baniard Hall, selfishly thinking of her own needs and desires. She could feel the edge of her sharp vengeance blunting, like an old knife rusting in the backwater of a turbulent stream. She feared that she would lose her resolve to kill the Wickhams long before the year was done.

She had to leave. If she stayed, she would forget why God had left her on this earth. If she stayed, she would betray her family's memory. If she stayed, Grey and his unhappiness would engulf her, fill her with longings for a future that could never be. Not while a single Wickham lived.

If she stayed, she would have to face the truth. She had fallen in love with him.

The sky was clear. No clouds covered the waning moon. Allegra peered out from her small dormer window and nodded in satisfaction. It would be bright enough to see the road, but not so bright that she couldn't melt into the shadows if she were followed. She wrapped her spare shift and a second pair of stockings into her neckerchief, added her comb, and tied the bundle firmly. She would put on her straw hat later. As for Papa's bloodstained handkerchief...She sighed and fingered the yellowed square. She would carry it on her person, in her bosom. The trip to London would be chancy and possibly dangerous, with the risk of highwaymen. She couldn't hazard losing the only memento she had.

She set the bundle onto her chair and reviewed her plans. All was in readiness. She lifted the cover of a large crock and sniffed the chunks of raw meat within. Faugh! If she'd had to delay another day, the other maids would surely have smelled the rank odor coming from her room.

It had taken her three or four trips to the kitchen, in as many days, to spirit away the meat from under the cook's nose. And another two days in the stillroom to extract the white juice from several heads of lettuce, then wait impatiently for the juice to dry into brown cakes. She had crumbled the cakes into bits, and mixed them in with the meat. The dogs would be asleep in no time. The dried juice was a potent narcotic; Allegra had even heard stories of surgeons using it to produce sleep before an amputation.

Humphrey had gone to spend the night with his woman. She'd heard Andrew whispering it to Verity. It would be simple enough to throw back the bolt on the gate and vanish into the night.

She counted out her coins once more. A fair amount; Ridley had been generous in the two months she'd been here. There was enough to pay for the mail coach from Ludlow to London, and even provide for stops at inns along the way. London in three days. And then Wickham.

She frowned. But how was she to live in London? She remembered Lady Dorothy's invitation. She might pay a call on that good gentlewoman. But she'd still need money. If she could hire a solicitor to search for Wickham, it would make her task simpler. But where was she to get money, even if she chose to steal it? Mr. Briggs and Mrs. Rutledge kept their accounts safely locked away. As for Ridley—she had no idea where he kept his purse.

Ridley. She frowned. All those knives. Covered with jewels. One of them alone would buy her passage halfway around the world, if that's what it took to find Wickham. One blade, out of all that array. Why not? Ridley would scarcely miss it.

She snuffed her candle and opened her door. It must be well past midnight. The Hall was quiet and dark. She would leave her bundle and the crock of meat in her room for now. If, heaven forfend, she were caught going toward Ridley's rooms, no one could accuse her of trying to run away. She could tell a fanciful tale of sleepwalking, or some such.

There was enough moonlight filtering through the windows to bathe the passageways in a dim light. Allegra moved slowly and quietly, feeling her way with her hands whenever she turned a dark corner or descended a staircase. She found herself at last outside the door to Ridley's dressing room. She had no fear of disturbing Jagat Ram; his room was on the other side of the passageway. Without any hesitation, she opened the door and tiptoed into the dressing room.

She looked up as she passed the portrait of Lady Banyard. Even in the gloom, that pale face glowed. "I have not forgotten," she whispered, feeling as though she owed expiation to every Baniard going back in time. The last of her line.

She opened the door to Ridley's closet, pausing for a moment as the heavy, familiar scent of incense assailed her nostrils. No doubt Grey had had an unhappy day, and had needed the comforting memories of his Calcutta past. She could only guess, of course. Since the night of the box room, she had been shunned and ignored by him and everyone else at the Hall, including Mr. Briggs. Like a leper. It had been an agony for her—to wonder if Grey were suffering, and to feel helpless to reach him. But there was no light shining beneath the door to his bedchamber tonight. At least he slept. She prayed it was a sleep of peace and tranquility.

She looked around the room. The carved sandalwood shutters at the windows caught the moonlight and cast lacy shadows across the carpet and the mounded cushions of the couch. The glow of the moon didn't quite reach the collection of knives and swords above the mantelpiece, but Allegra could see the dim luster of metal and the dark shine of jewels even in the gloom. She scanned the weapons quickly. There was one, she remembered, that had several large stones in its hilt. If she was going to be a thief, she might as well be sensible, and take the one that she could most easily pawn. She stretched forth her hand to reach for the knife she wanted, a small, exotic dagger crusted with jewels.

A thief. The thought gave her pause. She lowered her hand and leaned her arm heavily on the mantel, overcome with sudden guilt. She was prepared to be a murderess if she must. That was for the family. But to sink to thievery…She sighed unhappily and rested her head against her arm, closing her eyes to ward off the pain. What had become of Anne Allegra Baniard, who could never gather eggs from the henhouse without feeling that she was robbing the poor chickens of their young? She sighed again. There was no going back, recapturing the innocence of her childhood. But sometimes the going forward was painful and tinged with regret.

She heard a sound behind her and opened her eyes. The room was bathed in bright light. She whirled to find Grey Ridley standing in his doorway, holding a large candleholder before him. He swore viciously and slammed the candles onto a nearby table. The flames from the tapers fluttered for a moment, casting frightening shadows on his angular face.

"What the devil are you doing here?" he growled.

Chapter Thirteen

Allegra stared in shock, her hand pressing to her bosom as though she could still her racing heart.

Grey Ridley was as terrifying as she had ever seen him. He stood scowling in his nightshirt, bare-legged and barefooted, a tall, powerful, hard-muscled man. His near-nakedness—the long legs uncovered from the thighs down and darkly dusted with hair—only added to his air of intimidation. He looked like a primitive savage, a barbarian emerging from the past, save for the very civilized pistol he clutched in one fist. He set it down next to the candles and took a menacing step toward Allegra. His eyes narrowed in cold fury. "I asked you what you were doing here."

She found herself stammering, desperate to invent an excuse. "Forgive me, milord. I didn't think…A moment of your time…That is to say…" she gestured vaguely toward his night clothes, "I didn't realize you had retired for the night." Think. *Think!* What reason could she give for wanting to speak to him at this hour?

His mouth twisted in a mocking smile. "I retired early tonight. Almost sober, you'll be pleased to know. I sat up awhile with the poems of Andrew Marvell." The smile deepened to a suggestive smirk. "You are familiar with his work?"

She understood his meaning at once, and blushed at the pointed sarcasm.

"Yes," he said dryly, "I thought you would be. *To His Coy Mistress* is a favorite verse of mine. 'Tis amusing to see how other men play the fool." His voice took on a sudden harsh edge. "But that's quite beside the question. I asked what you are doing here. Must I repeat it again?"

"I…I came…" She twisted her fingers together and stared down at the carpet.

His next words caught her with the awful suddenness of a thunderbolt. "To barter your body for your freedom? Was that it?"

God help her. She suppressed a cry of dismay. But perhaps a false confession was the only way out of this dilemma. It would give her a few moments to delay while she racked her brains for a plan. "Y-yes," she said, beginning to back toward the door. "But now I see that you…"

"*Yes?* And yet, when I came in, you were at the mantel. Deep in thought, it seemed to me. Were you plagued anew with uncertainty?" There was a dreadful stillness about him as he waited for her reply.

She shook her head violently. "No!" No matter what else happened tonight, she didn't want to add to his doubts about his manhood. "Not one whit, milord. But when I saw that your rooms were dark, I hesitated to disturb you." She curtsied and backed closer to the door. "I'll trouble you no further tonight. If it please Your Lordship, you have but to name the hour and I'll return here tomorrow evening." God forgive the lie, by tomorrow evening she would be well on her way to London. She put her hand on the door latch behind her. A few more steps and she would be free.

"You'll stay, damn it!" His eyes glowed with a dangerous light. "This is a business compact, is it not? I'm selling you your freedom. Under the circumstances, I think I have the right to choose the conditions of the sale. And since you're here, and I've been wakened from a sound sleep, I choose here. And *now.*"

She was trapped. If she refused him, she had no doubt he would guess that she'd been trying to run away again. It would probably mean the humiliation of a thrashing at his hands. And imprisonment in her room, that was certain. Her hopes for London would be dashed—perhaps until her bondage year was over. But if she agreed…She sighed. Godamercy, what did it matter? Mama had endured far worse. She nodded in assent.

"Good. Shall we agree on terms? I had thought to take three months off your bondage as my part of the compact."

It seemed absurd to negotiate like this. She would give him her body, he would take his pleasure of it, and then she'd be gone. She would leave his bed and his house long before dawn. So why bargain? But her pride goaded her. She thrust out a defiant chin. "Ten months. The remainder of my bond."

"You have a high opinion of yourself. Six months, and not a day more. You're a fine stillroom maid. I hate to lose you too soon. I'll release you in January."

She wondered if this was how a whore felt. She paused, half tempted to bolt for the door, then submitted and moved slowly toward him. What did he expect of her now? She stood before him and waited for him to make the first move.

He crossed his arms against his chest and glared at her. "Well?"

"Milord?"

"I told you I'll not woo you."

Her heart sank. He *did* expect her to play the whore. She screwed up her courage and put her arms tentatively about his neck. But when she reached up to set her lips on his, he jerked his head roughly aside.

"You can do better than that," he growled.

She dropped her hands and stepped back, bewildered.

He raked her body with his lustful eyes. "I want to see if you're worth six months. I've forgot since that day at the pond. Show me."

She sighed in resignation. A whore was expected to accommodate her patron. Hands shaking, she began to undress. She remembered that he liked her hair loose; she pulled off her cap and unpinned her topknot, then tossed her head so the thick curls tumbled down over her shoulders. She took off her gown and stays and stepped out of her petticoat, shivering as though she had a chill.

She had fastened her gaze on a painting behind him before she had begun; she couldn't bear to look in his eyes as she disrobed. It wasn't that she feared to be naked before him; in some strange, perverse way, she *wanted* him to look at her. But the room was so bright, and his face so harsh and cold—filled with a hostile wariness that challenged her to please him. It shamed her that a moment which should have been tender, warm, and sympathetic was stark and impersonal. A business compact, he called it.

Though she moved as slowly as she dared, her heart pounding, it didn't take her long to shed her garments. In a few minutes, her shift was all that remained to protect her modesty. She hesitated, then loosened the strings and allowed the soft muslin to slide over her hips to the floor.

Grey uttered a low cry, as though the sight of her naked body had torn the sound from him. It gave her heart. Whatever else he felt—anger, hatred, cold mockery—he clearly desired her. She found the strength to look him full in the face, then smiled shyly. "What now, milord?"

One shaggy eyebrow angled into his broad forehead. "Improvise," he drawled.

She swallowed hard. If she was to save a shred of her pride, find some humanity in this night's business so that she wouldn't feel as though she'd been violated, she would have to crack that cynical mask. To return Grey's coldness with concern and gentleness.

She moved to him again and lifted her hand to his face. Though he had refused her kiss, he allowed her touch. Such a beautiful face, she thought. Even when he scowled, as now he did, she found pleasure in that face. She caressed his cheek and felt the muscles of his jaw tense under her hand. She explored the cleft in his chin, enjoying the sensuous curves beneath her fingertips. She stroked his lips, and knew a thrill of triumph when he gasped and closed his eyes.

I want you, Grey Ridley, she thought suddenly. This was no longer a foolish contract—her body for her liberty. She was a woman in love, hungering for him to love her in return, if only for a brief moment. God forgive me, she thought. Would it be so wicked of her, to allow herself one night of pleasure? Only one? She would still be on the road to London in the morning.

She tried to kiss him again, longing to teach him with her lips the secrets of her heart. Again he turned his head aside. She refused to be discouraged by his obstinacy. The more he resisted, the more her need grew. Her eager mouth sought the curve of his chin, his Adam's apple, his throat, and rained soft kisses on his flesh. He tasted and smelled wonderful; her body quivered with the nearness of him.

With unsteady fingers, she unfastened the neck of his nightshirt, pulling it open to expose his chest to her searching mouth. She sighed and nuzzled her face in the dark patch of curls. How silken sweet a man's body could be.

She ran her hands over his shoulders and down his arms, luxuriating in the strength of the muscles and sinews she could feel beneath the fabric of his garment. The thrilling sensation, the power she felt merely from touching him, made her pulse race madly. She teased herself, resisting the urge to put her hands beneath his nightshirt and touch his bare skin. It was more exciting, more tantalizing only to imagine the heat of his flesh on hers.

She looked up at his face. His eyes were open, watching her. His mouth was set in a stubborn line, still fighting her allure. But his eyes, his eyes…She read desire smoldering in their tawny depths. Desire, and something else. She saw it clearly now, though perhaps she had merely learned to peer beyond his eyes and see what was in his heart. And what she saw was fear.

She had refused him before, led him to think that she was willing, and then rebuffed him. Clearly he was not about to give in to his weakness again.

You foolish, dear man, she thought. What must I do to make you take the gift of my love?

She renewed her efforts to woo him. She put her arms around his neck and pressed her naked body close to his. She shivered, feeling the hard length of him against her, the shaft that was already rigid and waiting to claim her. It was almost too thrilling to be endured. Her flesh was on fire, her blood pounded in her ears.

And still he stood like a statue, cold and unyielding. She moaned softly, feeling a sudden flush burn her cheeks. What was she doing, humiliating herself like this? He would not melt, he would not bend. It was clear that he intended to take her, at the last, as Squire Pringle had taken Mama. Forcibly, brutally. An object to satisfy his lust, and nothing more.

It was too much to bear. She dropped her arms and turned away from him, weeping bitterly. She ached for the touch of his hands on her body, for the warm sweetness of his mouth, for the human contact that would drive away her shame. "In the name of pity," she whispered, burying her face in her hands, "touch me or I shall die of longing."

She felt his hand on her wrist, swinging her around to face him. He pulled her roughly toward the table, and turned her so that the candlelight fell full on her tear-washed face. He stared at her for a long time, his expression closed and filled with doubt. "Do you truly want me?" he growled at last, then looked away as though he feared her answer.

"More than honor itself."

"*Truly?*"

She choked on a sob. "Can't you see it in my eyes?"

His features relaxed into a smile of relief and gratitude. "Then come to my bed, fair Allegra," he said hoarsely. He lifted her in his arms and carried her into the shadowy enchantment of his bedchamber.

It was dim here, the only light coming from the candle glow that spilled obliquely into the room from Grey's closet. The sheets were cool as he laid her on the bed, and the damask bed curtains stirred and whispered a silken song. Allegra turned her head and rubbed her cheek against the pillows. The linen smelled of him, musky and masculine and captivating.

She watched him with hungry eyes as he pulled his nightshirt over his head and threw it to the floor. The thick patches of hair on his chest and groin were like dense, dark islands on the knotted expanse of muscle and flesh. And out of one island there grew something large and proudful and impatient. Something that made Allegra quiver with more than a little anticipation and fear.

He climbed onto the bed. But instead of lying beside her, he knelt at her feet like a humble servant. He took off her shoes and reached for the garters tied above her knees. His hands were warm, caressing her legs as he stripped the stockings from them. He bent and kissed her knees, his lips soft and tantalizing on her flesh. "Sweet," he murmured.

He shifted on the bed and perched above her, his body a cage that kept her lovingly imprisoned. His hungry mouth found her breasts; his kisses roused her with strange and new sensations, a delight of feeling that left her breathless.

She writhed beneath him, eager to give as well as to receive, to learn every inch of his dear body. She stretched forth her arms, touching him wherever her searching hands led her. She discovered a tufted patch of hair at the nape of his neck, and stroked it gently, luxuriating in the softness against her fingers. His skin was smooth and hairless on the sides of his ribs; she curled her hands around him, feeling the bones and rippling muscles that responded to her touch.

But, after a while, she couldn't think, let alone caress him. His mouth at her bosom had continued its hungry assault, nipping at her flesh, sucking at the tender, sensitive nipples until she wanted to cry out with the dizzying joy of his lovemaking.

She moaned in greedy frustration. She wanted more. She burned for his mouth on hers. Trembling, she took his face between her two hands and raised it up to hers.

"I haven't even kissed your sweet lips tonight," he said. "What a fool." He chuckled, but there was a tremor in his voice. He leaned toward her mouth.

"No," she whispered. "I want to kiss *you*. As though it were the first time."

"And so it is, my fair Allegra," he said, his eyes dark with warm tenderness. "Take your kiss, then."

She pulled his mouth down to hers and touched his lips, shyly at first, and then with all the yearning passion in her heart.

He sighed in pleasure, relaxed, and lowered his body to hers, stretching himself full length on top of her. She could feel every part of him, from the hairy legs that rubbed against hers to the weight and strength that took her breath away; from the warmth of his breast to the overbearing maleness that pressed impatiently against her closed thighs. She gloried in every sensation. She was conscious, as never before, of her own delicious nakedness. Alive to the feel of this man wherever their flesh touched, as though her body were possessed of a hundred tingling, sensory fingers.

Their mouths hadn't separated since that first sweet joining, as though neither wished to break the thrilling contact. Grey's lips were soft on hers, and parted slightly. Allegra hesitated, then thrust her tongue into his mouth in an excess of violent emotion that surprised her with its ferocity.

He started and groaned at her unexpected burst of passion, grinding his mouth against hers and meeting her tongue with his own. She clung to him. Nothing existed for her but their burning mouths, the pledge and promise of this first glorious kiss.

At length he lifted his head from hers and drew in a great gulp of air. "God help me," he gasped. "I want you so much, I can't wait." He prodded her legs apart with his knee, and positioned himself so that his hard shaft pressed against her moist, throbbing portal.

She was in an agony of longing and sudden, thrilling dread. Mama had cried in anguish beneath Squire Pringle. Always. She felt as though she were stretched on the rack, awaiting…God knew what torment. Yet she loved him. How could he hurt her?

He began to rock gently against her hips, his manhood merely grazing and stroking the soft entryway. The sensation was wonderful, but her fear was driving away all thoughts of pleasure. Dear heaven, she thought. Good or bad, let it be done with! She couldn't wait another second. She put her hands around him, grasped his firm buttocks, and pulled him into her with all her might. She flinched with the sharp, tearing pain of his entrance.

"Sweet Jesu," he cried, "you're so tight!" He gasped in surprise and delight, then grunted as his body shook with violent spasms. She felt the thrill of his impassioned thrusts, and then the warmth of his seed as it flooded into her. "Too soon," he said with a groan, collapsing against her. "Too soon."

She lay quietly, feeling him within her. After that first hard entrance, the ripping of her maidenhead, it had not been unpleasant, despite the lingering pain. Far from it. And now? Without quite being aware of how she could control such a peculiar muscle, she tightened herself like a sheath around his shaft, and was thrilled at the jolt of excitement that one small movement sent through her body. He had felt it as well. He moaned in pleasure and kissed her softly. Pleased with the result, she tightened the muscle again, and felt herself growing warm with renewed ardor. She forgot the few twinges of remaining soreness. She arched her body to his, praying he would understand and move inside her again, thrill her once more.

Instead, he withdrew and sat up beside her, scowling down at her body. "Why didn't you tell me?"

She looked down at herself in surprise. Her thighs were spotted with blood. "I...I didn't think it would matter."

He swore softly. "Not matter? That you were a virgin? Damn it, I hurt you. I should have been more careful."

"No, Grey. No. It was sweet pain."

He shook his head as though he wished to clear it of a sudden bewildering thought. "But...a virgin?"

"Why should you have thought otherwise?"

"But...I thought...Wickham. Lord Ellsmere. In the Colonies. I thought that was why you sought him."

She smiled ruefully at his mistaken conclusion. As though the insignificance of a woman's honor could have set her on her terrible course. "I never met the man," she said simply.

He lifted her hand and rubbed his fingers across the calluses that still remained on her palm. "Never met him? And yet you endured a life of misery to come to England. Because you want to kill him."

"No," she said softly. "I *must* kill him. Or never seek for peace in this world."

"In God's name, why?"

She turned her head away from his searching gaze. The dark concern in his eyes. Her vengeance was her own. And the Baniards'.

He sighed at her silence and rose from the bed. Allegra lay in warm contentment, eyes closed, unwilling even to move. She heard the soft fall of Grey's bare feet on the carpet, moving toward his closet; then the room was still. She wriggled against the scented smoothness of the sheets. She wouldn't get up until she had to. Let this sweetness last, she thought, if only for an hour or two. It would be the dearest memory she carried to her grave.

"Allegra." She stirred and opened her eyes at the sound of her name. Grey sat on the edge of the bed, holding a small basin of water and a sponge. Though she protested that she wasn't a helpless child, he gently bathed her thighs and washed away the bloody evidence of their passion. It was such a humble gesture—this proud, noble man ministering to her most intimate needs—that she wanted to weep. When he had finished and put the basin aside, she pulled his head down to kiss him tenderly on the mouth.

"That was scarcely your chore," she murmured.

He perched on the edge of the bed. "But it was my fault," he said with remorse. He stared at her, lost in thought. Then he suddenly began to smile, an expression of such warmth and joy that the dim room seemed to brighten. "Of course! That was the why of it…in the box room."

She returned his smile, glad to give him the reassurance he needed, though it be false. "I tried to tell you it had naught to do with you. I was afraid. As many maidens are, I suppose. And so I…lost my courage and pulled back at the last."

"And tonight?"

"If we risk nothing, we gain nothing."

"And what did you gain tonight?" he growled, his joyous smile turning to a frown. "I hurt you."

She smoothed away the frown with her fingers. "Foolish man. I've been hurt for much of my life. By those who meant to do so. *That* is pain."

He laughed bitterly. "And I've never hurt you by my deeds and words?"

"You strike out at the whole world, but your blade is always pointed at your own breast. How can you hurt me?"

He jumped up from the bed and angrily began to pace the room. "Why do you forgive my cruelties with such generosity? I scarcely merit it! Are you a fool? Or a martyr?"

She couldn't bear to quarrel with him. Not tonight, when she would never see him again. Better to go quickly, before her heart was broken further. "Shall I leave you now, milord?" she whispered.

He stopped his pacing, looked at her, then shook his head. "Not yet."

"Shall I bring you something to drink?" There could be a flask of gin in his closet, or the remains of one of her cordials. She sat up and swung her legs over the edge of the bed.

He hesitated. "Is it your wish that I should drink?"

She shook her head. "Not when it makes it easier for you to indulge that cruelty you so dislike in yourself." She moved across the room and stood before him, holding out her arms. "Take me, instead of the drink."

"Oh, sweet woman," he groaned, and clasped her to his bosom. "God knows you're more intoxicating than any drink I've ever known." He kissed her passionately, his tongue tasting her, savoring her mouth; then he dropped his head lower and buried his face in the softness of her neck. "Christ's blood," he muttered, "but I want you again."

She ran her fingers down his spine and felt a thrill of joy when he quivered at her touch. "Why, then, here I am."

"No." He pushed her away with both his hands, like a man resisting temptation. "I fear to hurt you again. There will be other nights."

"No. Tonight!" She tried to hide the desperation in her voice. He mustn't guess that tonight was all they had.

"I dare not. I...Wait." He chuckled softly, crossed the room, and rummaged in a small cabinet. He turned to Allegra and held out a crock that looked strangely familiar. "I have a clever stillroom maid, who mixed the most remarkable unguent for me. 'Tis very soothing. Shall we try it?" He gave her a sly wink.

She had never known he could be so playful. It warmed her heart to see it. "'Twas meant for the scratches of a bear," she said, pursing her lips against the smile that hovered near her mouth.

"And tiger scratches?" He grinned. "For I fear I'll be in danger of attack if I refuse this impatient cat before me."

She laughed softly. "The tiger will be a purring kitten if you only oblige me."

He chuckled. "And then, perhaps, if I oblige you well enough, you might reward me with scratches of a different sort." He jerked his head toward the bed. "Go and lie down."

She did as he instructed, allowing him to open her legs and smooth the fragrant cream into her tender flesh, probe the soreness within. His fingers moved back and forth, in and out—stroking, soothing, igniting her senses anew with hot desire. She arched her back to his hand, wondering how it was possible to shiver and burn all at once, to feel contentment and a desperate yearning for something more at the same time.

"Godamercy," she breathed, "can anything be more wonderful than that?"

"I trust so," he said with a smug laugh, and moved on top of her. When he entered her, his shaft gliding silkily to its warm berth, she cried aloud. Alarmed, he looked down at her and frowned. "Damn it, I've hurt you again."

She laughed shakily. "That was joy, not pain. And if you stop again, I swear on my recipe books that I *will* scratch you."

"'Tis on your head, wench. No quarter given."

"No quarter asked," she whispered, and abandoned herself to the ecstasy of his lovemaking. He thrust gently at first, the smooth strokes working her into a frenzy of delight. But when she cried out and clutched at his shoulders in an excess of passion, the gentle thrusts became a pounding rhythm. He slipped his hands under her hips and pulled her even closer to his pulsing loins.

It was not enough to have him within her; she wanted every part of him to be hers. She clung to him, wrapping her arms and legs tightly about his body. He was her life, her blood, her soul, her heart. And this night would end too soon. She would be alone again with her awful task. She savored every moment of this brief joy. And when her body—stretched taut with ever-increasing desire—gave way in a drenching rush of release and fulfillment, her heart burst as well, and a sob escaped her throat.

Grey's release came a moment afterward. He gasped and trembled and shivered, then was still. "Oh, God," he groaned, struggling to catch his breath, "was there ever creature sweeter than you?" He kissed her lips and cheeks; then he kissed them again and frowned. "Tears?"

She stroked his dear face. "Tears of happiness. When I die and go before God for judgment, and he seeks to know the one hour of my life I would sell my soul to relive, I shall tell him of this night."

"'Tis only one of many. I promise you that," he said hoarsely. "I knew the first day I saw you—in the lower parlor, after the maids had washed your beautiful hair—I knew you'd be good for me." He smiled, a wry smile. "But I must be heavy for you." He moved off her with reluctance and sat up. "My oath, you're bleeding again." Before she could stop him, he had fetched his basin.

"I wish you wouldn't," she said, as he dabbed at her legs. Somehow, it didn't seem right. He was the master, she the servant.

"It gives me pleasure."

She had a sudden recollection. The bent head. The tender care. "As it gives pleasure to Mr. Morgan?" she asked softly.

His head jerked up and he stared at her. "How did you know?"

"I saw you once. By chance."

He sighed and put aside his basin. He seemed embarrassed by her knowledge. "Absurd, to play such a role."

"But if it brings you a measure of peace…"

He covered his eyes with his hand. "I shall never have peace. Never atone for what I did."

For what he did? Dear heaven, could it be true? "Did you…" her voice shook with the dread of it, "did you *kill* her?"

He nodded. "Yes. I killed her. And I killed our son, as well." He sounded tired and resigned.

"I don't believe that! Lady Dorothy said it was a childbed fever."

He shook his head. "She begged me not to duel with Osborne. She had known him since her childhood." He laughed bitterly. "But I was headstrong and proud. He'd goaded me into it. God save me, I could have refused the quarrel. I could have shown mercy. I knew it was envy on his part. Because I was rich. And he'd come back from a failure in the Bermudas." He turned and looked at Allegra. His eyes were shadowed with pain. "She begged me on her knees…Her body was swollen with our child. Oh, sweet God! Who knows why a man chooses the darker path? He had insulted me…my pride…"

"Oh, Grey." Allegra wrapped her arms around him and held him close.

"And after I killed Osborne…" He shuddered and drew away from her, as though he felt unworthy of her embrace. "She sent for me, in the agony and pain of her stillbirth, and put my dead son into my hands. She insisted that I hold it, that poor little thing. She would have it so, she said, that I might suffer as she had suffered."

He gulped, stared at the ceiling, then went on. "And while I wept over my child, she lay there—amid her bloody sheets—and cursed me. And told me she had done it on purpose. Because she had come to hate me, and my name, and…Oh, God!" His voice caught in his throat. "And my child in her womb."

"On *purpose?* Merciful heaven, what are you saying?"

"I don't know what potion she took to force her labor too soon. Perhaps you, with your lore of the stillroom, would know."

Allegra gasped. It was scarcely to be believed. She knew, of course, what Ruth would have taken. A distillation of juniper, mixed with mercury. Mama had secretly used it herself, more than once, to rid herself of Squire Pringle's foul seed. She frowned at Grey. "But then how can you say that you killed her?"

"Don't you understand? I drove her to it. She had no other way to show me her hatred and her pain, save by destroying what I held most dear." He brushed the tears from his eyes. "Poor helpless Ruth, suffering with the grief I'd caused her."

It was still almost beyond comprehension. "She destroyed the child in her own womb?"

"She found an apothecary to give her something. It was not meant to harm her, only the child. But, in her unhappy state, she must have taken too much of it. It ended by poisoning her as well. By the time I knew of it, it was too late to save her. I sent for a doctor in secret. But he looked at her and departed." He groaned. "I hear her voice, over and over again, cursing me. Sometimes I think only gin can drown out her screams."

"And you told no one? Not even your friends? Not even when the gossip began? The whispers of murder?"

"How could I? I was the cause of it all."

She shook her head, shocked as much by Grey's acceptance of guilt as by the horror of Ruth's actions. "But that's monstrous!" she cried.

"Yes," he said, bowing his head. "I can never forgive myself."

"No! *She* was monstrous!"

He scowled savagely. "Are you mad? I drove her to it. That sweet, good woman. She was a saint. And I broke her heart."

Allegra felt a sudden, unreasoning hatred of the dead woman for blighting Grey's life. It was a hatred that felt very much like jealousy, but she drove the ugly thought from her mind. What kind of woman would kill her unborn child to revenge herself on her husband? "Put aside your thoughts of guilt, Grey," she begged. "How long can you torment yourself for what's done? It cannot be recalled."

He waved his hands as though he wished to fend off her reasoned words. "'Twas my fault entirely. I drove her to it." His voice cracked. "And God cursed me for my wickedness by transforming me into a coward."

"*Your* fault? Did you guide her hand to the foul nostrum? We're creatures of our own free will, Grey. She chose her means of revenge against you. It was a cruel, willful deed. She *chose*. Don't you understand? She chose foolishly and unwisely, to be sure. But she was willing to kill her own child out of spite for you. I don't wish to speak ill of the dead, but...God help me, I could not have made such a cruel choice. But she did. And now her spite reaches from beyond the grave to play sad havoc with your life."

He gripped her by the shoulders and glared at her. "What do you know?" he growled.

"I know that your pain breaks my heart. Forgive yourself, Grey. Let her go."

"I have no right. Unworthy wretch, she called me. And 'tis so. Why should I know peace?"

She pounded on his chest in frustration. "Listen to me, Grey Ridley! How can you call yourself unworthy? Jagat Ram would give his life for you. The rector at the almshouse called you an angel of mercy. Even Mr. Briggs admires you in his way. And as for me...I had room in my heart for nothing save thoughts of vengeance. Yet you crept into my life, into my very soul, and made me love you."

"What?" He stared in disbelief.

She hadn't meant to tell him. It seemed too cruel, knowing she must leave. But perhaps those were words he needed to hear. "I saw you at your worst, and still discerned the good man you were. The good man you *are*. Take my love and let it heal you at last. Put away the dark past, live again in sunshine. Foreswear the excess of drink that makes you cruel, and let Mr. Morgan rule your heart. Promise me!"

"You love me?" His face was filled with wonder.

She nodded, helpless to stem the flow of tears. "Will you promise?" she whispered.

He took her into his embrace, and kissed her tears and laughed gently. "I give you leave to reproach me with your sad eyes should I become the monster again." He pulled her down to lie beside him on the bed. "Come, you dear woman. Let me fall asleep with you in my arms. And wake to your gentle smile." He wrapped them both in the coverlet and sighed in contentment. "I think I'll dream of you."

Her own sigh was filled with grief and pain. "I'll dream of tonight," she said. "Forever."

"So solemn? There will be many more nights like this."

Her heart was breaking. She clung to him. "Yes, of course." She kissed him fervently on the mouth, and rested her head on the pillow of his warm breast. She heard his breathing relax into sleep, felt the rise and fall of his chest beneath her head. Felt again the wonder and joy of lying in her lover's arms.

After a little while, she carefully extricated herself from his arms and slipped out of the bed. She turned away from his sleeping form; she couldn't bear to look at him where he lay. One glance at his dear face and she would be undone, her vow in tatters. She hurried into his closet and dressed quickly, then took the jeweled knife from the wall and tucked it into her bodice.

She was about to slip from the room when her eye fell upon Grey's small writing desk in the corner of his closet. She had debated with herself about writing him a note. The more she thought of it, the more it seemed the honorable thing to do. She had no hope that they would ever meet again. Her search for Wickham could take her anywhere. And if she found him, and found the courage to do her duty, her final journey could be to the gallows. But she couldn't leave without a last message to Grey.

She poured out her heart on the paper, assuring him that she would love him forever, and begging him to forgive himself and find happiness again in his life. Her tears flowed as she wrote, dropping to the page and nearly blurring some of the words. She sanded the letter, folded it, and found a stick of wax to seal it closed. "Lord Ridley," she wrote on the outside, in her formal hand. Grey, my love, was what she longed to write.

Numb with pain, she groped her way through the dark passages to her room. Only there did she realize that she'd carried the letter away from Grey's closet. It would be folly to return to his rooms. If she continued to move around the Hall in this fashion, it would take but one light sleeper to raise the hue and cry.

Instead, she propped the letter against the seat of her chair. One of the girls would find it and give it to Grey. She tied on her hat, tucked her bundle under her arm, and picked up the crock of meat.

The dogs succumbed to the narcotic in no time. Allegra was soon hurrying away from the Hall. Just before she disappeared into the darkness of the trees that would lead her to the front gate, she turned and looked back. Through a blur of tears, she could just make out the candlelight from Grey's closet. Her heart twisted in grief. The candles would burn low and sputter. Would he waken to the sound and find her gone?

"Sleep in peace, my love," she whispered. "God knows, if I were free to love you all my life, I would."

She sighed and plunged resolutely on. If she was about to take a life in London, she prayed that she had at least helped to restore a life at Baniard Hall. A life for a life.

It was small comfort to her breaking heart.

Chapter Fourteen

He refused to open his eyes too soon.

Grey Ridley lay in his bed, grinning. He resisted the urge to stretch, to make any movement that might disturb her. He would wait until the desire to look at her sweet face overcame him; only then would he open his eyes. For now, it was pleasant just to lie there, drifting in that hazy world between waking and sleeping, and recall last night.

Had he ever known such pleasure with a woman before? The encounters with whores and tavern wenches, the fleeting liaisons with easy women in the Court—had they ever been much more than temporary release for his frustrations, his unhappiness, his sense of unworthiness?

It had never even been as good with Ruth. At least not the physical part of their love. She had been so frail and delicate. He'd always felt as though he would crush her beneath him if he weren't careful. Of course, that was what had made him love her so much—that fragility, that gentle helplessness. Women like Ruth needed to be pampered and petted, to be worshipped, not overpowered by a man's strength. It had always seemed right, to love her that way. To protect her and care for her, and receive clinging devotion in return.

But Allegra, with her burning intensity…it was as difficult to imagine her passive and languid in his bed—as Ruth had been—as it was to imagine Ruth's hands touching him with Allegra's intimacy. Ruth responding with Allegra's fiery kisses. Allegra's passionate cries of pleasure. He felt like a man this morning; it was a feeling that he'd almost forgotten in the year and a half since Ruth's death.

A man? There was that grin again, spreading across his face without his willing it. A man? My God, he felt like a *giant!*

And that delicious minx, with her bold kisses and caresses. An inexperienced virgin, no less! He felt himself growing warm just imagining the lusty romps they would share as she learned the ways of passion. What a joy it would be to teach her!

He allowed himself a few moments to savor the sweet daydream, then realized his folly. To think of her was to feel his body growing tense with desire, to be helpless as his loins stirred with need. To think of her was to want her. Desperately.

Perhaps he'd open his eyes after all. See the time by the ebony clock on the mantel. If it was still early, he didn't think that Allegra would need much persuasion to linger in his bed for another quarter of an hour or so. He turned his head to where he knew she would be, and opened his eyes.

He sat up with a jerk and swore aloud. *Gone*, damn it! Where the devil was she? He felt disappointment and unreasoning anger in equal measure. How dare she abandon his bed? Had he given her leave? One night scarcely entitled her to such independence!

He shook his head and began to laugh, suddenly aware of his own absurdity. The sun was streaming through the windows and the clock showed nearly eight. It was later than he thought. Ram would be coming soon with his breakfast. Allegra had her duties. And her modesty. He could scarcely blame her for wanting to be discreet. The gossip in the Hall could be cruel. And that harpy, Rutledge, was only looking for an excuse to upbraid the girl.

He climbed out of bed and retrieved his nightshirt from the floor; he slipped it over his head, searched and found slippers and morning gown. He smoothed his hair and retied his ribbon, glancing over at the bed as he did so. If he could do nothing about its disheveled state, at least the master of Baniard Hall could look orderly.

And still the grin persisted. What was it about Allegra that so captivated him? It was more than just her passion. More than just the deep intensity of her soul that excited him. He had poured out his heart to her last night, telling her things he'd never spoken of before. Not even Ram had been privy to such an intimate confession. He should be regretting his indiscretion. But instead he felt light and free, as though the secret of Ruth's terrible ordeal had weighed like a heavy crime upon his soul.

Why had he told Allegra? He had wept last night, felt pain, passion, the awakening of emotions long buried. And all because of her. It was as though the fire of her own life force had warmed his moribund heart and stirred it back to life.

He went to the window and gazed out at the expanse of sun-filled lawn. It would be a fine morning. The first of September already. The raspberries would be ripe on the bushes, and the sheep would be fat and lazy on the hillsides. How should he spend such a glorious day? He couldn't wait for tonight to make love to her again. Perhaps he'd send for her. Invent some excuse—he needed her advice at the apothecary's in Newton—and spirit her away in his carriage for the whole day. He chuckled softly. He hadn't made love in a carriage since the reckless days of his soldiering.

And then he'd buy her a gown. He wanted to see her in something beautiful, something that did justice to her loveliness. Something low cut, but modest enough to hide that charming birthmark just above the nipple. Like a little half-moon, fawn-colored against the pale flesh of her breast. He felt unexpectedly proprietary about that birthmark; it was for him to see, and no one else.

If he admitted it to himself, he felt proprietary about the girl as well. Torn between giving her her freedom—the only decent thing to do—and keeping her with him for always. She'd leave for London the minute her bond contract was terminated. He had no doubt of that. But he wanted her to stay, and not only for his own sake. He wanted to keep her from seeking out Ellsmere and ruining her life. Perhaps now that they had become lovers, he could persuade her to confide in him. To tell him the why of the dark hatred that drove her. If she was willing to confess that she loved him, surely she'd trust him with her secrets.

He shook his head. *Love.* Who would have thought that any woman would ever again find him lovable? He felt a glow of satisfaction and gratitude, wondering how he could repay such devotion. Such a dear gift. Not with his own heart, surely. He wasn't ready to love again. Perhaps he was no longer capable of it. Still, that sweet creature...

"Christ's blood," he muttered aloud. It was absurd. He was an addlepated fool! Had it been so long since a woman had excited his desire that he could possibly imagine it was love?

He heard a sharp rap. "Good morning, Sir Greyston." Ram stood in the doorway, holding his usual breakfast tray, complete with its bottle of gin.

He smiled in pleasure. His appetite was keen this morning. "I'll breakfast in my drawing room," he said. After last night, his bedchamber seemed too private, too intimate, for an invasion of servants.

He settled into a comfortable armchair in his drawing room and patted a small table beside him. "Set your tray here, Ram," he said, "and pour me a cup of that chocolate. And then go and tell Mrs. Rutledge that I wish Allegra to attend me here."

"*Chocolate?*" Ram looked pleased.

"Chocolate. And bring me a chop or two to go with that bread and butter, on your way back. I'm famished." And grinning like an idiot again, he thought, struggling to suppress his smile. Though it was probably ridiculous to try to hide anything from Ram. He wondered how long it would take his valet to fathom what had happened here last night. Or any of the servants, for that matter.

Briggs came into the drawing room as Ram was leaving. He looked worried and distracted. "Your pardon for this disturbance so early, milord. But I think it were best to take a man with you if you plan to stroll in the park this morning."

"What the devil are you talking about, Briggs?" he said impatiently. "I'm perfectly sober, as you can see. I don't plan to fall down." He saw the pained look on Briggs's face, and remembered Allegra's words. "You have concern for my safety?" he asked, making an effort to sound civil.

"Yes, milord. Andrew found his dogs drugged this morning. Sleeping like kittens. There may be villains lurking in the park. The gardeners are out searching now, and Andrew has gone down to the dovecote to see if any birds are missing."

He frowned. "And my horses?"

"Hale and sound, and every one of them in his stall."

"The manor house?"

"I don't think anyone broke into the Hall. If they're still about, they're on the grounds."

"But how the devil could anyone have gotten into the park? The wall…?"

Briggs shook his head. "I myself saw to every inch of its repairs in June. And, since then, one of the gardeners inspects it by the week."

"Then how could the villains get in?"

The unpleasant voice of Mrs. Rutledge interrupted from the doorway. "Not 'villain,' Your Lordship," she purred. "'Villainess.' As to the 'how' of it, Humphrey was not at his post last night. He abandoned his lodge for a doxy. And so the creature was able to make her escape."

He felt the first cold stirrings of dread. "Escape? What creature?"

Mrs. Rutledge was enjoying her triumph. "Why, Allegra, of course," she crowed. "I myself went to her room to fetch her, when Cook noticed her missing at breakfast. Her room was empty. Her belongings are gone. I even sent Verity to look in the stillroom before I came to disturb you with the news of her disappearance. I've just now learned of the dogs. And Humphrey's dereliction that made the girl's flight possible." She smirked at Briggs. "Humphrey was *your* responsibility, Mr. Briggs!"

Grey rose angrily to his feet and glared at Mrs. Rutledge. He pounded his fist on the mantel beside him. "And *you* will answer for the girl's disappearance!"

The woman's fleshy lower lip quivered. "I'm well aware of my responsibilities, Your Lordship. If the girl chose to leave, I couldn't keep her from going. But I've already set the footmen on a search of the Hall, from top to bottom. If the jade has stolen anything, we'll soon know of it."

He muttered a dark oath. She was right, of course. A servant had a right to leave a master's employ. And unless anything was missing, dissatisfaction with the employment wasn't a crime. Nor was hasty flight. Not unless Grey wished to broadcast the fact that Allegra was a bond servant. He waved the housekeeper from the room. "Go about your business."

She curtsied and backed toward the door. "Good riddance, I say," she sniffed. "Miss High-and-mighty." She was out the door before he could explode.

He took out his anger on Briggs instead. "A pox on you! Do I pay you to be careless? What kind of useless fools do you hire? I want Humphrey sacked."

"It will be my pleasure, milord," Briggs answered grimly. He hesitated, then cleared his throat. "By your leave, I'll call off the gardeners' search. One can assume that the girl made a clean escape. If she was clever enough to feed a narcotic to the dogs, she would have planned everything with care. But there is the matter of her indenture contract…Do you wish to have it known? She can, of course, be hunted down for a runaway."

Her contract, he thought, his heart curdling with bitterness. They had made love twice. Perhaps, by her reckoning, each coupling was worth six months. He had begun by treating last night as a business affair. Why should he be surprised when the little baggage did the same?

"Tear up her contract, Briggs," he said savagely. "She bought off the remainder of her term last night."

The steward could scarcely conceal his surprise. "Bought off?"

"You heard me," he snarled. "I let her go."

Briggs sighed. "She was a fine stillroom maid. And a young woman of intelligence. I regret her leaving."

"Then you may mourn her. I'll not." Why did Briggs stand there as though he had lost a boon companion? She was just a chit of a girl, and not worth anyone's grief! He regained his chair and picked up his chocolate cup. Let the man see that *he* didn't give a damn!

"Your pardon, Sir Greyston." Jagat Ram emerged from his closet, his brow wrinkled with concern. "That blade...from the Nawab of Behar...the one with the rubies..."

Was he to be bedeviled by everyone this morning? "Yes, yes! I know the one. What of it?"

"'Tis gone, Sir Greyston. It was there last evening, when I left you for bed. I am always noticing your collection when I pass through your closet."

Damn her! Not content with betraying him, she had to steal from him as well? "Those stones will fetch a king's ransom," he muttered.

Briggs pressed his lips together in disapproval. "By your leave, milord, I'll have a warrant sworn out for the girl's arrest. For thievery. It shouldn't go unpunished. At the least, we should demand the return of the blade." He frowned. "That would explain her haste in leaving. I didn't think the girl was capable of it."

He laughed sardonically. "She's capable of attempted murder, or have you forgot? But let her go. I'm well rid of the minx. If it cost me a knife..." He shrugged off Briggs's protests. "She'll be bound for London, of course. To kill Lord Ellsmere. If I knew where the man was, I'd send him warning. A-a-ah!" He threw up his hands in disgust. "Why the devil should I care? If it makes her happy to see him dead..."

Briggs nodded in resignation. "As you wish, milord."

"Leave me now. Both of you. I'll ring for you when I want to dress, Ram."

He watched them file out of the room; then he lifted his cup and saucer and hurled them into the cold fireplace. The thick, dark chocolate oozed down the brass of the andirons. Damn her forever! Lies! All of it! The gentle warmth and understanding that had wormed from him his darkest secrets, the words of love, the intense sincerity in her eyes. All false. And the passion? Had that been pretense as well? Merely dutiful payment for her liberty?

Bah! He was the coward of Baniard Hall. He was the *dupe* of Baniard Hall. He had sunk so low in his own eyes that the hussy had found it simple to flatter his masculine pride, to gull him into thinking that she cared for him. A sly scheme to win her freedom, and nothing more.

He hesitated, then reached for the bottle of gin at his elbow. It burned in his mouth and his throat, hot and astringent. But it couldn't burn away the sweet taste of her lips. And, no matter how frantically he drank, head thrown back and gulping great mouthfuls like a rum-soaked tippler, it couldn't numb his brain to the memory of her face.

He slammed down the half-filled bottle, buried his face in his hands, and wept.

Grey Ridley held his candlestick next to the dark-green brocade that covered the walls along the great staircase. He shook his head and frowned. What an unpleasing color. What had possessed him to move into Baniard Hall without first changing the decorations? It was clear that old Baron Ellsmere had had neither the funds nor the taste to do justice to the fine architecture of the building. Odd that it had never troubled him before.

Perhaps, as Ram kept trying to tell him, he was regaining his sense of balance. Emerging from the cold darkness that had nearly destroyed him. Noticing things that had escaped him when he'd come to the Hall a short year ago.

He laughed bitterly. Or perhaps his sudden discontent with Baniard Hall had more to do with his present state of mind. The place had never felt like a lonely prison until...until she was no longer here to brighten its rooms. Perhaps that was why he now found it ugly.

He sighed and made his way slowly down the dim staircase, shielding his candle on the way. He crossed the entrance hall, opened a door, and descended another staircase to the lower ground floor. The kitchens were quiet. The servants' hall was dark. And Mrs. Rutledge's room. Only Briggs's office still showed a light beneath the door. He shook his head. The man was a glutton for work.

He sighed again. Nearly a week since she'd gone. And he was going mad. He could snap at his servants, as before. Pretend apathy, as before. Drink himself into insensibility and pray for a dreamless sleep. Just as before.

Yet everything was changed. He had worked like a dog in the almshouse and found no peace. He had engaged a whore for a night to help him forget, and had ended by sending her away in disgust. He had cringed as never before at the whispers of his servants, wondering if they knew how Allegra had made a fool of him.

He had even put aside his gin after the third day. Strangely, he had lost his taste for it. It was as though there was no room in him for anything but seething rage. It had purged his need for drink, burnt away the layers of indifference that had protected him, until he felt as though he had been thrust into a great furnace and melted down into one pure element: pain.

And beyond that, nothing but emptiness.

He opened the door to the stillroom. The little minx had had cures for everyone's ills. She'd rid the coachman of his stones, freed the cook's helper from her insomnia, and cured an epidemic of fever among the grooms. Perhaps he could find, among her bottles and nostrums, a cure for his discontent and gnawing anger.

He set down his candle and looked around the orderly room. Everything—bottles and jars, flasks and packets of powder—was clearly labeled in her graceful, florid hand. He wondered who had taught her to write so beautifully. Damn it, he wondered why it should matter to him! He uncorked a stone crock marked as a cordial and sniffed its contents. It smelled warm and spicy and vaguely familiar; she'd served this to him more than once. He took a deep swallow and replaced the cork. Perhaps he'd wait a while and see if it revived his spirits. If not, he could always try another.

He wandered around the stillroom, touching bowls and spoons and beakers. Rubbing his hands across the polished tin alembics. Fingering vials filled with colorful liquids. She had touched these selfsame objects. It haunted him, to know her presence was so near in this room.

He found her recipe book, still open and waiting, as though she would return in a moment and finish what she'd been writing. Idly, he flipped the pages, perusing her entries. It was strange to see himself mentioned at the end of almost every recipe: "His Ldshp. was pleased with this recipe for Barbados water." "His Ldshp. made a face at this imperial water, though he thinks I did not see it. Next time, add less ginger." "This *aqua composita* agreed with His Ldshp. He was in an excellent humor all the next day. Not a sign of the headache that had plagued him. Would that the ailments of his soul were so easily cured."

He scowled. Damn the wench! If she were so concerned with his well-being, why did she leave? He felt the anger growing again within him, the hot, helpless fury that tore at his vitals. With a savage growl, he picked up her recipe book and flung it against the shelves along the wall. There was a loud crash and a shattering of glass and stoneware. It brought him an odd measure of satisfaction.

He picked up the cordial he'd sampled, and reached for his candle. Perhaps tonight he'd be able to sleep.

"'Od's blood, milord! Is anything amiss?" Briggs stood at the doorway in his shirt and waistcoat, his face shadowed with concern.

In another moment, Mrs. Rutledge appeared behind him, yawning and hastily wrapping a voluminous cloak around her nightshift. "I heard a noise. Your Lordship...?"

He felt like a fool, a schoolboy caught where he oughtn't to be. "I wanted a cordial," he said defensively. "Is that so strange?" His words sounded false in his own ears. And they didn't explain why he felt it necessary to fetch the cordial for himself in the middle of the night, rather than ringing for a servant. "Why the devil don't we have a new stillroom maid yet?" he blustered.

"Your pardon, milord," said Briggs. "But Mrs. Rutledge hasn't been able to find a girl from the village who's willing and skilled at the art."

"Find someone in Ludlow then, damn it! Or train one of the girls here. Surely, for a few extra pounds…"

Mrs. Rutledge's face twisted in a sour grimace. It was one thing to be awakened from a sound sleep, her expression seemed to say. It was quite another to defend her hiring practices at this hour! "There's none of them can read *her* peacockish writing clear enough. All those high-flown loops and curls on the page. Her precious 'Lord Ridleys.'" As she said the words, the housekeeper curled her lip in scorn and wrote his name in the air with her finger. "She was always taking on airs. Putting herself above her station. Can you believe, milord, she even wanted *my* position?"

He frowned. Something wasn't quite right. What had the woman said? *Lord Ridley.* But all the entries in Allegra's book referred to him as His Lordship. "Where did she write 'Lord Ridley'?"

"Why I…in her recipe book, I suppose."

"No. I've only just looked through it. She never once writes Lord Ridley."

Mrs. Rutledge laughed nervously. "Oh, but she must have. I'm sure that…"

Christ's blood, the woman was blushing! And she looked as guilty as a prisoner in the dock. "*Where* did she write my name like that?" he demanded.

She was beginning to quake in fear. "A…letter," she whispered.

"What letter?"

Mrs. Rutledge looked for support from Briggs, but he scowled and folded his arms across his chest. "Answer His Lordship," he growled.

She gulped. "The day…the day she ran away. She left a letter in her room."

Grey fought the urge to strike the hag where she stood. "Now, by God, if you tell me you've destroyed it, I'll have you strung up by your thumbs!"

She gave a shaky giggle. "Of course not, Your Lordship. I'd never do such a thing! I meant to give it to you all along. I was only waiting until you were in a better humor."

He pointed to the door. "Fetch the letter, you jealous bitch," he said through clenched teeth. "You may thank God that you merely had the malice to withhold it, and not the courage to tear it up."

In the few minutes it took Mrs. Rutledge to scurry to her room and hurry back with the letter, Grey had paced the floor half a dozen times. She had written to him. And he had suffered, all this week, never knowing.

He snatched the letter from the housekeeper's fingers, broke the seal and unfolded Allegra's letter. His hands were shaking so violently that he could scarcely hold it steady at first. *She had written to him.* He took a deep breath, held the letter close to the candle, and read.

"My dearest Grey," it began. "It breaks my heart to leave you this way. God preserve me, I cannot promise even to return to you. The path that I have chosen, that I have sworn to take, will perhaps lead to my own downfall. But I have my duty. And the ghosts that haunt me are as real to me as those that haunt you. I beg you, Grey, to lay the past to rest. You can do no more to atone. Let it rest, and forgive yourself.

"As for me, forgive me and forget me. My course was set long before I met you. If I fail, nothing but death awaits me. If I succeed, I will have become a stranger to myself.

"They say that one sin breeds another. You are consumed with guilt for deaths for which you are blameless. What will become of me, when my hands are covered with blood I have chosen to shed? What will be left of your fair Allegra then?

"Live your life without me, Grey, and be happy. On those days when your soul is in pain, and drink seems your only release, remember the woman who loved you with all her heart and will love you forever. Allegra."

He turned away and covered his face with his hand. How could he have doubted her for a minute? How could he have heaped curses on her memory all this week? What a fool—to deny what his own eyes, his arms, his lips had told him. And now she was gone, set on her mad path to destruction.

My God! He swore to himself, filled with a sudden rush of panic. What if he was too late? He whirled to Briggs, the words pouring out of him in an anxious burst.

"Briggs! I know 'tis late. But I want you to write to Gifford in London tonight. Tell him to expect me on Saturday, at the latest. He's to open Morgan House at once."

A small, pleased smile tugged at the corners of Briggs's mouth. "Yes, milord."

"See if he can discover what has become of Tom Wickham. Baron Ellsmere, that is."

"Yes, milord."

He scoured his thoughts, then snapped his fingers. "The knife, of course! She will have pawned it, I should guess. Tell Gifford to inquire at all the shops."

The smile deepened. If his secretary could find either the knife or Ellsmere, he would surely find Allegra. "Yes, milord. You'll want Gifford to buy back the blade, of course."

"Certainly. It was a gift from a dear friend."

"Do you think you can find the girl, milord?"

"She'll have a week on me, but I doubt if she knows London. Where Gifford and I can go with certainty, she'll be finding her way. We may discover Ellsmere before she does."

"Shall I accompany you?"

"No. Ram will be enough. You're needed here."

"If I were you, I should take a second footman with you, milord. And armed. There has been talk of late. Highwaymen on the London road."

"Yes, of course." Highwaymen? He frowned in thought, his heart contracting in sudden fear. "My God, Briggs! What if she was harmed on the journey? She was alone when she left!"

The man's smile was filled with awareness. Grey wondered how much he guessed. "Be of good cheer, milord. I have no doubt she took the mail coach. A safe journey. I reckon she had enough money from what you paid her to buy a fare." He turned to the door. "I'll write to Gifford now."

"Wait." Grey held up his hand. "One thing more." He pointed to Mrs. Rutledge, who had been following the conversation with all the curiosity of a born gossip. "Rid me of that harpy."

Mrs. Rutledge squealed like a pig in a farmyard. "You *can't*, milord! I've served you well and faithfully."

"You'll go without a fuss, woman. And not a bloody reference from me!" He brandished Allegra's letter. "Or would you prefer to be arrested for stealing my correspondence?" He turned to Briggs as Mrs. Rutledge sputtered in outrage. "Sack the woman, and get me an *honest* housekeeper for a change. I'll pay good wages, but I'm damned if I'll allow my pockets to be picked any longer!"

The smile had become a grin. "*Yes*, milord!"

He returned the grin, pushed past a now-sobbing Mrs. Rutledge, and raced back to his rooms. He was glad to find Jagat Ram still up and waiting for him. "Prepare my clothes for a journey," he said. "We're leaving for London the day after tomorrow."

"London?" said Ram quietly. "Are you sure, Sir Greyston?"

He took a deep breath and shook his head. "No. I'm terrified. But I must find her."

Ram nodded. "Yes. I understand."

"Do you? She *loves* me, Ram," he said in wonder.

A gentle laugh. "Yes, I know."

That caught him by surprise. "Was I so blind, not to see? Or is it you, with your quiet ways, who manages to know everything that goes on in this house?"

"I do what I can to serve you, Sir Greyston."

He stared at Jagat Ram, cursing himself for a selfish clod. Had it been so long, and he so wrapped in his own miseries and drunken state, that he had failed to notice the man's loyal service? "You should go home," he said.

Ram shrugged. "In good time. When Allah wills it. For now, I am content, Sir Greyston. And you are needing me in London."

He scowled. Indeed. He would need all the help he could get to find Allegra. That foolish girl, to have run off like this. But the more he thought about it, the angrier he grew. "I may need you to keep me from strangling the girl when I find her," he muttered. "She could have told me of her plans. Damn it, she *should* have told me! Pray God she doesn't do anything rash before we find her. Proud, stubborn woman! She succors the whole world, takes on the burden of everyone's pain. Then the creature thinks that she must keep her own counsel. Wrestle her own dragons alone. 'Tis a foolhardy..." He stopped and glared at Ram, who had begun to chuckle softly.

"Why do you laugh?" he asked, his voice rising with indignation.

"I am thinking that that stubborn, proud woman has stolen your heart, if you will forgive my presumption."

"Stolen my...? Don't be absurd! 'Tis natural enough to have concern. The girl is a stranger to London, and she has embarked on a course of murder and folly. And anger, to be sure! I have a right to that. She stole my favorite knife, and ran away like a thief in the night. But stolen my heart?" He looked at Ram's wise expression, rubbed the back of his neck, and smiled ruefully.

"Yes," he said at last, "perhaps she has."

Chapter Fifteen

Summer was nearly over.

Allegra made her way down Great Russell Street toward Bloomsbury Square. The trees that lined the thoroughfare were tinged with the first colors of autumn, russet and soft gold glowing amid the dark-green foliage. The hawkers who cried their wares through the cobbled streets pushed barrows piled high with the bounty of the fall harvest. And the lamplighters were busily at work, cleaning lamps and replacing wicks. The coming of Michaelmas in two weeks would bring with it the enforcement of the Street Lighting Act. For six months, until Lady Day, the lamps would be lit from dusk to midnight. Allegra remembered Papa telling her of the glittering wonders of London on a wintry night.

She sighed. The time was passing, and she was no nearer her goal. She had been in the city for more than a week, and had precious little to show for it. She glanced down at her gown, a plain dark mantua of deep red cloth. It had been her one major purchase since she'd pawned Ridley's knife. It served two purposes. It was simple, yet handsome enough so that she could pass as a gentlewoman in the streets; a young woman who looked like a servant was subject to all manner of lewd entreaties by the London beaux.

And her new gown served another purpose. At her direction, the dressmaker had sewn a triangular pocket into the front bodice. It now held a very plain, but very deadly, dagger. To wear it near her heart was to remind herself of her vow. And whenever, in these past few days, she'd found her thoughts straying to Grey and the sweet ease of her life at the Hall, she had but to touch the dagger and feel its length pressing against the bones of her stays to be reminded of why she had come back to England. Why she wandered the streets of this vast, bustling city, wary of pickpockets, suspicious of every shopkeeper who held out his hand for a coin, yet eager to trust anyone who might help her to find Wickham.

A pox on that pawnbroker! No doubt he had marked her at once as an easy cully. With her simple country clothes and a costly knife that clearly was stolen. And she had been taken in. She had accepted his piddling offer for the blade, had even confided that she needed a solicitor to find a missing friend.

She laughed bitterly, catching the surprised stare of a passing clergyman. The pawnbroker must have been in league with that accursed solicitor all along. The two of them knew exactly how much money she had to spend. It had cost her half a crown a day. Double that amount yesterday, when the oily solicitor had smiled and sworn he had a friend who was sure he could find Thomas Wickham. It needed but a few extra coins, he'd said, to get his friend into the gambling house that Wickham was known to frequent.

And then this morning the rogue had told her that the search had been fruitless, and he would need another pound, at the very least, to continue to serve her. She had refused him, of course. She wondered now if he had ever done anything but take her money and share it with his confederate.

She reached Bloomsbury Square with its neat park and turned toward King Street on the east. She stopped a footman in front of one of the townhouses, and asked to be directed to the door of Dorothy, Lady Mortimer. She prayed that the woman had returned to London by now, and would remember her kindly.

She had hesitated to call on Lady Dorothy, fearful that word of her visit might get back to Grey. But she had no other friends in this city. And she was beginning to think—after her experience with the solicitor—that she'd need someone who traveled in aristocratic circles to find Lord Ellsmere. Random inquiries at taverns and shops had proved useless.

Lady Dorothy hurried to greet her almost as soon as she was ushered into the parlor. "My dear Allegra! You bring news from the country?"

She curtsied politely. "There's very little to tell, Your Ladyship. I've left Lord Ridley's employ."

"Oh." The smile faded from Lady Dorothy's face and she sank into a chair. She frowned down at the carpet, then lifted her eyes at last to Allegra and managed a faint smile. "You've come to London to be a lady's maid, then?"

"Not precisely, milady, though I thank you for remembering." She had already decided on the story she would tell. "I only want—"

Lady Dorothy interrupted her with an impatient click of her tongue. "Have you no messages for me?"

"No," she said, bewildered by the odd question. "Were you expecting any?"

"Not quite expecting, but…You have *nothing* to tell me?"

"Well," Allegra began, remembering Lady Dorothy's unhappy departure from Baniard Hall, "I feel sure that His Lordship has long since regretted your quarrels. But I have no message from him."

Lady Dorothy shook her head. "No, no! I meant Mr. Briggs. Surely he…" She buried her face in her hands. "Oh, I'm a fool. I was so sure I saw in his eyes…"

Allegra stared in astonishment. Could it be…? "Milady, can I bring you cheer?"

Lady Dorothy sighed and lifted her head, belatedly recalling her station. "Forgive me. This is scarcely your concern. What has brought you to my door?"

"I'm seeking a gentleman who once employed me. I wanted a reference from him. I heard he came to London. But I'm at a loss to find him. Beg your pardon, but you were so kind to me at the Hall, I dared presume to use your good offices to aid in my search."

"But *I* can give you references. I saw enough of your good character at Baniard Hall to speak for you."

"I thank you, milady. But I must have them from Lord Ellsmere."

"Thomas Wickham? I fear I don't know the man."

Allegra bit her lip. "Perhaps, someone else…?"

"Wait." Lady Dorothy frowned. "I think I heard something of him only the other day. I was walking in the Mall and met a friend. Oh, dear. What did he say? He'd heard the gossip at the Haymarket Theater. Yes, now I recall. Ellsmere is completely ruined, the poor man. He has been, for some time, thanks to his late father's gambling."

"Aye. I'd heard that was why he came to London. And is he here now?"

"For the moment. But only just. It seems that Providence has smiled upon him. He has inherited a small piece of property in Yorkshire. I think he's leaving from Gravesend this very week. Saturday, if I'm not mistaken. By packet boat, my friend said."

Allegra allowed herself a silent prayer. Thank the good Lord. Five days hence! How close she had come to missing Wickham. "And the name of his ship?"

"That, I know not."

She was filled with humble gratitude. God saw the righteousness of her cause. There would be time to learn the name of Wickham's ship and to engage passage for herself. She felt as though she were coming finally to the end of her long nightmare. "I thank you, Your Ladyship. I'll take my leave now."

Lady Dorothy rose from her chair and put a restraining hand on Allegra's arm. "No. Stay a little. At least tell me how things were at the Hall when you left." Her soft blue eyes held a silent plea.

Allegra debated with herself for only a moment. That fool Briggs would never speak for himself! "If you must know, Jonathan Briggs is miserable," she said. "He's desperately in love with you."

Lady Dorothy gave a cry of joy, her eyes filling with tears. She clasped her hands together and bent over them for a moment. "I knew it," she murmured. "My heart would not lie." She looked at Allegra in bewilderment. "But why has he never spoken of it to me?"

"Because he's penniless. And proud."

Lady Dorothy stamped her foot. "Proud? Oh, the muttonhead! I have a fortune. I could bring a marriage portion to our union that would keep us both comfortable. What more could he want?"

Her heart went out to the woman. "I, too, think he's a proud fool, milady. And I've told him so, more than once. But he refuses to court you, if he has nothing to offer."

Lady Dorothy's eyes flickered with hope. "You're his friend, I think. Can he not be persuaded? I should make it worth your while."

Allegra shook her head. "It would please me to have it so. And with no compensation save pleasure in your happiness. But he's a man of scrupulous honor. Surely you know that, milady. It would disgrace you both, he thinks, were you to stoop to marrying him. If he had a title other than gentleman, or a rich purse…But he has neither. And so he keeps his own counsel. And suffers in silence."

Lady Dorothy sighed in resignation. "I understand. I reckon 'tis that very honor which has drawn me to him. If he went against his own scruples to marry me, it would be a sad union. Shame would give way to recrimination. And from there to hatred. I've seen it happen with others, where the wife supports her husband." She sighed again, fighting her tears. "I must forget him, I suppose. But I thank you for your kindness in telling me. 'Tis a comfort to know he returns my love."

"I wish it could end in happiness, Your Ladyship," she said fervently. She curtsied and turned to leave.

"Wait. Where do you lodge?"

"The Bell Inn, in Wood Street, milady."

"Oh! But that's a dreadful, crumbling old place. Stay with me here. I should welcome your company. My brother Richard is still in the country. And I feel like a stranger in this city, after so many years in India. Stay with me."

"Alas, that will scarcely be possible. I planned to sail with Lord Ellsmere," she explained, realizing as she said the words how indecent that sounded. "That is, if he wishes to employ me again," she added, then stirred uncomfortably. That sounded almost as wanton.

If Lady Dorothy wondered about her traffic with Wickham, she was too gracious to show it. "Stay until the ship sails, then," she said. "Be my companion. And perhaps you can mix for me that most excellent eye balm you prepared at Baniard Hall." She bit her lip in sorrow. "I fear there will be a great deal of weeping in the weeks to come."

Allegra hesitated. It would be a pleasant stay, and she liked Lady Dorothy. But she had one concern. "If Lord Ridley should come to visit, I shouldn't want him to know of my presence here. I fear he would persuade me to return to the Hall." That was surely no lie, she thought with a pang of regret.

"I doubt that he would wish to visit. Not after what happened. The rupture in our friendship…and with Richard away…But he'd never learn of your stay, in any event. You have my word on that." Lady Dorothy twisted her fingers together in concern. "Is he still drinking so much?"

"No, milady. I think he is somewhat improved."

"How glad I am to hear that. Perhaps the pain of Ruth's death is beginning to fade at last. Perhaps if he hadn't worshipped her so much, if he had seen her clearly, it would have been easier for him."

Allegra found that an odd thing for Lady Dorothy to say. See Ruth clearly? "What should he have seen?" she asked.

"It may simply be gossip, you understand. But I've heard talk lately that the Pickerings—Ruth's family—boasted among their friends of having cheated Grey."

"What do you mean? How cheated?"

"They were rich in land but heavily in debt, so 'tis said. They scraped together a considerable dowry. Largely borrowed, I think. To make it seem that Ruth had no need of a good marriage. And then, once the vows were given, they contrived to have Ruth prevail upon Grey for vast sums of money at every opportunity. He gave it willingly, and never asked for an accounting. Thanks to that, the Pickerings are now almost free of their debts. They only regret that the golden goose died with Ruth. Or so I've heard tell."

"Oh, poor Grey!" cried Allegra without thinking. "That is…" she blushed, "His Lordship. To be duped so foully. Small wonder the Pickerings hated him so when his wife died, and spread the vile rumors of murder."

Lady Dorothy nodded. "And Ruth must have known of their devious plot. There's no way she could have been innocent. Oh, I wish I could tell Grey of it. But he would only see the good in her, and despise me for staining her memory."

Allegra gulped away her unhappy tears. "He'll see the truth when he wishes to see it. And not a moment before, Lady Dorothy. 'Twould be folly to malign a dead woman."

Lady Dorothy eyed her shrewdly. "You must call me Dolly. For we're sisters, I think, sharing the same heavy burdens of love. Come." She slipped her arm through Allegra's and turned to the door. "I'll have my servants fetch your furnishings from the Bell. Come. Walk with me in the garden until candlelight. Talk to me about Jonathan. And I'll tell you of the Grey Morgan I knew long ago."

"Right this way, Mistress Mackworth. Cap'n Smythe be waiting in the roundhouse." The grizzled seaman guided Allegra up the ladder that led from her cabin in the aft of the ship to the open poop deck. "Mind the pitch of the ship," he said, taking her by the elbow and steering her to the door of the large cabin.

"We're well away at last," she said, scanning the distant coastline and the sunset sky. "Have we left the Thames yet for the open water?"

"Not a quarter of an hour ago." He pointed toward the still-bright west and a cluster of houses along the shore. "There be Leigh-on-Sea, at the mouth of the river."

"And we have had our clearing from the customs men? With no disturbances, I trust?" She'd stayed secluded in her cabin, well furnished with food, since coming aboard Saturday afternoon. She had no wish to be closely questioned by the authorities while they inspected the ship for contraband; she was carrying far too much money for a woman of her seeming humble station. She had even arranged a small payment to the searcher of the customs so that he would leave her and her belongings in peace.

The seaman nodded in answer to her question. "Aye. All's shipshape."

"And who will be at the captain's table?" she asked. She knew it would be Wickham, of course. She had questioned the mate and learned that Wickham had paid for his meals, as she had. Her heart beat in wild impatience to meet him at last. But she was curious about the other passengers. Since Captain Smythe had stayed ashore at Gravesend to observe the Sabbath, they had all been left to their own devices.

"Not too many at table," replied the seaman. "Most of 'em has chose to furnish their own meals. Cap'n Smythe and the mate, to be sure. And the lord what come aboard just afore you did, on Saturday. And there be one other gentleman, what rowed over from Tilbury Fort as we were weighing anchor."

He opened the door and ushered her into the roundhouse. It was a large and airy cabin, which served the captain for his quarters. Near the expanse of windows, a round table had been set with a fine white linen cloth and an abundance of pewter plates, cutlery, and drinking cups. There was a flask of wine and a jug of ale on the table, as well as a bowl of steaming squash and a platter of fresh bread and cheese. A seaman in a white jacket and head cloth stood nearby, holding a large dish of roasted pigeons. Clearly, Captain Smythe believed in his comforts.

But Allegra scarcely had eyes for her surroundings, nor for the captain and his mate who had jumped to their feet at her entrance. Her attention was on the man who sat beneath the windows and leaned back in his chair, one leg crossed over the other.

She had been prepared for his youth—he would be no more than twenty-four or -five now, by her reckoning. But she wasn't prepared for his softly round and pleasant face, the boyish smile that played at his mouth, the jovial good humor in his eyes. He wore a small peruke, but he hadn't quite managed to tuck up every lock of his reddish-gold hair under it; several wisps straggled onto his neck. Moreover, his shoulders were dusted with an excess of white powder that had shaken loose from his wig. His dark-gray suit was ill-fitting, and his carelessly tied cravat was beginning to fray.

At the captain's introduction, he smiled broadly, struggled to disentangle his legs, stumbled against the table, and managed at last to haul himself to his feet. "Mistress Mackworth! A pleasure!" he boomed, holding out his hand.

She nodded, but kept her hands at her sides. "Lord Ellsmere." She forced herself to sound civil. But giving him her hand was more than she could manage.

He didn't seem to notice the slight. He continued to beam as the mate seated her, then regained his own chair. "I' faith, when Captain Smythe told me there would be a gentlewoman at his table, he failed to mention how beautiful she was."

"You are too kind, milord," she murmured, and contrived to return his smile as warmly as she could. Perhaps she could use his geniality to her advantage. She had planned to creep into his cabin tonight, stab him, and throw her knife overboard; since there were at least a dozen passengers on the ship, it would be difficult to connect the killing to her. But if Wickham proved as agreeable and tractable as he seemed, her task would be even simpler. She could lure him onto the deck at any time during the voyage, kill him, and push him overboard.

She shivered at her own cold-bloodedness. It was one thing to plan his murder. But if she found the courage to carry it out, could she live with it on her conscience for the rest of her life? Be still, Mama, she thought. I *will* avenge you all.

"You're shivering, ma'am," he said, shaking his head. "Let me send for something to cover your shoulders."

"No. 'Tis not the cold. Only a sudden troubling memory."

"Then I charge myself with cheering you this evening." He reached for the glass decanter. "Let me offer you some of the captain's excellent wine." He filled her cup, then set the wine bottle back in its place on the table. As he did so, the large, turned-back cuff of his coat caught at his own drinking cup and toppled it, spilling the remains of his wine onto the cloth. He grinned, shrugged, righted his cup, and calmly refilled it. "I've christened your cloth, Captain Smythe," he said with a laugh.

"We've seen rough waters, Lord Ellsmere. 'Tis not the first spill."

Nor yet the last, I'll wager, thought Allegra wryly, watching Wickham's ungainly movements. She felt a surge of unreasoning anger. *This* was her adversary? *This* was the man she was sworn to destroy?

He took a large swallow of his wine and smiled at the captain and the mate. "I count on you gentlemen for a fair voyage," he said. "The last time I made a sea trip..." He looked beyond their heads and his smile deepened. "But here's our other messmate, come to join us at last. Bless me, but I think I know you, sir!" He jumped to his feet in pleasure.

"Yes, we've met, Lord Ellsmere. When I bought Baniard Hall from you."

Allegra froze in shock at the sound of the deep voice behind her. In another moment, Grey Ridley had moved to the table and was holding out his hand to Wickham.

Dear God, she thought, feeling the sudden pounding of her heart in her breast. She didn't know whether she was glad or dismayed to see him. If he had followed her, it could only mean that he wanted to keep her from her sworn path. But, oh! How handsome he looked, how wonderful to see his dear face again!

He shook hands with Wickham across the table, then turned to Allegra and reached for her fingers. "'Tis Mistress Mackworth, the captain tells me." At her dumb nod, he lifted her fingers to his lips and kissed them softly. She trembled, remembering the feel of those lips on her mouth and body. "And I am Greyston, Viscount Ridley," he finished. He released her hand and sat down beside her.

"Your Lordship," she murmured, giving him a tender smile that held all her love in its depths.

He smiled back with his mouth, but she heard the hard crunch of his jaw, and saw the cold light in his eyes. "I trust we shall have a pleasant voyage, ma'am."

She stared at him, bewildered and confused. Why was he angry? Was he so unforgiving at her leaving?

Captain Smythe motioned to his servant, who brought around the meat. "Your man doesn't intend to join us, Lord Ridley?"

"No. Jagat Ram prefers the solitude of his own cabin." He poured himself a cup of wine, then held it up to the captain's servant. "If you'll be so kind as to put a bit of water in this."

"You're guarding your drinking, sir?" said Captain Smythe.

"Yes. I found that I was beginning to do damage to my constitution with an excess of gin."

Allegra felt a thrill of joy at his words. "And you have foresworn gin, milord?"

"For good and all, ma'am. I need to keep my wits about me. I have lately discovered that the world is peopled with creatures, such as yourself, perhaps, who act rashly and foolishly. If I'm to keep them from their mad course, I must be sober." His eyes were like glittering knives of cold, carved amber. His voice was sharp with sarcasm.

Allegra turned away and bent to her food. It would be twice as difficult for her now. She had not one adversary, but two.

Wickham's hearty laugh filled the cabin. "That sounds far too serious and calculated, Ridley. When last we met, you had nothing more in mind than to retire to a quiet refuge in the country. You no longer enjoy the Hall, then?"

"The country has served its purpose to refresh me, sir. I now find that there are certain things missing from it. And until they can be restored or replaced..." He glanced briefly at Allegra and scowled. "But you, Lord Ellsmere. How fare you, since you sold the Hall?"

Wickham stabbed his pigeon with his fork and smiled ruefully when a gob of grease spurted onto his waistcoat. "Not well. Not well at all, sir. My father, alas, liked fast women, slow horses, and every game of chance devised by man. And expected me to pay for his pleasures after his death."

"Which you have, most commendably, so I've heard."

"I' faith, it was a formidable task that took me the better part of two years to accomplish. And most of my inheritance." His face brightened. "But, having said that, I must tell you that I have renewed prospects. My mother's aunt—a dear old creature—has just died in the fullness of her age, and left me her house in Yorkshire. Whitby, in the North Riding. A charming seacoast town. Besides the house, there's a bit of land and a modest income that goes with it. A man could take up farming quite comfortably. In point of fact, you find me on my way there now, sir, to take up residence."

"And with great good humor, I think," said Grey. "You seem happily resigned to your lowered station."

For the first time, Wickham's jovial expression deepened into a frown. "I'm not a man of driving ambition, Lord Ridley. It ruined my family."

And mine as well, thought Allegra bitterly. Why was Thomas Wickham such an ordinary, reasonable young man? She wanted to hate him. She *needed* to hate him!

"And may I ask why you are aboard, Lord Ridley?" said Wickham.

"I'm searching for a bond servant of mine. A runaway. I had reason to think she might be going to Yorkshire."

"But that's a serious offense, milord," said Captain Smythe. "Why don't you call in the authorities, and get a warrant for her arrest?"

"'Tis a capital crime, sir. And I wouldn't see the wench hanged for it." He cleared his throat; it was a strangely ominous sound. "Which is not to say that the saucy creature doesn't deserve to feel my hand across her backside when I find her!"

Allegra's head snapped up in alarm, only to find him smiling grimly at her. She gulped and tried to keep her voice from shaking. "But a bond servant, Lord Ridley. It seems so cruel. Wouldn't you consider releasing the woman from her contract?"

"I was prepared to do so, but she betrayed my trust. Now, I'd need a great deal of persuasion to be convinced. Listen, now…" he said, ticking off the points on his long fingers, "she ran away in the night. She refused to tell me of her plans, though she had every reason to think I'd be sympathetic to her. And she's a damnable thief. Would you trust a woman like that? No matter how many letters she left you?"

"It would depend on whether or not you believed her letter," she murmured. Surely he couldn't think that her avowal of love was merely another devious trick! "Did you believe it?" she whispered.

His glance softened, reminding her of the tender lover he had been that night. "I did. And I do." Allegra felt relief flooding through her. He believed in her love. He forgave her. Then his eyes grew suddenly hard and she trembled. "But it scarcely assuages my anger at her running away," he growled. "The wench still owes me for that."

Captain Smythe laughed as he rose from the table. "I should not want to be in that girl's shoes when you do find her!" He turned to his mate. "Come, Baines. To work. The sky was clear this evening, but old Godwin was complaining of grief in his bones. And his bones never lie."

"Aye, Cap'n. We shall have storm by morning."

"Well, as the old tars would say, 'Bid the wind blow devil, the more wind the better boat.'" He nodded to his guests and left the roundhouse, the mate trailing behind.

Ellsmere sighed. "I do dislike rough seas. I fear I haven't the guts for them. Begging your pardon, ma'am."

"I find it helps to take the air," said Grey. "If I were you, I should avoid the solitude of a cabin, and seek the deck when you can."

Allegra had had her share of seasickness on her voyage from America. "But to look at the horizon riding up and down only makes it worse."

Grey raised a mocking eyebrow. "I think that Lord Ellsmere would be infinitely safer on deck, with his eyes closed and in full view of others, than he would be below. Who knows what dangers lurk where no one can see?"

She had a sudden fear that Grey might tell Wickham of her plans. She laughed nervously. "Will you have Lord Ellsmere shrinking from empty shadows, milord?"

"I'd only warn him of genuine dangers should I deem it necessary," he said pointedly. "As I'd warn anyone in danger. Including my missing bond servant, who would be wise to take heed."

She was growing quite weary of the hostile edge to his voice. "That...*saucy* creature?" she asked, her lip curling in disgust.

His eyes narrowed. "She'll pay a forfeit that she'll not soon forget."

"That sounds exceeding cruel, Your Lordship," she said through clenched teeth. "You're quite sober now, I see. But are you any kinder than you were in your gin-soaked days?" She rose abruptly from the table, smoothing her skirts. "By your leave, gentlemen," she murmured, and swept from the room, leaving a scowling Grey behind her.

She closed the door of her cabin and threw herself on the bunk. Curse him! He couldn't stop her—not even with his angry threats. Not when she'd come this far, endured so much!

She looked around the snug cabin. Like the roundhouse, it was comfortably appointed, with a large bunk between the bulkheads, and a small table and chair. Captain Smythe treated his passengers well, if they had the money to pay for furnishings.

She laughed bitterly, remembering her passage over from the Carolinas only this past spring. Cramped into a dark hole just above the stinking bilge, starving most of the time, fearful that one of the seamen would see the woman beneath her boy's disguise and rape her.

As for the Baniard family's voyage in the convict ship all those long years ago...She shuddered. She would never, *never* forget that horror. Nor the fact that the Ellsmeres had been the cause. By God, whether Grey tried to interfere or not, Thomas Wickham would never see the coast of Yorkshire!

She sat for a long time, her thoughts in a turmoil, while the light faded and the cabin dimmed. She lit her lantern and watched it sway gently with the movement of the ship. She thought she heard sounds in the passageway beyond her door; Grey and Lord Ellsmere must have gone to their own cabins by now.

Grey. She ached to throw herself into his arms, to beg him to make love to her. But she had her duty. And that came first. Perhaps she would search for him, force him to understand that she couldn't live her own life until Wickham was dead. Perhaps if he saw her desperation, he'd leave her in peace to do what she must.

She opened the door and stepped out into the passageway. She knew which was Wickham's cabin; she'd asked the mate almost as soon as she had come aboard. But she didn't know where Grey was berthed. She hesitated, frowning at the several doors that opened onto the dim passage.

Suddenly, one of them opened, and Grey was there, tall and menacing. Allegra's heart constricted with dread. His hand shot out and clamped around her wrist. He pulled her, protesting, into his cabin and slammed the door. The hanging lantern above his head cast terrifying shadows across his scowling face. He wrapped her tightly in his fierce embrace and glared down at her.

"You may kill him in the morning, if you must," he growled. "But tonight, damn it, you belong to me!"

Chapter Sixteen

His mouth ground down on hers in an all-consuming kiss. She gasped as he forced his tongue between her lips, thrusting it savagely into her mouth as though no part of her was safe from his overbearing possession. His hands roamed her body; he clutched her flanks through her skirts and held her against his swelling loins until she trembled with longing. Her fear melted away, to be replaced by a burning hunger, a desperate need.

It was still so new to her—to make love with a man. Her body scarcely remembered the hard fullness of him within her, the sensation of intimate flesh pressing against flesh. But her heart recalled the thrill.

She threw her arms around his neck and welcomed his kiss, gliding her tongue sensuously against his. He groaned and dropped one hand from her body to fumble with his clothing. In another minute, he had gathered up her skirts to her waist. He slid his hand along her bare thigh, lifted her leg and guided it to wrap around his hip. She felt his rigid manhood against the moistness of her cleft and held her breath, anticipating his loving entrance. Instead, he growled like a beast capturing its prey, tightened his grip on her thigh, and plunged wildly into her.

She cried out and clung to him, returning his impassioned kisses with her own. She had forgotten how glorious it was. And when he began to move, rocking against her sensitive flesh in a tantalizing rhythm, she felt the stirring of sensations that were new and strange and frighteningly wonderful. It was as though there were a taut band somewhere within her body, a band that twisted tighter and tighter with each thrust of his loins. She knew it would snap, she knew it would explode. And what would follow after that, God alone knew. She only knew it was sweet agony to feel the tension building.

"Godamercy," she breathed, throwing back her head in rapture, "don't stop."

He scowled down at her, then abruptly withdrew his shaft and pushed her away. "No," he muttered darkly, "not yet, my impatient Allegra. I'll know every inch of you first." He reached for the bodice of her gown and began to tug roughly at the hooks.

She returned his frown, feeling her rising excitement die. He meant to torment her before he satisfied her—or himself. And not out of love. But because the cauldron of rage still boiled within him. She thought at first to leave, to storm out of his cabin, to refuse to be a party to his ill humor.

Then her common sense reasserted itself. She hadn't forgotten his threat of chastisement. He had every right to take his hand to her—she still belonged to him, by law. No matter what they had bargained that night. He might even have brought the accursed contract with him. She'd find no refuge with Captain Smythe if she sought his protection.

She sighed. Better to accept Grey's lovemaking, even in anger, than to feed his wrath by resisting. He was perilously close to the edge; she could see it in his eyes. If she dared to reject him now, and shatter his fragile pride…

The knife! In a sudden panic, she remembered the knife in her bodice. She pushed away his fingers and clutched at her bosom. If he should find it hidden there! "You needn't be my maidservant, Grey," she said, forcing herself to sound calm and reasonable. "I can do for myself." She turned away, working at the fastenings of her gown and stays. She could hear behind her the sounds of his own clothing being removed— the clump of shoes, the rasp of velvet breeches, the silken whisper of cravat and shirt. As she finished her own disrobing, she felt his hands on her bare shoulders.

"Don't turn around yet," he ordered.

She tensed as he slid his hands down her back to cup the soft roundness of her buttocks. It was not quite a caress; his hands were hard, urgent—kneading the tender mounds with a roughness that bespoke his continuing anger, not his passion. She felt a thrill of renewed fear. Was this merely a prelude to something more painful? Would the fondling end with the sharp smack of his hand against her bare flesh? Worse still, would she suddenly find herself sprawled across his knees, like a child, awaiting a humiliating punishment?

By all the Saints, she wasn't about to wait like a meek bird to find out! She whirled around and glared at him, her chin thrust forward in defiance. "Do you intend to beat me, or make love to me?"

His face told her that she'd been foolishly rash to challenge him. His thick brows were drawn together in a scowl, and his mouth was set in a tight line. He seemed to be debating with himself over what would bring him the most satisfaction.

She gulped at the savage look in his eyes, and took a step backward. At that moment, he reached for her, swept her into his arms, and tossed her onto his bunk. He threw himself on top of her and kissed her hard, his mouth demanding a response. She sighed—there was as much relief as pleasure in her reaction—relaxed, and lifted her arms to his neck.

His hands on her wrists stopped her. He stretched her arms over her head and held them there, pressing her into the softness of the thick straw pallet. She laughed gently and tried to pull loose; she wanted to touch him, she wanted to explore his dear body with her fingertips. But instead of releasing her hands, he tightened his grip. "Grey?" she said tremulously, and struggled against his hold. It was useless. His hands were like chains, shackling her to the bunk. She felt like a helpless prisoner, weak and powerless against her captor. She writhed in a ferment of impotence. "Let me go!"

"I told you that you belong to me tonight," he growled. "I intend for you to know it." Though she resisted with all her strength, he jammed his knee between her closed thighs and spread her wide, then planted his burning shaft at the juncture between her legs. But instead of entering her, he glided back and forth against her tender flesh, a sensual stroke that roused her in spite of herself. Again and again he rubbed his firm manhood against her, teasing her to a fever of longing and desire. She ceased her struggles and closed her eyes, aching to feel his hard length within her, to quench the flames that had begun to burn in her loins. She arched her hips to meet him, desperate to force him to take her, to enter her. To satisfy her unfulfilled need. And still the torment continued.

She opened her eyes to look at him. His face was granite-like and impassive. She groaned in frustration. "In the name of God, Grey," she pleaded, "have a little mercy."

"As you had mercy, when you ran away without so much as a word to me? Damn you, I nearly went mad, wondering how you could leave me like that."

She twisted and twitched beneath him, her arms helpless and pinioned, her body equally trapped, a captive of her own desire. "And so you torture me now?"

"No, God help me," he muttered. "I want you as much as you want me. But be warned. I won't be gentle with you tonight. I can't. Not yet."

"I don't care," she whispered, and closed her eyes again.

She gasped at the shock of his savage entrance. He buried himself deep within her, thrusting again and again with a fierce, pounding tempo that shook her to her very soul. He was hard and strong and brutal, each stroke of his manhood a conquering assault that was very close to pain. She felt as though she would explode and dissolve into nothingness beneath his demanding possession. She cried out, torn with the desire to be released from her agony, yet never wanting him to stop.

In response to her fervent cry, he let go of her wrists, slipped his hands under her writhing hips and pulled her even closer to his surging loins. She could feel the jolt of each wild thrust deep within her belly. Again and again, until she thought she'd be ripped asunder. She lost all sense of reality. She clung to him, raking his back with her nails in an excess of passion. She was floating, trembling, soaring. Helpless beneath his ferocious attack, yet heedless of her own will. Pain was pleasure. Surrender was joy.

She felt the hot flames racing madly through her body. Burning her flesh, blazing into her face, roaring in her ears. Release came in a final explosive shudder as Grey convulsed above her and collapsed. She could feel the hot wetness of his sweat on her breast, the pounding of his heart against her ribs. His ragged breath was a heavy rasp next to her ear.

At last he stirred. "Damn you, you perverse witch. If ever you leave me again…" His tone was more gentle than his words. He lifted his head and kissed her. There was warmth and peace in his eyes, in his kiss.

She gazed at him in wonder, sensing—with that flash of intuition that was so much a part of her—what had happened. She had atoned, with her body, for all the years of pain he had suffered. All his anger, all his helpless rage, had come pouring out in that one savage act of love. "Are we forgiven now?" she asked softly.

He frowned. "Forgiven?"

"For abandoning you."

He swore softly, rolled over and sat up, rubbing the back of his neck in uneasiness. "I must have been mad, to use you so roughly. I should beg *your* pardon, not the other way round. Of course you're forgiven."

"Both of us?"

"What do you mean, both?"

"Myself…and Ruth."

He started at her words and looked away; he stared for a long time at the swaying lantern, his brow wrinkled in thought. After a while, he turned to Allegra with a rueful smile and shook his head. "I never thought of it until now. I suppose, all unaware, I *was* angry and unforgiving. That she should die. That she should leave me."

"As did your saucy wench." She smiled and pulled him down to lie beside her, feeling a warm contentment that flooded her with joy.

He grunted. "My saucy wench risked a great deal."

"Would you have punished me instead of making love to me?"

He stroked her bottom with a tender hand. "It did cross my mind," he said dryly.

"For running away?"

"No. I had Briggs tear up your bond contract."

She was glad of *that* news! "For stealing your dagger, then?"

"No. I reclaimed it from that rascally pawnbroker in Change Alley."

"Then why did you follow me? And threaten punishment in such a cruel way at supper?"

"Because, my fair Allegra, my sweet thief," he said, kissing her with a tenderness that made her tremble, "you had stolen my heart. And then had the temerity to go away."

"Oh, Grey," she said, nestling in his arms. "You know I didn't want to. I meant every word in my letter."

He held her tightly and kissed the top of her head. "I know," he said gruffly.

"I'm sorry about stealing that beautiful knife. I had no other way. No means to support myself in London."

"'Tis forgotten. I told you, I reclaimed it. The pawnbroker even directed me to the Bell Inn to find you. You'd already gone. Where were you?"

"With Dolly. That is, Lady Dorothy Mortimer."

"Poor Dolly. And Richard. I treated them badly at the Hall, drunken fool that I was."

"I think they understood, and are only waiting for you to hold out the hand of friendship again." She sighed unhappily. "Poor Dolly."

"Such a deep sigh? Simply because I was uncivil to her? It can be remedied."

"'Tis not you. 'Tis Jonathan Briggs."

"Briggs? Uncivil? Did he dare to insult my guests?"

She laughed softly. "Of course not. His only failing is pride. And a too-tender heart."

While Grey shook his head in disbelief, Allegra told him of the hopeless, silent love that had blossomed between his steward and Lady Dorothy. "That bloody fool, Briggs," he exclaimed at last. "To refuse to speak up! And all for the want of money?"

"'Tis his sense of honor, and he refuses to bend."

"And this was happening while Richard and Dolly were at the Hall? Under my very nose? Was I too blind to see it?"

"You were too intoxicated most of the time to see it," she chided, then snuggled against him to soften her reproach.

He snorted, but returned her embrace. "And you're as saucy as ever you were in the Hall. I once demanded a kiss from you as a forfeit for your insolence. I think the price has now gone up."

She felt the sudden, unexpected hardness of his member against her body and giggled. "As have other things, milord."

He laughed outright at her sally. It warmed her heart to hear. "Come to me then, you devil," he said. "I'll never get enough of you." He covered her body with his and took her lips in a sweet kiss. And when he made love to her this time, it was with a tender gentleness that left her trembling and weeping for joy.

After a little while, he stirred. "I have a powerful thirst. Look in my sea chest. I think Ram left me a flask of good claret."

She eyed him with curiosity and more than a little disquietude. But she obeyed, fetching the wine and filling a tumbler with the ruby liquid.

He took the proffered glass and laughed softly. "Take the frown from your brow, my sweet. I drink a bit of wine for the pleasure of it. No more than that. I drank gin for forgetfulness. I wasn't sunk so deep into corruption that I couldn't tell the difference."

"And now?"

"I don't want to forget a moment with you," he said hoarsely. "Not a solitary hour." He reached out and stroked the side of her face with a gentle hand. "Until you came along, only my toil in the almshouse made sobriety worth my while." He finished his wine, stood up, and pulled her into his arms. "If we haven't reached Yarmouth by morning, I'll have Captain Smythe make for the port. Ram can arrange for a carriage to take us back to the Hall."

She pulled free of his embrace and shook her head. "No, Grey. I cannot."

"Damn it, are you still set on your bloody course? You'll come back to Baniard Hall with me. I'll not hear a word of rebellion!"

She stamped her bare foot at his high-handed tone. "Am I still your bond servant?"

"Of course not. I told you…"

"Then I can travel where I choose. And I intend to follow Wickham to Yorkshire."

He scowled. "Why do you always call him Wickham, not Ellsmere?"

Her lip curled in scorn. "Wickham is the name of the whole low-born, accursed family. 'Tis how I shall always think of them. Ellsmere is a dishonest title for an unworthy line."

"And so you'll kill him?"

She felt the bile in her mouth, bitter with her hatred. "I'll follow him to the ends of the earth. Until I stand at last on his grave."

He grabbed her savagely by the shoulders. "In the name of God, *why?*"

"Please, Grey," she begged, "let me do what I must."

"Choose life," he said fervently. "Choose the future and forget the past, as you so often urged me to do."

He mustn't sway her. He mustn't! She had her honor and her duty. "Don't you understand? I have no future until the past is laid to rest."

She saw the warmth fade from his golden eyes, until they were like hard amber. "Until Wickham is dead?" he asked angrily.

"Yes."

"Will you persist in your folly? By God, Allegra, if I must, I'll have you dragged back to the Hall in chains. For the theft of my knife."

She glared at him. "If you do, you'll live with a wraith. An empty shell of a woman, and nothing more."

He sighed, momentarily defeated, and held out his hands. "Come to bed. We'll speak of this in the morning. Perhaps I can persuade you at last to trust me, to open your heart to me. Come to bed, fair Allegra."

Despite the warm comfort of his arms, she slept fitfully, waking just before dawn to the violent heave and pitch of the ship. The light was gray at the window, and the panes rattled against the rising wind. She could hear the creak and groan of the ship's timbers, and the squeak of straining ropes and tackles. The captain's augur had spoken truly: there was a storm brewing.

Allegra eased herself from the bunk and quietly donned her garments. If it wasn't blowing too hard yet, perhaps she'd walk on deck for a while. Her brain teemed with confused thoughts; the fresh air might clear her head. If she told Grey, if she trusted him, would he urge her to turn from her course? Or, having learned her family's dire story, would he instead understand and give her his blessing?

She moved along the passageway and stepped out onto the deck, drawing in a surprised breath at the force of the wind that assailed her. It tugged at her skirts and whipped tendrils of hair around her face. The air was chill; she thought at first to fetch her cloak from her cabin, then changed her mind. She wouldn't stay out that long.

The sky was still quite dark; she could see only dimly the forms of seamen in the masts above her, as they hastened to trim the sails against the wild wind. The seas were high; cresting waves crashed into the bows, sending up sprays of briny water. Allegra tasted salt on her tongue.

Clinging to the railings and handholds, she made her way down to the main deck. The wind was quieter here. She found a thick coil of rope, well sheltered by the forecastle, and sat herself down. The main deck was a ferment of activity, with seamen hurrying to stretch canvas over the open hatches, or tighten ropes and stays, or scurry aloft at the mate's bidding.

The growing storm was as busy as the sailors. It rattled the yardarms in their chains, blew fiercely through the rigging, lifted the ship to each surging wave and tossed it down a moment later. Allegra felt as though she were a serene island in the midst of all this turmoil and hubbub; if she sat here quietly, perhaps the world and all its troubles would pass her by.

"Begging your pardon, Mistress Mackworth, but you'd best seek your cabin." The mate, Baines, stood before Allegra, his frowning face crusted with salt. "'Tis not likely this blow will stop anytime soon."

"Are we in any danger?"

"Lookee." He pointed across the port bow. In the brightening dawn, Allegra could just make out the dark outline of flat-topped cliffs. "Cap'n's afeared we be too close to land. We was blown in at Winterton Ness. And now we be forced to run west. If the wind don't turn, we could run aground. Or be driven in at Cromer Bay."

"Is that so dreadful?" Somehow, the thought of a bay didn't seem very threatening.

He laughed sharply. "They don't be calling it the Devil's Throat for nothing! Go below, ma'am. 'Twill be safer."

She nodded and rose from her perch. The ship was now tossing violently on the stormy seas. She made her careful way across the deck to the ladder that led up to the quarterdeck. She was reluctant to go inside; she would have to deal with Grey, and her own roiled emotions. Slowly, she climbed the ladder, then paused, her hand going to her bosom.

Wickham was there. His eyes were squeezed shut and he inhaled great gulps of air, as though he hoped to placate his queasy stomach by the act. He had buttoned his waistcoat carelessly, his wig was askew, and his cravat flapped in the strong breeze. Clearly, he had only just reached the deck in time. Sweet heaven, thought Allegra. Was there ever a more sorry figure of a man?

No! She mustn't pity him! He was her family's sworn enemy. She slipped her hand into her pocket and fingered Papa's handkerchief; she knew by heart the shape of every dark stain on it. The feel of the old fabric gave her courage. Let it be done and over. Let the door to the past be closed, once and for all. Then, perhaps, she could find a future with Grey. She squared her shoulders and reached for the knife in her bodice.

But, wait! Why risk a thrust with her dagger? If she didn't kill Wickham at the first blow, he could raise the hue and cry. She glanced around her. The quarterdeck was deserted. The dim gray light of dawn would shroud her dark deed. And the quarterdeck railing, against which Wickham leaned for support, was invitingly low. A quick push, and he would be gone. She hesitated for a moment and breathed a prayer. For you, Papa. Mama. Lucinda and Charlie.

She moved toward her quarry then, her heart pounding in her breast. He opened his eyes as she reached him; he smiled warmly, without the slightest hint of embarrassment at being found in such a low state. She noticed his eyes were a clear blue, as guileless as a child's. "Mistress Mackworth," he said.

No, she thought. *Baniard*, you villain.

"In the name of God, Allegra! No!" Grey stood, shirt-sleeved, at the cabin door. With an angry growl, he raced across the quarterdeck and captured Allegra in his arms. She had only a moment to register shock at his sudden appearance. Then a huge wave crashed against the ship. The vessel shuddered like a living creature, and she and Grey were toppled overboard into the boiling seas.

She choked and gasped, flailing her arms wildly to keep herself afloat in the turbulent water. Curse her tight stays—she could scarcely move, let alone breathe! And her skirts were growing heavy with seawater, dragging her down. She felt panic building within her; then Grey's arm was around her waist, strong and reassuring.

"I'll not let you go!" he cried over the hiss of the foam.

"I can't…" she gagged on a mouthful of salty water, "I can't swim very well!"

"Don't be afraid. I'm here. You'll not sink." He looked up at the ship; the wind had shifted, and the vessel was slowly turning away from the looming shore. "Ellsmere!" Grey called out. "Get help!" The snap of the wind carried off his words.

Wickham cupped one hand to his ear, straining to hear, and raised his other arm in a gesture of helplessness. Then, his face brightening with a hopeful smile, he clambered onto the railing and dived into the water, splashing into the churning waves at some distance from them.

Grey began to shout as loudly as he could, striving to hail the ship. It was a futile effort; the vessel was already moving rapidly away from them. He turned about and pointed toward the distant shore. Wickham, floundering in the water, nodded his understanding.

Grey smiled grimly at Allegra and turned his face toward the water. "Grasp the top of my breeches," he gasped. "And hold tight! God willing, we'll reach the shore before the full blast of the storm!"

The tempest hit when they were halfway there. Rain and savage winds buffeted them; they were at the mercy of the furious elements. Allegra's fingers were numb from the cold water and the effort of clinging to Grey. She lost all sense of time, of reality. There was too much water, too much wind, too many merciless waves.

After a little while, the darkness closed over her.

Chapter Seventeen

She woke to a cold mist on her face. She sat up and rubbed her arms; her gown was damp and covered with fine sand. She felt chilled to the very marrow. She frowned down at her feet. Her shoes were gone. And her hair combs as well: she was aware that her wet locks hung loose to her shoulders, tangled with bits of seaweed. But she was safe. She was on land. Thanks to Grey.

Grey! She jumped to her feet, staring in panic at the empty, mist-shrouded beach before her, the swelling waves that rolled up on shore. "Grey!" she cried.

"Peace, Mistress Mackworth. He's safe."

She turned to see Thomas Wickham smiling behind her. He had lost his peruke; the pale red-gold of his own hair, hanging in matted curls, made him appear even younger and softer than before. He pointed up the beach to where the sandy expanse gave way to jumbled rocks and chalk cliffs. "Ridley lies yonder. Just beyond that cluster of rocks. And sleeping like a babe." He gave an apologetic laugh and tugged at his earlobe. "'Tis all on my account, I fear."

"How so?"

"He brought you in to shore. Then, weary as he was, and seeing that I was foundering, he swam out again to help me. It was doltish of me to have jumped in after you. I suppose I thought you'd be swept away before I could fetch help." He shrugged good-naturedly. "Lack of common sense, I suppose. I never made a good planter in the West Indies. I' faith, I always grew the wrong crops!"

She looked up at the sky. It was still leaden and stormy, though the rain had stopped. The heavy mist made it difficult to see more than a short distance in any direction. For all they knew, Captain Smythe's ship could be somewhere out there, just beyond their view. Searching the coast for signs of them. "Do you know what time it could be?" she asked.

"By my stomach, I'd say it was well after noon."

She shivered. Though the wind had died, the air was cold.

Wickham gestured vaguely toward the water. "The North Sea. 'Tis never warm. I remember coming to Yarmouth in July, as a child. My mother kept a fire going the whole time."

"Begad, we could use your mother and her fire right now."

Allegra whirled at the dear voice, and found herself enveloped by Grey's arms. Heedless of Wickham's presence, he pressed his lips to hers. "You taste of salt," he murmured, gently plucking the seaweed from her hair.

Wickham chuckled. "Perhaps the captain was deceived, but I knew it was an affair of the heart. For all your fanciful tales of a runaway bond servant, Ridley!" He held up his hand, forestalling Grey's reply. "We'll speak no more about it. 'Tis none of my concern. As to fire..." he fumbled in the pocket of his coat, "I have a tinderbox, if we can find some dry wood."

Grey scowled at the sparse vegetation that grew among the rocks and crowned the low cliffs. "'Twill take a powerful big fire to warm us and dry our breeches. And as for Mistress Mackworth's skirts..."

A fire seemed vastly unimportant to Allegra. Sooner or later, her clothes would dry on their own, no matter how many skirts she wore. "But how are we to be found?" she asked with some trepidation.

Grey put his arm around her in reassurance. "To begin, they will have charted where we went overboard. Or thereabouts. I met Jagat Ram in the passageway, not five minutes before I came out on deck. I have no doubt he'll persuade Captain Smythe to turn about and search for us. And then, for all we know, we may be nigh onto a village. Ellsmere and I can climb the cliff to look around."

"I'll come with you," she said.

He looked down at her stockinged feet. "Not without shoes."

"Oh, but..."

"Will you forever be stubborn?" he growled. "The rocks would cut your feet before you'd taken half a dozen steps. Foolish creature!"

She glared back at him. He might have resolved to be sober, but he hadn't yet resolved to be civil!

"Come now, Ridley," scolded Wickham. "No need to be sharp with the girl." He smiled at Allegra. "I saw a shallow cave, just down the beach. The sand is dry, at least. And you'll have shelter from the wind." He handed her his tinderbox. "And if, by some miracle, you should find a few dry twigs..."

She watched the two men start off for the cliffs, searching for a cut in the pale rock face that would lead them to the top. Then she moved down the beach until she found the cave that Wickham had described. It was a small hollow, perhaps nine or ten feet wide, and only a little taller than an ordinary man. She wondered if Grey would be forced to duck his head when he came in. The walls were irregular, toward the rear of the cavern, where the daylight scarcely reached, she thought she could discern a narrow opening.

Godamercy, but it was cold! She was half tempted to strip off all her soggy garments, then changed her mind. There was an odd kind of warmth in the snug embrace of her stays, damp or not. But perhaps if she took off her petticoat, the skirt of her mantua would dry a little more quickly. She stepped out of the petticoat, then sat and made herself comfortable on the sand. It was blessedly dry; that alone made it seem warm. She sat back and sighed, trying not to notice that her stomach, which had enjoyed neither breakfast nor dinner, was beginning to grumble. She was cold, and she was wet, and she was hungry. She sighed again. Perhaps she'd sleep until the men returned.

She sat up suddenly. Surely she didn't have her wits about her today. There was a small clump of reeds growing out of a crevice in the cave. She'd been staring at it for the past quarter of an hour without really thinking. But it was *dry*. And there was another patch, now that she came to notice it, that grew near the rear of the cave. If she could collect enough of the dry grasses, she might start a fire. She'd seen several pieces of driftwood on the beach; even damp, they might catch, if they had enough of a start.

She stood up. Perhaps there were other caves, similarly blessed. She moved to the rear of the cavern, meaning to gather the reeds here first before she explored the beach. She stopped and peered into the gloom. Upon closer examination, she saw that the narrow opening made a sharp turn and widened suddenly into a roomy passageway, perhaps five feet across. And there seemed to be a glow of daylight coming from a great distance. Another opening in the cliff? Better and better. She might find more reeds, even a sturdy bush or two, untouched by the rain. She started down the dark passageway, keeping one hand on the wall to guide herself.

It was sheer good fortune that she trod upon a stone, which dug into her stockinged foot. She winced, stopped, and knelt to toss the offending pebble out of her path. God save her! She gasped in alarm, blinking her eyes in the dimness to be sure that they weren't deceiving her. Not one pace in front of her, the floor of the cave vanished. Completely. With shaking hands, she examined the space, discovering a pit that extended the whole width of the passage, from one side to the other. She cast the pebble into the hole and was dismayed to hear the hollow splash of water far, far below.

A dangerous place, my girl! she thought to herself. And one that only bore exploration with a lighted torch. Carefully, she made her way back to the outer cavern, determined to venture afield no more without the company of the men.

She hadn't long to wait. She heard a cry and a clatter of stones, and raced out of the cave. Several yards up the beach, Wickham lay sprawled on his back, surrounded by branches and twigs. The knees of his breeches were scraped white from rubbing against the chalky stone, and the palms of his hands were covered with scratches.

In another moment, Grey appeared at the top of the cliff—his arms filled with a like amount of wood—and scowled down at Wickham. He tossed his burden to the beach, piece by piece. Then, unencumbered, he scrambled easily down the slope of the cliff to where Wickham lay.

"You bloody fool," he growled. "I told you to drop the wood first!"

Wickham smiled sheepishly and rubbed at his red palms. "There was scarcely a day as a child when I didn't come home like this." He rolled onto his knees, then awkwardly attempted to stand. He flinched in pain. "And once a month I'd sprain this very ankle."

"Damn it, man, can you walk?"

Wickham took a tentative step forward. "Not easily, but…" He shrugged. "'Twill be better in a day or two. It always is."

With Grey's arm around his waist, he limped to the cave and sank to the ground. He reached into the pocket of his coat and pulled out his cravat, which was folded into a small packet. "Here you are, Mistress Mackworth," he said, handing it to her. "I thought you'd enjoy to have this."

She unwrapped the linen and found a branch clustered with gooseberries, and two small pieces of fruit besides. They seemed to be a sort of shrunken apple—stunted by the cold easterly wind, no doubt. "How kind of you," she said, staring in surprise. "But you?"

"Ridley and I can wait to eat. I have a plan for supper."

Allegra frowned at Grey. "Supper? Are we to stay here, then?"

"You can't walk far without shoes. And now, it would seem that Ellsmere, here, can scarcely walk at all! Besides, there's too much fog up and down the coast. We could see nothing from atop the bluff. As soon as the mist lifts, I'll climb again."

Allegra held out the filled cravat to Grey and Wickham. "Please. I'll not eat alone. I shall take the berries. You share the rest." Though the two men were stubborn, insisting that the food was for her, Allegra prevailed at last. "We're comrades in mutual distress," she said. "And I warrant I'm more able to endure hunger and suffering than the two of you."

They ate slowly and silently, savoring every mouthful. The apples were consumed—stems, seeds, and all—and Allegra gnawed on the gooseberry branch to get the last of the flavor after the fruits were eaten.

"That was a splendid dinner!" said Wickham in a jovial manner. "But now, Mistress Mackworth, let me repay your kindness." He reached down, unbuckled his shoes, and held them out to Allegra. "Until my ankle heals, I scarcely need these."

She gaped, taken aback by his generosity. "They are…somewhat large," she stammered.

"No matter." He took his cravat and tore it into thin strips, which he handed to her. "You can tie the shoes to your feet. They'll not take you far, but at least you may walk among the rocks without cutting yourself."

"But…your cravat…" she murmured, still shaken by the goodness of a man she was sworn to hate.

He shrugged and tore off another strip. "I needed it, in any event, to make my sling."

"Sling?"

"One of my few skills," he said. "You may have noticed that I find the physical world a trial."

Allegra glanced at Grey, then looked away, forcing herself to keep from smiling. They could scarcely deny Wickham's words!

"You may smile," he said genially. "I'm quite used to it. But, as I said, I'm a master of the sling. My mother—a most remarkable, clever woman—taught me when I was a boy."

"And your prey?"

"This is what I've explained to Ridley here. I told you I'd stayed in Yarmouth as a child. There's a most remarkable occurrence in this part of the country, and at this season. All the swallows of England have begun their winter migration. They use this very coast as their starting point on their way to Holland, and thence to warmer climes. Not a soul knows why. 'Tis one of God's delightful mysteries, I suppose. But if the wind is off sea, as now it is, they must wait for a gale, or at least a freshening, for they're windbound creatures. I saw them wheeling overhead as Ridley and I tramped the bluffs. If I've guessed aright, the birds should begin to gather by the thousands on the beach and rocks as the day ends. I'll find a place to set myself. If I'm fortunate, and haven't forgotten all my mother's lessons, we should have a fine supper!" He limped off down the beach, picking up stones as he went his way and stuffing them into his pockets.

Grey and Allegra spent the rest of the afternoon gathering driftwood and reeds. They found a small stream of fresh water flowing into the sea. While Grey chipped at a large rock to make a hollowed-out vessel in which to carry the water back to their cave, Allegra scavenged for shells they could use as cups. Wickham's shoes were large, and slipped about on her feet, but she was grateful for them nonetheless.

By the time daylight was beginning to fade, and Tom Wickham had come limping back to them, triumphantly holding a mass of dead birds aloft, Grey and Allegra had managed to get a hissing fire going at the opening to the cave.

They worked as comrades, equal in labor. After Wickham had cleaned and plucked the birds with his penknife, Grey took them to the stream to wash them. Allegra fed the fire, then threaded the birds on green sticks and roasted them to a fine turn.

It was a jolly meal. Their clothes were dry at last—Allegra had put on her petticoat again; it was snug and warm—and their bellies were satisfied. The two men had even agreed to call each other by their Christian names, though Allegra pretended that it was modesty alone that prevented her from calling Wickham "Tom."

She sighed in contentment and licked her fingers to savor the last of her birds. "They wanted a bit of salt. You should have washed them in the sea, Grey."

He grunted and raised a mocking eyebrow. "Did I complain about your cooking?"

Tom Wickham held up his drinking vessel. It was the black, shiny shell of a mussel. "We can search for these in the morning," he announced cheerily. "I' faith, there might even be wild ducks on the bluffs! We shall live and prosper like Robinson Crusoe until we're found." That thought seemed to delight him, and he beamed at them both.

Allegra nodded in acknowledgment. Even in America, there had been much talk of Defoe's novel when it had first appeared.

Grey looked beyond the entrance to the cavern. "The wind has come round, I think. The clouds seem to be blowing out to sea."

"With our swallows, more's the pity," said Wickham.

Allegra peered at the clear sky. "If the ship comes back," she asked, "will they see our fire now?"

Grey nodded. "In all likelihood. But only if we keep it going all night. I'll stand guard."

"No, Grey," said Wickham. "We'll share."

"*All* of us," said Allegra firmly. "Comrades. Remember?"

In the end, and with a great deal of grumbling from Grey, it was agreed that Allegra should tend the fire only until the moon rose, and then she was to waken him. "Only until then," he warned, taking her in his arms to kiss her good night. "It should be an hour, at most."

As the men curled up in sheltered corners of the cave, Allegra tucked her legs under her skirts, settled herself comfortably, and sat beside the fire, half in and half out of the cavern.

The soft air, now blowing off the land, was warmer than it had been all day. The wood had finally begun to dry, and the fire burned merrily, sending up showers of sparks into the sky. The rhythmic splash of the waves against the shore and the gentle breathing of the sleeping men were the only sounds to break the dark stillness. Allegra found it pleasant just to sit and let her thoughts drift.

After a while, the full moon rose out of the sea, large and orange-gold as a pumpkin ripe on the vine. She frowned. Like the pumpkins she'd cultivated in Gammer Pringle's fields. She saw herself as before, sweltering in the hot sun, her hands raw with blisters, her back bent and aching as she dug and raked and hoed. She frowned more darkly, filled with bitter memories, as the moon rose higher in the sky and turned to a pale, shining silver orb that bathed the sand in its luminous glow.

And still the haunting memories persisted. The moon had beamed down in just that fashion over Baniard Hall. Midsummer's Eve. Four days before she'd turned seven. And Charlie had taken her out into the park, under the brilliant moon, to catch fireflies in a bottle.

She looked at Wickham, sleeping peacefully. Why did he still live, when the memories gnawed at her heart, sharp as the fangs of a serpent? How could she face her conscience, when she had supped with him, and laughed with him, and taken his proffered gifts? She ground her teeth together and savagely pulled his shoes from her feet.

She groped for the knife in her bodice. Hadn't everything in her life been leading toward this moment? Eight long years of hatred pressed against her heart, just beneath the blade. It consumed her like a bitter, dread disease; she would never be cured without the shedding of Wickham's blood. Softly she rose to her feet, crept to his side, and peered down on him where he lay.

He was smiling in his sleep. Curse him and all his family! Had Mama smiled for a single moment, through all the years of hell? Allegra pulled out her knife and stood with it poised above him. The bright blade glittered in the light cast by the fire. Now, she thought. *Now*. While the memory of her family's suffering was fresh in her mind.

The knife began to shake in her hand. She clasped her wrist with her other hand to steady it. Was she a fool? Was she a coward? Why did she hesitate?

She heard Grey's hoarse whisper behind her. "*Do it*. And damn your soul forever."

She turned, her face contorting in agony. The knife dropped from her grasp, landing softly on the sand. "I...I cannot!" she gasped. She clapped her hand to her mouth to stifle her cry of pain, and ran out of the cavern. She raced along the moonlit beach, her thoughts in turmoil. Where could she run? Where could she hide, to escape her failure?

"Allegra!" She heard Grey's pounding footsteps behind her, and then she was in his arms, captured by his strong embrace.

"Let me go!" she cried. "Why didn't you let me do it on the ship, while my resolve was still upon me?"

"Foolish child," he said tenderly. "You couldn't have done it then, either."

"But I *should* have! I have no right to live whilst that man lives!" She struggled in his arms, tossing back her head in helpless frustration. The full moon cast its cold, bright eye on her, condemning her with its unforgiving gaze. She wanted to die. To sink into the sea for shame.

"For pity's sake, Grey. Let me go."

He sucked in a sharp breath. "Christ's blood! The moon on your face...So white, so pale. That face. My Lady of the...!" He swore again. "You're a *Baniard!*"

She closed her eyes and buried her head against his chest. "No," she said with a moan, "the very last Baniard. The only one left to avenge the family."

"How dull-witted of me," he muttered. "I should have guessed. Not only the painting. I should have questioned how the Ellsmeres came to own the Hall. Especially after I heard stories of the Baniards in Newton. Disgraced, they said. Exiled for treason."

"Convicted falsely on the word of John Wickham. And his son, Thomas. They never told you that, I'll wager." She bit her lip, fighting to keep her chin from trembling. She felt lost and desolate. "I had a family once, Grey. And now they're gone. All of them."

He pulled her down to sit beside him in the sand, and held her tightly in his arms. "Tell me. For the love of God, tell me at last, Allegra."

Strange how the memories came creeping back in painful bits and pieces, like stragglers from a battle. "Do you know the leopard on the front gate? On the coat of arms? It lost its paw the day they dragged Papa from the Hall to arrest him. I think half the folk in the parish were there to watch. And jeer and throw stones, calling him words I'd never heard before. Mama had to hold my brother Charlie, to keep him from murdering the constables. I had a sister, too. She would have been a duchess today, with a loving husband and children. We were so happy. Life was sweet."

"And then?"

"They were all sentenced to transportation to the American Colonies, there to work as bond servants. Life slavery for Papa. Seven years for the others."

"And what of you?"

"I was to be left behind. Put into a workhouse as an orphan. But Mama begged the judge to let me come with her and work for nothing."

"You were only a child?"

"Not quite ten."

"How long ago was this?"

"A little more than eight years." It seemed like a lifetime.

"My God! Eighteen? You're so young! I thought…" His voice caught. "Your eyes are filled with grief. So old."

"'Tis the pain of living," she whispered. "After the sentence was passed, they let Papa leave the prison and come back to us at the Hall. Only to settle his affairs. I found him in the garden one cold afternoon. He was sobbing like a babe. Big brave Papa. I think my childhood died that day."

"Oh, my poor Allegra," he groaned. "Lean on my heart and weep. Shed your child's tears now."

Her eyes were dry. Her heart was numb. "Don't you understand? I have no tears left for myself. Only hatred for Wickham."

"What happened to your family?"

She sighed. "Papa had a little money left, after all the debts and costs of the trial were paid. I don't know what happened to it. Perhaps he used it to bribe the magistrate. I know we were not at first meant to travel all on the same ship. But, in the end, we did. Clapped under hatches in a suffocating little space. Mama and Lucinda earned a bit of money for our food by washing the seamen's clothes. I don't remember much of the voyage, until the very end. I was seasick and frightened." She sighed again, her heart so heavy with grief that she could scarcely breathe.

"Lucinda was too beautiful," she went on at last. "Why did God make her so? Too beautiful for safety. And one day, three of the sailors found her alone and…" She gulped. She found that she was trembling violently, despite Grey's solid embrace. She'd never told it all until now. Never spoken the dreadful words aloud. Now, it was as though the story was bursting to come forth with such urgency that it shook her whole body, like a wind rattling against the shutters of a house.

"The damned villains," muttered Grey.

"Papa had endured prison, and shame and disgrace. But Lucinda's rape was more than he could bear. When he found out, he tried to attack the seamen. Not even Charlie could stop him. The sailors beat him with their fists until he was bloody. I screamed so much I couldn't talk for two days after. Mama nursed him as best she could, but he died the day before we reached Charles Town. We buried him at sea."

Grey choked on an oath. "My God, how can you tell me this without weeping?"

She shook her head. "I don't know. I used to weep, sometimes, when Mama showed me his bloody handkerchief. But no more."

"And what happened in Charles Town?"

"Charlie was sold first. To the brutal hell of a rice plantation. And Lucinda, my dear sister…I see her face even now. Her lips were still swollen from all the savage, cruel kisses, and her pretty eyes were the eyes of a wounded animal. She was bought by the owner of a tavern. But we could hear the whispers in the crowd, the sly laughter. It was in truth a brothel, I learned later. Lucinda must have understood. She broke away from the man who bought her and dashed into the street. There was a horse and carriage. She ran into its path. 'Twas what she wanted, I think. She died there on the road, her blood soaking into the dust. So far from home. Poor Lucinda."

He swore again. "And Squire Pringle bought your mother as a house servant?"

She nodded. "And raped her almost every night, for five years."

She could feel his body jerk in surprise. "Sweet Jesu, I didn't know!"

"I told Mr. Briggs the story, that day in the stillroom."

"I didn't hear that part. Oh, my precious Allegra. Forgive me. Forgive me! I must have seemed no better than your Squire Pringle."

"No." She stroked his face in tender reassurance. "I was only afraid of you that first day. When you kissed me."

"And you bit my tongue, which I deserved. But who taught you to defend yourself so fiercely?"

"I don't know. Mama didn't have the strength to fight. At first, we got letters from Charlie. They were of some comfort, though filled with rage and bitterness. I tried to keep up Mama's spirits by talking of the day when the terms of bondage would be over. Seven years, Mama, I'd say. And then we'll start anew, you and I and Charlie. I talked to her of buying land, of finding a place in Virginia or New York. But when Charlie's letters stopped, all the hope faded from her eyes. I think her heart could bear no more pain."

"Allegra, my dear one."

She sighed. "I begged her not to die. I swore over and over that I'd seek out the Wickhams and kill them. That I'd avenge all the wrongs done to us." She wrapped her arms around Grey's neck, clinging to him for strength. "I couldn't save her, Grey. Not with all my promises. It haunts me night and day. I couldn't save her."

He kissed the side of her cheek, her delicate earlobe. His kisses were a sweet comfort. "And what of Charlie?" he said. He sounded almost reluctant to ask, as though he had little desire to prolong the suffering that her narrative brought her.

"I heard two years ago that he had drowned in the swamps, trying to escape." A small, sad moan burst from her throat. "Oh, Grey, I'm so tired."

He kissed her more fervently. "Dear, sweet Allegra. I wish to God I could take away your pain."

"Then tell me why I couldn't kill him tonight!" she cried bitterly.

"Because they taught you too well, your fine Baniards. They taught you to be better than your enemies. To show goodness and mercy. To cherish life, not death." His voice was warm with admiration.

"But I made a promise!"

"What were you—only fifteen? It was a child's promise, given in a moment of agony and desperation. A child's bargain with God, perhaps. In hopes of saving your mother. Forgive your enemies. Walk away from such a dreadful promise, and learn to live again." He took her face between his hands and kissed her full on the mouth. "I want to make love to you now," he whispered. "I want to give you the gifts of joy, and life, and love."

He laid her back on the sand and took her body with a tenderness that erased her pain and soothed her soul. She hadn't imagined it could be so sweet—to be caressed and cherished. He murmured soft words of praise and comfort that cheered her heart. He tucked back her skirts with loving hands and entered her, thrusting gently while he rained kisses on her face and neck and bodice. He asked for nothing. He seemed only to concern himself with her ease. To stroke her face and body with his caring fingers, to stroke her soft core with his undemanding shaft.

And when he peaked in a gasping climax, he scarcely moved within her, as though he feared to visit his fervent emotions upon her overwrought soul. She felt his warmth pouring into her, like a final sweet benediction, and knew that she would sleep peacefully tonight.

At last he stood up and held out his hands to her. "Come. 'Twill be cold if we linger here." He put his arm around her and guided her back to the cave. "I'll be gone at dawn," he said. "Long before you waken. If the sky holds clear, I should find a village nearby." He kissed her once more, then sat before the fire to tend it during the long night.

Her sleep was dreamless, sweet and serene. She awoke to Tom Wickham's cry and the feel of rough hands on her bosom.

Chapter Eighteen

"Sink and scuttle me, here be a pretty handful!"

Allegra gasped, desperately blinking away the last of her sleepiness, and glared up at the strange man who knelt over her. His face was ugly and weather-beaten, his clothes stank of tobacco, and his greasy hair was topped with a sailor's bonnet. He squeezed her breasts and grinned. "A choice morsel, or I'll be hanged."

Anger drove away her fear. She slapped at his filthy hands and scrambled to her feet. "You'll be hanged soon enough, my man," she said, her lip curling in disgust, "if you forget your manners!"

Brazenly she pushed past him to storm out of the cave. Godamercy! There was a knot of men on the beach—nearly a dozen, she guessed—as evil-looking as the one who had disturbed her sleep. Beyond them, riding the first swell of the waves, was a dark ship. It sat low in the water, as though it carried a heavy cargo, and its sails were furled. A small boat, filled with boxes and bales, was drawn up on the beach; another boat, similarly laden, had just pulled away from the ship and was moving toward the shore.

Allegra scowled, feeling the beginnings of trepidation. The ship carried no colors, no flag to identify its home country or port. There could be no reason for it to be in this isolated place—no reason except one. She remembered what Papa had said, whenever he read of a new customs tax imposed on goods coming to England: thanks to the heavy duties, smuggling was almost a national vocation!

She shaded her eyes and peered up at the sky. The sun was already high. Midmorning, she reckoned. She had slept late. She wondered how early Grey had left, how soon he could possibly return. In the meantime, if she and Tom Wickham could convince the smugglers that they meant them no harm, they might be safe enough.

Wickham! She scanned the scene with a frantic eye, belatedly recalling that his desperate cry had wakened her. Suddenly the group of seamen parted, and she saw him in their midst. He was barefooted; he had tied the remains of his cravat around his injured ankle for a brace. His coat was torn, and the pockets bulged oddly. He smiled at Allegra in reassurance and took a few limping steps in her direction.

Just then, one of the smugglers stretched out a foot and thrust it in front of Wickham's leg. The poor man tripped and fell heavily, sprawling forward on his face. From out of his pockets spilled handfuls of mussels. He struggled to stand up; the seaman shoved him down again, to the accompaniment of raucous laughter from his companions.

"Oh, you villains!" cried Allegra, reaching for the dagger in her bodice. "Devil take it," she muttered. If her ugly intruder hadn't found the blade already, it was still on the floor of the cave, where she'd dropped it last night. She hurried to Wickham and knelt before him. "Tom, are you hurt?"

He shook his head and waved an arm toward the assembled men. "Not at all. My comrades and I were having a friendly conversation. I merely told these fine gentlemen how you and I were washed overboard, and were planning to go for help as soon as my ankle would allow me to travel." He scooped up the mussels from the beach, returned them to his pockets, and stood up, helping Allegra to her feet. "Now, if you gentlemen will permit us to have our breakfast, you may go on about your business with no hindrance from us." He offered his arm to Allegra. "Come, my dear."

His cool assurance bolstered her own courage. She reached for his arm, but felt it roughly jerked away by the seaman in the bonnet. "Breakfast later," he said. "First, I be wanting *my* refreshment. A sweet taste o' this wench."

Wickham drew himself up and glared at the man. "That good woman is my wife," he announced. "You will show her the respect due a lady." Again he offered his arm. "Come, madam."

Allegra exhaled a long breath as the seaman released her and fell back, shamefaced. Thanks be to God that Wickham's ruse had discouraged the villain. "Husband," she said, and took his arm.

They had scarcely taken half a dozen steps up the beach, however, when one of the other men cried out. "Hold, blast ye!"

Reluctantly they turned. The seamen were advancing on them, their faces dark and filled with menace. Wickham maintained his proud stance in the face of this new danger. "You have aught to say, my good man?" he asked.

The seaman grinned unexpectedly, revealing rotted teeth. He jerked his head in the direction of the man in the bonnet. "I goes along wi'

Gregory here. My jockum be mighty hungry arter a long voyage." He clutched at his groin and joggled it suggestively.

"Why, as to that," said another, leering at Allegra, "I'm for a little sport. And what's the 'arm? 'Taint as though she be an unspoiled dell, what don't know the touch of a man." He scampered forward and tried to grab Allegra.

"No, damn you, you cowardly louts!" Tom Wickham gave him a violent push to the ground and thrust Allegra behind him. "When you can, run for the cave," he said in a low, urgent voice. "We might be able to hold them off at the entrance."

She nodded, praying that her knife was still there.

Another sailor tried to rush Wickham. He struck the seaman full in the face with his clenched fist and grunted in satisfaction as the man went down. Arms poised to strike again, he whirled to another. Just then, a large rock came flying through the air at him. Wickham cried out, clutched at his temple, and sank to his knees, blood pouring from between his fingers.

Cackling in triumph, Gregory darted forward and kicked him as he sat bent over on the sand. "Be we cowardly louts? Or just brethren o' the sea? Share and share alike is my motto. Aye, shipmates? And if this here gentleman be calling us friend, why then he'll share his lady. And wi' a right good will. Aye, mate?" he asked Wickham, giving him another savage kick.

"For God's sake, Allegra, run!" he gasped.

But it was too late. She found herself surrounded by ugly, grinning faces. She spun around, seeking an avenue of escape. It was useless. She cried out in panic as she felt her arms grabbed from behind and held firmly. "Filthy dogs! Let me go!"

Wickham growled in fury and struggled to his feet, lashing out at the sailors around him. Once more he was beaten to the ground and forcibly held back by several of the men.

Gregory scraped off his red bonnet and bowed to Wickham, a mocking smile on his face. "Your worship," he said. "We gives you the right to watch us play in-and-in wi' your lady." He turned to the others. "Bein' as how I found her first, I take the first turn." He fumbled with his breeches, uncovered his straining member, and nodded at his fellows. "Lift her up."

Allegra shrieked as she felt her ankles grabbed by two of the sailors, her body raised off the ground, her legs spread wide. She writhed and jerked convulsively, cringing as Gregory slid his rough hands along her skirts and pushed them up to her hips.

He ran his hands along her naked thighs and snickered. "I likes my wenches small, so's they scream when I go in 'em. Be you small, woman?"

Another sailor stepped forward, one finger held up in an obscene gesture. "I'll find out for ye, Gregory lad. Tuck back her skirts to her prat, and we'll see what kind o' pintle-case be there."

"Damn you! *Damn you!*" Wickham fought against his captors, nearly choking on his outrage.

"Avast, ye scurvy devils! Did I set ye to work, or to go whoring?" A man in a large cocked hat came storming up the beach and angrily smacked the head of one of the men who held Wickham. "Leave off!" he roared. "Be ye men, or red savages? Loose the wench!"

Allegra gasped in relief, shaking and sobbing as she felt herself lowered to the ground. She smoothed down her skirts with trembling hands and rubbed her arms; her flesh felt soiled by the vile touch of these men. She ran to Tom Wickham and knelt before him. "Did they hurt you?"

He put his arm around her and gave her a comforting hug. "I was teased by my schoolfellows many a time," he said. "It hurt worse."

The man in the cocked hat scowled at Gregory and jerked his thumb in Tom and Allegra's direction. "Now, who be these two?"

Gregory cleared his throat and kicked at the sand. "Beggin' your pardon, Cap'n, but they be travelers, washed up from a passing ship. I found the woman in the cave."

Tom set his chin in a hard line. "We were quite prepared to let you go on your way," he said. "We had no quarrel with you. But these ruffians chose to make free with my wife." Even with the blood still oozing down his cheek, he managed to look dignified.

Allegra hesitated for only a minute, then pulled Papa's handkerchief from her pocket. She dabbed carefully at Wickham's bloody face, then folded the handkerchief into a bandage and tied it around his temples. "Why don't you leave us in peace?" she muttered.

The captain scratched his chin. "We be on a bit o' business, you understand."

Tom sighed in annoyance. "If you've brought in half the tea of the Indies, it matters naught to us! Carry on your business, and then leave. We're only hoping to be rescued."

Gregory swore softly. "Cap'n, we can't leave 'em here."

"We'll send 'em off, then. Toward the village."

"But Cap'n, such a pretty wench. And we be long at sea. A little sport afore we sends 'em off. Why not?"

"Well…" The captain wavered, his dark eyes surveying Allegra in a way that made her shiver.

The seaman with the rotted teeth stepped forward and tugged at his forelock. "Beggin' your pardon, Cap'n, but arter we lets 'em go, what's to keep 'em from tellin' of this place? And 'twere the best spot we ever come across."

"And growing more chancy with every trip," grumbled the captain. "I be thinking 'tis time to find another anchorage."

"All the more reason to let us go, then," said Tom.

The captain shook his head. "Not yet." He gestured down the beach toward the cave. "Bring 'em along until we be done unloading. Then I'll think on what to do with 'em." They were marched at a brisk pace toward the cavern, Tom struggling valiantly to keep up with his injured ankle. Allegra was dismayed to find that her knife was gone, though Tom's shoes still lay discarded in the corner.

The captain signaled to the men in the boat that had just come ashore. At once, several seamen picked up something that appeared to be a broad, heavy platform and started up the beach with it. With a great deal of swearing and sweating, they carried the contrivance into the cave and placed it across the deep pit.

Allegra had to admire the cleverness of the rogues as they crossed the crude "bridge" to the tunnel beyond. They had a safe and secure lair for their dishonest traffic. The tunnel was light enough to see their way; small openings in the cliff above let in the daylight. It was only when the passageway opened up to a huge underground cavern, which echoed with their voices, that the smugglers struck flint to the many torches that lined the walls.

The captain pointed to a corner of the cavern that was farthest away from the entrance. "Put 'em there," he said. "There be no way they can escape without our seeing."

Allegra and Tom sank to the ground, grateful to be ignored while the smugglers went about their business. There were a great many boxes and bales to be carried in and stacked inside the cavern. From the markings on some of the chests, Allegra guessed the contents to be calico. It was a contraband Indian cloth that many American and English women wore and used in their furnishings, despite the laws against it. There seemed to be boxes of tea, besides. And—from the pungent smell that soon filled the cave—tobacco as well.

Tom Wickham flexed his bandaged ankle and scowled. "I made a mess of it, as is my wont. A clumsy knight errant. I couldn't even warn you properly when I saw that lout, Gregory, go into the cave."

He couldn't be reproaching himself! Not after all his gallantry. "No, no," she protested. "Your alarum woke me. The villain would have overpowered me else, while I slept."

He scratched at his ear, his face reddening. "Your...your pardon for my presumption. To call you wife. I thought it might help to save you."

She hid her smile as best she could. His boyish embarrassment was oddly charming. "It was very noble of you. *Have* you a wife?"

"No."

"A sweetheart, then?"

"In the past. But...A looby like me...I'm not so great a catch."

"Don't be absurd," she chided gently. "I'm sure that any young lady would be proud to be seen on your arm." Oh, dear, she thought, seeing his face turn a deeper shade of red, she shouldn't have said that! Tom Wickham was far too artless to accept such a personal remark. She cleared her throat and made a great show of watching the seamen at their tasks. "The ship rode low," she said at last. "I think it will take them all day to unload it."

He nodded. "All to the good. I saw Grey leave before daybreak. I feel sure he'll return with help long before nightfall. In the meanwhile, would you care for some breakfast?" He grinned and pulled a few of the mussels from his coat pocket. "They clung to all the rocks on the edge of the water. 'Twas simple enough to gather them. I knew you'd be hungry when you awoke."

"But you must have walked far. And with your injury. How kind of you."

He waved away her compliment. "My mother taught me to be chivalrous. Now..." He looked around the cave to see if they were being watched, then fished in the pocket of his waistcoat and produced his penknife. "I should have preferred my mussels steamed over a fire. And we could use a bit of water to wash off the sand, but 'tis sustenance."

Hiding the penknife from the view of the smugglers, they managed to feed themselves after a fashion. Allegra used her skirts to clean the shells as well as she could, then handed them to Tom, who inserted the point of his knife between the shells and gave the blade a quick twist to open the mussel. They soon had mastered the knack of swallowing the slippery bivalves without chewing, so as not to grind their teeth on sand. It was a strangely jolly meal, for all their predicament. A warm interlude of companionship that left them smiling and sated.

But as the afternoon dragged on, Allegra began to grow more and more uneasy. Though Tom seemed to make an effort to be cheerful for her sake, she could read concern in his face, as well. The smugglers had spoken several times about their confederates: men from the nearby villages who would come with wagons and transport the goods to Norwich for sale.

Why would they speak openly of such matters? thought Allegra. Unless…She shivered. Unless they had no fear of being betrayed. What was almost worse, the villains leered and snickered each time they passed her, nudging one another in the ribs and exchanging sly whispers.

By the time the smugglers had carried in their last box and chest, Allegra knew it must be evening. The last few loads had been accompanied by men holding dark lanterns to guide them through the dimming passageway. She looked at Tom and bit her lip. "So late. Why hasn't Grey returned by now?"

He patted her hand. "Soon, I have no doubt."

She watched uneasily as the seamen made themselves comfortable, unwrapped packets of food and began to pass around flasks of rum. Clearly, they intended to wait for their accomplices. And if the hours stretched by, and the intoxicating spirits flowed freely…

"I think they mean to kill us," she blurted at last.

Tom shook his head. A red-gold curl drooped over the handkerchief around his temples. "Will you frighten yourself for naught? Why should they? If they meant to, they would have done it long since."

"They're waiting for their friends." She had a dreadful sense of foreboding. "That pit drops to the bowels of hell itself. Who would ever find us?"

"Come, come," he said. "You forget that *we* are waiting for our friends as well." He smiled his encouragement. "My mother taught me to look for the bright side."

"And in the meantime," she said bitterly, "will I be their amusement to while away the hours?"

The smile faded. "As to that, Allegra…" He traced a meandering pattern in the dirt with his finger. "I've been dwelling much on that thought in the past hour or so. I feel sure that Grey will come, of course. You mustn't be afraid. But in the event that…" He hesitated and cleared his throat. "I shall defend you, as best I can. I think you know that. But…" He fastened his blue eyes on hers. They were warm with sympathy. "If… if you should prefer death to dishonor, my two hands are at your service. I'm a clumsy oaf, God knows. But I can do that for you, should it be your wish when the moment comes."

"God be merciful," she whispered, feeling the tears burn in her eyes. "Why are you such a good, kind man?"

He laughed gently. "I told you. I was raised to be chivalrous."

"And I was raised to hate you!" she cried. "You fool! I followed you onto the ship only to kill you." She buried her face in her hands. "How can you be kind to me when you're a Wickham and I'm a Baniard?"

She heard the sharp intake of his breath. "My God! The little girl with the sad eyes."

She raised her head and stared at him through her tears. "What do you mean?"

"I went down to the quay at Bristol to see your family board the convict ship. You clung to your mother's skirt, poor little thing." He swore softly and pounded the dirt with his fist. "They told me later you had died. All of you."

"Only I survived. I..." She looked up in alarm as Gregory and several of the other seamen swaggered across the cave toward her. The captain stayed where he was, but his grinning face clearly approved his men's actions.

Gregory took a pull from his bottle of rum, tossed it aside, and wiped his mouth on his sleeve. "Give us a kiss, wench," he said. He clutched Allegra's shoulders and jerked her to her feet.

Tom was on his feet as well. "Damn you," he said, and leapt for Gregory's throat. A shot rang out. Tom gasped and clutched at his breast.

Allegra screamed. She felt rough hands on her body—tearing her bodice, pulling her arms, clutching at her hair. A whirlwind of filthy, panting men swirled around her. She prayed God to give her strength to endure.

There were more shots, echoing against the rock, and suddenly the cave was filled with smoke and noise and confusion. Shouts. Cries. Angry curses. The harsh metallic clash of steel on steel.

Unexpectedly released, Allegra shrank against the wall of the cave, holding her tattered gown to her breast. There seemed to be dozens of armed men in the cave, battling the smugglers. She saw Baines, the mate. And Jagat Ram, wielding a large blade. She recognized several more of the sailors from Captain Smythe's ship.

And then she saw Grey. Tall and strong and noble. He carried a large staff which he used to soundly beat any smugglers foolhardy enough to come at him with knife or sword. "Oh, Grey," she whispered, and wept for joy.

The fighting was over in a matter of minutes. Outnumbered, the smugglers threw down their blades and pistols and allowed themselves to be marched out of the cave. Allegra found herself enveloped in Grey's comforting arms.

"Thank God you're safe," he muttered, kissing her in a frenzy of relief. "The sheriff suspected this coast of harboring smugglers. He gave us half a dozen of his armed men for safety's sake."

"Why did you take so long?" Her body began to shake convulsively, giving in at last to the tension of the past hours. She clung to him for support.

"We had to sail along the coast. And wait for the wind. As luck would have it, Captain Smythe had put in at the first village I came to. But when we saw the smugglers' ship at anchor, we waited until dark to make our own landing." He clutched her to his breast and groaned. "My poor dear Allegra. I thought I'd die when I heard you scream. Are you hurt? Did they harm you?"

"No, but…Oh my God! Tom!" She threw herself out of Grey's arms and looked wildly about.

Tom Wickham had dragged himself to a sheltered corner of the cave, and now lay gasping, his hand pressed to the spreading stain on his chest. He smiled faintly as Allegra and Grey knelt at his side. "My mother would be pleased. That I died defending a lady."

"Don't be absurd," said Allegra as brightly as she could. "We'll bring you to a surgeon. Why, in no time at all…"

His eyes were suddenly solemn. "Don't," he said. "We have no time for lies."

"But you can't die!" She brushed at her tears.

He closed his eyes for a moment. "Lord, I feel as though I were filled with broken glass." He managed another smile. "Don't weep, Allegra. I' faith, I've led a pleasant life. I can look back over twenty-five years with few regrets." He reached out with his bloody fingers and grasped Grey's wrist. "But there's much to be told. Is Captain Smythe's ship at anchor?"

"Yes."

"Send for my sea chest. Then listen to me. I'll want you to write it out, Grey, so I can sign it." He coughed for a moment, then was still.

While Grey gave instructions to Baines to fetch Wickham's sea chest, Allegra tore bandages from her petticoat and pressed them against Tom's wound. She found a bottle of rum and a bowl of water, then bathed his face and gave him something to drink. The blood had long since dried on the handkerchief around his forehead; it was almost the same color as the stains from Papa's blood.

"Don't speak now, Tom," she said. "Rest for a little while."

"No. Listen to me. I must put things right before I go." He sighed, then coughed softly. "How shall I begin? My parents lived apart much of the time. My father and I were...not on amicable terms. I lived away at school, or stayed with my mother and her family in Yarmouth. My father...he stayed in Shropshire with his own father, or came down to London to gamble. Perhaps I tell you this to explain my ignorance. My blind stupidity to what happened. I knew there was bad blood between my family and the Baniards. From the time of the civil wars. But all I ever heard from my father and grandfather was envy. That the Baniards had great lands and wealth whilst the Ellsmeres...the manor house at Holgate. That was all."

Grey stared in surprise. "Sir Henry Crompton's manor?"

"He bought it from my father, after we moved into Baniard Hall. At least I thought he did, at the time. He'd been my father's friend and gambling companion in London." Tom looked at Allegra, his face twisted with remorse. "I was with my father when he found the treasonous letters. God forgive me, it was what I testified in court. It seemed so accidental at the time—to come across a riderless horse in the woods. So haphazard that I could truthfully swear it hadn't been all arranged. And of course the horse was traced to a known Jacobite who'd escaped to France." He took a deep breath and winced.

"I think I was my father's dupe in the matter. To seal his plot against your family. How damning it must have been at your father's trial for a soft-faced youth to give his innocent testimony. And self-righteous, as only a boy can be. I was convinced, you see, that your father *was* a traitor."

"Never!" cried Allegra.

He ran his tongue across his lips. "Let me go on. I know not how much time God has granted me." He blinked as though he were fighting to focus his thoughts. "My mother died, and I went away to school again. When I returned to Baniard Hall, I found that my father had sold the house at Holgate to Crompton. But I never found any record of money changing hands. Not even in my father's papers after he died."

"What are you saying?" said Allegra.

"I think Crompton guessed what my father had done. And took the house at Holgate for his silence. The year before my father died, he gave part of the Baniard woods to Crompton as well."

"Good God, man," said Grey. "Can you prove this?"

"Not anymore. Five years ago, I found some letters and papers in my father's desk. One of them was from an underling, detailing the expenses he would incur upon leaving the Baniard household and resettling in

Virginia. He demanded recompense from my father. Another letter was from someone who had signed the name…." Wickham closed his eyes and groaned. "Oh, God, it hurts."

Allegra choked back a sob. "Rest for a bit, Tom. Please."

"No time. The letter. Yes. It was signed Tiberius."

Grey frowned. "A secret name?"

"No doubt. The letter…this 'Tiberius'…confirmed that my father had forged the papers that convicted your father, and asked for compensation in exchange for his silence. In the name of friendship."

"Where are the letters now?"

"My father destroyed them. But not before I confronted him and forced him to tell me the truth. That it was so. He even bragged about it, once the secret was out. And told me how he'd bribed a Baniard servant to steal your father's seal. It was how he authenticated the forged letters."

"Dear heaven," breathed Allegra. She felt as though a great weight had been lifted from her shoulders.

"Do you remember the name of the Baniard servant?" asked Grey.

"Alas, no. But I feel sure that 'Tiberius' was Crompton, though 'tis only a supposition." He clutched at Allegra's fingers. "I tried to find out about the Baniards, truly I did! Hoping to undo some of my father's wickedness. But the news from America…the whole family had died, they said. I left for the West Indies after that. There was nothing I could do to put things to rights. I never saw my father again. But I beg you, Allegra…" his blue eyes glistened with tears, "forgive me for the harm I've done you."

She stroked his pale cheek. "Oh, Tom. You've been my friend today. My champion. God knows you have my forgiveness. And more."

"And…" he grimaced in pain, "can you forgive my father for being venal and weak?"

She turned her head aside. He was asking too much. She was glad when one of the sailors appeared, carrying Tom's sea chest.

"Good," he murmured. "There's paper and pen, Grey. Begin it: I, Thomas Wickham, fourth Baron Ellsmere, do freely confess the plot invented by my father, John Wickham, third Baron Ellsmere, to discredit and blacken the name of the Baniard family of Baniard Hall, Shropshire. And in particular Sir William Baniard, Baronet." He closed his eyes. His upper lip was beginning to bead with sweat, and his voice had taken on a peculiar rasping quality.

"Peace," said Grey. "Let me write it as you told it, and then I'll read it back to you."

While Grey wrote, Tom closed his eyes in sleep, a small frown marring the innocent youthfulness of his face. Allegra watched over him, her thoughts churning. At last Grey was finished writing. Tom seemed to sense the moment, even in sleep. He opened his eyes.

Grey had written a faithful account, only leaving out the name "Tiberius" and its possible connection to Crompton. What was important, he explained to Tom, was that the Baniard name should be cleared. An unproven conspirator, after the fact, was of little matter. Tom nodded his agreement, managing to sit up with Allegra's help. He took the pen from Grey and—in the presence of Captain Smythe as a disinterested witness—signed the paper.

He fell back to the ground, gasping. His face was gray and his body had begun to tremble. Allegra tried to urge him to rest, but he shook her off. "Grey...in the chest. All I own. The house and land in Whitby. The deed is there. Let me sign it over to...to Allegra." He sighed in finality as he signed the deed and held it out to her.

She choked back her tears. "You don't have to."

"I do. An atonement, however small. The wrongs we've done you. 'Tis the least the Wickhams owe the Baniards." He gazed at Allegra. There was a faraway shadow in his soft blue eyes. "We might have been friends and neighbors. Was I...was I your champion today?"

"The bravest in the land," she whispered.

He smiled then, a smile of such sweetness that it broke her heart. "Your brave champion. 'Tis...'tis the best thing I ever did in my whole clumsy life..." He sighed again and closed his eyes and slipped away.

"Sir Greyston, the dawn is breaking."

Grey struggled up from sleep and took the cup of coffee that Jagat Ram offered him. He looked around the cabin of Captain Smythe's ship and noted that his chests were gone. "Have you transferred my conveniences to the prize ship?"

"All but your bed furnishings here."

"And Mistress Mackworth's? That is to say, Mistress Baniard's?"

"She hasn't yet asked me, Sir Greyston."

He nodded. "I'll go to her." He frowned, wondering at Allegra's mood this morning. She had been like a haunted wraith since Tom Wickham's death last night, agreeing numbly as he brought her back to the ship, persuaded her to don fresh gown and shoes, urged her to take a bite of supper. She had fallen into an exhausted sleep at last.

It had taken most of the night for Captain Smythe's people to return the contraband goods to the smugglers' ship. Baines would captain the prize and bring both cargo and brigands to the authorities in London, while Captain Smythe continued on his voyage north. There would be a fine reward for everyone involved.

He was surprised not to find Allegra in her cabin. Even more surprised to learn from a seaman that she had asked to be brought ashore before first light.

After a worried search of the cave and the beach, he found her at last sitting on a jumble of rocks at some distance from the cavern. She was lost in thought, staring out at the rising sun. Her hair blew loosely around her head—a soft ebony halo—and her cheeks glowed pink from the brightness in the eastern sky. But the remote expression on her face gave Grey a chill of dread. "Sweet Allegra," he said, sitting down beside her, "are you well?"

She lifted her head and stared at him. Her eyes were empty. "I don't know what to do," she said. Her voice was the high-pitched singsong of a lost and frightened child.

He smiled gently and tried to gather her into his arms. "'Tis simple enough. Marry me and come back to Baniard Hall."

She flinched from his embrace. "I can't. I have nothing to give you, Grey."

"You have all your love, and all your sweetness."

"No! Don't you understand? All that time, all those years. I had only my hatred to sustain me. And now Tom is dead, and I have nothing. I never thought beyond killing the Wickhams. All those years. And now—nothing. No purpose in my life."

"No purpose? There's you and me! And our future. I *love* you!" He took her by the shoulders and pressed his mouth to hers. Her lips were cold and unresponsive.

She pushed him away and shook her head. "I think I must be as dead as poor Tom. I have no feeling, no joy. No sorrow, even. The world is an empty, hollow place, and I'm frightened. Don't waste your time on me, Grey."

He swore softly. "And what will you do?" he said, his lip curling in bitter sarcasm. "Spend the next two years in a bottle of gin?"

She groaned. "I don't know. Go away. I don't know."

He felt helpless, frustrated, boiling with unreasoning fury as he watched her move farther away from him with each word. How could he reach her? "Damn it, I love you!" he repeated, his voice dropping to an angry growl. "You gave me a reason to live again. Why can't I do the same for you?"

Her dark eyes were wide and blank. He had never seen such desolation in all his life. "Because I'm dead," she whispered.

"You're alive!" he bellowed, and slapped her across the face as hard as he could. And then a second time. He raised his hand to strike her again.

"Stop!" she cried, holding up her arms to ward off the blow. "That hurts!"

"Yes!" he said, grabbing her by the shoulders and shaking her with all his might. "Because you're alive! So long as you can feel pain, you can feel joy! There's time enough to join the Baniards in the cold emptiness of death."

She was beginning to tremble violently, her mask of control crumbling. She tore at his hands on her shoulders. "Leave me alone."

"How many more times must I strike you to bring you back to me? To bring you back to life? You said it to me once. Let the dead rest. You can't atone for something that wasn't your doing. You can't bring them back by destroying your own life!"

She stared at him, wild-eyed. "I have no right to live!"

"They're dead and you're not. Accept it!" God forgive me, he thought, and struck her once again with the flat of his hand. She recoiled in pain, her hands going to her face, and collapsed into a fit of convulsive sobbing.

He pulled her into his arms and cradled her quaking form against his breast. He felt his own tension easing as she wept. Somehow he knew that the bitterness of the past was draining out of her with every burning tear she shed. The tears she had refused to shed for eight long years.

Her face was ravaged and swollen by the time she lifted her head from his chest. But there was a serenity in her eyes that he'd never seen before. He held her face in his hands and kissed her over and over again, tasting the salt of her tears. She needed him, and he felt humble and proud to serve this creature who had so completely stolen his heart.

"Lord Ridley, if we're to catch the tide, you'd best come aboard now."

He looked up. One of the sailors waited at a respectful distance, waving his arm in the direction of the ships. He stood up and helped Allegra to her feet. "Do you come with me, love? Baniard Hall needs the whisper of taffeta in its rooms."

"Not yet," she said. "Let me go away for a little while. To Whitby. To Tom's house. My house. Just for a while."

"Are you sure?"

"Let me bury the ghosts. And my hatred. Once for all." She laughed sadly. "Who would have thought a Wickham could be so endearing? Why should I feel grief at his death?" She sighed. "Let me go to Yorkshire on Captain Smythe's ship. You can return to London." She must have seen his unease. "Don't be afraid, my dearest Grey," she added. "I'll learn to live and laugh again. I promise you." She reached up and stroked his cheek. "Do you mind?"

"I mind very much. But I love you. And I'll wait." He smiled warmly. "Better still, I'll come for you. In a month's time." He felt his voice catch in his throat as he recalled all the dark and lonely days until this sweet woman had come into his life. "And then," he said, feeling his heart swell with love and gratitude, "and then I'll never let you go away again."

Chapter Nineteen

"I'm pleased with Mrs. Carey, the new housekeeper, Briggs." Grey slipped into the coat that Jagat Ram held out to him, admired the cut in his dressing-room mirror, then turned and examined his steward. Jonathan Briggs looked positively miserable. Still pining for Dolly, that was clear. The bloody fool, he thought. To keep his silence. As though wealth, or the lack of it, had aught to do with matters of the heart! "The other servants are comfortable with her authority?" he went on.

"Yes, milord. She has a natural air of command."

"And a beautiful daughter as well," he said with a sly smile.

Briggs looked shocked at his suggestive tone. "Milord?"

He laughed softly. "Do you really think, with Allegra waiting for me in Yorkshire, that I'd look at another woman? Even in the days when I was drunk, I wouldn't have been that much of a fool. Now that I'm sober…"

Briggs shuffled the papers he held. He was too proud and honorable to show resentment, but he couldn't completely hide his aching heart. "You're very fortunate, milord. Allegra—Mistress Baniard, that is—showed herself from the first to be a fine woman. Though we knew nothing of her noble birth then. Very fortunate indeed."

"Yes," Grey agreed. "I only remarked on the housekeeper's daughter because I was thinking of you."

"I, milord?"

"Yes. Isn't it time you yourself were getting married? I should like to see you settled. And the Carey girl is a handsome wench. She'd make a fine bride. I'd be more than willing to give her a small dowry, so you could set up your own household on the grounds. Come. What do you say?"

The mournful expression on Briggs's face was slowly turning to one of horror. "Married?" His voice sounded choked.

Grey watched as his valet tied his lace cravat in neat folds, then gave it a final pat. "Yes, Ram. This will do very nicely to be married in. Have the tailor finish the breeches as we agreed." He frowned at Briggs. "So silent? Well, perhaps the Carey girl isn't to your liking. But one of the other girls here at the Hall? Barbara can sulk. And Margery whines. But Verity has her charms."

Briggs's face was turning red. "Milord!"

He shrugged. "Not interested? Perhaps it's just as well. I need your services at the moment. And a sighing lover wouldn't suit my purposes." He raised a warning finger to Jagat Ram, who scarcely managed to hide his smirk. God knew how he himself had sighed for Allegra every minute of every hour since he'd returned to the Hall!

"Your purposes, milord?" said Briggs.

"You know that I've sent Gifford to Court with Baron Ellsmere's deathbed confession. I should like to be able to give Allegra the king's pardon of the Baniards as a wedding present. If you could but add your voice and influence to Gifford's…"

"London? But I'm needed here, Lord Ridley."

"Not for the next few weeks. 'Tis a quiet time. The harvest is in, and the cottagers are feeling mellow. Well disposed toward the Lord of the Manor. And with the capable Mrs. Carey here…"

"But…London. I have few friends at Court, milord. And my brother's title is modest. I fear my influence will be trifling. Surely you yourself…"

He shook his head vehemently. Every day he was getting stronger, seeing the past with a clearer eye, feeling the jagged wounds heal. He had stopped missing the gin after that first week. He had looked for joy in his days, and had struggled to bury the darkness of the past.

But he wasn't brave enough yet to face London society. He had stayed cooped up in Morgan House while Gifford had inquired after Wickham and sent his men to scour the pawnbrokers' shops for the knife. And, on his way back to Shropshire, he'd only stayed in London long enough to refresh himself and see that Baines delivered the prize ship and the smugglers to the proper authorities. He wasn't ready to risk the humiliation of being seen at Court or in St. James's Park or in any of the clubs or coffee houses where Viscount Ridley had been greeted with warmth not so very long ago.

"Stay at Morgan House and assist Gifford in whatever way you can," he said. "I charge you, as well, with a difficult undertaking. This will be your burden alone. Gifford has more than enough to do."

"Whatever you wish, milord. I stand ready to serve you."

"'Tis the matter of my friends. I should hope to have Lady Mortimer and Lord Richard Halford attend my wedding. But we parted on a note of acrimony. You are to bring them my warmest greetings and my humble apology."

Did he only imagine the sudden light in Briggs's eye? "Yes, milord," said the steward.

"Peacemaking takes time, you understand. Friendships must be nurtured. Lady Dorothy is particularly sensitive. I fear I hurt her exceeding much."

"But with her capacity for forgiveness, her sweet nature, her kind and generous spirit..." Briggs stopped abruptly, blushing to the roots of his blond hair. He cleared his throat and studied his shoes. When he continued speaking, his voice was low and strained. "I'll call upon the lady directly I arrive in London. And assure her of your amity."

Grey scowled. "It will take more than a simple assurance. I charge you to call upon the lady every day." He had to turn his head aside. It was difficult to look upon the expression of mingled joy and pain on Briggs's face without smiling.

"Every day?" he croaked.

"Every day. And I order you to take her to the theatre at least twice a week. And strolling in the Mall, if the weather holds." He stared up at the ceiling in thought and scratched his chin. "Oh, and take her for tea at Mr. Twining's Tea Shop in the Strand. The ladies seem to like it, as I recall." He waved an indifferent hand. "And any other amusements you can think of, that Lady Dorothy might enjoy. If you need a proper suit, have Gifford direct you to my London tailor."

"But, milord, I..."

"Damn it, Briggs! Do you work for me, or do you not? You're to do all this in my name. And with a right good will, by God, whatever your personal feelings in the matter! If you find Dolly's company a trial, you'll simply have to endure it for my sake. Now go away, and let me talk to Ram."

"Milord." Briggs set his jaw in a hard line and backed from the room.

Grey turned to Jagat Ram. "Now, you said you received a letter from Gifford this morning?"

"Yes, Sir Greyston. And—as you instructed me—I have not opened it." He pulled a letter from his pocket and handed it to Grey.

"Good. If it requires a reply, I'll expect you to get my letter in the post without Briggs knowing of it." He tore open the letter and read it quickly, smiling in pleasure at the message. "I knew I could depend on Gifford."

Ram raised a dark, inquisitive eyebrow. "May I ask, Sir Greyston?"

"You may not."

Ram chuckled. "I am thinking you are very satisfied with yourself."

"Satisfied, but scarcely content." His body ached with longing and desire. "Three weeks, Ram. I think I'll go mad until I see her again."

Ram nodded. "Is it that Mr. Morgan will be needing to work in the almshouse a great many days?"

He laughed softly. "'Tis not the days that trouble me, my friend. 'Tis the nights!"

The ruins of the old abbey came up out of the soft fog like the bare bones of a mythic and long-gone sea creature. Allegra felt the damp mist on her face and smiled. It had been a sweet and comforting month. Her soul had been washed clean of its rancor, like the sea rocks when the tide came in; the hatred and bitterness had blown away with the strong, heather-scented wind that swept over the moors and out to sea. She was glad she'd had this time of solitude. She had found peace.

She heard the tinkle of a sheep's bell beyond the crumbling walls of Whitby Abbey, and then a shepherd emerged from the mist, leading his flock. He tugged his hat in her direction and she responded with a polite nod. The inhabitants of the town had left her alone most of the time—not out of a sense of exclusion, but because they respected her privacy.

She had found them to be a warmhearted lot. They had been fond of Tom Wickham's aunt; they seemed to assume, as a matter of course, that the old woman's beneficiary was equally deserving of their friendship. And the several tenants who paid rent on her land were positively deferential.

She passed the abbey and took the footpath that followed along the top of the cliffs and led toward Robin Hood's Bay. The air was colder here, smothered by the mist, the drifting white blanket that came in off the North Sea and hung along the shore on windless days. She could hear the cormorants wheeling and shrieking somewhere below her. She passed several small thorn trees, their branches twisted inward, as if to shelter themselves from the northerly gales and the corrosive salt air. The wild beauty of the place took her breath away.

"Oh, Grey," she whispered. How she yearned to share this serenity with him. To walk the sandy beaches and climb the heights. To stand on the cliff when the wind blew strong, and feel the rain on their faces. And still there were four long days until his arrival. *Saturday, the twenty-fourth,* his note had said. *I adore you.*

She moved inland from the cliff path, making her way into the tree-filled hollow that sheltered her small cottage. Fingers of fog had managed to penetrate even this snug dell; the autumn-stripped trees were enveloped, and strings of mist threaded the last of the roses near the door. The cottage was old and cozy, still bearing in its rusty sandstone walls the distinctive diagonal chisel marks of the Yorkshire masons.

She hurried inside to the large sitting room that occupied most of the ground floor, lit a fire in the grate, and put away the few purchases she had made in Whitby. In a short while, the room was filled with warmth and the kettle on its hook had begun to boil. She made her tea, then cut herself a chunk of cheese and several pieces of bread, and sat by the window to enjoy her supper.

It began to grow dim, the gray evening descending like a soft veil. She lit the candles, pulled out her knitting, and settled in for a quiet hour or two before bed. She was beginning to nod before the fire when she heard a noise outside. At this hour? she thought. Who could it be? She hurried to the door and flung it wide.

A tall figure stepped out of the mist. "I couldn't wait another day," he said gruffly.

"Grey!" She threw herself into his arms, welcoming the sweetness of his kiss. His mouth was cold from the sea air, and his cloak felt damp beneath her fingers. But the warmth in her heart turned the October twilight to summer. "Come inside," she said. "You must be chilled to the bone."

"And worn to the bone as well. I rode all the way, scarcely stopping."

"Alone?"

"I couldn't bear the thought of a slow carriage journey. And Ram is no horseman."

She gulped back her tears of joy. "Oh, you foolish, dear man. Have you had supper?"

"Yes. An inn outside of Malton. But if you have a barn for my horse, and a hot bath…"

She pointed toward a small stone outbuilding. "I think there's fodder there. Tom's aunt kept a cow."

He kissed her again, but made no move to release her. "Allegra," he said. His voice was soft and hoarse.

She saw the doubt in his eyes. "Did you fear I'd stop loving you?"

He pressed her to his chest and groaned. "I'd lie in bed at night and wonder if I'd merely dreamt it all. If my sweet Allegra would still be waiting for me."

"Waiting and eager, my love," she murmured.

He kissed her exuberantly then, patted her rump and laughed. "No more eager than I, woman! Get me into that bath—then show me to your bed. I've been dreaming of this night for weeks. 'Twas enough to make me want to go back to the gin!"

While she heated water and filled the tub, he undressed before the fire. She felt shameless—watching him, admiring the lithe strength of him, the easy grace, the potent body that filled her with desire.

He grinned and lowered himself into the tub. "Hussy! You once accused me of having wicked eyes. What am I to think of a woman who looks at me the way you do?"

She tossed her shoulder at him. "Think what you wish," she said pertly. "'Tis my pleasure to look at you if I choose."

He snorted. "And what do I have for *my* pleasure?"

"In point of fact," she said, bustling to a cupboard in one corner of the room, "you can have Barbados water. Your saucy stillroom maid hasn't forgotten what pleases you." She poured out a small glassful of the soothing liquid and brought it to him in his bath.

He downed it quickly and smacked his lips. "As good as I remembered it. I'm not sure I've made a wise trade. A stillroom maid for a wife."

"I can do both, you arrogant dog."

He held up his glass for more and leered goatishly. "You can do many things."

She reached for the glass. With a sly smile, he dropped it a moment before she could grasp it, and curled his fingers around her wrist instead. She squealed in surprise as she felt herself pulled into the tub on top of him. "Grey!" she cried, pushing against his wet, hairy chest.

"*This* is my pleasure, woman. You in my arms." He embraced her shoulders with dripping arms and kissed her—a burning, searching, hungry kiss that left her trembling.

She put her hands beneath the warm water and felt his body, sleek and strong. It gave her a thrill of joy and anticipation. She ran her fingers down his ribs, kneaded the flesh of his hips, stroked the knotted muscles of his thighs. She purred in contentment. What heaven!

She giggled, aware suddenly that her skirts were soaked. "Godamercy, my gown. Let me up, Grey," she laughed.

"Alas," he said, echoing her laughter, "what's to be done?" He helped her to stand, then climbed out of the tub himself. He glanced down at his wet body; his member was swollen and erect.

She stifled further laughter. "What a peculiar bath, to have produced such a result."

"Indeed! We shall have to see if the bath has affected you in like manner." He reached for the fastenings of her gown and undressed her with impatient hands, stopping only now and again to pull her into his arms and kiss her. At last she stood naked before him. He cupped his hands around her breasts and rubbed his thumbs against her nipples until she gasped in pleasure. "Yes," he said. "Hard and firm. 'Tis a most peculiar bath. A strange malady."

"Can you recommend a cure, milord?" she whispered.

"That I can." He scratched enticingly at the small birthmark on her breast and bent and kissed it. "Charming. I remember it from the day I came into your bedchamber, and your shift fell from your shoulder. It was all I could do to keep from kissing it."

"'Tis yours now," she said, wrapping her arms around his neck. "And all of me."

"Then come, love." He spread his cloak in front of the fireplace and laid her down upon it. He extinguished the candles in the room; the glow from the grate cast warm shadows across the walls and sparkled in his topaz eyes as he knelt over her. He kissed her face and neck, and when she arched her body in rapture, he kissed her breasts and swirled his tongue around the hard, eager points.

Writhing, she raised her hips to his firm member, aching to feel him within her, but he chuckled softly. "Not yet. 'Tis too much joy to tease you." He thrust his manhood against her thighs, gliding it sensuously from her loins, across her belly and up to the sensitive hollow between her breasts. When she moaned and wriggled in delicious pleasure, he pressed her breasts together with strong hands to capture and enclose his burning shaft. He was warm and silken-soft and hard all at the same time; she felt her senses quickening with the plunge and slide of his manhood. She scratched at his knees in a frenzy of wild delight; in response he clutched her breasts more firmly and increased the vigor of his strokes.

She cried out in pain and tugged at his hands. His fervor had carried him beyond gentleness. "No more," she whispered. Her voice was tentative, fearful to make him think she didn't want him. "Come into me now, Grey. Please."

His eyes were dark with passion. "I don't want it to end so soon."

"Will it end if you don't move in me?"

"Not so quickly."

"Then don't move," she said, opening to receive his hard thrust. He was thick and full, and the feel of him within her, even quiescent, made her tremble and burn, as though an icy flame were racing through her body. She remembered the first time they had made love, when she'd discovered the strength of that odd internal muscle. Now she tightened it around him and was delighted to hear his gasp of pleasure. But when she did it again, and then a third time, he groaned.

"You witch," he said, panting, "do you think I can keep still for that?" He kissed her hard and began to move against her hips, rocking and thrusting in a wild rhythm that drove her to the edge of madness. Her body was on fire, her loins quivering and pulsing in answer to his all-consuming need. And when he climaxed in a roar of triumph, she cried aloud and wrapped her legs around him, never wanting to let him go.

He sighed and buried his head in her neck. "I think I'll never stop marveling at the joy of loving you. And when we're married, I'll want you every minute of every day. 'Aha!' the servants will say, when they see you vanish into my rooms. 'His Lordship is harrying Her Ladyship again.'" He kissed her on the tip of her nose and smiled warmly. "If it pleases you, I think we'll leave here in a day or so. I've already spoken to the rector in Ludlow about marrying us. We can take the mail coach home."

"To Shropshire?"

"I thought we'd stop in London first. I want to see how Briggs is faring."

"Mr. Briggs in London?"

He laughed. Rather smugly, it seemed to Allegra. "He's squiring Dolly around the city. Upon my orders. Perhaps by now he's managed to get up the courage to kiss her hand, if nothing more."

She frowned at him. "You've thrown them together? Knowing of Mr. Briggs's pride? Oh, Grey, how could you do such a thing?" She jumped to her feet in annoyance, then sank again to her knees as a wave of vertigo swept over her. "How...very strange," she said, blinking against the odd sensation. "For a moment I thought I should faint." She turned to him, her eyes wide with concern. "I pray I'm not coming down with a fever."

She had expected sympathy, not a shout of laughter. "'Od's blood!'" he cried happily.

She scowled. Even loving him, she found his humor unseemly. She could be truly ill. "What is it?" she demanded.

"Don't be angry," he said, drawing her back down into his arms. "Tell me, when I was holding your breasts before, and you pushed my hands away...Was it because they hurt?"

"Y-yes," she stammered, taken aback. "They've been quite tender all this week. I scarce know why."

"And your flux? Has it come as usual?"

Though she had lain with him, this still seemed too intimate a discourse to hold with a man. "No. 'Tis late. No doubt, the disruption in my life…the ship and the storm and the cruelties of the smugglers." She shuddered.

"Oh, sweet heaven," he groaned, holding her more tightly. "Have I atoned enough that God would bring me such happiness?"

"Happiness?" She gaped at the unexpected thought he'd put into her head. She felt like a naive fool. "Oh, Grey, am I carrying a child?"

He sounded very close to tears. "Our child," he choked. "Yes. It must be so. I remember that Ruth…" He cleared his throat and stood up, turning away to hide his fervent emotions from Allegra. "We'll marry tomorrow. In Whitby." He helped her to her feet and kissed her with such love and tenderness that her heart burst with the joy of the sweet burden she knew she must be carrying. She would give him the child he had so longed for. She would replace his dreadful loss with the precious fruit of her womb.

He sat her before the fire while he fetched a fresh shift from her trunk, then dressed her as a loving parent would; he filled a warming pan with coals and carried it to the bedchamber above to heat the sheets for her comfort. She felt pampered and petted. And when he carried her to bed and tucked her into the circle of his arms as he drifted off to sleep, she knew that she would only have sweetness in her life from this moment on.

Grey scowled at the long, steep flight of steps that led up from the town of Whitby to the old Church of St. Mary's, with its square Norman walls and its battlements. "Are you sure you don't wish me to hire a cart? And take the road?"

Allegra reached out and smoothed the frown from his brows. "Dear Grey, I've been coming up and down those stairs for nearly a month, each time I came into town to the shops. I'm merely pregnant. I'm not a helpless cripple."

"But nearly two hundred steps," he growled. "At least let me carry you."

She giggled. She had never loved him more than at this moment, when he was behaving like a schoolboy in love. "I'll be too heavy," she said, lifting her basket filled with ribbons and laces and a pretty new pair of shoes. "You should never have bought me all these trifles."

"When we get home, I want to buy you everything. Gowns and jewels and…" He frowned again as two farmers passed them and chuckled and nudged each other in the ribs. "Damn it," he muttered, "why does everyone stare at us?"

"We're the town attraction. At least since you spoke to the rector of St. Mary and asked him to marry us. It doesn't take gossip long to spread in a small village." She pointed up the hill to the ruins of Whitby Abbey, which stood at a short distance from the church. Beyond the ruins was a large, gray stone manor house. "That's where the Cholmleys live, I'm told. They're the only gentry in Whitby. The Lords of the Manor. But with the family away in London, and Abbey House unoccupied at the moment, *you*, my love, are the only nobility here." She grinned. "And a viscount, into the bargain! 'Tis an event for people who only know farming and shipbuiding."

He seemed scarcely to be listening. His eyes were warm on her face, examining her as though he couldn't get enough of her. "Do you know how adorable you are when you smile? I want to kiss you until you beg for mercy. Right here on the street."

She felt herself blushing. "At least wait until we're married."

"Why, then, my bride," he said, holding out his hand, "shall we?" She nodded and slipped her fingers through his, allowing him to lead her up the stairs.

They had scarcely taken half a dozen steps, however, when a young woman darted up from the street and curtsied. In her hand she held a large and somewhat bedraggled flower, which she held out to Allegra. "It bean't right for a bride to be wi'out flowers on her weddin' day. 'Tis the last from my mam's garden." She pressed the blossom into Allegra's hand, turned scarlet, and skipped away.

Allegra was still staring after her in surprise and pleasure when an old woman came hobbling up the stairs, leaning on a stout walkingstick. Allegra recognized her as one of her tenants. Several townspeople crowded at the foot of the stairs, looking expectantly up at the crone. She smiled—a toothless grin—reached into her basket and pulled out a bunch of dried rosemary. "We be wishin' ye well, your worships." She lifted her stick and gestured at the long, meandering staircase. "Every bride and coffin in Whitby travels this way." She handed the fragrant herbs to Allegra, then turned toward the assembled villagers. "Well," she scolded, "what be ye waitin' on? They won't bite. An' that's the truth, sure as rain."

One by one the townsfolk shuffled up the stairs to shyly hand Allegra their bouquets—a handful of sea grasses and reeds, purple heather from the moors, a fading rose—until Allegra's arms were filled with their bounty and her eyes misted with tears. She felt warmed and welcomed by these strangers—a reminder, lest she forget, that there were more good people than evil ones in the world. She smiled at Grey, too moved, too overwhelmed to say a word.

He grinned. "Begad, a most excellent village! We shall have a wedding as has never been seen before!" He turned to the old woman. "Does Whitby have a tavern with enough ale to quench a town's thirst?"

She nodded vigorously. "Aye, Your Lordship!"

Grey fished in the pocket of his coat and pulled out a sack of gold coins. "Then tell your tavernkeeper to roast what meats he has, and tap every keg, and make us a wedding feast for every soul in Whitby to enjoy!" He silenced the cheer that rose from the crowd with a wave of his hand. "Those of you who wish it, come to the church and see us married. It would be our honor. But first…" He winked at Allegra and lowered his voice. "I will have my way, you saucy miss." He turned again to the townspeople. "Find me four strong lads with a stout chair who aren't daunted by these steps." He kissed Allegra's hand, his eyes filled with love. "My lady shall come to her wedding in style."

And so she did—borne on the most elegant chair the good citizens of Whitby could find, her arms filled with her fragrant and humble bouquet. The clergyman blessed their union to the accompaniment of huzzahs from the spectators; then everyone trooped back down the hill to celebrate and dance and drink their toasts to the bride and groom.

It was night before they climbed the steps again on their way home from the merry tavern scene. They waved to the townsfolk who wished them a good night, and made their way slowly up the hill.

They were silent, filled with the wonder of their love, the clear stillness of the night, the beauty of the large, full moon—so bright that it blotted out the stars. They passed the tombstones in the churchyard, old and weather-beaten, and watched the face of the moon play hide-and-seek through the ruined Gothic arches of the old abbey.

Grey stopped suddenly and dropped to one knee before her. "I salute you, my love," he murmured. "Anne Allegra, Viscountess Ridley. It has a fine sound to it. It suits you."

She felt a surprising pang of anger and regret, like a sharp knife to her heart. "They should have been here to share my joy," she said, feeling the hot tears flow.

He rose to his feet and pulled her into his arms. In the bright moonlight she could read the uneasy doubt on his face. "Allegra, I hoped…my gift…Will it be enough to ease your sorrow, I wonder?"

"What is it?"

"I had a letter from Gifford. Just before I left Wenlock Edge. He and Briggs have obtained the king's pardon. The Baniards are absolved of their crimes. Your father's good name is restored."

Her rush of joy was followed by bitterness. "The king's pardon came too late."

"Will you still nurture your hatred? Let it go."

"I thought I had," she said. "When Tom died. But I think I'll hate John Wickham forever." She sighed. "Take me to bed, love. And make me glad to be alive."

They held the candle between them as they mounted the steps to their bedchamber. They undressed quickly and lay down together on the large, curtained bed. Though Grey was a solicitous and tender lover this evening, Allegra found herself chafing with a vague discontent. His caresses, his kisses, the way he touched her body with gentle hands. She felt a distance in his manner tonight, a diffidence, a…a lack of *passion*, she thought suddenly. Had the ceremony of their marriage destroyed the spontaneity that had brought excitement to their previous encounters?

And then she remembered his behavior all day. She sat up in bed and put her hands on her hips. "Am I to have eight months of this?" she demanded. "Eight months of being treated like a fragile child's poppet whenever you take me to bed?"

He sat up in his turn and scowled at her. "What do you mean?"

"I have a body that was tempered by a great deal of work, Grey. You can be more forceful when you make love to me. I'll not break."

"'Tis only your condition. I have concerns. That's natural enough."

She flounced out of bed and stood in the center of the room, glaring at him. "Then you shall not have me at all, milord. Not until I'm brought to bed with our child."

"Rebellion? So soon as we're married?" He crooked a finger at her. His eyebrows arched devilishly in the light of the candle. "Come here, you saucy wench."

She shook her head and danced around the room, waving her arms at him like a teasing child. "You'll have to catch me."

He growled and leapt out of bed, charging her like a wild bull. Laughing, she managed to elude him at first. But he was fleet of foot and the room was small. She found herself backed into a corner, unceremoniously tucked under his arm, and flung across the bed. She tried to scramble away, but he pinned her down, one large hand on the flat of her belly. The other hand pried her legs apart. "You imp, is this forceful enough for you?" he said, and plunged his fingers within her.

She gasped and writhed at his loving assault, managing at length to wriggle from under his imprisoning hands. And when he rose on all fours to pursue her, she caught him off guard with a violent push and toppled him onto his back.

Pressing her advantage, she straddled him and positioned herself above his eager, poised member. "How do *you* like a timorous lover, milord?" She lowered herself gently onto his shaft, and watched his look of surprise turn to one of anticipation. But—though he thrust upward with his hips, urging her to move—she kept her body still, his member captured and restrained within her. He groaned in frustration and she grinned.

Lifting her forefinger, she began to scrawl words across his hairy chest. Letter by letter she spelled out her message, forcing him to speak it aloud while he gasped and twitched at the sensuous touch of her finger. "Allegra is not fragile," she wrote. She dotted her "i's" by tickling delicately at his nipples.

"No more," he muttered at last. "Grey is not a patient man!" He grabbed her around the waist, wrenched her off him, and threw her onto her back. He thrust himself wildly into her, wringing a cry of ecstasy from her lips. He was as forceful as she would have wanted him to be, riding her with a passion that left her senses reeling. By the time they climaxed in a burning, drenching thrill, he had taken her in every position he could devise.

She lay exhausted, warm and contented. But after a little while, she began to giggle. "I have no doubt our child slept through all of that."

He nuzzled his head against her neck and kissed her and nibbled at her ear. "For what I have in mind for you in the next few months," he said, "I hope he's a very sound sleeper!"

The night had grown cold. They dressed for bed, crawled between the heavy blankets, and fell asleep entwined. The happiest day of my life, thought Allegra, just before she drifted off.

She woke to the sounds of a struggle, a muffled cry, the gurgle of a choked voice. The bed was empty. She groped for flint and candle, striking a light with shaking fingers. She scrambled off the bed and held the candle high.

Grey knelt on the floor, straddling the slight, well-knit figure of a man. He had one hand at the man's throat and the other on his hand, which clutched an evil-looking knife. As Allegra watched, Grey wrenched the blade from the man's fist and sent it spinning across the floor. "The bloody rogue tried to kill me as I slept," he growled.

Allegra frowned down at the stranger. How dare he disturb their sweet idyll? A thief in the night, no doubt. His dark, greasy hair was loose and wild, and his face was twisted into a savage scowl. He shook his head from side to side, clutching at Grey's hand on his throat. He uttered a foul oath, then looked squarely at Allegra for the first time.

She gasped and fell back a step, one hand going to her bosom. "Godamercy," she breathed. *"Charlie?"*

Chapter Twenty

Charlie gulped the last of his ale, banged down his tankard and rubbed his sleeve across his mouth. "Have you nothing stronger than this, Annie?"

Allegra frowned in dismay. "I have a few cordials that I distilled."

"But no brandy?" He sneered in Grey's direction. "Did you marry a toupet man who doesn't drink?"

Grey muttered darkly. Allegra put a restraining hand on his arm, her eyes begging his silence. For this was Charlie—alive! Her own dear brother come back to her. She couldn't bear to see a quarrel between the two men she loved the most.

She had wept and hugged Charlie, ecstatic to see him. She had assailed him with questions, so bubbling and happy and unbelieving that she scarcely waited for him to answer one before asking another. He had seemed uncomfortable with the extremity of her emotions, turning her aside at last with a brusque request for food and drink.

"Will you have more cold mutton, Charlie?"

"No." He stood up and restlessly paced the room, then stopped and looked at Grey. "Ridley. There was a rogue of that name who bought Baniard Hall from young Ellsmere, I heard."

Grey lowered his shaggy brows and clenched his jaw. "I am that man, sir."

Charlie let out a shout of laughter. "Zounds, Annie, but you turned out to be a shrewd one! You were a sweet little chicken. But I never thought you could look after yourself so well. 'Tis a pity there wasn't a Wickham heiress. I might have married and screwed the whore to get back the Hall myself." He laughed bitterly. "A nice bit of revenge that would have been, eh?"

Allegra pressed her lips together. "Charlie, Grey is the man I love. I won't have you talk that way."

Her brother shrugged. "If you choose to feather your nest on your back, Annie, why should I give a fig?"

"Now, damn you, sir!" Grey leapt for Charlie.

"No! Grey!" Allegra rushed to intervene. "Please, love," she said, putting her arms around Grey's neck. "Do you think that Charlie suffered less than I?"

Grey untwined her arms and took a deep, steadying breath. He nodded at Charlie. "You were a gentleman once, sir. I trust you haven't forgotten that. This is my wife, my viscountess. And your sister. Kindly have the honor to show her respect, and we can be friends, as God intended kin to be." He hesitated, then offered his hand.

Charlie muttered a soft oath to himself and accepted Grey's gesture of peace. He looked abashed at his own behavior. "My hand, sir. 'Tis difficult to forget the past, you understand."

"For Allegra as well. Bury your anger, and rejoice that you've found one another again."

"Aye." Charlie resumed his pacing, stopping to peer out at the night sky and drum his fingers against the windowpane. "So Tom Wickham is dead. I came here to kill him when I heard in London that he'd inherited this place. It must have been recent, his death."

Allegra sighed. "Scarcely a month ago. He…he died in my arms," she added, chewing at her lip.

Charlie's mouth twisted in a cruel smile. "I should have liked to see that."

She started to protest, then kept silent. Was Charlie's hatred any more bitter than her own had been? Best to shift the discourse. She could tell him of Tom's bravery at another time.

She looked toward the window; it would soon be dawn. Grey had long since donned shirt and breeches, but she was still in her nightshift. Perhaps she would go upstairs and put on her gown. "Have you slept at all tonight, Charlie?" When he shook his head, she reached to help him off with his coat and make him more comfortable. "Let me fetch fresh sheets for the bed, dear one, and then you can take off your boots and sleep for a little while."

The coat was well cut and of a fine, expensive cloth, but uncommonly heavy. Allegra frowned. Was that the outline of a pistol in a deep, inner pocket? "You were in London?" she asked. "What did you do there?"

He rubbed his nose with the back of his hand. "This and that. There are few opportunities for a man who must use an assumed name."

Godamercy! In all the excitement, she'd never told him the glad news. "Not any longer! Oh, Charlie. You can be Charles Baniard again. And forevermore. We're free! Tom willingly confessed his father's plot before he died. The king has granted his pardon. The Baniards are absolved. Oh, Charlie," she cried again, throwing her arms around him, "don't you understand? You're *free!*"

"Free?" He snarled and shook her off. "Three years ago I escaped from the plantations. A runaway. For two years I tried to leave America. I was a fugitive, living on the road, stealing food and clothing, milking untended cows and eating grass to keep myself alive. Through rain and cold and bitter nights. And always fearing that I'd be discovered. I managed at last to find a ship, and served like a dog 'tween decks to earn my passage. I came home to learn that John Wickham was dead, Tom Wickham vanished, and the Hall sold to this caitiff." He gestured angrily in Grey's direction. "*Free?*" He spat the word. "There's a rope waiting for me, on some gibbet, for returning from transportation." He gave Allegra a sarcastic bow. "Or would you like 'Charles Baniard' to openly turn himself in? If I escaped hanging, they'd merely send me back to the plantations. So much for being 'free.'"

Grey stepped forward. His face was like stone, but his voice was calm and reasonable. "I still have influence at Court, I think. I can plead your cause in London. A pardon, at the very least, from your wrongful sentence. If I speak to the right people, perhaps I can have your title restored. Baronet, was it not? And then we might arrange a sinecure or small pension from the king, in compensation for the loss of your estates. I think it can be done. Give me the name of the plantation owner as well. I'll send him a fat settlement, to satisfy him and keep him from making mischief against you."

Allegra's heart swelled with gratitude. How good and generous of Grey. She slipped her arm through his. Dear heaven! She felt the unexpected tremble of his body, the quivering in his arm, and stared in sudden shocked remembrance. How could she have forgotten his humiliation in Ludlow, the dreadful story of his London disgrace that Dolly had told? And now, to return to London again, to brave the Court, the scorn of society…Oh, God, how difficult this must be for him! "Are you sure you want to do this for Charlie, my love?"

He looked down at her. She could see the veil of fear and haunting doubt in his eyes. "'Tis for you, Allegra," he muttered. "Not for him."

"But perhaps Gifford…or Briggs…"

He sighed tiredly and passed a hand across his mouth. "And if they failed? How soon would it be before I saw reproach in your eyes?

Contempt? It was a mad dream I had, to think I could hide away in Shropshire forever. Let me face my demons and prove my worth, if I can. With a worthy cause." He squared his shoulders and managed a thin smile. "Come, Baniard, what do you say to that?"

Allegra blinked back her tears. How she loved him—this good, brave man. She wondered if her brother would ever appreciate Grey's sacrifice. "You see, Charlie," she said, "your little Annie made a fine choice for a husband. God willing, Sir Charles Baniard will be restored."

Charlie curled his lip in bitterness. "'Tis the least I'm owed, after what I've endured."

His unhappiness was breaking her heart. "Oh, please, Charlie, forget the past. Learn to enjoy life again. As I have."

"Forget the past? Do you know what the rice fields are like? Stinking marshland and heat and the merciless flies and mosquitoes. Degradation and brutality, day after unending day. I cannot imagine that hell, with its fires, could be any worse." As he spoke, his voice had risen to a sour whine.

Allegra frowned. "All of us endured misery," she snapped. "And learned to surmount it." She softened her tone. "Remember your Baniard pride," she chided. "Pride and patience, Grandfather used to say. Remember? What happened to your Baniard pride?"

"*This* is what happened!" he cried. He gathered his shirt at his shoulders and pulled it up to bare his back. The thick welts were like ropes of flesh, crossing one another in a sickening overlay of scar upon scar. If there were muscles beneath that tormented flesh, they were no longer visible.

Allegra fell back, gasping, her hand going to her mouth. "Oh, sweet heaven."

Charlie whirled and slammed one hand down on the table. "And *this* is what happened, for trying to escape once before." The first two joints of his little finger were missing, and the tip of the stump was bluish-black, as though the wound had been sealed with pitch.

"Oh, Charlie." Allegra began to cry, overwhelmed by her dear brother's sufferings.

"Damn it, Annie," he said in disgust. "I hate bitches who cry. My whore would feel my fist if she ever shed a tear in front of me."

"Now, by God, sir, I've had enough!" Grey reached out and smacked Charlie on the side of his head, a savage blow with his open hand. "You will guard your tongue, sirrah, or I'll thrash you like an unruly child!"

Charlie shook his head to clear it, then glared at Grey, his eyes narrowing like a viper. His hand darted into his boot top and produced a knife. "Have at me then, you damned queer cove! I'll slice your face for you!"

Allegra wrung her hands in anguish. "For the love of God, stop. Both of you. How can you do this to me, when you're both so dear to my heart?"

There was a moment of deadly silence, then Grey slowly relaxed and pulled her into his arms. "Forgive me, Allegra."

Charlie drew in a long, tortured breath and returned the knife to his boot. "No, I'm to blame. I've known naught but rough companions for a long time. Annie. Little Annie. I'm sorry." He sighed. "Do you know how much you look like Mama? I wish I had known where you were in Charles Town. I could have come to lay flowers on her grave."

"We'll put a monument to the family in the park at Baniard Hall," said Grey gruffly. "They'll not be forgotten." He cleared his throat. "Now, let's look to the future. Allegra and I will leave for London as soon as we can. 'Twere best if you stayed here. Until I can obtain a pardon for your escape, you shouldn't be seen abroad."

"Yes," said Allegra, grateful that peace had returned. "Stay here, dearest Charlie. This place…" She had a sudden thought. "Let me give it to you. Tom Wickham bequeathed it to me, to the Baniards, the day he died. You should have it. 'Tis only fair and proper. And there's a small income, which should help."

Charlie looked around the sitting room with a critical eye. "It will serve, I suppose. But if I'm to be marooned here for a time, I want my whore with me. She's a hollow-hearted bitch, but a strong moll who works like a horse. I left her in York when we came up from London."

Grey nodded. "I'll search her out. What's her name?"

Charlie snickered. "Lord! I know not. They call her Glory. That's all. I left her at the Black Dog Tavern, the other side of York, on the Selby road."

"I'll arrange for her to join you here. And, before we leave for London, I'll find a lawyer in Whitby to arrange for this cottage to be legally conveyed to you. Along with the land and its tenants." Grey frowned in thought. "If you need money, I can leave some with you. And I'll arrange with my secretary to send more. Say, another hundred pounds."

Charlie assessed him as though he were seeing him for the first time. "You're very free with money. Did my sister marry a rich man?"

Grey shrugged. "A turn of fate. The gods treated me kindly through the years."

Charlie's face was a twisted mask of resentment. "Whilst I was breaking my back," he muttered.

Hearing the tone in his voice, Allegra felt a sharp stab of pain. God willing, the reversal of his fortunes would set Charlie on the road to peace and joy again. All the ugliness, all the bitterness, would vanish, and her dear sweet Charlie would return. Just as before. She smoothed back the hair from his drawn face, his scowling brow. He looked so much older than his thirty years. There were even a few streaks of gray at his temples. "We'll send for you as soon as we can, dear one. You'll see. Everything will be put to rights."

He stared at her. His dark eyes—so like her own—were the eyes of a cornered, haunted animal, a gasping creature who seeks the last refuge and prays to be left alone to live.

"Annie," he murmured sadly, "the world hasn't been right for more than eight long years."

Chapter Twenty-One

"Oh, Dolly, I can only guess what it cost him." Allegra finished the last of her tea, put down her cup and sighed.

Lady Dorothy nodded with understanding, and motioned the waiter for the bill. "To have done so much for your brother, and in less than a month."

"I can scarcely believe it yet. A full pardon for Charlie. His title restored with all honors. Even a respectable pension. And the house that Grey rented for him on St. Martin's Lane…I'm sure it cost more than Grey said, and that he's paying for it himself."

"Have you seen your brother since he came back to London?"

"Only once. He called upon us at Morgan House. He's still so bitter. So…" It seemed almost disloyal to speak against her dear brother, "so ungrateful for what Grey has done. As though he'll settle for no less than compensation from the whole world for his suffering. As though Grey hasn't suffered on his behalf."

"And Grey never spoke of how he contrived it all?"

Allegra shook her head. "No. Day after day those first two weeks he forced himself to go to Court. Alone. And came back hours later trembling, his face ashen. He wouldn't speak of it, even to me. Oh, Dolly! The humiliations and insults he must have endured, the laughter of his old friends…'Twas a wonder he didn't go back to the gin. I don't think he was forced into a duel, but I'm sure he was challenged upon more than one occasion. It took him days to arrange an audience, but he saw the king once, and Walpole twice. And they granted his requests for Charlie. Perhaps their acceptance will go far to smoothing his way in society again."

Dolly smiled in sympathy. "He was always a little proud. A bit too confident. I have no doubt that society, in its cruelty, was only too glad to see him taken down a peg. Richard has urged him to take him along as a companion. Even if only to a coffee house or a gentleman's club. But Grey always refuses."

"And goes alone, no matter what it costs," said Allegra, feeling her husband's pain as her own. "What can I do to help him? We're invited to an assembly at Burlington House next week. 'Tis the first entertainment that Grey has accepted. I fear it greatly. What if he should feel the need for bravado in my presence? Oh, Dolly!" she cried again. "Why do men put themselves in the way to be hurt? Why are they so stupidly proud?"

Dolly laughed bitterly. "You ask *me?* That muttonhead, Jonathan Briggs! I've done everything short of throwing myself into his arms! I even had Dick mention to him, as though it were a stray thought, that I'd put aside a generous marriage portion. Should I choose to wed again, of course." She sighed. "I almost thought he'd kiss me last night. And then…"

"Are you sorry that Grey contrived to force you together?"

"I know not. 'Tis such sweet torture. But such pain, fearing that Jonathan will never surrender his pride." She stood up and smoothed on her knitted silk gloves. "I must go. I'll walk with you to the Mall, and then find a chair to take me home."

Allegra adjusted her warm cloak and picked up her muff. She nodded solemnly at the proprietor of the tea shop, who bowed low and wished Their Ladyships a pleasant afternoon. But when she and Dolly emerged into the chilly November day, she burst into a giggle. "It still seems so difficult to accept—that I'm Lady Ridley."

"I needn't ask if you and Grey love each other. I can see it in your eyes whenever you're together." Dolly smiled up at the sky and blinked. The thin afternoon sun sparkled on her tears. "I'd give up my title and my fortune to know such happiness." She sighed and brushed at her cheeks. "Do you like Morgan House?"

"More and more. 'Tis the most beautiful place I've ever seen."

"There aren't many detached mansion houses like it in London. Not anymore. Between the Great Fire and the expense of keeping up a townhouse as well as a country seat, few peers will spend the money on a great mansion. Most of them are gone now. But Grey lavished a fortune on Morgan House when he came back from India. Of course, until he bought Baniard Hall, the Ridleys had no estate save the one in London."

Allegra sighed. As magnificent as her new house on Piccadilly was, she ached to go back to her childhood home, to take her place as its mistress for the first time. "Grey has given me full discretion to refurnish Baniard Hall to my taste. As soon as we return to Shropshire."

"When will you go?"

"Not until Grey is sure that there are no claims against Charlie. No fines that must be paid. I think he's waiting for a letter from America. The release from his bondage."

"Look!" interrupted Dolly. "There's Grey now." Moving westward from the Strand, the two women had reached the edge of St. James's Park and the wide promenade known as the Mall. Despite the chill day, it was crowded with strollers—the cream of London—hoping to be seen, to exchange gossip, to flirt and arrange trysts.

Grey smiled and nodded as they approached. Allegra's heart caught at sight of him. Even among the throng, he was the most splendid of men. His tall frame was clad in a handsome dark-gray velvet coat, and his superb waistcoat was of striped silk. Even in the city, he declined to wear a periwig, tying back his own abundant brown hair and finishing it with a sprinkling of powder. A cane with an elaborately carved head was looped around his wrist with a silken cord; although it was the latest fashion, Allegra knew he carried it only to mask the fact that he wore no sword.

"Dolly," he said, taking her hand and kissing it, "how agreeable to see you." He looked at Allegra. She needed no further greeting than the love shining deeply in his amber eyes, the pleased grin on his face.

Dolly smiled in return. "You seem merry today, Grey. I should like to stay and learn the reason why. But, alas. I have a pressing engagement. Will you hail me a sedan chair?"

They said their farewells and waved good-bye to Dolly; then Allegra turned to Grey. "In truth, you *do* look merry."

He shook his head. "No. Say rather astonished. Or perhaps bemused by my own blindness. Yet strangely lighthearted as well." He held out his arm. "Come. Walk with me in the Mall. Tell me I'm not completely mad."

"Godamercy, Grey, what happened?"

"I was at Button's Coffee House in Covent Garden for most of the morning. I took a dish of coffee. A pipe of tobacco. I read the journals. The most extraordinary news. The Pickerings are ruined! Ruth's family. All of them. They've gone back to Kent, their tails between their legs. Heaven forgive me, but I felt a sense of retribution as I read the words. God knows their accusations of murder in Ruth's death, their challenge to me, were the beginning of my downfall."

"They had no right, *ever*, to accuse you."

He squeezed her arm. "Dear, loyal Allegra. But, you see, that was not the source of my present gladness. Or confusion. While I was reading the *Daily Post*, several of my old acquaintances approached. Comrades in arms from our service with the Guards. They were as pleased with the Pickering downfall as I. They swore their friendship was undimmed, and begged me to call upon them now that I'm back in the city!" He seemed awed, overwhelmed by the wonder of it. "I'd avoided them until now, fearing…Ah, well. Perhaps I fled London in foolish haste. In any event, my friends told a remarkable tale. For months now, the Pickerings have bragged of pushing Ruth into marriage with me. For the money alone." He stopped and stared at Allegra, his face twisted in consternation. "Was I blind? Was I merely her dupe? She was forever imploring me to pay her family's debts. I did it out of love, of course. But…was I a fool?"

What could she tell him? That his suspicions, after all this time, were closer to the truth than he guessed? No. It seemed too cruel. "I have no doubt she loved you deeply, Grey," she murmured.

From the look on his face, she wondered whether she had put his doubts to rest. But he merely nodded and continued walking.

"Ecod! Is this not my adversary from Ludlow?"

Allegra stifled a gasp at the sight of Sir William Batterbee, bearing down on them from across the lawn. Her heart sank. There were several men at his side, each as ostentatiously dressed as he. And though most of them were unarmed, Batterbee himself wore a sword hanging from an embroidered velvet sash around his waist. He doffed his feather-trimmed cocked hat and gave them a mocking bow. "Lord and Lady Ridley," he said.

Grey's jaw was like granite. "I have no quarrel with you, sir. Nor do I wish one."

Batterbee smiled, an oily grimace. "Nor I with you, Lord Ridley. My friends here…" he smirked at his companions, "they're all acquainted with the circumstances of our last meeting." Allegra winced as the gentlemen beside Batterbee snickered. "And since then," he went on, "I hear you've insinuated yourself back into Walpole's favor. On behalf of your new wife's family. I shall not presume to quarrel with a man who holds that kind of power. Or *money*."

Allegra felt Grey stiffen beside her, and clung more tightly to his arm. No matter what Batterbee said, she was determined that her husband not be goaded into a quarrel.

"Yes," said one of Batterbee's friends, a mincing peacock who pranced forward on the balls of his feet. "Weren't you telling us, Billy boy, how much it must have cost Ridley to ruin the Pickerings?"

Grey growled deep in his throat. "Now, by God, sir, that's a damnable lie!"

"Peace, Farrell," said Batterbee, parting his friend on the shoulder. "Though it may appear that our friend Ridley can only fight on the field of mammon, and with a weapon made of guineas, there's no *proof* that the Pickerings owe their downfall to him."

Grey let out a curse, shook free of Allegra's grasp, and leapt for Batterbee. "You dog!"

Batterbee jumped back in alarm and drew his sword. "In God's name, Farrell, give the man a blade and oblige him to fight fairly!"

Grey bared his teeth in a snarl and brandished his cane. "Not this time, you filthy mongrel. I bloodied your mouth with my fist when last we met. It will please me now to thrash you to a pulp with my cane!"

"Ha, sir!" cried Batterbee, raising his sword. "On your head be it, then!" He lunged at Grey.

To Allegra's amazement, Grey parried at once with his cane, turning aside Batterbee's sword as though he himself were similarly armed. He feinted, thrust, dodged. At length, he looped his cane around Batterbee's blade, gave a ferocious twist to his wrist, and sent the sword spinning away onto the lawn.

Allegra sagged with relief. Only then did she realize that Grey had paled during the encounter, and the cane was now trembling in his hand. But his voice, when he spoke, was strong and sure.

"Now, Batterbee," he said sardonically, "shall we begin with a few strokes for your insults to my lady in Ludlow?" He raised his cane and delivered a sharp blow to the seat of Batterbee's breeches.

"'Odds fish!" Batterbee leapt in pained surprise, wavered, then turned and fled, leaving his foppish hat in the dirt of the path.

There was no time for Allegra to enjoy Grey's triumph. Out of the corner of her eye, she saw the peacock, Farrell, begin to remove his glove. If he threw it in Grey's face, there would be no hope of avoiding a duel. Forgive me, Grey, she thought. She took a halting step forward, stumbled, and cried out. "My ankle! God preserve me!"

Grey turned to her and scowled. "Are you hurt, madam?" Without waiting for a reply, he scooped her into his arms.

She bit her lip in seeming pain. "Take...take me home, for the love of God."

He watched as Batterbee's friends withdrew from the scene, then frowned at the spectators who had crowded around. "Send for a hackney coach," he ordered.

Morgan House was only a few minutes away from the Mall. Scarcely had Allegra settled into the carriage and rested her leg on the seat opposite than the coach was passing through the gateway of the mansion and pulling up to the wide doors. Without a word, Grey lifted her out, carried her past the bowing footmen to her rooms upstairs, and gestured for her maidservants to leave. When they were alone at last, he threw her unceremoniously onto the bed. "You can walk normally now," he growled.

She sat up, her heart pounding in sudden uneasiness. "What do you mean?"

His lip curled in disgust. "Did you think I was a blind fool? Were you so afraid of being humiliated by your coward of a husband?"

"No, Grey, I…" She chewed on her lip and turned away. What else could she have done? Allowed the glove to be thrown, the challenge to be given?

"If I need you to rescue me," he rasped, turning toward the door, "I'll tell you. Until then, leave me in peace." He stormed from the room. She could hear his angry footsteps thudding down the passageway, and then the loud slam of his door.

He sent word through Jagat Ram that he would sup alone in his rooms. She spent a tormented evening, wondering if she should go to him. Wondering—with even more torment—if he would come to her. There had scarcely been a night, since they'd come to London, when they hadn't made love. Joyously, rapturously. Now she sadly dressed for bed and wondered if she had damaged his pride beyond repair with her well-meaning interference.

Morgan House had quieted and the servants gone to bed before she decided to confront him. She tiptoed down the darkened passage, shielding her candle against the night air. She shivered and clutched her wrapping gown more tightly to her bosom. It was cold here, so far from the warmth of a fireplace.

She opened the door to Grey's sitting room. There was a faint light coming from his bedchamber beyond. She hesitated, wondering if she should knock, then boldly opened the door and stepped into the room.

He was sitting in his shirt-sleeves, at a little table in the center of the dimly lit room. His elbows were on the table, his chin resting in the palms of his hands. His face was a mask of anguish. Set before him on the table was a large bottle of gin and a glass.

Allegra felt the sinking of her heart in her breast. She put down her candle with a trembling hand. "Grey?"

He looked up and scowled. His eyes were haggard. "Get out."

"No. You need me."

"The only thing I need is the gin." He peered up at her in the gloom, his mouth twisting in an ugly smile. "You needn't look so frightened, my dear wife. I haven't touched it yet. I've been sitting here for hours and wondering why." He reached for the bottle.

"In the name of God, Grey. Don't."

He slammed the bottle back on the table and jumped to his feet. He was powerful and menacing above her. Terrifying in his uncertain mood. "Damn it!" he roared. "I'll bloody well drink it if I choose to!" He eyed her up and down with contempt. "Or do you have some woman's trick to stop me, equal to your artifice in the Mall? Are you able to faint in a convincing manner? Ruth was good at that. Perhaps a few tears? A heartfelt plea? I'm minded that you were prepared to grovel before Batterbee in Ludlow. To save me from disgrace."

She flinched at his cruel words. "I thought the monster I knew in Shropshire was gone," she said in a bitter whisper.

"Monster?" He turned away from her and slapped his hand on the table. The bottle and glass rattled ominously. "'Tis a little late for you to regret your choice of husband, madam. I am as I am. A monster, if you will. And a coward." He shrugged. "Perhaps we'll not walk in the Mall anymore. To spare you further shame."

Oh, the man was impossible! "*Shame?*" she cried. "I'm proud to be your lady. Your wife! I married a good and strong man. Aye, and a brave one besides!"

"Who cringes at the sight of a blade. Or hadn't you noticed?"

She stamped her foot in frustration. "Is that the only bravery there is for a man?"

He laughed—a thin, sharp bark. "Not when he possesses it. But when 'tis gone...Ah, how he misses it." He turned back to the bottle. "At least, with the gin in me, I didn't feel the scorn and contempt so keenly."

She snatched the bottle from his hand and flung it into the fireplace. The liquor flared up in a bright burst of flame, casting a satanic light across the room. "'Tis false courage in that bottle," she cried. "False manhood!"

His eyes glowed in fury. His arms shot out to pull her close to his breast. "Damn you! Do you want a man? Is that it? Then you shall have one!" He ground his mouth on hers in a cruel kiss.

She moaned softly. He was resolved to take her, willing or no. She saw it written clear on his face. She trembled in dismay, feeling sick at heart. Helpless before his desperation.

"No, let me go," she begged. She struggled against the power of his grasp, but he wrenched her to the floor and knelt and bent her back across his arm. Her wrapping gown had fallen open. With his free hand, Grey clawed at the lace of her nightshift and tore the garment to her navel. He lowered his head and curled his hot mouth around one nipple, kissing and sucking in a frenzy of passion and rage-driven need. Allegra writhed beneath his angry kisses.

By the time his lips had traveled a path upward to her neck and chin to find her mouth and savage it with his tongue, she had ceased her struggles. There was no reaching him in that prison of self-loathing he had built. She closed her eyes, allowing the bitter, burning tears to seep from beneath her lids.

She heard him groan and opened her eyes. For a moment he stared in disbelief at her tear-stained face. Then he groaned again, released her, and turned away. Wrapping himself into a tight knot, he buried his head in his arms. His shoulders shook with violent sobs. "Oh, God, Allegra," he choked, "will it never end?"

She was beside him in an instant, cradling his head in her arms. "Grey, my love. My sweet, dear Grey. You don't have to do more for Charlie. You've done enough. Take me home to Baniard Hall. Why do you need to stay here, with pigs like Batterbee eager to attack you? Let's go home."

He raised his head. The haunted look on his face was like a silent shriek of pain. "How shall I go? Like a whipped dog, as I did before? To hide behind the gin? I *must* stay."

He sighed and rubbed the heel of his hand across his wet eyes. "I keep hoping that the next time, or the next…There's no logic to it. I fought in a score of campaigns. Bloody battles that sent men screaming from the field in wild fright. And I was fearless. Fearless! But now…Sweet Jesu. Do you know how it feels? There's a numbing chill in my bones. The blood pounds through my head, roars in my ears. Such…such terror in my gut, I can scarcely describe. As though the grave were opening to me. My hands, my sinews…weak, useless." He moaned and pulled her into his arms, holding her close. "How do I begin to understand it, Allegra? Where do I find the key to free myself from these chains?"

"But today you were able to fight Batterbee. And against the smugglers' swords, with only a staff, you were fearless."

"I know. A cane. A staff. But when I put a sword in my hand, and feel the cold steel against my fingers, I see Osborne's face in the throes of death. I hear Ruth's cries of accusation." He laughed sardonically. "How easily her soft voice could ascend to a whine."

"Perhaps it happens because you regret having killed him."

"Osborne? Not a whit. He was a pompous, arrogant man. I always felt that he deliberately picked a quarrel with me."

"But surely you didn't mean to kill him?"

"No. He was a terrible swordsman. I meant only to disarm him. But the field was wet, and he slipped and fell against my blade before I could withdraw it."

"Then why should you think of him? Or Ruth, for that matter?"

"Perhaps I still feel responsible. For her grief. For her death."

"Once and for all, Grey Ridley, you didn't kill her! Why do you continue to torment yourself with guilt?"

He held his head between his hands, grimacing in agony. "God alone knows." He looked at her, seeming to notice at last the torn state of her clothing. "And I torment you with my vile behavior. Forgive me. Forgive the monster you married."

"Oh my dear love," she said, getting to her feet and holding out her hand to him. "Come." She led him, unresisting, to his bed and helped him to undress, feeling a maternal tenderness she had never known before. This good, strong, brave man was also a wounded soul who needed her; her heart swelled with the wonder of it.

She shed her own garments and lay down on the bed, her arms outstretched. Waiting, willing, eager for the touch of his flesh on hers. The warm possession and conquest of his manhood. If her body could be the vessel that received all his pain and left him at peace, she could think of no greater joy in life.

Their lovemaking was gentle and tender—a sharing and giving of warmth and comfort and deep understanding. When it was over, they lay side by side, lost in their own worlds, staring up at the canopy of the bed.

Allegra stirred at last, uneasy to express the thought that troubled her, yet needing to have the words spoken. "You're not staying here in London…that is, you're not forcing yourself to face the likes of Batterbee because you fear *my* scorn? I don't want you to suffer on my account. I shall love you no matter what you do."

He leaned up on one elbow and kissed her. "No," he said gruffly, "I do it for myself. For my honor." He bent and kissed the soft flesh of her belly. "And to be worthy of our child."

• • •

"Have I neglected to mention that you're looking splendid this evening, Lady Ridley?"

Allegra held out the skirts of her pink satin mantua and gave a graceful curtsy. "Thank you, Lord Ridley. My husband is generous in his clothing allowance."

Grey smirked and kissed her hand. "Your husband would like to throw out every gown and every petticoat and shift you own, and keep you naked in his arms forever."

She tossed her shoulder at him. "My husband is a wicked man, sir."

He leered—as lecherous a smile as he could make it. "Yes. With wicked thoughts. But, alas. He must wait, and suffer, until later." He kissed her hand again. "In truth, my love, you do look beautiful. His Majesty thought so."

"How could you tell?" Allegra had been surprised and delighted when King George arrived unexpectedly at the Earl of Burlington's assembly. A soldier, with little interest in fashion, he had appeared plainly dressed in a dark, tied-back wig and a simple coat, waistcoat, and breeches of snuff-colored cloth. His only decoration had been a large, diagonal sash of pale-blue silk.

Allegra had paid her respects with a curtsy, and even managed to murmur a few words of gratitude for his kindness to the Baniards. But the king had responded with a blank stare, then turned and murmured to his companion. Allegra remembered what Grey had said—that His Hanoverian Majesty had never bothered to learn English. "How could you tell?" she asked again. "That he thought I was beautiful?"

Grey grinned. "He'd have to be blind not to think you so. Besides, I know a few words of German. And Burlington translated the rest for me, after the king had gone."

The king's appearance, though brief, had added luster to the already festive evening. Lord Burlington was a good host. One of the richest men in the land, if not the most prominent, he had supplied his guests with everything they needed for their pleasure. A corner in the Great Hall had been set aside for the service of tea, and another for conversation and the playing of innocent games of cards. There was music and dancing in a drawing room, food and drink in an eating parlor. Burlington had even set aside a small closet for the more serious gamblers and card players.

Allegra was feeling mellow and contented. The guests they'd met had been warmly friendly to Grey, and gracious to her as his new viscountess. For a few moments, she found herself thinking that perhaps no one would ever challenge him to a duel again. His fears would quietly fade away, and that would be the end of that.

She laughed softly. Foolish Allegra. Foolish hope. As though a *man*, full in his pride, would ever let that happen! Sooner or later, God preserve him, Grey would feel the need to force a challenge, face his demons once again, prove his manhood in that absurd way of all men.

Grey jerked his chin toward a man who had just come in at the far door of the Great Hall. "Egad, there's a French dog," he said, using the fashionable expression to describe someone who was overdressed. "Have you ever seen such a foppling?"

Allegra stared. In a society where masculine simplicity of dress was the ideal, the man certainly called attention to his person. His red satin suit and waistcoat were thickly embroidered with silver, and his white silk stockings had a line of roses stitched up their length. His cravat and cuffs were of heavy lace, and his flowing white periwig was so full that it almost covered his shoulders. He wore a large, decorative sword, and carried a cane as well. He made Batterbee and his friends look plain by comparison.

He lifted his head and smiled sourly across the room at Allegra. "My word!" she gasped. "'Tis Charlie!"

Grey snorted. "So it is. And determined to show society that he has returned to his former glory. I have no doubt I'll see the bills next week."

"What do you mean?"

"Your brother has developed the unpleasant habit of declining to pay his bills. When pressed, I'm told, he has been known to say 'send them to my rich brother-in-law.'"

"Oh, Grey, you mustn't allow it! Not even for my sake."

He turned and stroked her cheek with loving fingers. "Allegra, the man has suffered greatly. Grant him a little license. A little time to come back to himself. He's not as strong as you are, I think. To overcome the past."

The sneer remained on Charlie's face as he made his way across the room toward them. "Well, Annie," he said, "is this assembly worth my time? I've just left a masquerade at the Haymarket Theatre. Now there's a lively place! Half the mothers in London sit up and wonder if their daughters will return home still virgins—after a ball at the Haymarket." He took a restless turn about the corner of the room, surveying the guests gathered in cozy groupings. "What a mess of dead fish. They scarcely look worth my while. Is there gambling here tonight?"

Allegra bit her lip. "Why must you gamble, Charlie?"

"Why?" he grumbled. "Because I shall never have enough money to satisfy my hungers. I have eight years to reclaim, Annie. Eight long years of whores I never bedded, claret left untasted. Missing roast beef to warm my belly on a freezing, hungry night. I didn't lead a charmed life. Like your husband here," he added bitterly.

"Charlie. Dear one." She put her hand on his sleeve. "Why don't you go back to Yorkshire for a while? Find peace in that sweet cottage, as I did."

"Yes. It was pleasant. Glory was as happy there as a Cheapside matron, the simpleminded slut." He shrugged. "But I sold it."

"What? Sold it? But why?" She felt a twinge of inexplicable loss, remembering her own happy days in Whitby.

He rubbed his nose with the back of his hand. "I had a gambling debt to pay."

"Faugh!" muttered Grey. "I've been hearing reports of your traffic in London for the past two weeks. Your gambling and wild living and all the rest of it. You haven't lost that much, to need the proceeds from the cottage. Not even at the cockpit."

Charlie threw Grey a glance of such malevolence that it shocked Allegra. "Am I under your watch?" he snarled. "No, I didn't need the money. I didn't want the bloody place. It was tainted by the Wickhams."

Allegra clasped her hands in dismay. "Oh, Charlie. Forget the Wickhams. Forget the past. Why don't you settle down and marry?"

He chuckled, an ugly sound. "Marry? When I have a woman like Glory? You haven't seen her, have you? She's well named. Ignorant and crude, to be sure. But glorious. The face of a goddess, and the willing body of a Greek slave. The best damned whore I ever had. Maybe I'll bring her to one of your teas at Morgan House, Annie. That should horrify your refined friends. Eh?"

Allegra frowned. "If you intend to be cruel, Charlie, I don't want to talk to you anymore tonight."

He pouted in anger. "Why, then, a pox on you, Annie. And a pox on this lot. I'm off to Belsize, where the gambling is good and the company doesn't prance around as though their noses were in somebody else's arse." He turned on his heel and stormed from the room before Grey could vent his rage.

"Do you still have hope for him?" asked Allegra with a sigh. "I think perhaps *my* Charlie is long gone, all his sweetness and goodness beaten out of him."

They wandered through the rooms for the next quarter of an hour or so, stopping to chat with Grey's old friends from the Guards. As they passed the gaming room, Lord Richard Halford called out to them from the doorway. They exchanged greetings, then followed him back into the closet.

"Are you gambling tonight, Dick?" asked Grey.

"No longer. The stakes have grown too high." He pointed to one of several tables in the room at which sat Sir Henry Crompton and two other gentlemen. "It would appear that Crompton cannot lose tonight," he went on. "He has already vanquished half a dozen players, and frightened off the rest." Even as Richard spoke, the two gentlemen at the card table scowled in disgust, pushed their notes of hand toward Crompton, and abandoned the field of battle.

Beaming in self-satisfaction, Crompton leaned back in his chair and patted his fat belly. He snapped his fingers at a footman and sent him off to fetch a glass of sack, magnanimously tossing a coin in the servant's direction. He looked up and saw Grey; the confident smile turned to one of uneasiness. "Ah, Ridley," he said, "I hear you had a disagreement with my cousin Batterbee in the Mall last week."

Grey flicked a small speck of dust from his ruffled cuff. "I was resolved to my satisfaction, Sir Henry."

"Indeed." Crompton uttered a sound that was halfway between a nervous laugh and a wheeze. "My cousin seemed to think that you would have beaten him bloody with your cane. Like a common stableboy!"

Grey's voice was edged with steel. "And so I should have. I don't make idle threats."

Crompton's ruddy face turned a deeper shade of red beneath his lavish periwig. "Begad, sir, you're not a man to be taken lightly."

"Then, I wonder…" Grey eased himself into the chair opposite Crompton and smiled. "Would you dare to play cards with me, sir?"

"I warn you, sir, I'm invincible tonight."

"I'll chance it."

Allegra snapped open her fan in annoyance. "Really, Grey. Must you?" To gamble on their first night out in society, and with that villain Crompton!

He looked up at her. Though he smiled in reassurance, there was a dark shadow behind his eyes. "Trust me in this, Allegra," he said softly. "Take a turn around the rooms with Richard. Have a bit of supper. You haven't lost me for more than an hour or so."

He fished in his waistcoat pocket, pulled out a silver coin, and placed it under one of the candlesticks that sat in each of the four corners of the table. At once, the groom of the chambers, who was responsible for the cards, hurried forward and set two fresh decks before Grey. "Now, Crompton," he said pleasantly, shuffling the decks with deft fingers, "shall we begin with all-fours? Five thousand pounds a game?"

Crompton drew in a rasping breath, but nodded his assent. Several spectators crowded around at the smell of fresh blood.

Richard was at Allegra's elbow. "Come," he said. "You're pale before they've even begun. I know Grey at cards. He needs to concentrate. Not concern himself with a wife who might faint."

She agreed and reluctantly allowed Richard to lead her away. They found an empty table and chairs in one corner of the Great Hall, and sent a servant to fetch some tea. They drank the brew together, and laughed at the antics of one of Burlington's dogs, a little spaniel who leapt and played with the fringe hanging from the draperies at the nearby window.

Allegra sighed. "I wish Dolly had come. I do so enjoy your sister's companionship, Richard."

He frowned. "I scarce think she would enjoy herself. Even on such a pleasant occasion as this." He scratched his ear under his short gray wig. "I think my sister is bewitched. At one moment she's happy. And then she's cast into a pit of despair, sighing and moaning. I had hoped that she might marry again. A woman shouldn't be alone. I thought that was her intention as well, especially when she asked me to get Mr. Briggs's advice on her marriage portion. But though she seemed concerned with his opinion—she sets great store by Mr. Briggs, I think—I've seen no suitors on the horizon."

Allegra hesitated. It wasn't her place to reveal Dolly's secrets. But she was dismayed to learn that the happy face her friend showed to her and to the world vanished into gloom once she was alone with her family. "Whatever her distress, I feel certain that time will heal it." A vague enough response. If Dolly wished to confide in her brother, it was up to her to do so.

Richard pulled his watch from his pocket. "Shall we see how Grey is faring?"

The closet was now empty, save for the two players and the servants; the spectators had long since tired of the game and gone on to supper.

Grey appeared as cool and composed as he had an hour before. But Crompton was a changed man. His large wig was slightly skewed on his shaven head, his waistcoat was unbuttoned as though he had needed more room to breathe, and his florid face seemed twisted into a permanent scowl. The scattered stacks of notes in front of Grey clearly explained Crompton's disarray.

Grey smiled. "Jack *and* game, sir," he said, throwing down his cards.

Crompton groaned, pulled a handkerchief from his pocket and mopped his sweating brow. "No more," he said. "You've bested me tonight, sir. As it is, I'll trust you to be a gentleman, and not take those notes to my bank until I can secure the funds."

Grey leaned back in his chair and tapped his long fingers together. "What if I were to give you the opportunity to recoup, sir?"

"Recoup?"

"There's sixty-five thousand pounds in notes of hand here, by my reckoning. I propose one turnup of the cards. Double or nothing. High card wins. What do you say to that?"

Crompton chewed on his thumbnail and stared at the chandelier overhead. "That's a deal of money, sir."

Grey laughed. "Come. Aren't you a gambler? Think of it. One hundred and thirty thousand quid. On the turn of a card."

Crompton wavered, then nodded. He pulled out a shilling and thrust it at the groom of the chambers. "But I'll buy the deck this time," he muttered.

Grey shrugged. "As you wish." He held out his hand and motioned to Allegra. "Come, madam, be my luck."

She moved to him and put her hand on his shoulder, smiling her encouragement and love. But her heart thumped in alarm. There was a great deal of money at stake. She scarcely knew if Grey could afford the loss. What had possessed him to behave so recklessly tonight?

Crompton slapped the shuffled deck in front of Grey. "You choose first."

Allegra was awed by Grey's cool confidence. Without a moment's hesitation, he turned over the deck to reveal the queen of hearts. He grinned up at her. "Of course."

Crompton gulped and stretched forth his hand to the cards. His plump fingers were moving and twisting like eels in a barrel. He grasped the deck, withdrew his hand, clamped his fingers around it again. He turned the card at last, sucked in his breath, and slapped the card onto the table with the face down. "God damn you, sir," he muttered. He looked up at Grey. His face was haggard, drained of color. "If we can discuss this like honorable gentlemen, Lord Ridley..."

Grey's voice had turned to ice. "I'm not a gentleman, Sir Henry. I'm the coward of Baniard Hall. Remember?" He motioned to one of the hovering servants. "Fetch a quill and ink. Sir Henry has a promissory note to write."

Crompton began to bleat, his words tumbling out of him in a highpitched quaver. "I do humbly beg your forgiveness for my intemperate words, Your Lordship. And for the scene in Ludlow. And for whatever disrespect I may have shown formerly to your good lady. I'm a simple man. This will ruin me."

Grey smiled; he suddenly reminded Allegra of a Carolina water snake about to strike. "I had thought of that, of course. And so I'm prepared to be merciful." He indicated the notes on the table before him. "I'll be content with this. A wedding present for my wife."

Crompton's fat jowls sagged with relief. "You have my gratitude, sir."

"Wait." Grey held up a cautionary finger. "There's one thing more I want from you."

Crompton managed a thin smile. "You have but to name it, sir."

"The Baniard woods that adjoin my land."

Crompton rose to his feet, his face purpling. "You're mad, sir! I'm building a manor house there."

Grey raised a bored eyebrow. "I'll have it torn down."

Crompton was beginning to sputter. "By God, I'll not countenance this…this blackmail! I would rather borrow money to pay my debt to you than give up that land. There's a fine income there. I bought it from my friend Lord Ellsmere, God rest his soul, the year before he died."

Grey shook his head. "No," he said softly. "'Twas a gift, I think. Would you admit to that, Tiberius? That's what you called yourself to Ellsmere, was it not? In your secret correspondence?"

"What?" Crompton sank back into his seat, quivering like fish jelly. "You…you have no proof of that."

"Ah, but you see, John Wickham was careless. He saved his letters, and left other proofs to his son, Thomas. I have Tom's dying statement as well. If I should show any of those proofs to Walpole…"

Crompton was almost in tears. "I didn't learn of Ellsmere's evil plot till long after all the Baniards were dead. I take no responsibility for what happened to them!"

"But now, you see, they've come back to life. I think my wife is entitled to her family's woods as compensation."

"Yes, of course," blubbered Crompton. "But Ellsmere's letter…"

"It will stay in my possession. I give you my word to destroy it the minute I hold the deed to the woods in my hand. I'll send my secretary around to you tomorrow. Now, as to these winnings here…" He pointed to the notes on the table. "Madam my wife needs something in which to carry them home. Take off your peruke."

"By God, sir, you go too far!"

Grey bared his teeth in an ugly scowl. "Your wig, *Tiberius*." He gave a sarcastic laugh. "Blackmail, you see, is a dirty business. Even if your victim is a man you claim as a friend."

Crompton pulled the wig from his head and slammed it down on the table. His shaved pate was damp with sweat, as red and blotchy as his face. He stormed to the door amid the titters of several guests who had just come into the room. At the last moment, he turned and shook his fist at Grey. "You bloody rogue! You stone-hearted villain! Your wife made a cuckold of you with Osborne, and you never even knew it! May it bring you nightmares now!"

Grey roared and leapt for Crompton, but was restrained by Richard's strong grasp. "God's teeth, Grey, let it go! Look to your lady. She's exhausted."

Allegra sagged against the table, trembling. It had been too much for her—watching the battle of wits between Grey and Crompton, bursting with pride yet fearful that at any moment Crompton might draw his sword. "Please," she whispered. "Take me home."

Grey drew a long, steadying breath and put his arm around her. By the time Richard had gathered the notes into Crompton's wig, Grey was beginning to smile sheepishly. "Stupid of me to allow Crompton to vex me that way. I've been wondering about Ruth and Osborne every day for the past week. Rethinking every moment of my life with her. Every disturbing encounter that I saw with Osborne. I suppose when Crompton said the words aloud, I knew I couldn't hide the truth from myself any longer." He sighed. "Come, my fair Allegra. 'Tis time for home and bed."

Richard grinned and pressed the filled wig into Grey's hand. "I haven't seen such a performance since you cozened the Viceroy of Bengal into giving you his prize stallion. By God, I wish Peter had been here tonight!" He patted Grey's shoulder. "Now take your wife home. I'll see you upon the morrow."

They made their way home to Morgan House in the dark of night, their footmen running ahead with lighted torches to show the coachman the road. Allegra could only marvel at the wonder of the man beside her. He had avenged the Baniards, forced Crompton to pay for all his wickednesses, given her back her family's lands intact. And all without raising his voice, let alone drawing a sword.

She slipped her arm through his. "You're the bravest, kindest man I know, Lord Ridley."

He looked down at her and smiled. "Are you tired, Lady Ridley?"

"Not *that* tired."

"Good." He kissed her gently. And then not quite so gently. By the time they reached Morgan House they were burning with desire. Grey groaned when he saw Briggs waiting in the vestibule, holding a sheaf of papers in his hand. "Why must the mail be delivered day and night in this damned city?" he muttered. "Well, what is it, Briggs? Can't it wait until morning?"

"No," said Allegra, seeing the look on the steward's face. "The man is shaking like a leaf. What is it, Mr. Briggs?"

"'Tis only…A distant cousin. My grandfather's sister's son, I think. He has just died."

"Oh, alas," she murmured in sympathy. "Was he dear to you?"

"I never even knew of him. But…but he's left me some money. An income from a trust. Some property in Scotland." He stared at them, bewildered.

"But that's wonderful news!" she said. "How much has been left to you?"

"He bequeathed three hundred a year to my elder brother."

Allegra's heart sank. Three hundred a year could support a gentleman in moderate comfort; no doubt Briggs would get less than his brother. Scarcely enough to bring to Dolly in marriage. "And you?" she asked.

"Two…" he gulped. "Two thousand. A year! The lawyer says that my cousin felt that since my brother Arthur has the family title and holdings, the bulk of *his* fortune should come to me."

"Oh, Mr. Briggs!" Quite forgetting her position, Allegra burst into happy tears and threw her arms around his neck.

He sputtered in embarrassment and untwined her arms. "Milady, you shouldn't. It isn't proper."

Grey scowled. "And is that bloody letter the only thing that's keeping Lady Ridley and myself from our beds tonight?" He stifled Briggs's stumbling apology with a grunt. "I suppose you expect me to allow the wedding feast here at Morgan House. The sooner the better, I should guess. Before Christmas. Or the day after."

Briggs had never looked so happy. Nor so young. "Wedding?" he squeaked.

"Well, I assume you plan to ask Dolly."

"Y-yes. Of course. I…"

"If I recall Dolly's habits, she likes to read late into the night."

Briggs's face lit up as though he'd been struck by a wondrous revelation. "Do I have your permission to call upon her *tonight*, milord?"

"Of course."

"You don't object?"

Grey's stern expression melted into a grin of delight. "You bloody fool! If you hadn't asked, I would have thrown you out on the spot!"

Chapter Twenty-Two

"Mr. and Mrs. Jonathan Briggs, Esquire. Oh, doesn't it have a lovely sound?" Dolly's blue eyes glowed with happiness.

Allegra glanced out of the open door at the cold December afternoon and tucked Dolly's hood closer to her neck. "It sounds just as it ought," she said.

Dolly hugged her against her bosom. "Thank you for the wedding dinner, and the day, and for being my friend, and…"

Allegra laughed. "Go to your new husband. He's waiting in the carriage. You'll be at your house in Bloomsbury Square?"

"For a week or two. And then Jonathan wants to visit his brother, Sir Arthur. We both regretted he was too ill to travel to the wedding." She kissed Allegra on both cheeks and hurried out to her coach.

Allegra sighed and leaned against a marble pillar in the vestibule of Morgan House. It had been a lovely day: the simple ceremony amid the grandeur of St. Paul's Cathedral; the bride bubbling with joy, the groom alternately beaming and pinching himself to be sure it was all happening. Morgan House had sparkled, the servants in their blue and crimson Morgan livery had been properly attentive, and the cooks had outdone themselves. Grey, splendid in his red ribbon and star of the Order of the Bath, had presided nobly over the festivities in the Great Hall, raising his glass to toast the happy couple.

"May you know the blessed felicity we have found," he'd said, and Allegra's heart had overflowed with love.

"So pensive? When our guests await you?"

Allegra turned and smiled at the sound of Grey's voice in the entrance to the vestibule. "Grant me a moment's quiet contentment, my love. Dolly looked radiant, didn't she?"

"As do you."

She looked down in pleasure at her pale-blue silk mantua. The front, from bodice to hem, was trimmed with diamond buckles and bows. "Such extravagance, Grey. Even for Christmas."

He took her into his arms and kissed her. "I want to give you all those things you missed. All those things you were so cruelly denied."

She sighed. His words had touched a painful spot, the one blight on the day. "I wish Charlie had come."

"Patience, my sweet. There's much anger in your brother. We can only wait until it fades. Perhaps if he had something to do, a position in Court…" He frowned in thought, gazing up at the painting on the domed ceiling. "Gifford is good at arranging things."

Gifford is good at arranging things. She stared at him, struck by a sudden thought. The answer to a mystery that had been nagging at her. "*You* did it. You and Gifford. That…that cousin who was completely unknown to Mr. Briggs. Who left his fortune to the younger brother, not the elder. Surely an odd bequest. Unless you and Gifford…!"

He shrugged. "Nonsense. I'm sure we all have distant, unknown kin."

"Who would leave a fortune to a stranger they had never made any effort to meet? It *was* your doing, wasn't it, Grey?"

He was beginning to look uncomfortable. He cleared his throat and tugged at his lace cravat. "Don't be absurd. Why should I throw money away like that?"

"You were prepared to gamble away a fortune to Crompton."

"That's a different story. I would have challenged him again and again until I had won it back."

She shook her head. How blind of her not to have guessed it before. "You're the unknown benefactor, Grey. And that's that."

"I'll deny it till my dying day."

She threw her arms around his neck. "I love you, Grey Ridley. An angel, they called you at the almshouse."

"Faugh," he said gruffly, turning away in embarrassment. "What need I of so much money? I have wealth enough to maintain myself for five hundred years."

The dear man. Her eyes filled with tears. "How was I lucky enough to find you?"

"Hmph! You tried to kill me, as I recall."

She put her hands on her hips. "And you tried to beat me, you brute!"

He pulled her close and patted her rump through her gown. "I wonder what would have happened that day had I succeeded in pulling down your breeches?" He stroked her firm bottom again, his hands immodest and suggestive in their movements.

She tried to ignore her thrill of pleasure, and managed to glare at him in mock annoyance. "You're quite tenderhearted about it now, you rakehell. But I bit your tongue merely for kissing me. Remember? What do you suppose might have happened if you had gone beyond kisses?"

"Shall we discover the answer now?" He held her in his possessive embrace and pressed his lips to her bodice.

She struggled halfheartedly. "Godamercy, Grey. Our guests await."

His mouth burrowed deeper among the folds of her lace neckerchief. "I want to send them all home and take you to bed."

"I can scarcely wait to get back to my stillroom in Baniard Hall," she said with a giggle. "Surely I can concoct a love-dampener! Now, behave yourself." She allowed him one more kiss, then took him by the hand and led him into the drawing room.

Most of their guests had departed when the wedding couple had left. Allegra had given instructions to the butler to move the remaining company—some two dozen ladies and gentlemen—into a smaller room, and to see to a light supper should the party extend into the nighttime hours.

She liked the small drawing room in Morgan House. It was handsomely furnished, warm and intimate. Above the fireplace hung a portrait of King George, which His Majesty had given to Grey upon the occasion of his knighthood for bravery in battle. It seemed fitting to bring the company here. Most of the men who had chosen to linger with their wives were Grey's old army companions. With Allegra's consent, Richard Halford had urged them to stay a little longer. The friendship and approval of these men, she knew, would go far toward dispelling Grey's lingering doubts about his bravery.

Twilight had begun to fall when a footman approached Allegra at the tea table, where she was serving several guests. He bent and whispered in her ear. "Milady, Sir Charles and Lady Baniard are here."

Allegra scarcely had time to register surprise at the announcement when Charlie came swaggering into the room. He was more elaborately dressed than he'd been at Burlington House; his coat and waistcoat were a mass of thick embroidery, with gold braid scrolled around every button and buttonhole. He carried a feather-trimmed hat under one arm, and his chased sword hilt was covered in gems. "Annie," he said loudly, and beamed at the assembled guests, clearly pleased to have an audience. "I regret to have missed your friends' marriage. But I was busy getting married myself. At St. Mary le Bone."

Allegra bit her lip in dismay. St. Mary le Bone was a crumbling old church, known chiefly for clandestine marriages. What had possessed

Charlie to choose such a place? And with *whom?*

She didn't have long to wonder. Charlie beckoned to a shadowy figure in the doorway. "Come, wife. Allow this fine company to pay homage to the Lady Gloriana Baniard."

The woman who stepped awkwardly into the room was the most beautiful creature Allegra had ever seen. Her small lace cap scarcely hid an abundance of brilliant crimson curls piled helter-skelter on the top of her head. Her skin was like porcelain, clear and peach-tinted. Her features were exquisite, well-defined, striking. Her large, luminous eyes were a sparkling, moist green, like emeralds covered with dew, moss in the rain. She looked strong and healthy; not a fainting flower bud, but a fine, robust blossom. Allegra wondered if she had been born of Gypsies—wild and free and magnificent.

But her cheeks glowed with garish spots of color, and her full, rouged lips were a shade of red that nature had never intended. She wore several beauty patches on her face, a necklace, eardrops, and a quantity of rings and bracelets. Her gown, though clearly costly, was gaudy—a bright scarlet figured silk that scarcely suited a bride. Moreover, the bosom of the gown was cut to an immodest level, the rounded swell of her breasts covered neither by a neckerchief nor a scrap of lace. And the embroidered satin apron that she wore over her gown scarcely concealed the fact that she was in the final distended phase of pregnancy.

No one in the company moved, too stunned and embarrassed by this bizarre scene even to look at one another. In the deathly silence, Charlie laughed. Allegra was aware for the first time that he must have been drinking. His eyes were slightly glassy and his voice was loud and slurred. "Are you surprised, Annie? I had to guide the slut's hand to sign the register. She can't even read or write. But she's a beauty, eh?" He whirled to Grey, his eyes dark with some deep emotion. "Eh, my rich brother-in-law?"

Grey clenched his jaw. "Why don't you take your wife home, Charles?" he said quietly.

"No. I want everyone in the room to rise and bow to my bride." He chuckled. "*Gloriana.* I didn't even know that was her real name until she told the vicar." He made a face at the woman. "Come in, Glory, damn it. Why do you hesitate?"

Allegra could read confusion and dismay in Gloriana's eyes, the desire to flee her uncomfortable surroundings. But she held her head at a proud and defiant angle as she shuffled clumsily into the center of the room to stand beside Charlie.

There was the sound of suppressed snickering from one of the guests. Grey scowled and immediately stepped forward, holding out his arm to Gloriana. She chewed on her lip, clearly uncertain what to do. Deftly, Grey took her hand and slipped her arm through his. "Come, Lady Baniard," he said, "let me introduce you to the company." He led her to Allegra. "My wife, Lady Ridley."

Allegra held out her hand and smiled, hoping to put the poor creature at ease. "Gloriana. Sister. Welcome to Morgan House."

Charlie doubled up with laughter. "That's the first time any woman has ever called you sister, eh, Glory? Mostly, they call you foe. Did I tell you, Annie, where I found this slattern?"

Gloriana pouted and looked around the room. "Charlie, don't. It aren't right, in such fine company."

He sneered in her direction. "Scarcely married an hour, and you begin to sound like a mewling wife. Shut your mouth before I shut it for you."

"In the name of heaven, Charlie," cried Allegra, "is that a way to speak to your wife?"

Gloriana shook her head. "He don't mean nothin' by it, he don't. He got a good heart."

Charlie laughed at that. "And a good something else to tickle you with when you need it. Eh, girl? Now, Annie, let me tell you where I first saw Glory. Have you been to the theatre at Lincoln's Inn Field?"

Allegra nodded, if only to humor her brother until she could think of a way to get him home. She exchanged a worried glance with Grey. It was clear he was just as concerned, but unwilling to humiliate Charlie in his present mood. His slightly drunken state. "Yes," she answered, "we saw a clever play there last week."

"Perhaps you don't know, but oftentimes there's entertainment in a different part of the theatre. Contests of skill. They help to pass the time for the spectators who might arrive too early for the play. Gladiators," he explained. "As in the days of Rome. Half naked. They battle each other with staffs and flat blades until blood is drawn. Very amusing. Very profitable, if one casts a bet on the winning combatant." He grinned and chucked Gloriana under the chin. "The women gladiators are the most wondrous to watch. Glory never got a scratch in all the times I saw her. By God, what a fighter!"

Grey muttered under his breath as Gloriana hung her head. "Now, sir, 'tis time you leave."

Charlie's eyes narrowed and he put his hand on the hilt of his sword.

"Charlie. Dear one," said Allegra quickly, stepping between the two men. "Go home, I beg you."

"No. I came here to celebrate my wedding." He patted Gloriana's rounded belly. "And my imminent child. Oh, yes, it's mine." He glared at one of the guests who had scarcely stifled a laugh. "Once I found the whore, I made sure that she wouldn't ever again dare to earn money on her prat."

"Did you lock her up?" asked Grey in disgust.

"No. I blacked her eye if she even cast her peepers on another man's nocker."

Allegra gasped. She wondered if Gloriana was as humiliated by this scene as she was. Charlie's wild recklessness, his descent into foul street language, his insults to the woman he now called "wife."

But there was no deterring her brother, she realized. If his behavior was a kind of revenge upon the world, there was no sending him home until the scene was played out to his satisfaction. She sent a signal to Grey with her eyes, hoping he'd understand and agree. "Come, Husband. Help me to introduce Sir Charles and Lady Baniard to all our guests."

The introductions went more smoothly than she would have dared hope. Most of the company appreciated Grey and Allegra's awkward position, and made every effort to be civil. That seemed to mollify Charlie somewhat; he even managed to smile and exchange a few harmless pleasantries with several of the gentlemen. And when Richard Halford bowed solemnly to Gloriana, then turned and invited Charlie to accompany him to his club in the next week or so, Allegra began to breathe more easily. Perhaps the evening wouldn't be a disaster after all. Charlie was becoming more sober, more aware of himself and his pride, and Gloriana—awkward and out of place—was beginning to flag with weariness. Perhaps they wouldn't even stay for supper.

Suddenly Richard stared intently at Gloriana, his brows knitting together in a pensive frown. "My faith, madam, but that's an unusual pendant you have on your necklace."

She put her hand to her throat. Hanging from her strand of creamy pearls was a brooch—a large, milky opal surrounded by a ring of emeralds. "Charlie give it me," she said.

"I only saw one other like it before. A good friend of mine, Sir Jocelyn Middleton, had it made up especially for his wife upon the occasion of their marriage. To his own design. It was meant to be the only one of its kind."

Charlie laughed. "Then the jeweler gulled him. For here's its mate."

Richard continued to frown. "May I ask where you got it, Sir Charles?"

"I bought it, sir."

"But where?"

Charlie had an odd look on his face. "Why do you ask?"

"Because last year Middleton and his wife were set upon on the Oxford Road by a masked highwayman and his confederates. The jewel was stolen, among others."

Charlie rubbed his nose, seeming to be abashed. "Ah, that would explain it."

Strange, thought Allegra. She had suddenly realized that Charlie always rubbed his nose whenever he seemed to be disconcerted. Or backed into a corner. "What would it explain?" she asked.

He rubbed his nose again and looked sheepish. "In point of fact, I bought the bloody thing at Jonathan Wild's Lost Property Office. The man makes a living at locating stolen property, and no questions asked. That pendant had gone unclaimed for a year. And so I bought it."

"It remained unclaimed," growled Richard, "because of the family's sad history. The highwayman called himself Lord Bee. And never a more depraved villain has lived. After stealing their money and their jewels, he killed Middleton in cold blood and raped his wife in a most savage manner." He turned to Allegra. "Forgive my unseemly frankness."

Charlie shook his head. "Truly a tragic story. I shall forbid Glory to wear the accursed jewel ever again."

"'Tis more tragic than you might imagine. Lady Middleton was never herself again. She died of an overdose of laudanum a month ago."

"What a dreadful story!" said Allegra. "And they never caught this Lord Bee?"

Richard shrugged. "No one knows what he looks like. I remember only that Lady Middleton said that as he was violating her she bit the fiend's hand. He pulled off his glove to tend the wound afterward. The wretch has a missing finger. 'Twas the only thing she remembered of that fearful event. Her coachman saw it as well, and can still attest to it."

"Sweet Jesu," muttered Grey.

Allegra felt the blood drain from her face. It couldn't be Charlie. It couldn't! Yet what did she know of him? Of the man he had become since those long-ago, happy days at Baniard Hall?

Richard glanced at the tight faces around him, his eyes narrowing. "Middleton was a good friend of mine," he said. "May I trouble you to show me your hands, Sir Charles?"

Charlie drew himself up and jammed his hands into his pockets—the picture of outraged indignation. "You may not, sir," he said. "Nor will I stay another minute in this company to be insulted. Come, Glory." He turned toward the door.

Richard blocked his way, his jaw set in determination. "Forgive me, but I shall prevent you, sir, until I've satisfied myself. I give you my oath on that. If I must knock you to the floor, I intend proof of your innocence. Or your guilt. I have but to send for the coachman. I hired him after Lady Middleton's death. He's just outside in the courtyard."

Cornered, Charlie looked wildly to Allegra, his eyes dark with entreaty. "Annie, don't hate me. I had no choice. I was a hunted man."

The tears flowed from her eyes unchecked. Tears of pity. Of sympathy. "Dear one, I understand." Had she not been prepared to commit murder herself?

Gloriana tore the jewel from her neck and threw it down. "Damn you, Charlie! You swore you never killed no gentry cove!"

Grey slipped his hand under Charlie's elbow and looked around the room at the other guests. Few seemed to be aware of the drama taking place. "Come," he said, pulling Charlie gently toward the door. "No need to call attention to these proceedings. My man Gifford will find a lawyer. Someone with influence at Court. I feel sure we can intercede on your behalf."

"*No!*" As they reached the door, Charlie shoved Grey up against a large, marble-topped side table and drew his sword. Richard let out a bellow and leapt forward, his hand on his own blade, while several of the guests jumped to their feet in alarm. Instantly, Charlie raised the point of his sword to Grey's throat. "If anyone moves," he snarled, "I'll not hesitate to kill him." Richard came to a halt, and the few servants in the room stood immobile, eyes wide with terror.

"Oh, Charlie, don't do this," implored Allegra.

"Why not, Annie? Do you know what will happen to me? At best, transportation and slavery again. More likely, the road to Tyburn for 'Lord Bee.' I have quite a reputation, you'll soon discover. They'll sell broadsheets on my life as the death cart makes its way to the gallows. No, thank you. I'm for the open road instead." He laughed darkly and prodded Grey with his sword point. "But if my rich brother-in-law wishes to stop me, let him fight for the privilege."

Grey growled in frustration. Backed to the table, the sword at his neck, he had nowhere to turn. "This is madness, Baniard."

Charlie's mouth twisted in a cruel smile. "Not at all. In truth, I *do* want to fight you, Ridley. I've heard much of your cowardly demeanor on the field of honor. 'Tis still the gossip of London. I should like at least one amusing memory to take with me." He jerked his head in Allegra's direction. "Annie, get Halford's sword and put it on the table next to... the coward of Baniard Hall? Isn't that what they call you, Ridley? I should like to see you on your knees, quaking in fear."

Richard drew his sword. "*I'll* take your challenge, sir," he said quickly.

Charlie glared at him. "The devil you will! If you move, Ridley dies on the instant. Annie, the sword!"

Trembling, Allegra took Richard's sword and placed it on the table beside Grey. She dared not look into his eyes, fearing to see the irrational terror in their depths. At Charlie's barked command, she backed away from her husband.

"Pick up the blade, Ridley."

Grey shook his head. "It will only be the worse for you. Give it up."

Charlie flicked his sword arm, leaving a red slash on Grey's neck. Grey winced. "They say you weep, you're so afraid. You shake like an old tippler. Is it so?" He lunged more savagely. A bloody stain appeared on the shoulder of Grey's coat. "I call you coward. I call you milk-livered craven! Will you fight me?" Charlie swung his blade at Grey's leg. Grey grunted with the pain as the sword bit deep into his calf.

Allegra gasped in horror. How could Grey stand there and allow himself to be attacked? "Charlie, please!"

Grey wiped the sweat from his brow. "Why are you doing this?"

Charlie's face twisted with hatred. "You sleep in my house. In my father's bed. You fornicate with my sister and pretend it gives you the right to Baniard Hall!" He lunged again. Grey held up his arm to protect himself, and swore as the point of the sword caught him on the wrist.

"Godamercy!" Allegra cried out with the awful realization of her brother's purpose. In some dreadful way, Grey had come to represent everyone who had ever hurt Charlie, the embodiment of all his bitter hatred, resentment, and envy. His painful grievances, nurtured through years of torment, had somehow come to be laid at Grey's feet. Oh, God! she thought in horror, her heart torn in two. "Defend yourself, Grey," she begged. "He means to *kill* you!"

Grey lifted his head and looked at her. The haunting fear in his eyes was mixed with something else. Uncertainty. She remembered that Grey had killed someone Ruth loved. And had been consumed with guilt because of it. She wished she could rush to him and give him all her comfort. Instead, she brushed at her tears and managed a brave smile. "Do it for me, Grey," she whispered. "And for yourself. No matter what happens, I love you."

He rubbed his hand across his mouth. Allegra wondered if he was thinking of the gin. Then he took a deep breath and picked up the sword.

"Charlie, I beg you," said Allegra with a sob. "Remember the old days."

"Did you?" he snarled. "You betrayed us all by marrying a usurper, by having Wickham in your power and doing nothing!" He sneered at Grey. "Now, Ridley, show me if you're a man."

Grey lifted the sword. His knuckles were white from the tightness of his grip, and his hand shook as though he had the palsy. He clenched his jaw and made a tentative pass at Charlie's blade, turning it aside for a moment. He took the opportunity of that moment to move himself away from the trap of the table at his back, then lunged again. His steps were sure, though his arm still quivered.

Charlie laughed and parried easily. "Is that the best you can do, coward?"

In some strange way, Charlie's taunts seemed to strengthen Grey. Allegra watched in wonderment as his movements grew more confident, his sword arm steadier. He seemed to be reclaiming his skills and his courage at the same time. He was on the attack now, not merely defending himself from Charlie's savage thrusts.

The calmer and surer Grey became, the more frenzied grew Charlie's onslaught. He feinted, he attacked, he dodged, he cursed aloud, eyes burning with murderous hatred. He thrust wildly, his blade held low, and lost his balance, sinking to one knee.

At once, Grey leapt forward and stamped on his sword, pinning it to the floor and dislodging it from Charlie's grasp. "It's over, Baniard," he said. Then he looked at Allegra, his eyes brightening with tears of relief. "It's over," he said again, and uttered a choking sound that was halfway between a groan and a joyous laugh. He retrieved Charlie's sword from the floor, handed both weapons to Richard, and beckoned to one of the servants. "Fetch the watch," he said hoarsely. "Tell them to bring handcuffs and leg irons."

Charlie backed toward the door. He looked like a cornered animal, his shoulders sagging, his hands drooping under the skirts of his coat. Allegra felt a moment's sharp pity and regret for the ruin of her brother's life. And then she saw the pistols in his hands.

He trained them on Grey and the others, then jerked his chin at his wife. "Damn it, Glory! Don't be a useless whore. Lay hold of my sister and come to me."

Allegra cried out in shock, feeling herself held and imprisoned within a grip that was astonishingly strong. She struggled against Gloriana, but it was useless. She was being dragged toward her brother. Grey and Richard moved in unison, reaching out to help her.

"Hold!" cried Charlie, brandishing his pistols. "Don't take another step if you value Annie's life. She'll remain unharmed if you keep your distance. Otherwise, Glory is quite capable of breaking her neck. I only want her as a hostage to see us safely out of here. And those diamonds of hers will be a nest egg for Glory and me."

Grey doubled his fists in helpless fury and glared at Charlie. "By God, if she's harmed…"

Charlie laughed, an evil sound. "Annie is my sister. There are still blood ties. But as for you…" He raised his pistol and pointed it at Grey. "Baniard Hall was *mine*, you whoreson! You never had a right to it. Let it come to your widow. She, at least, belongs there."

"No!" Allegra screamed as Charlie squinted down the barrel of his pistol.

Suddenly he stiffened, his eyes wide with shock, and dropped to his knees like a stone falling to the ground. The pistols tumbled from his hands and he leaned forward, grimacing. Allegra could see, between his shoulder blades, a strangely carved knife in the shape of a snake. It was imbedded to the hilt. She looked up. A small, hidden door had opened in the paneling, and Jagat Ram stood there, his dark eyes burning.

"Oh, God. Charlie!" Allegra broke from Gloriana's loosened grip and rushed to kneel and put her arms around her brother. She hesitated, then lowered him gently to her lap. "Grey, send for a surgeon."

Charlie gasped and shook his head. "Too late, Annie. Let me die."

Grey ordered his servants to bring strong spirits for Charlie to drink, and set a pillow under his head. But it was clear there was no hope. Already his eyes were beginning to glaze. Allegra removed his periwig and smoothed the damp hair from his forehead. She fought against her tears, wondering how she could feel such pain for a man whose loss she had mourned years ago.

"Don't cry, little Annie," he whispered. "'Tis better this way. Think of the shame of a Baniard at Tyburn Tree. And I'm so very tired of this life. Let me sleep." He closed his eyes, then opened them again. His face was soft and serene, washed clear of the anger and bitterness that had haunted him for so long. "Do you remember the place on Wenlock Edge where we used to go? And look out over the whole valley?"

She nodded. "'Tis still as beautiful as ever."

"Bury me there." He glanced up at Gloriana, standing forlorn and apart, a stranger in every way. "Take care of my child. And my poor sweet whore."

Grey knelt beside him. "I give you my pledge on that, Charlie."

Charlie smiled faintly and lifted trembling fingers. "And your hand, Ridley?"

"Willingly, Brother." Grey clasped Charlie's hand in a strong, vital grip.

"Queer little sister." His voice was beginning to falter. "Rum little poppet, my Annie. You could laugh for joy at a rainbow, and weep at the sight of a chained dog." He sighed—a deathly, hollow sound. "You would have wept for me, Annie. I was a chained dog for too long."

"I know," she whispered. "I know."

His mind was beginning to wander. He muttered incoherently, words and phrases jumbled together as though he were reciting a list. Or cataloging his life. "So tired...damned bloody villains...sleep at last..." He smiled at Allegra, his face radiant, the years and pain melting away. "Do you remember when it snowed at the Hall, little Annie? And you made angels in the snow? So white and clean and pure...like our lives then. Life was never so bright and clean again...in the whole accursed world..." He coughed once and then was still, his dark eyes staring sightlessly. Grey stroked his lids closed with gentle fingers.

"Aw, Charlie. What a rum gent you was." Gloriana stood above his prostrate body, her hands twisting at her apron. She seemed lost and abandoned, and suddenly very young—her unspoiled beauty at odds with the harsh, artificial coloring of her rouge.

"Come and sit down," said Richard, putting his hand beneath her elbow.

She shook her head. "He were good to me sometimes." She gasped, uttered an oath and crumpled to the floor, clutching at her swollen belly. "Damn your eyes, Charlie," she said with a grimace of pain, "why couldn't you wait to see your brat?"

Chapter Twenty-Three

The dawn sky was a pale, milky yellow, like the cream rising in a wooden tub. One star lingered in the west, a glittering crystal shard that twinkled in the frosty air. From beyond the garden wall of Morgan House came the clang of a dustman's bell and the clamorous bawl of a fishmonger. The church bells began to ring—close and majestic from St. James, just across Piccadilly, softly musical from the more distant St. Martin's in the Fields.

Allegra sighed and pulled her fur-lined cloak more closely around her shoulders. There was comfort in the everyday sounds, in the cold winter air that swept her mind clean of dark thoughts. She felt weary, but it was the weariness of someone who has come through a long journey and reached safe harbor at last.

"Why don't you go to bed? You haven't slept all night, the servants tell me."

Allegra turned and smiled at Grey. There was a small plaster on his neck, and he limped from the wound to his leg, but his face mirrored her own serenity. "In a little while, love," she replied.

He crossed the gravel path of the garden, took her into his arms, and kissed her tenderly. "What a good heart you have. Gloriana is well?"

"'Twas a long, difficult night for her. But she's sleeping now."

"And the babe?"

She smiled in joy and wonder. "Oh, Grey, he's beautiful! He looks just like Papa. And Glory said she'll name him William, if I wish it. After Papa."

He nodded in satisfaction. "All the more fitting, since he's the new baronet."

She gulped, the tears rising to her eyes. "Sir William Baniard, Baronet. It sounds just right."

"And it *shall* be right. I assume you wish to bring Gloriana and the child back to Baniard Hall."

"Of course. She's unlettered, but not unintelligent, I suspect. And she has no one in this world, poor thing. Perhaps, in the seclusion of Shropshire, we can help to educate her to her new station."

He grinned, clearly pleased with himself. "As the mother of the Lord of Baniard Hall."

"What do you mean?"

"It seems only fitting that justice should be served at last. And Baniard Hall returned to its rightful owners. I'll arrange the details with Gifford. We'll live there, of course. When we're not here in London. But I intend to entail the Hall to the child, to be held in trust for him during our lifetimes. Are you agreeable to that?"

She nodded, too overcome with emotion to speak. Once again, God willing, there would be a William Baniard to preside in splendor over Baniard Hall.

"We should leave London soon," he said. "Before winter makes the roads impassable."

"As soon as Glory can travel." She patted her flat abdomen. "And while I still can."

"Sir Greyston." Jagat Ram stood solemnly at the entrance to the garden, waiting for Grey's nod before coming forward and greeting them both with a little bow.

He and Grey exchanged a long, silent look; then Grey smiled. "You'll be returning to Calcutta now, of course."

"Of course. It is Allah, I am thinking, who led me to that little door at the very moment when…" He stopped and bowed again to Allegra. "I am regretting that it was your brother, milady."

"I'll never reproach you," she said. "I would have done the same, God forgive me."

Grey shook Ram's hand, then threw his arms around the other man and clasped him to his breast. "Six years, my friend," he said hoarsely. "I'll miss you."

"But you no longer need me. Lord Halford told me of the duel."

Grey shook his head in amazement. "I don't know what happened. For the first time, with a sword in my hand, I didn't think of Ruth. Nor of Osborne dying." He turned to Allegra, his eyes brimming with love. "I thought only of you. In danger. My sweet, precious Allegra."

"I should have died if anything had happened to you."

He held her hands and kissed them, then looked around the garden and laughed. They were alone. Ram had discreetly vanished.

Allegra sighed. Ram's appearance had reminded her of her brother again. "Poor Charlie. How twisted with hatred he had become. Was I as mad as that, with my obsession to kill the Wickhams?"

"For a little while, perhaps. We were both a bit mad. I think I'd be in Bedlam by now, if you hadn't come along."

"No. For all the dreadful days and nights of too much gin and self-destruction, I think you were always fighting to save your soul."

"Not very well. Not until you."

She stroked his dear face, so handsome and strong. "Oh, pooh. Have you forgotten the angel of Hosier's Almshouse?"

He chuckled. "The garden will need planting in the spring."

"Then Mrs. Morgan will come and work beside her husband." She patted her belly again. "If nature will allow."

"How strange is life," he said, musing. "Ripples on a stream. The odd twists and turns. Those hours I spent at the almshouse, before you came into my life, were the sweetest I'd ever known. The only warmth in a life that had become well-nigh unbearable. And yet..." he stared at her in wonderment, "I should never have found them, but for my despair."

She nodded, understanding him, and herself, with sudden bright clarity. "And I. I came looking for revenge, my heart dark with hatred. And found love and joy. Such promise from such pain."

He scratched his chin in thought. "I remember a verse from one of Shakespeare's plays. About finding happiness in adversity." He frowned, then began to recite. "'There is some soul of goodness in things evil, would men observingly distil it out...'" He shook his head. "I've forgot the rest. But it ends, 'Thus may we gather honey from the weed.'"

"And so we have, my love. The sweetest honey of all." She looked up at the heavens. The day was brightening, but the sky was beginning to cloud over—an icy, brittle whiteness that shimmered with the promise of snow.

With gentle hands, Grey lifted the fur hood of her cloak and tucked it around her face. "Come inside before the snow falls."

Her face felt alive with the cold, invigorated by the crisp air. "Winter is here for certain. Perhaps it has already snowed on Wenlock Edge." She thought of the winters at Baniard Hall—sitting before the fire in cozy warmth while the wind blew around the old stones and the snow fell in clean, white drifts. Papa would tell stories of the civil wars, and Mama would serve a hot claret punch, redolent of cloves and oranges.

Allegra felt a sharp pang of longing. Baniard Hall in the glory of winter.

"Oh, Grey," she whispered, snuggling into the warmth of his arms, "take me to my home."

Marielle
(The French Maiden Series - Book One)

Armed with only a disguise and her wavering courage, Marielle Saint-Juste goes on a perilous mission to free her brother from unjust captivity. But when she enters the prison of Louis XIII, it isn't her wounded brother she finds, but a mysterious stranger—and her destiny.

In this French dungeon, a love illuminates the darkest shadows in two hearts. Marielle will not only face her deepest fears, but change her life forever.

Lysette
(The French Maiden Series - Book Two)

Lysette, the Marquise de Ferrand, is left penniless after her husband dies. With nowhere else to turn, she ventures across the turbulent French countryside to the safety of her brother's home. But when she meets Andre, Comte du Crillon, her plans change. She cares not that he's married; using her beauty as her weapon, she sets out to seduce him.

But little does she know, there's another man in her midst, waiting for the perfect time to take her for himself. It is in his arms that Lysette is destined to find that true love and sanctuary she seeks.

Delphine
(The French Maiden Series - Book Three)

Unable to deny the attraction that simmers between them, Delphine and Andre fell willingly into one another's arms on their long journey from Canada to France. But after an impassioned night, come morning, the ship has docked, Delphine wakes alone, and Andre has fled.

Scorned, Delphine soon finds herself determined to avenge her broken heart. But a love that will not be denied soon gets in the way of her journey to vengeance.

Dreams So Fleeting

Born the illegitimate daughter of a great French nobleman, Ninon knew only a harsh life of cruelty and hardship. It wasn't until the dashing Count of Froissart, Philippe, whisked her off to a different world did she begin to have hope for a better future.

But she soon learns her new life isn't void of misfortune. A slave to both his powerful title and an unbreakable marriage vow, Philippe's love remains just beyond Ninon's reach. Could she dare give her heart to the handsome and cunning rogue, Valentin, instead?

Gold as the Morning Sun

Seeking to ease her ailing father's mind as his body fails him in his final days, Callie Southgate agrees to marry the mail-order groom sent to her from back east. When she meets her husband, she is timid around the handsome but mysterious man. But when they marry, she finds passion she never knew in his embrace.

Jace Greer, a con-man and bank robber, is given the perfect opportunity to start over when the stagecoach carrying a mail-order groom is ambushed, leaving Callie's future husband dead. Taking on the deceased man's identity as his own, Jace continues to Callie's home in Colorado with the hope of leaving his murderous past behind him.

But as true love blooms between Jace and Callie, secrets Jace tried to keep buried begin to surface, threatening their futures—and their lives.

The Ring

Prudence Allbright believes Lord Jamie's declarations of love—so much so that she vows to follow him to the Colonies. It is onboard the ship that will take her to him that she meets the honorable Dr. Ross Manning, and a flame of passion ignites.

Ross is determined not to defile the memory of his late wife, but night after night he longs to hold Prudence in his arms. When Prudence discovers Jamie has already gone back to England without her, Ross knows he may have only one last chance to claim Prudence as his own. But can love stand against the secrets of Prudence's past?

My Lady Gloriana

In this twist on the Pygmalion story, a duke makes a wager that he can bed the uncouth Lady Gloriana. But the bet takes on a life of its own...

The year is 1725. Lady Gloriana Baniard is a beautiful fish out of water. Brought up on the mean streets of London, she is a brash, blunt, obscene force of nature. But thanks to a brief marriage to a disgraced aristocrat, she is forced to live with his noble family and endure the humiliating process of learning to be a lady. Rebelling, she runs away to Yorkshire, where she intends to be a blacksmith, a skill at which she excels. She knows she'll need a manservant to front for her. When John Thorne appears, she hires him, stirred as much by his irresistible attraction as by his strength.

John Haviland, Duke of Thorneleigh, is an arrogant, indolent gambler and womanizer. Having seen Gloriana just once, he yearns to make her his own. When he learns she has run away from her family, he makes a wild bet with his wastrel companions—he will find the lady and bed her. Disguised as a humble servant, he becomes her assistant, learning the blacksmith trade. The clash of wills between these two proud people creates more sparks than a blacksmith's anvil, as Gloriana learns to be a lady, Thorne learns humility—and desire deepens to love.

Printed in the USA
CPSIA information can be obtained
at www.ICGtesting.com
JSHW031709140824
68134JS00038B/3592

9 781682 302163